Praise f

"Robin Maxwell off   1948–
who will grow into t   yn /
of scandal, intrigue, a   spellbound as
Anne's inevitable desti

—Susan Holloway Scott, author of *Duchess*

"Absolutely superb! *Mademoiselle Boleyn* is one of the most lush and beautiful historical novels I have ever read. I seriously could not put it down."   —Diane Haeger, author of *The Perfect Royal Mistress*

"Reading Maxwell's brilliant new novel, it's easy to see why Anne is the 'Boleyn girl' who changed the course of history, and why she is the source of never-ending fascination. We are finally able to catch a glimpse of Anne Boleyn before her enemies vilified her, while she was still just a young woman looking for true love. I couldn't put it down."   —Michelle Moran, author of *Nefertiti*

"Anne Boleyn fans will cry, 'Huzzah!' when they learn that novelist Robin Maxwell has returned to her Tudor roots. In this saucy romp, a prequel to her *Secret Diary of Anne Boleyn,* Maxwell writes in the remembered voice of a child—a tricky feat indeed. Readers will find much to delight in, from finely drawn secondary characters like Leonardo da Vinci to scintillating descriptions of the French glitterati and the royal court. Frothy and French in its main setting, Maxwell's work nevertheless conveys a gravitas that foretells Mademoiselle Boleyn's eventual fate, especially in the novel's exploration of the motives of Henry Percy, Anne's first love and her ultimate betrayer."   —Vicki Leon, author of *Working IX to V*

Books by Robin Maxwell

The Secret Diary of Anne Boleyn

The Queen's Bastard: A Novel

Virgin: Prelude to the Throne

The Wild Irish: A Novel of Elizabeth I and the Pirate O'Malley

To the Tower Born: A Novel of the Lost Princes

Mademoiselle Boleyn

ROBIN MAXWELL

 NEW AMERICAN LIBRARY

New American Library
Published by New American Library, a division of Penguin Group (USA) Inc., 375 Hudson Street,
New York, New York 10014, USA • Penguin Group (Canada), 90 Eglinton Avenue East, Suite 700,
Toronto, Ontario M4P 2Y3, Canada (a division of Pearson Penguin Canada Inc.) • Penguin Books
Ltd., 80 Strand, London WC2R 0RL, England • Penguin Ireland, 25 St. Stephen's Green, Dublin
2, Ireland (a division of Penguin Books Ltd.) • Penguin Group (Australia), 250 Camberwell Road,
Camberwell, Victoria 3124, Australia (a division of Pearson Australia Group Pty. Ltd.) • Penguin
Books India Pvt. Ltd., 11 Community Centre, Panchsheel Park, New Delhi - 110 017, India •
Penguin Group (NZ), 67 Apollo Drive, Rosedale, North Shore 0632, New Zealand (a division
of Pearson New Zealand Ltd.) • Penguin Books (South Africa) (Pty.) Ltd., 24 Sturdee Avenue,
Rosebank, Johannesburg 2196, South Africa

Penguin Books Ltd., Registered Offices: 80 Strand, London WC2R 0RL, England

First published by New American Library, a division of Penguin Group (USA) Inc.

First Printing, November 2007
1   3   5   7   9   10   8   6   4   2

REGISTERED TRADEMARK—MARCA REGISTRADA

LIBRARY OF CONGRESS CATALOGING-IN-PUBLICATION DATA
Maxwell, Robin, 1948–
Mademoiselle Boleyn / Robin Maxwell.
p.   cm.
ISBN: 978-0-451-22209-1
1. Anne Boleyn, Queen, consort of Henry VIII, King of England, 1507–1536—Childhood and
youth—Fiction. 2. Courts and courtiers—Fiction. 3. France—History—Francis I, 1515–1547—
Fiction. I. Title.
PS3563.A9254M33 2007
813'.54—dc22   2007017339

Set in Bembo
Designed by Daniel Lagin

Printed in the United States of America

For my mother, once again . . .

*T*here they are. The cliffs of Dover. The seas are so rough that one moment the castle and the smudged white line neath the headlands are visible, and the next they're obliterated by a moving mountain of dark green water under this ship. I'm desperately queasy—sure my olive complexion matches the waves. Mayhap that is why I've a vague feeling of unease returning home.

I should not.

I'm seventeen and already have a brilliant life behind me. And *everything* to look forward to.

It *is* reminiscent, though—the churning whitecaps, roiling black skies. Eight years now since I've set foot on English soil. *Eight.* Like the sign of infinity woven across the narrow Channel. Last time I stood on Dover beach, my new life in France was days away from beginning. I remember it, in detail so perfect it might have been yesterday. . . .

The Sisters Boleyn

*O*n a stormy October dawn, all of us were gathered on the sand—royals, nobles, clergy—waiting, watching for the blustery weather to clear for the passage. King Henry's sister Princess Mary was crossing the Channel to marry the French king. I and my own sister, Mary Boleyn—three years my senior—were most privileged to be part of the wedding entourage.

"Ow!" My sister, Mary, hand to her face, was squeezing back tears threatening to fall. Our father had just pinched her cheek, viciously, from the sound of the cry.

"Thomas, please . . ." My mother's tone was one—if dogs could speak—of a beast begging its master not to kick it.

"Her cheeks need pinking," he growled. "She's pale as a walking corpse."

"She is *afraid*," said my mother. Suddenly I thought her brave, for by her persistence she risked Father's wrath. "Look at the weather, husband. The ships bob as though they'll be torn from their moorings. Mary's never been to sea."

"That is not the *sea*, Elizabeth," he said as if to a stupid child. " 'Tis merely the English Channel. And if our cowardly daughter cannot face the thought of four hours on a boat, then perhaps we shall leave her in France . . . permanently."

At that, a sob erupted from Mary's throat, despite her attempts to stifle it.

As my father uttered a curse on all women and turned away in disgust, his eyes fell briefly on me, but they made no contact with my own. Indeed, he did not even see me, the insignificant nine-year-old that I was then. Dark. Gawky. And far too skinny for his taste, or fashion for that matter.

Beauty of the day demanded translucent skin of peaches and cream. Cherubic faces. Dimples, if possible. High, voluptuous bosoms. That was a perfect description of Mary Boleyn. Still, 'twas not enough for our father.

Nothing was.

My appearance, in any case, was of no account, as I was already betrothed. The Butlers, a family in Ireland on my mother's side—all of our high family connections were on my mother's side—had been fighting for years over a great inheritance of property. My marriage to a son of that feuding clan—one James Butler—would, it was believed, settle the matter once and for all. The fortune would be directed where it properly belonged—in my father Thomas Boleyn's hands.

Did I like my cousin James, my future husband? Did it matter? Had I a say in whom I should wed?

No. No. No.

I rarely thought on my future. Girls were routinely ripped from their families when they married, sometimes—if distances were great—never to see them again. Letters might be written. Gifts sent. But couriers were waylaid by bandits along the road. Ships sank. Hoped-for heirs were born dead or, worse, born *girls*. Over time, family ties with daughters unraveled like a thick rope whose cords, one by one, were severed, till hanging together by a single strand, finally snapped under the weight of years and disinterest. Even memories faded.

The women might never have lived at all.

As for that October journey to France, I stood waiting on the windswept beach unafraid. Mayhap that is too self-possessed a description of myself. But I *was* experienced. A veteran, not only of the Channel crossing, but of life in a foreign court.

The reason was that my father had the previous year sent me—at a most tender age—to live in the Low Countries. My dark eyes too large for my face, a skinny reed of a thing, I had taken up residence in the Hapsburg city of Malines, in the Netherlands.

I do admit to being scared the morning I was deposited in the redbrick palace, very much alone and at the mercy of my mistress, Archduchess Margaret of Burgundy. She was daughter to the Holy Roman Emperor, Maximilian. He was the patriarch of the Hapsburg family—highest royalty in our world. Feared. Respected. Learned. Intermarried with every dynasty on earth.

And inconceivably rich.

Maximilian, I'd heard had astounded Europe's heads of state when he'd named a woman regent of the Netherlands. But Margaret shocked them further when she became the most powerful female on the continent. The court she presided over was the most exquisite ever. Father must have known that everyone who was *anyone* sent their children to this court for training. The greatest poets, scholars, architects, painters, sculptors, and musicians of the day gathered round Margaret like a honey-soaked queen of the hive.

My first sight of her, though, was a bit of a shock, as she was an ugly creature by anyone's standards, even attired in the richest gown and adorned with diamonds and rubies at throat, wrist, and finger. But I was clean amazed by her first act—kneeling down and embracing me. She'd said something in French that, at the time, I could not understand, but I did remember the words.

Once I'd learned the language, I discovered that they meant, "Look at you. You are gorgeous. A tiny, dark jewel."

The Palace of Malines, three stories with many windows and pretty stone arches, was furnished in the grandest manner. As I was led up the stairs and into the nursery, the paintings and tapestries that adorned every wall, the music that filled every chamber, dazzled my country senses.

But for all the palace's grandeur, the true heart of the court was the rooms that housed the royal offspring, as Margaret had a strange affinity for children, of which she had none of her own. She instead doted wholly on her dead brother's litter, whom she brought up with all the love and tenderness of a mother.

The females, Eleanor, Mary, and Isabella—being mere girls—were of course less highly valued than the one male, Charles. He was fourteen to my eight, perhaps a bit haughty despite a dangerously jutting lower jaw and a flabby bottom lip.

In those first weeks, I admit, I missed my family—my mother most of all—my dogs second, brother, George, third. And even Mary, though she always had a way of making me feel small and stupid. I tried not to dwell on what I was missing but soon realized it was easy.

There was so much at the Burgundian court to do and see and *learn*.

I was very fortunate, for Archduchess Margaret, for no apparent reason, had taken an especial liking to me. True, I watched all the honorable ladies at court and imitated them to perfection. Dwarf that I was, I danced with the most spirit, if not grace, and accompanied myself on the lute and clavichord with the sweetest, tremblingest voice.

And I offered, as my mother had instructed me, to *help* at every turn. Small things counted. Picking up a dropped handkerchief. Lifting a skirt trailing unnoticed in the mud. I soon noticed that Margaret was insisting on having me near her all the time. Not long after my arrival she wrote to my father saying she found me so bright and pleasant that she was more beholden to *him* for sending me than he should be to her for having me.

In the Malines schoolroom, French was drilled into me, so that in the shortest time possible I'd become fluent. My penmanship and spelling, on the other hand, so appalled my tutor that I was frequently slapped. History, politics, and the immense Hapsburg landholdings—great swaths of Europe ruled by the children's grandfather Maximilian— were of prime interest to Charles. But whilst his sisters' eyes glazed over at lectures of monarchs and kingdoms, and their ever-shifting borders, enemies, and allies, I sat quiet at a cat and *listened*.

Charles, for whom this intelligence meant *everything*, would catch me out the corner of his eye as I concentrated on the tutor's sometimes unfathomable lessons; then he looked at his sisters, who were scribbling silly notes to one another. I could not tell if his appraisal of me was approving or harsh, for at first he did not deign to speak to me.

One morning after the girls had skipped out of the classroom, I'd paused to examine a map of Europe that the tutor had left behind on the table. I was looking for England, and whilst I could see London clearly marked, there was no sign of Edenbridge, the village where I'd grown up. I did not notice that Charles had also lingered behind. I looked up to find him eyeing me suspiciously.

"I've never met an English child before," he finally said. "Are they *all* like you?"

His question was mystifying, but I did my best to answer.

"No," I said, "some of them are boys."

He laughed sharply, and I learnt in that moment how enjoyable it was to entertain one of my betters.

"Why are you talking to me?" I ventured. "You never talk to your sisters."

"Why would I want to talk to them? They're boring as boulders."

This time *I* giggled.

He grew serious all of a sudden and very puffed up. "I'm going to be the Holy Roman Emperor one day," he announced.

I gave him an impish grin. "And *I'm* going to be the Queen of England."

"You're outrageous!" he cried.

I shrugged my shoulders, not at all sure if his words were a compliment or an insult. But after that, we became friends.

Whenever he could, Charles would sneak me away from the schoolroom and take me touring through his little world—the Palace of Malines—and I was game for almost anything.

His favorite place in which to show off was *la Première Chambre*. It was a large hall with almost no furniture, but boasting a most astonishing collection of tapestries and paintings. A few were religious. There was one that shocked me—a naked man with a dog. But the bulk of them were portraits.

Being a boy, Charles cared very little for the tapestries, but the gallery of royal ancestors and political allies set him afire with storytelling. He delighted in regaling me with the high points of Burgundian history, the most lurid details of his family, and the tallest of tales. Sometimes they were one and the same.

"My father, the archduke Philip, died when I was little," Charles told me as he stood proudly before a portrait of a young and very dashing nobleman. "He was a beautiful man, don't you think?"

I nodded vigorously.

"His name *said* so. 'Philip the Handsome,' he was called. I hardly remember him."

Charles's face twisted with something that was meant, I'm sure, to be grief, but that pugnacious chin and lip of his perverted it to something almost comical in my eyes. I stifled myself and was relieved when we moved on to a portrait just next to his father's. It was a woman in the garb of a Spanish infanta. What he said then was anything but humorous.

"My mother, Joanna, was so in love with my father and beside herself with misery when he died that she wouldn't be parted with his body." Charles grew thoughtful. "Some say the Spanish are prone to morbidity, but hers was so severe she wandered around Europe for two years, carting his moldering corpse with her."

I was so young that even though I understood the word "corpse" I was yet unclear about the "moldering" part, but the gist of it was horribly understandable.

"She is still alive, my mother. And altogether *mad*. She's been kept locked away for her own safety ever since." He brightened then. "But their marriage was a good thing all in all. It allied the Hapsburgs with Spain—my mother's parents were Ferdinand and Isabella. It means our empire now surrounds our most hated enemy, Louis of France." Charles came to his full height and suddenly looked very imposing to me. "When all the male elders in my family are dead, I shall rule a *vast* territory."

"That is . . . very good," I managed to stammer.

"You know," Charles said, strolling along to another group of portraits. These hung strangely from the ceiling, each by two chains. "Your Tudor monarchs have been our family's friends and trading partners for decades."

"I didn't know," I said, beginning to blush at my ignorance. "I've never been to court in England."

"Then you probably do not know him," he said, pointing up at one of the chain-hung portraits, "though you would have heard of him. He died before you were born."

There stood a gaunt, severe-looking man. At least I recognized the English garb, and I could see he was a king by his crown.

"It is *your* king's father, Henry VII. When his wife died, he tried to marry my aunt Margaret, but she wouldn't have him."

"Why not?" I said, finding my voice and a question that did not sound completely stupid.

"She'd had two husbands already and did not want a third."

"But she could have been Queen of England!" I cried, suddenly confused. *Why on earth would anyone refuse to be the Queen of England?* I wondered.

Charles looked offended, and I suddenly realized I'd blundered. To his credit he dismissed the idiocy of an eight-year-old naïf and moved along to the next portrait—a young noblewoman. To my amazement Charles swiveled the wooden panel round on its chains. I could see painted on its back a coat of arms, a Tudor rose, and some writing, in English.

He read the motto written there. " 'Faithful and Obedient.' This is King Henry VIII's sister Princess Mary." Charles suddenly became the one doing the blushing. "She is my betrothed."

"You're going to marry an English princess!" This news somehow delighted me.

He let the panel swing back so we could view the sitter. She had pale, luminescent skin and delicate features, but only the smallest hint of fair hair was visible under her headdress.

"She's prettier in person than she is in her portrait," I said, surprising myself. Surprising, for it was a lie. One I was about to get caught in.

"I thought you'd never been to court," said Charles, eyes narrowing like those of a lord of the Spanish Inquisition. "So how would you know?"

In that moment, trapped by my own perversity, I was determined not to be humiliated, even if it meant another sin of deceit.

"My father is a very important man at court," I said. *That was true enough.* "Sometimes the royal family visits our home in Edenbridge." *Another lie. I'd never met a one of them.* "King Henry has a farmhouse near ours—'Haxted.'" *Thankfully a fact.*

Charles screwed up his face again. "I think you're lying to me."

It was the first "moment of truth" in my short life. "Well, you will never know if I am . . . ," I said, putting on my prettiest little-girl's smile and batting my eyelashes the way I'd seen the court ladies do, ". . . will you?"

Rather than angering Charles, this obvious fibbery seemed to delight him. He laughed.

"You're a very strange child," he said and, turning, strode across *la Première Chambre* toward the door. "Would you like to see the library?"

"Which breast are you meant to cut off?"

"I believe it is the *right*," Archduchess Margaret answered.

Margaret and her charges—I was now included in everything—had gathered in her beautifully appointed bedroom, *la Seconde Chambre*, a place where none but the Hapsburg ruler and her intimates were allowed. The costumes we were to wear for the latest of the archduchess's frequent entertainments were laid out on one side of her large bed.

I was, as was often the case these days, taken aback by Charles's question, as well as by his aunt's imperturbable response.

"Of *course* it must be the right," he said. "A flat chest on that side would have made it more easy to pull back the arrow."

The theme of this entertainment, "Queen of the Amazons," had been Charles's idea. In studying his Greek, his imagination had been captured by the story of the Amazon women, a warrior tribe who lived without men and fought brilliantly with bows and arrows on horseback. They had, each of them, sacrificed a breast to make their archery skills more precise. Margaret had adored the idea for a masque, and immediately set her seamstresses to work on the performers' attire.

The archduchess, of course, would play the Amazon queen, and we girls her warriors. Charles would be king of the unlucky invaders of their land.

I really should not have been surprised at this adult exchange between Charles and Margaret. In the short time I'd lived in the Netherlands, I'd observed that he was treated like a full-grown man by his aunt, and she so adored him that she spoiled and indulged him excessively.

"How will you achieve the look?" he demanded of Margaret.

"Binding the breast, I suppose. Over the shoulder. On the diagonal."

Together they stood looking down at her costume, a fabulous bejeweled creation woven so thickly with silver threads that its "breastplate" appeared metallic. A *real* silver helmet topped by long, puffy white feathers looked as though it could have been worn on the battlefield.

"The bodice will have to be refashioned so the bandaged shoulder will be hidden, don't you think?" Charles said. "And the material over the right chest should be pulled tighter and flatter, so the missing bosom is more dramatic."

Margaret smiled and gave Charles a kiss on the cheek. "You are so clever. I'll send it back to Régine today. Now," she said, "what about these Amazon women?" Margaret turned to Charles's sisters and me.

The three of them had been paying no attention whatsoever to the conversation and were sitting on the other side of the great bed looking bored with the whole affair. I, on the other hand, had been quietly ogling the costumes trying to reckon which was mine, and hanging on Charles's and Margaret's every word. I flushed red with embarrassment at being caught.

But they were far from displeased.

"I think we've found your sword-bearer," Charles said to his aunt. "Our little English adventuress looks ready to wade into battle this instant."

Now Margaret's smile fell on me. As she knelt down, Charles handed her one of the smaller outfits. She held it to my shoulders and scrutinized it carefully. Up close Margaret was uglier than ever, with misshapen cheeks, lips fat and eyes bulging.

I looked up to see Charles holding out a sword.

"It's heavy. Bend your arm when you take it," he said. "But if you're going to be the queen's sword-bearer . . ."

Suddenly his sisters were aware of the foreign interloper being singled out for some honor by their brother and their aunt. One by one they hopped off the bed and came to stand round us.

I had never been confronted by jealousy before, but now it was all too apparent.

I stared at the jewel-studded sword, a magnificent artifact. I looked at Charles. At Margaret. And then at the three furious little duchesses. I thought mayhap I should insist on giving the honor to one of the girls. They were royal kin. Certainly more deserving than me of the exalted role of sword-bearer.

Then suddenly it struck me. *It wasn't my fault they weren't paying attention.*

With my fiercest Amazon warrior's expression, I bent my elbow, tightened my shoulder and wrist, and received the sword hilt from Charles.

Though the weapon was merely a prop, its weight nearly took my arm down, but I was determined not to fail in my first royal posting. I held firm, every muscle trembling and straining. Finally, with a terrible grunt, I raised it aloft, right over my head.

Margaret gasped. "Good girl!"

"That's the way!" Charles was laughing with pleasure.

I was insanely pleased with myself. Even that triangle of female jealousy directed like daggers at my neck could not diminish it.

Even if you were a girl, I was quickly learning, *it behooved you to keep your eyes and ears open.*

I vowed to myself that I always would.

Too, the Fates played a hand in my single year of education in the Netherlands.

Malines was suddenly abuzz with news of Europe's most recent bloodletting. My king, Henry VIII, had gone to war with France.

"Does *everyone* hate France?" I asked Charles as we waited for the audience to assemble for our masque. We and the other performers stood milling round behind a huge mural of a Greek isle that encompassed a full third of the *Première Chambre*. My Amazon costume was, by far, my favorite ever.

"Absolutely everyone," he said. "But in this case other factors spurred Henry on. He's been smarting from a long succession of heirs born dead. My poor aunt Katherine can't seem to give him a living child. Besides, he's young, virile, vainglorious. He *needs* a war. All monarchs do. King Louis is doddering, hunchbacked . . . and French. Who better to fight?"

As though seized by a warrior spirit, Charles sliced the air above his head with his prop sword.

"Apparently Henry made a decent show of it," he continued. "Built some giant guns, cleared a whole forest to build a fleet of ships. Then luck was with him for the invasion. And weather. He managed to take two French towns with hardly a casualty on either side."

"England *won* against France?" I said, proud and delighted.

"Aunt Margaret calls them 'pathetic victories' as battles go. And Henry must be mortified about what happened in Scotland."

"Scotland? What happened there?"

"While he was in France his poor, childless, helpless queen won the greatest battle on English soil in the kingdom's history. At a place called Flodden Field. The idiot Scots king, James—the man is *married* to Henry's other sister—decided in his infinite wisdom that Henry's absence in France was the perfect time to *invade* England."

Musicians had begun the tune that would announce the players' entrance onto the "stage." Margaret was making last-minute adjustments to her nieces' costumes. But I was desperate to hear the end of Charles's story. And he was clearly enjoying telling it.

"It's already legend," he said, "how my aunt Katherine's troops demolished the Scottish army. Slaughtered ten thousand. Killed her sister-in-law's husband, King James, in battle, and secured the borderlands. She brought glory on her adopted country and made heroes of the men who fought there. Of course, Henry will take all the credit."

"How can he," I asked, "if it is already legend?"

"You can see for yourself," said Charles, calling after me as Margaret herded her Amazon warriors past him onto the stage to a great musical fanfare. "He is coming here for a visit!"

Henry did come, riding at the head of his spotless troops, into the Netherlands—the brave conquering hero. Then, in the presence of Margaret and her court, he celebrated with feasts and masques and joustings his own splendiferous glory.

Amidst jugglers, contortionists, and fairy-dusted dancers, he nibbled on quail thighs and tongue-of-songbird soup, basking in the great entertainment mounted for him by his friend, ally, and soon-to-be kin the Holy Roman Emperor. My first, and last, sight of Maximilian found him a handsome and vital man despite his advanced age and the family's "Hapsburg lip."

I was one of the fairy-dusted dancers there to witness the English king's triumph, but more especially King Louis' embarrassing defeat. I must confess that Henry did enchant me that night in Malines. He was my king, and astonishing to look at: tall—taller by a foot than most men—broad shouldered, with muscular thighs, and arrayed in his silks like a sun god, his thick, curly red gold hair like a halo round his handsome face. His teeth were straight and very white, and when he laughed, the sound boomed across the noisy hall. He took delight in throwing his meaty arm round Maximilian's shoulder, and hugging him like the family he would soon be.

Henry's men—including my father—danced attendance on their king. Never having been at the English court before, I'd not witnessed Thomas Boleyn in this subservient role. I took a strange enjoyment watching him bow and scrape and grovel. Laugh when I knew he was not amused.

Quite ignored by him, I stayed very close, attending Margaret at the table. I heard Henry, deep in his cups, command my father to kiss his foot. His loyal servant blanched, then forced a simpering smile and dropped to one knee. Henry's guffaws brought Father back to standing. All a jest. Everyone laughing—Maximilian, Margaret, Charles. Even my father.

Henry's arrogance was utterly charming.

Or so I thought.

Some months after the English king left the Netherlands, I was coming into the schoolroom early, but heard voices. Raised voices. It took only a moment to recognize them as those of Charles and Archduchess Margaret. I froze in my steps and, realizing I had not yet been seen, flattened myself on the wall outside the door.

"But the delays on my marriage will surely be *insulting* to Henry," I heard Charles say.

"Your grandfather simply wishes to put Henry in his place," Margaret replied.

Charles's grandfather? That must be the emperor Maximilian, I thought. *He is delaying Charles's marriage to the English princess?*

"But why, Aunt?"

"You saw the man," she said. "His hero-mongering and self-aggrandizement. All for a few forgettable victories in France. Truly, he is the King of Hubris. Honestly, Charles, Henry needs a little comeuppance."

"But I *will* have Princess Mary in the end?" Charles's voice was almost a whine. "She is so very pretty."

"You shall have her, darling. Have no doubt of it."

The conversation seemed over and suddenly fearing I'd be caught,

I ruffled my taffeta skirts and came round the corner, "hurrying" in through the door. I pretended surprise at finding Charles and his aunt there. A moment later the three duchesses came fluttering in and I breathed a sigh of relief.

I'd not been caught, but as I later learned, the story was far from over.

Charles was teaching me the game of chess in the far corner of his aunt's library, what had come to be my favorite room of the palace. Besides another twenty portraits hanging on the walls, matching busts of Margaret and her second, beloved husband, and several massive tables, there were over three hundred manuscripts—some of them quite ancient—a collection of printed books, and rolled maps of the world, all carefully arranged on polished wood shelves. On one wall hung a gigantic unfurled scroll of the Burgundian family tree, two *thousand* years of rulers, all of whom Charles knew by heart.

The chess was slow going. I was barely nine, and try as I did, I kept mixing up the proper movements of the knights and the castles. But Charles was insistent about continuing. I thought he did not so much want me to learn the game as he wished to *teach* it to somebody. He had been exceedingly patient.

I was glaring down at the board, my head in my hands, quite sure I was about to be checkmated, when Archduchess Margaret *exploded* into the library, shouting unintelligibly. This was extraordinary, as she was normally so calm and measured in her voice and movements.

Charles and I were paralyzed by the sight of her flying at us like a runaway horse. But as she closed in, we began to make out her ranting.

"The nerve of him! The conceit!" She was almost upon us, and we both reared back on our stools. "And the *stupidity*!"

"What, Aunt?" Charles cried. "Of whom are you speaking?"

Suddenly Margaret's wild eyes focused and, to my horror, fixed on *me*. My first thought was that my father had somehow insulted her, but the archduchess soon disabused me of that notion.

"King *Henry*." She fairly spat the name, then turned her livid face to Charles. "He has revoked your betrothal to Princess Mary."

"I am *jilted*?!"

"That is not the worst of it," Margaret added in an ominous tone.

I was wishing for magic just then. Some wizard to come and spirit me away, poof! All disappeared. Instead I felt pinioned to my chair, lumpish and gawking.

"Henry has promised his sister to his newly vanquished *enemy*."

"You cannot mean King Louis?"

"Oh, but I do," said Margaret. "Ancient, scurrilous Louis."

Charles sat unmoving except for his eyes, which darted back and forth in his head as though he was calculating his losses. The indignity of it. The fair and lovely bride now but a dream. He looked like he might weep.

Margaret saw this. "It's all right, Charles. It's better this way."

I could see Charles did not believe his aunt, but she tried all the same.

"Why would you wish to marry the sister of a backwater fool who calls himself a king? A monarch without so much as a single heir? Your grandfather was right. Henry is an insubstantial king. A less-than-consequential ally."

"But England and France bound by such a high marriage?" Charles argued quite rightly. It was a dynastic disaster for the Hapsburgs.

Margaret's face grew very red and her eyes fell alarmingly on me again, as though I were somehow responsible for this appalling betrayal. I was English. That was enough.

Without another word she took hold of Charles's arm and yanked him up so hard that his stool toppled over with a crash. Then she marched the boy who would one day become the much-feared Holy Roman Emperor across the library floor. Just before he disappeared out the door, he shot me a strange half smile that told me I was absolved, in his eyes, from my king's treachery.

But it was the last time I ever saw Charles.

Within days, my father had summoned me home to England to

prepare for a *new* European journey, this time in the wedding party of Princess Mary, now betrothed to everybody's enemy.

This, then, was how I came to be standing on Dover beach that October day, my slight frame swaying in the gale, long black hair whipping my cheeks, skirts billowing. My sister threatened with expulsion from our family for her cowardice. And my mother showing rare bravery against my overbearing father.

CHAPTER 2

*M*aking space tween my bickering family and myself, I picked my way through the myriad courtiers and ladies, caught sight of pudgy and demure Queen Katherine (I could not imagine her even *wishing* to take credit for the Scottish victory) and her dour Spanish waiting women, avoided a red-robed whale of a man—Henry's cardinal Wolsey—then gazed up in wonder at the white cliffs towering over my head.

The sound of soft but desperate voices piqued my ear. I shuffled through the sand and the crowd and hid behind a tent, its canvas door flapping loudly in the wind, till I could better hear the speakers. 'Twas the bride-to-be, Princess Mary, and her brother Henry. She was, in fact, more beautiful than the Malines portrait of her, though now she was near weeping, making clear her misery in the coming marriage to an aged wretch of a man—king or not. It made her ill to think of it. She was begging a favor from Henry, from the beloved sister that she was and always had been, that when old King Louis died, she might be allowed to *choose her next husband*!

"Absolutely not," came the gruff answer, Henry grumbling with indignation. "How do you get the idea that a *woman*, a princess of so much value to such a valuable throne, should choose a proper husband for herself?"

"I have done my dynastic duty with this match, Henry!" she cried, forgetting to whisper. Still, the tent flap was whipping and I worried it would drown out even a single word of this fascinating debate.

"If you do not promise me this," said Mary with more than a hint of steel in her voice, "I shall wait till we are mid-Channel, jump from the ship, and drown myself!"

I took a chance and peeked out from behind the tent. I *had* to see the look on the king's face. Mary's outrageous oath had already turned him scarlet, and he was moving toward royal purple, trembling with rage.

Mary, who saw she might have erred on the side of stridency, softened immediately and made a proud display of her feminine virtues. She shot an impish grin at Henry, one that was girlish, almost infantile, and when I saw Henry laugh, I knew 'twas the very smile she had delighted him with in childhood. Like magic, his color returned to normal, and he smiled back boyishly.

"You're a terror, Mary Tudor. Our mother would be turning over in her grave if she could see your behavior."

"Our mother would approve," she shot back saucily. "She would have given anything to have had a husband she truly loved, and not our lunatic father."

"Mary!" Henry cried, shushing his sister and peering around worriedly, just as I pulled back behind the tent. "Oh, *have* your chosen husband," he finally said. "But you make this old French king happy or I'll come over there and wring your pretty neck."

"Thank you, Henry!" I could not see, but from the sound of rustling brocades and the noises of smooching and smacking, I knew the princess had thrown her arms around her brother and was kissing him joyfully.

I sneaked away then and saw that my father was looking for me. The weather had cleared enough for the dinghies to be loaded with the trousseau trunks and nervous passengers.

The last thing I saw before stepping into my boat was Princess Mary saying what was clearly a passionate good-bye to a large, handsome fellow—Charles Brandon, the Duke of Suffolk. He was the king's boon companion from childhood, but now it appeared that he might be more than a friend to Mary Tudor—mayhap that husband-in-waiting.

With a lurch we were off, English soil quickly receding from my sight. All in all it had been a good day for me. I'd received none of the blows or pinches from my father, and I had learned a few juicy Tudor family secrets. I was younger than my sister, Mary, but more fearless in the face of the unknown—a foreign court full of French speakers and sundry mad monarchs. At nine years old I already felt a veteran and was frankly looking forward to a new adventure.

I was delivered of one immediately.

Escaping the only way I could from a dark cabin full of vomiting noblewomen, I stood in the open doorway leading out from belowdecks, watching as a black wave the size of a castle wall reared up in front of the ship's rail. The next moment, after a sickening slide, it was under us, but another watery behemoth was quickly bearing down. Wind so fierce it stung my cheeks raw drowned out my whimpers. Mayhap they were full-bodied howls of terror. I do not remember. What I *do* recall was the deckhand who found a stupid nine-year-old girl facing the elements during the third full day of a violent Channel storm.

I felt a viselike grip on my arm and heard the sailor cursing "the little fool" in the open doorway. He wrenched me inside just as another wave heaved a cage of chickens over the rail into the sea. He slammed the door behind us.

"Get ye downstairs with yer lady friends," he ordered me, "lest ye be swept away and drowned with those chooks."

I did not argue, but walked slowly down the steps and dark hallway. I needed no light to find the cabin door, just the smell of fear and the sound of girls screaming and puking.

No one would have recognized the cream of feminine English nobility in that captain's cabin, so wretched and undignified were they, hair flattened against sweat- and fear-soaked faces, gowns rent and stained with divers bodily fluids.

In near extremis was the princess herself. Mary Tudor was shrieking like an Irish banshee. She was a pitiful sight, Princess Mary, and none of her ladies could or would help her, as they all looked to be fighting horrors of their own.

I, who had actually seen my worst nightmare from the ship's door, picked my way through the miserable creatures and, with a clumsy curtsy swayed by the ship's roll, took up Mary's hand in my smaller hands and said, "All will be well, Your Grace. The storm is weakening." 'Twas a bald-faced lie, this, but its effect was instantaneous—as though I'd thrown a pail of cold water on a tantrumming child.

"Are you sure?" the princess said through chattering teeth.

"I heard two deckhands talking," I lied again. All this mendacity— should we perish—would surely lessen my chances for entry into heaven, I thought. But my words did calm the woman. And once she was in control of her senses, she found the strength to retrieve her royal demeanor, ordering all her ladies to collect themselves.

"The storm is lessening," she announced, and even as the ship tilted precariously, making her clutch the edge of the captain's bunk, Mary retained her authority. "We will *not* perish on this miserable Channel. God and my brother have sent me to France for a reason, and a little gale cannot deter them." She managed a weak smile and looked every one of her ladies—including my sister—in the eye until she had their silent agreement. Within moments they had reined themselves into a dignified, if frightened, female congregation.

It was then that I realized Mary Tudor was still tightly clutching my hand.

A mere two days after our arrival, the peaches and cream had returned to my sister Mary's complexion. On this morning she was all twitters and smiles, oohs and aahs, as we and two other English waiting women bumped along in a fine carriage preceding Mary Tudor, riding a magnificent white stallion on her triumphant entry into Paris for her wedding. She was her radiant self again as well . . . but only just.

There'd been another full day of stormy seas on that Channel crossing, and indeed our vessel never even made it into port. It had crashed upon some rocky shoals just before reaching France. Princess Mary had

had to be carried ashore in the strong arms of a sailor. Her trousseau chests, quite miraculously undamaged, were next to be hauled safely onto dry ground. Only then were we ladies—many of us wishing we *were* dead—taken to shore. Some kissed the ground. Others vomited one last time for good measure. Still others swore they were prepared to become French and never see England again, rather than set foot on another ship in their life.

But today, with the wildly cheering, gaily dressed crowds on either side of the procession waving banners, throwing rose petals, and calling Princess Mary's name, we were as pretty and merry as girls could be, and all memories of that dark, deathlike journey were burned away by the sunlight that seemed to set Paris ablaze.

As we passed through a massive gate in the city wall onto a wide thoroughfare, crowds grew thicker, and at every corner was a different musical sideshow or pageant. I could see on either side of us streets coming off the main avenue that were so narrow a cart would barely have been able to pass. Squeezed together along them were countless wooden houses, two and three stories high and not so very grand.

Towering above them to the left was a great fortress, which I guessed was the Louvre, and up ahead I could see the river Seine, with two bridges that crossed to an island in its center. I had learned of Paris and its environs during my year in the Malines schoolroom with Charles, who claimed he would need to know such things when he became a ruler.

"Look, Anne!" my sister cried, first pointing to a towering edifice on one end of the island, and then to a sprawling castle on the other. "Have you ever seen a cathedral so grand? And that palace! Is that where we're going to live?"

My new command of the French language had lifted my status a touch in Mary's eyes.

" 'Tis Notre Dame," I said of the cathedral. "But the old *palais* is now occupied by the Parlement and the courts of law. When in Paris, the king lives in the Palace of Tournelles. And see there," I said, pointing to our right to one of the only open spaces in the city. " 'Tis the Cemetery of the Innocents."

"You're a little know-it-all," Mary said to me, though her tone was light and indulgent.

"She's a little freak," said Mistress Joan Cavendish with a decidedly nasty tone. "That long, goosey neck, and those eyes of hers. Black, like a witch's."

"Leave her alone," Mary ordered. "Her eyes are pretty. Prettier than yours, you fat cow."

That shut Joan Cavendish up in a trice. She flung herself back into the cushions, altogether chastised. Everyone knew that Mary Boleyn was by far the most beautiful of the English waiting ladies, and therefore the most powerful—if women could be said to have any power at all. At least she was highest among the contingent of Mary Tudor's maids.

Mary was my protector in this society of callous Englishwomen, all of them higher in rank than the Boleyn sisters. *Would she also watch over me in the French court?* I wondered.

Now the procession had taken a right-hand turn before reaching the river and arrived at the front doors of the Palace of Tournelles. There waited a dignified and respectful crowd—all manner of French nobles, aldermen, and clergy.

I was surprised to see the castle was a rather dilapidated place, with great chunks of stone gouged out of the columns and lintels, and missing panes of glass in the windows, now patched with squares of oiled parchment.

But the servants who helped Princess Mary's entourage down from the carriage wore blue and gold livery as fine as some English noblemen's. Their collars and wrists flashed with jewels—paste, of course, but the effect was nevertheless startling. If this was the magnificence of French footmen, what, indeed, would be the habiliments of the King of France himself?

We were standing in our places when Princess Mary, flushed with the unexpected love and good cheer of the French crowds, clopped up on her giant steed, the animal all caparisoned in white satin and silver spangles. She sat tall and elegant in the saddle and, I thought, deserving of all the glory being accorded her. She was every inch a royal highness,

and in her blue, sparkling eyes there was not a trace of her four-day ordeal on the Channel, or her horror of marrying a withered old man.

An even greater cheer arose in the massed crowd, for suddenly the
great carven doors of Tournelles were pulled open and out walked
King Louis XII of France to meet his bride. Actually, *hobbled* would be
more precise.

He was worse than any of us had dreamed. He may once have been
of normal height but now, by virtue of his badly stooped back, was a
little man on spindly legs, swollen knees bulging like melons under his
silk stockings. His gray hair was so thin that even if it were clean, it was
still dull and stringy. His nose was a beak, his skin a wrinkled, pocky
map. The curve of the lips was downward, his jowls sagging. But the
most appalling moment came when he clapped his watery eyes on his
betrothed, beheld her loveliness . . . and smiled.

Louis' mouth revealed a pit of rotten brown choppers.

My heart lurched at that moment, in sympathy for the princess, and
I chanced a peek at her expression. Her own smile faltered so imperceptibly that surely no one had noticed but me. *Oh, she was a great girl,*
Mary Tudor! I wished her brother Henry could have seen that brave
moment. It must have been one akin to when a king marched over a
hill with his brave soldiers behind, to discover for the first time before
him the opposing army . . . ten times the size of his own.

Purple velvet-covered stairs were set beside Princess Mary's horse,
and two of the garishly attired liverymen helped her down. She walked
on the long carpet toward the ancient creature whose bed she would
soon share, smiling with brilliantly feigned joy. When they were at
arm's length, Louis began speaking words of love and appreciation to
her—in French, of course. No one had, apparently, told him that Mary
Tudor neither spoke nor understood a word of the French language.
She had never bothered with learning, so sure was she that her time in
France would be short.

In the end, no language of any sort was needed, for the princess
smiled her prettiest smile and, taking King Louis' head in both her
hands, kissed him full on the lips!

The crowd roared its approval. Louis was smitten. I winced at the gesture and I could around me hear Mary's ladies quietly muttering, "How revolting," "God help her," and a variety of "ew's" and "uuugh's."

But I had learned a lesson from Mary Tudor in that moment. Seen what *royalty* meant. Duty and honor came far before personal desire. Royalty rose above fear and petty considerations.

Royalty did not whine.

With that, we followed the king and his soon-to-be bride into the palace, and the reign of "Queen Marie" began.

So, too, did my French education.

The French Queen

CHAPTER 3

*H*opes that my sister, Mary, would be my protector were soon quashed. First, because we were separated for the most part, and second, because she, in her new, thrilling existence, had little use for a nine-year-old sister who knew nothing about the *important* goings-on in the French court. Like when Louis would begin renovations on this dark, falling-down wreck of a castle. Or who was sleeping with whom. Which silkwoman stitched the finest seam? Where had that ruby bracelet on the arm of Mademoiselle Vudois come from . . . and what favors had she had to provide to which monsieur to earn it?

And of course the new French queen's ladies-in-waiting were *drowning* in gossip—very quiet gossip, this—about the goings-on in the royal bedroom. What sexual techniques Marie—for that was what we were now meant to call her—was using to keep King Louis from deflowering her. The few times I saw my sister I heard that the queen had had tutoring from a long-in-the-tooth ex–royal mistress about the "French way" of pleasuring a man, with one's mouth—something that made me cringe with disgust to hear about.

Louis insisted he was intent on getting an heir from his young beauty, though his old body was defying him, the withered member having trouble remaining erect long enough to find its way into Marie's virginal canal.

She was far from encouraging the entry. Her long golden hair, the "French way," and her nimble, ivory-skinned fingers too quickly aroused her lover. The royal seed, it was whispered, was spilling everywhere but inside the queen's womb. She was delighted, of course, but one could not have said Louis was altogether displeased. In all his life the French king had never shared a bed with such a lovely, exotic, and younger-than-he creature as "his Marie." She had still not learned his language, just babbled charmingly in English with a French word thrown in here and there for good measure. She might as well have been an incoherent idiot for all he cared.

Every morning, noon, and night the king and queen played at *something*. They hunted to hounds and with hawks, riding their mounts at breakneck speeds that should have killed the man. On rainy days they walked the long galleries, visiting with his old friends or bursting in upon Marie's waiting ladies for protracted games of dice or musical entertainments.

Mostly, however, they indulged in the latest rage at court imported from Italy—playing "cards"—a deck of them. There were several games that could be played with these cards, all with fascinating names, but whichever was chosen was most often accompanied by gambling, a pastime to which no civilized person in Europe was a stranger. Of course, at a place such as this, the stakes were high and many fortunes, houses, and pieces of jewelry were won and lost on any given day of the week—Sunday not excluded.

At night it was dancing, everyone dressed and bejeweled to the limits of obscene elegance. And did the king dance, what with his huge knobs for knees and his round, humped back? *Dance he did*. He danced till he wheezed and coughed up blood. But nothing would stop him. He meant to show his bride that he was still a man in full. A glorious king of England's greatest enemy, and a fearsome stallion in the French Bed of State.

And where was I in all this excitement and perverse sexuality?

Living in the most mind-numbingly pious household in the entire court!

Louis' eldest daughter was Princess Claude, fifteen years old. He had no living sons, but French law apparently forbade a female from taking the throne as ruler. That honor was accorded Claude's husband, François, of the house of Valois—a tall man with a large nose, known for his flamboyance and his love of beautiful women.

"*Monsieur le Dauphin*," he was called.

So whilst my sister, Mary, arrayed herself in fine gowns, danced, and gambled in the innermost circles of high French society, I, in a Spartan chamber dominated by a large candlelit altar, did needlework. Till my fingers bled. And read Scripture till I could recite by memory in French and English, backward and forward, all four Gospels and the catechism. And Psalms. Claude loved the Psalms. Her ladies were inculcated with the devoutest of thought and morality, as though they were each and every one destined for a nunnery. The princess, regarded far and wide for her moral excellence, did not even employ a fool, for fools were well-known for their blasphemy and rude gestures.

We were denied the society of men, except at church and the greatest of state occasions, though in my first two months in France—after the wedding of Louis and Mary Tudor—there *were* no such occasions. It was day after day of embroidery and praying. But let me not forget *discussion* of the Bible and church ritual, and what it was to be a good, pious woman and wife.

Of course we were never allowed to play at cards.

"These cards have been forbidden by the Holy Father," Princess Claude told her waiting women one day. She had overheard two of them complaining that they'd yet to have the pleasure of the new, fashionable entertainment with which the whole court was abuzz. Then she fixed me with that sweet, crooked-tooth smile of hers and added, "Your King Henry has even complained that card playing has lured his courtiers away from their duties." Now her gaze swept the faces of all her household. "Surely we ladies have a gracious plenty of good works to fill our time."

I nodded in solemn agreement, but inside I was dying with curiosity. When we of Princess Claude's household, dressed all in our grays and blacks and browns, moved silently through the run-down corridors of the Paris castle, we would invariably see the games being played, sometimes by two men. Sometimes by three or four, all sitting round "card tables," which were themselves becoming more and more elaborate.

Most startling was that *ladies* were playing, not only with each other, but *ladies and men together*! They could be seen concentrating very closely on the large, sharp-edged cards that they held splayed, though discreetly, in both hands, and ones laid down faceup on the tables. But much of the time there was spirited chatter. Raucous shouting. Even name-calling.

Much as I revered Princess Claude, I longed to learn the secrets of card playing—to be a gaily dressed mademoiselle sitting at a table engaged in this small sport, laughing and gambling and whiling away the hours in light enjoyment.

But let me be clear. I am not—at least in retrospect—complaining. I was, after all, only nine. All my sister's talk of venereal matters made me very queasy indeed. I gagged at the thought of King Louis' naked body, and I shuddered at Mary's descriptions of the French queen's devious, though highly erotic, escapades with His Majesty.

I liked Princess Claude, who, only six years older than myself, was already married and had borne a child who had managed to live. She was corpulent, unattractive by most standards, with far too many moles on her face, and suffered with badly splayed hips and a club foot on one side.

She was also, without a doubt, the kindest woman I had ever known.

Once, asleep on the narrow pallet I'd been assigned in Claude's bedchamber, I had a nightmare about my favorite hound dying, drowning in the Eden River, which ran through the Hever estate.

I was awakened by a warm hand on my cheek. It was Princess Claude.

"Sweet Anna," she said quietly. "You were whimpering in your sleep. Are you ill?"

I sat up and felt my face was wet with tears. "Not ill, Your Grace," I said, wiping them away, and told her of my sad dream.

"You are homesick, that's all. It's to be expected. And I am sure your hound is very much alive. Tomorrow you should write your mother and confirm it."

Indeed, I found Claude's household a safe haven, and as she had taken an instant liking to me—much as Margaret in the Netherlands had—my existence was as warm and untroubled as a silken cocoon.

There were visits to Claude's chambers by her and François' tiny daughter, and though the king made no bones about his dismay at her sex, he was tender enough to the girl, chucking her under the chin and playing with her pale curls. Claude, on the other hand, held the babe close to herself, cooing and kissing her face and tiny pink hands. The visits were generally brief, with the buxom wet nurse whisking her out of sight for the feedings—a great relief to me.

"Motherhood," Claude said one day as I watched her daughter being carried out of the room after a visit, "is my greatest joy. More even than my joy in God's love." Her husband, François, she explained, had given her a strong, healthy child. Soon, she was sure, she would present him with the sons he so desired. "The boys of our union will provide France with an unbreakable bloodline, and the girls, wives to all of Europe's royalty." She blushed then and looked away. "It is a proud and blessed role." Her voice quivered. "And despite my ugliness and lame legs, no woman in the world is happier than I."

I saw Claude's anger emerge—*fury*, if truth be told—only when it came to the subject of the French queen. Marie, she insisted, was bound and determined to murder her father. He was being exhausted with the never-ending round of hunting and dancing, gambling and drinking—but most especially with nightly sexual excesses. For a prudish woman, the princess had a shrewd sense of carnal matters and kept well apprised of all the bedroom gossip regarding the king and queen. It was said that Claude had a spy in Queen Marie's household, though no one ever guessed the lady's identity.

I thought it a measure of Claude's honorable nature that she remained steadfastly kind to me, knowing full well that my sister, Mary, was one of the English ladies urging Mary Tudor on with her charade of a marriage, and actions dangerous to the health of Claude's beloved father.

For my part, I never spoke of either Mary Tudor or Mary Boleyn in Claude's presence. Pretended to be distracted by other matters when their names were mentioned. Purposely pricked my finger with a needle, or contrived that I'd dropped a stitch and needed to move to the window for light to pick it up. If the subject seemed to be straying Mary-ward, I offered to fetch the princess's clean linen or empty her chamber pot. Of course I never strayed too far too fast, so that I could secretly hear what was said. For 'twas *my* sister and *my* queen of which they were speaking, and even at nine I knew it was well to be learned in the details of scandal and vice.

Just better to be discreet about it.

As the youngest and lowest-ranking lady in Princess Claude's household, it was I to whom the task fell of taking her soiled monthly rags to the laundry. I did not mind the task itself, but the basement of Tournelles was creepily ancient and in the dim light with only torches flickering, it was easy to trip up on the rough cobbled floor, and I imagined it a fine lair for goblins and witches.

So I was hurrying toward the warren of washrooms, half-expecting something to jump out at me from the shadows, when all of a sudden I was face-to-face with a terrible apparition. It was almost my size, but the face was dead white and the hair gray, the eyes sunk deep into dark sockets. And it was grinning horribly at me.

I stopped in my tracks and made a noise—not a full shriek. Perhaps more a squeal, and I dropped the bag of bloody rags.

"What have you got?" said the creature in the voice of a young girl.

I hadn't yet collected myself enough to answer.

"Are you deaf?" it said.

All at once I realized my imagination had led me embarrassingly astray. I tried to compose myself.

"I am *not* deaf," I said.

"But you *are* clumsy," said the little French girl, who I now saw was very close to my age.

"And *you* look like a dead thing," I replied.

"So would you if you were covered in potash." With that, the girl bent over, picked up the bundle of menstrual rags I'd dropped, and started walking away. I now saw she wore a laundrywoman's smock and apron.

"Wait, I'm sorry!" I called out.

"No, you aren't." She was just about engulfed in the long hall's shadows. "You are a fine lady, and ladies do not apologize to laundry girls."

"But I am apologizing to you!" I shouted after her. "Please!"

She stopped and turned back into the flickering torchlight. Slowly, suspiciously, she walked toward me. On her ashen face she wore the grumpiest expression, so that when she made a short curtsy to me, the picture she presented was so comical I wanted to laugh. I didn't even know this girl, but I knew well enough that if I *did* laugh, she would be very cross.

"You needn't curtsy," I said. "I'm only nine."

"Youngster," she said flippantly. "I am ten."

"I know why you're covered with potash," I said a little smugly.

"You do?"

"You've been dripping water through ashes to collect lye," I said. "You'll mix the lye with oil to make soap."

She looked at me very hard. "Why would someone like *you* know something like that?"

"Because 'someone like me' had to learn to make soap. All ladies of the manor have to know such things, so they can oversee their staff and teach their daughters." I was finally holding my own in this conversation. "We just don't get as messy as you," I added, keeping a straight face.

She regarded me closely. I knew she was measuring her next words.

"That is because we make more soap in a castle than you and your mother do at your 'manor house.'"

'Twas a challenge, this, an invitation to continue the tit for tat. But I did not wish to risk offending this cheeky girl, the only person I'd met in France who spoke to me so.

I liked it.

I took a handkerchief from my skirt pocket and held it up in front of her face. She eyed it suspiciously, but then allowed me to wipe the ash from her cheeks.

"What's your name?" I asked.

"Lynette."

"Mine's Anne."

She looked down at the bundle of rags in her hands. "Are these yours?"

"Mine? No. I haven't started my courses."

"Your 'courses'?"

"Our monthly courses. It's what we call them in England."

"In France we call them a bloody mess."

I barked a laugh. "You do not!"

"Well, we do in *my* family. Nine women."

"Nine?"

"Lynette!" a female voice called impatiently from the dark end of the corridor.

"All of us but one are laundrywomen." She turned toward the voice. "Coming, *Maman*!" She looked me over one last time. "I've got to go."

She turned and I was already sorry about her leaving.

"See you in a month," she called back to me as she disappeared down the hall.

But as I started up the stairs, I was already wondering what excuses I could make before the month was out to come down and see Lynette again.

CHAPTER 4

*N*early three months after our arrival I received a sweet note from my sister saying she missed my company. That the other English ladies in Queen Marie's household were two-faced backbiters, and hated Mary for something over which she had no control—her beauty. She begged me to request Claude's indulgence for leave to visit with her for a few days. The princess, wishing to foster sisterly affection, agreed immediately.

I think I have never felt so small or inconsequential or naive as I did when, in the early evening on New Year's Eve, I stepped through the door of the queen's bedchamber, a room that had been almost carelessly decorated and, like the rest of Tournelles, was a place of faded glory.

Marie was just then rising from her bath. Of course in my memory she was still Mary Tudor, the little sister begging her older brother for a favor on Dover beach. The terrified green-faced girl whose fears I'd helped quiet in the captain's cabin of a storm-tossed ship. And I'd seen her from afar every Sunday since our arrival in France, looking appropriately solemn in the royal pew at King Louis' side as Archbishop de Lenoncourt droned out the Mass and a boring sermon.

But this creature before me was a different person altogether, from a different world—dripping wet, steam rising off her skin, now rosy pink from the bath. She seemed all-knowing. Exotic. Paradoxical. Nearly mystical. Her four ladies in attendance this night—my sister included—were dressed and coiffed and painted and fluttering about Queen Marie's naked body like butterflies round the most fragrant jasmine bush.

Two of them patted her limbs gently down with soft chamois towels; another lifted her hair so her neck and shoulders could be dried. The expression on Marie's face was unfathomable. I surmised that enjoyment of excessive pampering was a part of it. How many women on earth were so treated? But there was sadness, too. Or was it anger? And a twinkle of something else in her eye—mischief or cunning—I did not know which.

Queen Marie saw me enter her chamber and smiled a small smile of welcome. I closed the door behind me and suddenly felt a part of this new world. The royal French fleur-de-lis was everywhere apparent, its three blue and gold petals stitched into hangings and coverlets and pillows, the pattern carved into wall panels and bedposts, and repeated on all sides of the frame of a full-length looking glass into which the Queen of France now stared at her unclothed form.

"Powder," she said simply, and at that, her ladies began, with huge puffs of lamb's wool, to cover Marie's body with a fine, white, flower-scented dust that rose in a cloud all round her. She lifted her arms to be powdered there, and someone dusted the pale gold bush between her thighs.

"More wine," she intoned, her voice husky, and I was suddenly aware that the woman was tipsy. She took the goblet from Lady Elizabeth Blount and drank deeply, closing her eyes. She faltered where she stood, but her ladies steadied her, seeming accustomed to a drunken queen preparing for bed.

"What fragrance of oil would Her Majesty prefer tonight?" I heard my sister say. "Sandalwood? Patchouli? Rose and amber?"

"Let me have the patchouli," Marie answered. "It drives Louis out of his head. When I smell of it, I need only to stroke him a time or two and he finishes in my hand."

The king "finishing" in Marie's hand? What could that mean? My expression must have been so baffled the ladies began to laugh.

"Did you not warn your sister of Her Majesty's charade?" said Joan Cavendish to Mary.

"Rouge," the queen ordered, putting an end to her ladies' merriment. She seemed to be retreating inside herself, the spirited young woman I'd known now somber and troubled and consumed with inner conspiracies.

The waiting ladies went to work with their pots of paint, some of the reds mixed with wax for their queen's lips, powder for her cheeks, and oil for her small, hard nipples.

"Lubricate my breasts with lanolin," said Queen Marie. "If I surround his prick with my duckies and slide a few times, he'll spurt like a fountain."

Even inured to such cynicism, Lady Elizabeth made a small choking noise in her throat.

"I like to have choices," Marie added with a grim smile. Then, "More wine."

"May I suggest," I heard my sister say, "that Her Majesty might wish to be in control of all her senses tonight?"

She shot a hard glance at Mary, but it quickly softened as she saw the reason in her advice. "Yes, tonight especially," said the queen, sounding vague and dolorous.

Now the women lifted onto her delicate shoulders a pale pink silk dressing gown that looked to my eye to be made of a thousand folds and a thousand tiny seed pearls. She was ravishing, glowing youth and virginity her most seductive qualities.

Lady Jane Savage stood at a fancifully carven door that led into the king's chamber. "Are you ready, Majesty?" she said.

A look of the most pitiful helplessness suddenly crossed Mary Tudor's face. She was less a great and sophisticated queen than a frightened girl again. Here, now, as she stood poised to climb into her marriage bed with a randy old goat, there was no one—certainly not I—who had the power to quell her terror. Then, as if she slid over her face a gilded party mask, a smile appeared. "I'm ready," she said. "God help me."

Jane opened the door and the French queen swept from her ladies' presence into King Louis' apartments. With a click the door shut behind her.

There was silence among the ladies, so long and profound and sorrowful that I began to squirm inside my kirtle. Everyone stared at the door as though they had just sent the queen in to meet the devil.

Taffeta rustled. Elizabeth Blount sniffled. Then I heard the loud scrape of wood on wood. I looked up to see my sister dragging a small square table inlaid with silver and jewels, and decorated at each corner with a fleur-de-lis. From her exertions she looked up at us with an impish grin.

"Cards, anyone?" she said.

Not five minutes later I was at the table on Mary's right, with two other ladies in the other seats. There had been some argument as to who would be left out of the first hand.

I trembled with anticipation and some fear. *How quickly would I learn the games? Would I make a fool of myself? How long would these ladies let a child play with them?*

"I have nothing to gamble with," I nervously said as Mary shuffled the deck.

" 'Vie' is the word we use for gambling," she said. "Vying is gambling, and I shall stake you tonight. 'Stake' is the money we vie with."

I nodded, realizing my tutoring in card playing had just begun.

"What is the stake this game?" Joan Cavendish asked in a serious tone that sounded very much a ritual.

"Tuppence, till Anne learns," my sister answered.

The waiting women on our left and right slapped two small coins on the table before them. Mary put down ours.

"What shall we play?" said Joan, happy urgency tingeing her voice.

"Primero!" Elizabeth cried.

"Yes, primero!" Jane agreed excitedly, even though she was not to play.

"Too difficult for a beginner to learn," Mary countered.

"*Alouette?*" Elizabeth offered.

"*Alouette* has only two players. Let Anne learn a four-handed game."

"*Piqué.*"

"Too many rules," Mary countered. "And a shortened deck. Very confusing."

"*Glic!*" Jane shouted merrily.

"*Glic?*" Mary repeated with a sharp glare at the girl. Clearly my sister *had* retained her advantage over the French queen's waiting women. "*Glic* requires wit and nerve and is not for the faint of heart. 'Tis not a game to learn on. I say 'Ruff and Trump,' or 'One and Thirty.'"

"'One and Thirty,' then," said Joan Cavendish. "A few hands of that and—if she's clever—we can move on to something more exciting."

"Like primero," Lady Elizabeth insisted.

"Stuff primero up your arse," my sister said, snapping at the girl.

I quite liked Mary's strength, and especially that she was using it to protect *me*. The game decided, she slapped the whole deck facedown on the table. The girl to her left picked up roughly half of it. "That is called 'cutting the deck,'" Mary told me.

All the waiting women looked curiously to see which card showed up where the deck had been cut. It was clearly imprinted with eight stenciled red "hearts."

"Numbered cards are called 'pips,'" Jane explained, entering into the spirit of teaching a newcomer. "From one to nine, each is worth the number of pips on its face."

In turn, each of us cut the deck. I saw a red six of "diamonds" pip, and a card with a full-length picture of a man and a three-petaled black leaf, the leaf being called a "club." The man, I learned, was called a "knave," which was one of three "court cards," so called for the members of the court they represented. Aside from the knaves there were "kings" and "chevaliers" in each of four "suits," I was told, and they were all worth ten points apiece.

It was my turn, and I cut a card with a single black pip in the center and a few words in Latin above and below it—"*Deo Non Fortuna.*"

Everyone gasped.

"What luck has little Anne Boleyn to have found on the first cut of her first game the ace of spades!" said Joan.

"But there is only one pip," I said, bewildered. "Is this not the lowest card I could get?"

"In some games—though not in this one—the ace is worth *eleven* points, not one. It trumps even the court cards," Jane offered.

"Trump?" I asked.

"Trump," said Joan, irritation starting to build, "is simply a card in the suit that is decided beforehand will beat all others. You hold it in reserve for winning a trick."

I held my tongue and did not dare ask what a "trick" was.

"But the ace of spades," Mary said, "is singular, too, in that it is the only card with a motto on it."

I stared at the words and even with my poor Latin could translate it. "By God, not chance." I looked at the women. "Is that not strange, such a motto to be written on a playing card—a game of chance?"

"Can we just *play*?" said Joan, at her wit's end.

"Low card of the cut is dealer," Elizabeth declared, very businesslike.

The cards were suddenly taken up by Mary, who had cut the lowest—the six of diamonds—and from left to right she gave each of the rest of us three cards from the top of the deck, facedown, ending with herself.

"I am the 'dealer,'" Mary said. "And the player to the dealer's left is the 'elder.'"

Everyone picked up her cards and examined them with interest. I looked round and suddenly saw the players' faces go blank, as if to hide the pleasure or dismay in what they were seeing in their hands.

"The object of the game is simple," my sister continued, "to get a combination of cards as close to thirty-one as possible, without going over. I shall, one by one, begin offering each player more cards from the bottom of the deck. I shall ask them if they wish to (stick,) which means no, they do not wish another card—meaning they are close to thirty-one already. Or they may choose to 'have it'—one card, two, or three or more—till they decide to stick. If someone goes over thirty-one, they're out."

Mary began to deal, starting with the elder, who was Elizabeth. She decided to stick. Joan, across from Mary, asked for two cards, which she was given. Suddenly she looked smug and announced she was now ready to stick.

Next it was my turn. I had two court cards, worth twenty, and a six of hearts. Without hesitation I told Mary I'd "have it," and she dealt me a seven of diamonds. I was over thirty-one. My face instantly flushed scarlet.

"Are you out, then?" she said.

"I am," I said, mortified to have lost so quickly on my first hand of cards. But I was somehow relieved, too, having survived it and feeling a sight older than my mere nine years. By the night's end, I thought, I would be a veteran of card playing. I watched and listened as the first hand ended and Joan Cavendish won with a score of thirty.

The cards were shuffled again. But as the new dealer picked up the deck to begin, a sound was heard from the king's chamber. It was old Louis' cackling laughter. This sobered the ladies instantly. Everyone paused in the game, their hands forgotten. Elizabeth groaned softly. The stakes being played for in the king's bedroom this night were higher than at all the card tables in France combined.

"Will he be able?" Jane said in almost a whisper.

"Not likely," Joan replied.

" 'Twould be her bad luck," Elizabeth added.

Despite the gossip I'd heard of the game the queen played with the king, my expression must have given me away for an ignorant infant. My sister came once again to my rescue.

"If you haven't already surmised, the old French cocksman's cock is not what it used to be. He has yet to have penetrated Queen Marie. Till now he's been satisfied with her teasing and licking, rubbing and sucking. . . ."

My heart began thumping hard in my chest. I felt a bead of sweat begin to form on my upper lip. I gulped. "But tonight . . . ?"

"Tonight, Louis has announced, will be the night he takes her *fully*," Joan chimed in, sounding very adult. "He alluded to a bull."

All the waiting women tittered at that, and the thought of the withered old man as that fearsome beast made me giggle. At that moment, hearing my own voice, I realized I had neither laughed aloud nor giggled—nor even *chuckled*—for the whole three months in Claude's sober household. I'd barely laid eyes on a naked arm, no less a pair of rouged nipples and a powdered cunny. Had certainly not heard uttered "prick" or "duckies" or "finishing"—words far too vulgar for the French princess's ear. The thought of Claude witness to this night's happenings made me giggle harder. 'Twas apparently infectious, for suddenly all the ladies were laughing, and as sometimes happens for no reason at all, the hilarity increased, then multiplied out of control, till we were all doubled over, holding our bellies and wiping tears from our faces.

Mary Tudor's cry silenced all that.

It was a single scream, but terrible in its ferocity. The waiting women exchanged petrified looks.

"The pain of first penetration is said to sometimes be great, but that is if the man is exceedingly large . . . and Louis is not," Jane Savage offered, much the expert. "And the queen has been examined by her physicians and found to be quite normal."

Another scream pierced the night, even more alarming than the last.

My sister put down her cards and rose from her bench. She carefully made her way to the door separating the king's and queen's chambers, and as she placed her ear against it, the other women followed and gathered round her. I was surely not going to be left behind and so crowded with them. Clustered close together, our skirts of silk and taffeta, ballooned by fulsome petticoats, rose comically around us. But there was nothing comical about what next emanated from behind that door.

"No, no! God help me!!" Queen Marie cried. "Get off! Get off!!" Then the cries became wordless shrieks of terror. Over and over again.

We ladies were paralyzed with indecision. *What perversion was King Louis inflicting upon our lady?* But who were we to burst into the bedroom of the King of France? Husbands had the rights of life and death over their wives. Even if he was killing her, there was nothing to be done.

Then we heard the queen crying pitifully, "Help me! Please, someone help me!"

An anarchic look passed over my sister's face at those cries, and with a final inhalation of fortifying breath, she unlatched the door and opened it.

The clutch of ladies, myself at the rear, spilled into the king's bedchamber. Someone stumbled over the voluminous pink and pearl-encrusted dressing gown thrown down in a heap on the floor.

It took a moment to understand what we were seeing under the red brocade canopy of the great Bed of State. Queen Marie's pale white legs and arms were all that could be seen sticking out from under the prostrate nakedness of King Louis XII of France, all sagging buttocks, hunched back, and long stringy hair hanging down over his wife's red gold curls. He was very still. Too still.

Even I, pitifully naive in the ways of the world, could see he was dead.

"Get him off me!" Marie screeched at her ladies. "Get him off!!"

We proceeded to peel the still-warm but disgusting body of the French queen's husband off her trembling, naked form, and lifted her gently from the bed. Someone wrapped her dressing gown round her and sat her down on a chair. Someone else fetched wine. I brought a wet cloth and wiped her tearstained face. The ladies hovered and whispered discreetly.

But all that time an unasked question hung thick in the air. Surreptitious glances were tossed back and forth tween the ladies. One of them was caught in midair by the queen.

"The answer is no," she said. Her lips quivered. "The old goat never rammed me. He tried. Oh, how he tried. . . ." Her look was grim as she remembered the ordeal, and a single tear rolled down her cheek. " 'Twas horrible."

Then suddenly the queen blinked several times. It was as if she were looking to a distant horizon, seeing the first rays of sunrise—a new day dawning. She smiled, first a mere upward bowing of the lips. Then they parted and the curve grew wider into a full arc, exposing her pretty white teeth.

"I'm free," Mary Tudor said, as though she hardly believed it herself. "Sweet Jesu in heaven, I am finally free!"

CHAPTER 5

I had been too young to remember when the first Tudor king, Henry VII, had died and the eighteen-year-old giant Henry VIII—known for his strength and bravery on the jousting field, for his studiousness, religious piety, and, above all, golden-haired handsomeness—stepped up to receive his crown. Every "The king is dead, long live the king!" that rang out in England, from street corners and public baths in London, to sheep meadows and taverns in the smallest villages, was altogether sincere and exceedingly public.

Here in France, with Louis' slowly stiffening corpse being quietly rearranged by his wife's waiting women in the Bed of State, and dressed in bedclothes befitting a great king, the situation, I was soon to find out, was a sight more complicated.

"I am '*la Reine Blanche*' now," we heard Marie say very quietly. " 'The White Queen.' "

We ladies stopped our grim work and gathered round her.

"What are you saying?" my sister asked Marie.

She had grown very sober, but met no one's eye as she answered.

"French law clearly states that a dauphin succeeds a king after his death ... but only after it is assured that an heir is not growing in the womb of his queen. That would be *me*." She continued, staring straight ahead, speaking almost in a trance. "Tradition dictates that this husbandless royal female, now known as 'the White Queen'—white is used by the French for mourning clothes—must remain securely locked away from all society, particularly the society of men, for forty days. But I *have* no royal French brat growing in my womb," she added, "so such seclusion is entirely unnecessary." Then she went silent.

All of us contemplated Marie's words.

Suddenly the midnight cathedral bells began to toll, ringing in the New Year of 1515. And now the words began to spill from Marie's lips. "I want to go home. If I have to live in this crumbling ruin closely guarded for forty days with no dancing, no hunting or entertainments, I shall go *mad*! I won't do it. I won't!"

"Your Majesty." It was my sister kneeling at the queen's feet, imploring. "We must finish our work here."

"All right," she said.

We went back to work on Louis and when we thought the "scene" ready, we sent out a messenger with the dreadful news of the king's death.

The first to arrive at the royal bedchamber to view his body were his daughter, Princess Claude, and her husband, François—*Monsieur le Dauphin*. Despite her father's peacefully posed corpse, Claude was not in the least fooled. She could smell the patchouli oil. She could smell the sex.

"He has been ridden to death," I heard her say to François.

I had to hold my tongue not to say, *No, the king was the one doing the riding*.

Even to my untrained eye, the dauphin was obviously delighted Louis was dead: he was tugging at the bit like a newly broken horse. He had, of course, to stay appropriately sympathetic. François was many things, but an actor was not one of them. His feeble attempts at looking sad and giving comfort were comical to Marie's ladies, and we were forced to bite our lips till they bled, in order not to laugh. Claude must have been aware of her husband's true emotions, but such a public admission would have been so untoward, so humiliating, that she pretended to believe him and accept his comforting.

As she limped unregally from Louis' bedchamber to give the orders for preparation of the body, she nodded tearily to me. I rushed forward and kissed her hand, suddenly contrite that I'd been secretly laughing with the other waiting ladies, for I truly loved Princess Claude and was sorry for her father's death. She told me then that I might stay with my sister for the time being.

François had lingered a moment longer to gaze at the dead king, then came to bid the White Queen his condolences. Then he followed Claude out.

When we ladies looked to Marie, we saw she had changed. There was a distinct gleam in her eye.

"I have a plan." She beckoned us all into a small clutch and whispered. "I will need your help. *All* of you." Her gaze fell on me then. "Anne, you have the best French among us. That will be invaluable."

"I . . ." I was momentarily dumbstruck, but recovered myself quickly. "I am ever at your command, Your Majesty."

"Good," she said and, turning to the other ladies, began to spin her plan.

I was to be "invaluable" to a queen. Not the bearer of a prop sword in a court entertainment, but a member of a royal conspiracy!

The New Year was minutes old, but I knew without a doubt that 1515 would be a year to remember.

Several days were forced to pass before we could move on our course, though in that time I was recruited, with parchment and quill, to translate from English and set into French a letter from Marie to *Monsieur le Dauphin*. How many sheets of parchment were written and discarded I do not remember. But the correspondence had to be *just so*, Marie insisted—this letter of invitation to meet, very privately, with her. And it could not be wrongly worded to be misconstrued in any way whatsoever. It could not offend the dauphin. If, God forbid, the note should fall into any hands other than François', the consequences would be very dire indeed.

Finally Marie was happy with it. The content was simplicity itself, and my handwriting—which had not much improved since the Netherlands—was deemed acceptable. At least it was written in French.

My sister, who of all the ladies had taken most enthusiastically to the espionage, was chosen by Marie to pass the note to *Monsieur le Dauphin*, who, with his wife and the whole court, had been confined in the deepest mourning.

The Sunday after Louis' death the mourners finally emerged into public for the first time. The occasion of High Mass was chosen for the note passing. So strict was her confinement, the White Queen Marie was forbidden even to go to church. Mary and I, with the other waiting women, endured the Mass and the long, lugubrious sermon—the first of many to commemorate King Louis' passing. Claude wept openly and François, at her side, never let go of her hand. All of us worried that with the couple so tightly joined, Mary would lose the opportunity to secretly give the letter into his possession.

But the Fates were with us.

Claude fled quickly after taking the Sacraments, but François was held behind by Archbishop de Lenoncourt. Mary shooed the other ladies out of the cathedral, but allowed me to stay by her side and linger discreetly near the tall double doors. There were yet some churchgoers within the nave, and some clergy, so our actions could not be conspicuous.

Finally François came striding, alone, down the center aisle, tall and dashing and all in white—looking anything but a man in mourning. I noticed that his legs were impossibly long, but the calves were far too skinny for a man of his build. As he approached us, Mary and I curtsied low, but I peeked and saw her peering up at him with a conspiratorial grimace—one that served to stop him in his tracks. He stared down at her pretty face with both appreciation and amusement.

"*Les soeurs Boullan,*" he said, and smiled handsomely.

Mary looked suddenly confused, as she had learned as little of the French language as her mistress, Marie.

I whispered very quietly in her ear, "He acknowledged 'the sisters Boleyn.'"

"*Monsieur le Dauphin,*" she said—at least she knew that much—and took his hand, kissing it. No one but myself saw the folded note she slipped into his cupped fingers.

Then I whispered, so only he could hear, *"C'est de la part de la Reine Blanche."*

Surely he was startled by the gesture and the message from Marie, yet his expression changed not at all.

"Mademoiselles," François said, and bowed smartly to us before striding out the doors to meet several well-wishers.

Mary nearly collapsed with relief. "My part is done," she said, and smiled at me. "*Your* turn, little sister."

The secret meeting between the dauphin and the White Queen was not easily accomplished, and I was not there to witness its preparations. The details were later revealed to me, with much hilarity, by Marie and her ladies.

It had required the soldiers guarding Marie's door, after supper, to view her as she sat by herself, by the light of the fire, embroidering and wearing a distinctive gown, its skirt's design in rare stripes of red and white. It also required the guards to allow entry into the queen's chamber Mary Boleyn, who against the chill of the January evening wore—hood up over her head and face—a forest green fur-lined cloak.

My sister, appearing distracted, had shown only enough of her face to the guards to identify herself. The door was shut behind her. Once inside, the ruse began. Whilst pretending a loud argument had broken out between Mary Boleyn and the White Queen, the waiting women began undressing them both.

"Did I give you permission to speak to Monsieur Duprat?" Queen Marie cried. "If I know you, you're trying to seduce him. And he is a married man!"

"What if he *is* married?" Mary spat back. "His wife is swiving two other men! And besides, I was not trying to seduce him."

"I was not trying to seduce him, '*Your Majesty*,'" Marie corrected her. "I have lost my dear husband, and now, it seems, I have lost the respect of my waiting ladies as well!"

And so on . . .

It must have been a wonderful entertainment for the soldiers outside the door.

"Get out!" Marie finally screeched. "I cannot stand the sight of you! Guards, the door!"

As they swung the door inward, a green-cloaked figure, hood covering her "shamed" face, swept past the sentries and rushed away down the corridor. Both the men, I was later told, poked their heads in and looked nosily round, unable to hide their smirking expressions that said, "Ah, squabbling women." They saw White Queen Marie in her red-striped skirt, head down, back at her embroidery by the fire. But her needlework was less stitching than stabbing, as though each prick of the needle were viciously poking at Mary Boleyn.

Of course that woman by the fire *was* Mary Boleyn, and the green-cloaked lady hurrying to a secret assignation in the basement of the south wing of Tournelles was the French queen herself.

I had already arrived in the small, torchlit silkwoman's shop and was blushing madly as I tried to make intelligent conversation with François. But I was very nervous and used the familiar *tu* with him, rather than the more formal *vous*.

He was kind, even though he laughed at my nervousness, and told me that soon there would be two wonderfully witty ladies at court—ones he thought I would find particularly interesting.

"Who are they?" I asked.

"My mother and my sister," he said. "All that I have left of my family, both of whom I deeply adore."

I was honored to hear François speak of such personal subjects with me—a little nobody at his court. My mind was in a flurry—I wished to ask questions about these women, but surely anything I asked would be improper or impertinent.

I was saved by the entrance of Marie to the silkwoman's shop. She closed and locked the door behind her and threw back her hood.

"Majesté," he said, taking the White Queen's hand in his and kissing it, holding his lips on her skin a moment too long to be seemly.

Marie, in response, executed the lowest, most respectful curtsy I have ever witnessed a woman make. She did not immediately rise, instead waiting for François to take her shoulders and lift her from it. He was watching Marie closely, trying to discern from her expression, I thought, what his own tone should be. Whilst he was a male, and most probably the future ruler of France, he had, after all, been the one summoned to this secret rendezvous by the White Queen, who, for all he knew, might be carrying in her belly his rival for the throne.

The silence between them began to grow uncomfortable and I suddenly realized, coming to my senses, that my purpose there was as *translator*. I therefore screwed up my courage and began to speak in French to François, choosing my words with the utmost care and trying desperately not to blush. I explained that there was no possible way that Queen Marie was with child.

Monsieur le Dauphin seemed as desperate not to smile as I was to keep my composure, and at first I believed he was laughing at me. It soon became clear that his good humor stemmed from the intelligence I had just imparted to him.

"So there is no 'little Louis' growing inside the White Queen?" he asked me in French.

"Il n'y a pas d'enfant," I replied.

François wanted details, however. Proof. I translated the request to Marie.

"Tell him there was no penetration," she urged me. "Tell him I am a virgin still. Let his physicians examine me if he wants proof."

I did my best with that one, though, in my mortification, I wished for the earth to open up and swallow me whole.

Marie's declaration silenced François for a long moment. Then he told me very slowly and thoughtfully, as though he was choosing *his* words with great care, that such a situation was more than satisfactory to him, as he had no wish to wait forty days to take Louis' throne if there was no need. He quickly cast down his eyes in a show of reverence. Reverence for the late king . . . that fooled no one.

François was overjoyed. This news from the White Queen could not have been more pleasant.

He took her shoulders once again and kissed her on both cheeks. He was beaming.

"Je suis le roi," he said more to himself than either of us. He was, indeed, the King of France, with no impediment. If he had been any happier, I swear, he would have sung the words and danced a jig to them.

He had me tell Marie that as a formality he would be forced to have his physicians examine her, and begged her forgiveness for the inconvenience or embarrassment.

Then suddenly I caught him staring at this English beauty. This English *virgin*, through different eyes.

"Tell the White Queen," François said to me, never taking his eyes from Marie, "that she is looking particularly lovely tonight. That the green of her cloak sets off to perfection her eyes, which are bluer and more beautiful than the waters of the Mediterranean. And her lips . . ."

I began to translate and even to me, a naive child, it was abundantly clear that the man was flirting outrageously.

I could feel Marie trembling, though I could not then guess if her emotion was anger or requited passion. She merely bade me thank François for his indulgence, and for giving her her freedom.

He bowed low and thanked her for her honesty, which would bring him the crown in a timely manner. Then to my shock and delight he took up *my* hand and kissed my fingertips.

"La Petite Boullan," he said. *"Magnifique."* Then he turned and departed.

Marie opened the door and looked down the hall to make sure François had gone. "What a lecher!" she cried. "Far worse than his father-in-law. I do think he would have laid me down right on the floor had you not been here. Or, from what I've heard of him, had the two of us *together.*"

"Oh!" My expression was so shocked at the thought that Marie laughed aloud.

"Sweet Anne," she said. "You have done well tonight. Very, very well."

CHAPTER 6

"He's here, dear God, he's here!"

Mary Tudor—I could no longer think of her as "the French queen" or even "the White Queen"—stood at the window of her bedchamber staring down at the Tournelles Palace courtyard. Her waiting ladies, I among them, were gathered round her, peeking over her shoulders.

Gone was the icy and dutiful wife of King Louis. Gone were the dead eyes and monotone voice of the royal chattel. Gone, too, was all the pretense of her mourning for the old man's death. Here in front of us was a breathless, glowing, trembling young filly about to break down her stable door.

"Look at him, sweet Jesu, how he sits astride his horse! He is more beautiful than a Greek god." She tore her eyes away for a moment and turned to us. "Is he not?"

We all murmured our agreement, not simply because we wished to please our dewy-eyed mistress, but because Charles Brandon, the Duke of Suffolk, was indeed a handsome, well-made man. With long, luxuriant black hair and beard, he was broad of shoulder and slender of hip, with well-turned calves and meaty thighs.

"Oh, my love, my love!" she cried, turning back for another glimpse of Brandon as he dismounted with fluid grace and handed the reins to a liveried footman. "He just looked up here, to my window. Did you not see that?!"

"I think he did, Your Majesty," my sister, Mary, agreed, rather unconvincingly.

" 'Twas as if he knew exactly where I was without being told. I swear, our hearts are already beating as one. What about my hair? Is it pale enough?" She had been bleaching it with urine for weeks. Without waiting for an answer, Mary Tudor swiveled from the window and fairly dashed to her wardrobe. "Come, hurry."

No one argued. We had, but moments before, finished lacing and buttoning Mary into a fabulous black and tawny creation, sewn with hundreds of tiny diamonds and embroidered with golden lions. Now she was pointing to sky blue silk and cloth of silver.

"He loves me in blue. Says it reflects my eyes. My eyes! Jane!" she suddenly barked at Lady Savage. "The belladonna!"

The waiting woman found a tiny bottle on the cosmetics table and tipped a drop of the tincture into each of Mary's eyes. It was thought to make them sparkle.

"I want to be perfect for him. I *must* be perfect."

The Tudor princess, I thought, was on the verge of hysteria.

As we unlaced her sleeves and unbuttoned her bodice, slipping off the black and tawny, replacing it with the blue and silver, our lady prattled on, speaking to no one in particular. We mightn't have been there at all.

"My brother promised me, Henry did, that if I did my duty and married King Louis, when he died, I could marry whom I pleased."

I saw my sister and other waiting women exchange dubious looks, as though the young widow had suddenly lost her senses.

But *I* knew she was speaking the truth. I'd heard the promise made by Henry on Dover beach. Even in those long winter evenings after Louis' death, when the widow and her ladies passed the time playing cards and gossiping and sharing secrets, Mary had chosen to keep her counsel and tell no one.

I remembered that last glimpse of her and Charles Brandon together on the sand before she took to her dinghy for the Channel crossing. The longing on her face. I had not seen Brandon's expression, though, and I wondered now if he had been similarly overjoyed by King Henry's promise. Wondered, too, if Henry realized that the object of his sister's affection—her future alliance—was his best friend in life.

Charles Brandon might be a duke—the highest title in the land save king and queen, prince and princess—but he'd got the dukedom through favor, not through blood. I'd heard my sister and Elizabeth Blount quietly gossiping one day the week before his arrival as they'd folded the queen's linen.

"Charles Brandon's father was *Henry's* father's standard-bearer at the Battle of Bosworth . . . against Richard III," Elizabeth told Mary, sounding very worldly and mature. "He was one of the men who hacked Richard to pieces and placed the crown on Henry Tudor's head. That kind of loyalty does *not* go unrewarded."

"Indeed it does not," my sister agreed, equally knowledgeable.

"So Brandon's son was sent as a schoolmate and companion to *young* Henry. Charles Brandon was no scholar, but he was strong as a horse. Outgoing, like Henry was. They took to each other instantly. Perfectly matched with riding and fighting and wrestling . . ."

"Was it not just a year ago the king created Brandon a duke?" my sister asked.

Elizabeth nodded. "And now no one in England—save Cardinal Wolsey, I suppose—is more trusted by Henry."

Now Charles Brandon had arrived to fetch Mary Tudor home to her brother.

"My diamond earbobs!" the White Queen ordered Jane Savage. And to me she said, "Anne, fetch me the rose water."

"He does not care for cloying or exotic perfume like Louis did," she said as I scurried to get it. "Just the simple scent of homegrown English roses. Like me," she added. "He calls me his Tudor rose."

As I returned, Mary heaved a deep sigh and closed her eyes. "My love, my love, *my love*. He has finally come!"

The sky blue silk with cloth of silver, the diamond earbobs, and the rose water were all but lost on Brandon, as he was, after the briefest, protocol-laden exchange with Mary, whisked off by François, he having heard of the duke's prowess at feats of strength and warfare—things the French king, too, heartily enjoyed. The first several days of Brandon's mission were therefore spent in manly pursuits—jousts, wrestling, swordplay—all witnessed by the assembled court, of which Mary Tudor was an impatient, eye-rolling member.

He did claim her lace handkerchief as his token before riding onto the tilt field, and she swooned with the romance of the moment. But the length of his jousting lance, upon whose tip she placed her dainty cloth, was the closest Mary Tudor came to her love for the rest of the day.

Even at the feast and entertainments provided for the duke that night, Louis' widow was pushed so far to the background for Queen Claude and all the Frenchwomen of the court to have their fill of the dashing Englishman, Mary never had even a dance with him.

She was crushed. Furious. Beside herself with frustration. Finally she gave up trying in public to seek his attention and began to plot their assignation in private. Five long days after Brandon's arrival in Paris, Mary Tudor wove her silken web and lit behind it with the heat of her desire a dazzling fire, then lured the moth to his destiny.

The summons was a simple note to "My Dearest Charles," heavily scented with rose water, asking that the duke attend his princess so that they might discuss the details of her return home to England.

We ladies, in the meantime, had prepared the spider herself, this time with a care that made Mary's final seduction of Louis seem haphazard. Every last stray hair was plucked from eyebrow and nostril, every inch of skin powdered or perfumed; all twenty nails were buffed to sparkling. Gold dust in oil was applied to her cleavage and her eyelids. Care was taken when she was laced into her stomacher that the stays were pulled tight enough so that her form was made shapely, but that when the corset was removed, no marks would have marred her perfect white skin.

My sister spent two full hours brushing out Mary Tudor's wavy red gold hair, certainly one of her most spectacular features. It was decided that she would wear it long and free-flowing. At first she had us set in it a small diamond tiara—to remind Brandon of her queenliness. But later she thought better of flaunting her status, believing it would challenge his virility and perhaps dampen his ardor. *A man always wished to lord it over a woman*, she told us, *even if the woman outranked him*.

In the end we strung a garland of white posies through the curls. Indeed, the effect was ravishing.

Just before the appointed hour she sent us scurrying through the adjoining door into King Louis' chamber. It would be unseemly for the White Queen to be having an audience with the Duke of Suffolk alone in her bedchamber. Her waiting ladies were thought to be chaperones enough. No one had to know we were locked away out of sight—though not out of hearing—of the most romantic English rendezvous ever to take place on French soil.

Even through two heavy doors we could hear Brandon's knock. It was sharp and businesslike. Little did the man know what business lay yonder in that chamber. Of course we ladies were all pressed hard against the inside of Louis' door. Elizabeth Blount was on her knees trying to peer through the keyhole with promises that each of us would get her turn in that plum position.

He was inside now, and at first we heard very little, for Mary and Brandon were keeping their voices low. Elizabeth whispered to us that their actions were rather formal . . . even stilted.

Suddenly Elizabeth gasped.

"What? What!" we quietly cried.

"She's thrown herself into his arms! They're kissing!"

"Is he kissing her back?" my sister demanded to know. She had been most cynical of all the ladies about Charles Brandon's requited affection for Mary Tudor.

"His arms are around her," said Elizabeth, twisting her head for a better view. "He is *definitely* kissing her back."

"Sly bitch," Joan Cavendish said. "This must have been planned all along."

I smiled knowingly to myself as Jane Savage took her turn at the keyhole. But shortly there was no need for pressing close to the door, for Mary's and Brandon's voices rose so high in pitch that we could hear them very clearly.

"Are you mad, girl?" Brandon cried. "Henry would have our heads!"

"Henry has promised to let me choose my next husband. And I choose *you*."

"Your brother has sent me in all good faith on a state mission to bring you safely back to England. Truth be told, he is more concerned with me securing your dowry and the jewels Louis gave you as a wedding gift than he is about seeing *you* again. Sweetheart, we know very well we cannot do any such thing without Henry's express permission and blessings."

"I know nothing of the sort," she replied tartly.

"I am beneath you in rank—"

"You are the Duke of Suffolk!"

"In name only, as everyone is aware. And Henry made a point to say before I sailed that François is desperate that you should not marry a foreign prince hostile to his kingdom."

"What does that have to do with *us*?" she petulantly asked. I could hear the confusion in Mary's reply. She, who had never bothered to learn the French language, also had no grasp whatsoever of politics. Even *I* understood the implication better than she.

"If you and I marry," Brandon explained carefully, "we will be playing right into François' hands! Giving him exactly what he wants. Denying Henry what he needs."

"Damn Henry! And damn François! The man tried to seduce me when I was nine days a widow! I told you on Dover beach—"

"You told me you threatened Henry with suicide if you could not have your way. What else could he have said?"

The ladies round me were growing more and more agitated with these revelations. Finally it was my turn to kneel at the keyhole, and I was not disappointed. For at the moment I put my eye to the hole and fixed the couple in my gaze, Charles Brandon pulled away from Mary. I could see the expression on her face. 'Twas utter devastation.

"Charles, please!" she wailed, and threw herself at his back. She clutched him for dear life and began weeping sincerely. The sound of it stopped him in his tracks. "I thought you loved me. You *told* me you loved me. You said I was the most beautiful creature that ever walked the earth and that you would die to have me. Well, now you *can* have me."

He was silent, but I thought I could see his tall, manly frame trembling.

"Were you lying?" Mary demanded through her tears. "Were you playing me for a fool?"

"Of course I was not lying."

"Charles, I adore you. I have suffered agonies with a horrible old man to have you. But I did stay a virgin."

Brandon turned back slowly, his expression incredulous. "You are a *virgin*?"

She pulled herself up to her full height and smiled with chilly pride. "I am. François' physicians have confirmed it."

"Oh, Mary, Mary. My Tudor rose. I *do* love you." These last phrases were spoken more quietly than the others, and I could not discern the intent behind them—whether the man was trapped by his own promises, or simply shy to be saying them now that his protestations of affection might be acted upon. There were their physical differences—he was so large and muscular and dark, she so pure white and gold and delicate. *Did not opposites attract each other? Or just how succulent was the idea of Mary Tudor's surprising virginity after three months of marriage to a king?*

Joan Cavendish was trying to push me aside for her turn at the keyhole, but I pushed back, refusing to relinquish my place at such a pivotal moment.

Brandon was staring at Mary, deciding if such a claim was nothing more than an outrageous bluff. But she saw her advantage. She knew she was telling the truth—a "full house"—and decided to begin vying. Not waiting for another word, she flew into Brandon's arms. I saw one of her hands move low, and when I heard him groan with pleasure, I knew which appendage she had embraced.

My moment at the keyhole was unceremoniously ended when Joan shoved me aside.

"Dammit!" she whispered in the next instant. "They're moving to the bed. I cannot see them for the canopy curtains."

But truthfully, from that moment on there was no need for sight of the couple, for such were the sounds they made—so wild and ecstatic and raw—that each of us ladies, with her eyes closed, believed she knew what it was to be made love to by Charles Brandon.

I suddenly felt that secret place between my legs—part of me that had heretofore been used only for making water—now very much alive in a different way. This truly shocked me, but no more than having witnessed the power of a woman's passion, wit, and scheming in winning a man.

A woman fighting for the rarest of estates in our world—*a marriage for love.*

My life was changed that night—utterly—for I never believed such a thing was possible. And though I knew myself to be betrothed to an Irish churl named James Butler, I was struck by a pang of desire for that which Mary Tudor had boldly fought for and won.

I had clearly been dealt a lesser hand than she. I was not, nor would I ever be, as beautiful as she was, and neither was I royal. But I was more clever, and in my young heart a sight more courageous. Mayhap if I learned to "play my hand" for all it was worth, learn when to vie, when to bluff, when to fold, I, too, would attain a marriage for love.

Of course I might fail, as when no matter how hard I strove to win at cards, I was beaten by a better hand. But at the least I could watch and listen and learn from my betters. Then stake my fortune and future on the strength of my education.

It was worth a try.

The wedding of Mary Tudor and Charles Brandon was held four days later on French soil, a hurried affair in secret with just her ladies in attendance . . . and François, of course, unable to hide his delight that his rival's sister would not now be marrying a political enemy of France.

The blessings from Henry, as Brandon had predicted, were hard-won. At first the King of England, livid, refused their passage home, proclaiming that should they set foot on English soil, they would both be beheaded for treason.

Many tearful sessions were held tween the new Duchess of Suffolk and her husband, bent over the writing table composing letters of apology and pledges of fealty for their king—brother and friend. They pleaded their case in a hundred different ways, calling upon the love Henry bore them, with remembrances of childhood games and laughter, and even sorrows that they'd shared. Anything, *anything*, to soften the king's heart, which had turned so hard against them.

Finally he relented and the couple, mightily relieved, began preparing for their journey. Mary's ladies and I began packing our trunks as well.

One day, a fortnight before our return, Claude, who rarely ventured from her rooms alone, came to Mary and Brandon's apartments seeking—of all people—myself.

I'd seen little of the new Queen of France, and I suppose the joy of her surprise visit was plain on my face. We embraced warmly, and she touched my cheek as she had the time of my night fears, and all at once I was weeping at the thought I would never see her again, and said so.

She smiled that kindly smile of hers and said I should not be weeping, for she'd come with the news that I was *not* to be leaving for England with the Duke and Duchess of Suffolk, but was to stay there at the French court, under her care as one of her own waiting ladies. My sister, Mary, would stay in France as well.

I liked to think—and it might have been true—that our remaining with Claude was to do with her affection for myself. But I knew it had a sight more to do with our father, hard at work, scheming his schemes. He had no doubt calculated that his daughters' presence close in the inner circle of the French court benefited him more than our presence at home.

In any event, when the Suffolks rode out of Paris with a portion of

Mary Tudor's dowry but none of Louis' jewels, the Boleyn girls were there on the palace balustrade waving them good-bye. My sister was glowing, alive with the thought of her future adventures as the only English lady of François' new and exciting French court, as I—a mere child—could not be counted as such.

The news had to be broken to Mary that, as a waiting woman to Claude, she would be caught in a strange way between two opposite worlds. That glittering, intoxicating circle of roguish courtiers and their bejeweled mistresses might as well be halfway round the world in India if one was a lady in Claude's household, closeted every day and night, stitching and praying and learning the virtues of womanhood. If she stayed, my sister would live with the new queen under her stern and pious eye. Mary, when told, was indignant.

But there was nothing to be done.

CHAPTER 7

It was another late winter day in Queen Claude's household, breakfast and prayers behind us. So gray a morning was it in Paris that even sitting close by the window embroidering a thread of gold fleurs-de-lis on a linen shirt, I could barely see the design. The room was thick with French ladies and the queen, all of us at our needlework, but it was silent as a tomb. I thought I would go mad with the quiet and the tiny stitches that Claude would soon come round to inspect for perfection.

I chanced a look at my sister, Mary, who was beyond pretending interest in her small frame, holding a piece of cloth cut in the shape of a large hand. It would one day be a gauntlet for King François for his days spent hunting. Mary's deep sigh was so loud that several women who were gathered round an intricate tapestry looked up and fixed her with disapproving stares. When they'd gone back to their needlework, Mary made a face at me that very nearly wrenched a giggle from my throat, though I did successfully stifle it.

But she was not through with me. Quite sure she was otherwise unobserved, she moved her slippered feet in a dance move and jiggled her shoulders a bit.

Now I was forced to bite my lip to appear sober, for I knew she was signaling her desperate desire to go on to an activity far more enjoyable than endlessly pricking a cloth with a needle. This day, and two times other in the week, the ladies of staid Queen Claude's household were allowed—nay, *required*—to attend dancing lessons, certainly a high point in the otherwise stultifying daily schedule.

These happy sessions alternated with musical tutoring, for French noblewomen were considered incompletely turned out if they could not sing melodiously and accompany themselves on an instrument. My choice had been the lute, and my music master had conceded early on that I had quite the facility for lute playing, and that whilst my voice was still thin and reedy, it might one day, as I matured, become pleasing to the ear.

With a straight face I subtly moved my feet in the dance steps to answer my sister's secret communication. I looked out the window to the palace garden where the sundial normally gave us the time, but the gloomy weather prevented even a trace of shadow on the ground, and I was forced to shake my head at Mary, unable to tell her how much more torture we must endure before the hour of our dancing lesson. Suddenly she dipped her head back to her work. I froze.

Queen Claude was standing over my shoulder peering down at my golden fleurs-de-lis.

"Is my sewing terrible?" I asked her, trying to collect myself and not daring to meet her eye. Either she had not witnessed Mary and my little ballet, or she was ignoring it.

"It is better than your penmanship," Claude said, not unkindly. "But you *would* do well to keep working on both."

"Yes, Majesty," I said.

"Would you like to visit the nursery with me?" she asked.

"Now?" I said, realizing too late that the tone of my reply had been less than measured.

"Just a short visit to see my daughter and sister. You'll not miss but a few minutes of your dancing lesson."

I looked up at the queen, chastised, but found her smiling indulgently. Why she bore me such affection was a mystery to me. I had learned not to question such blessings, instead to enjoy them.

I smiled back. "I would be honored," I said.

★   ★   ★

"You needn't walk behind me, Anna," Claude said.

We were making our way through the run-down corridors of
Tournelles. The palace must have once been remarkable, but with its
chipped plaster walls and pillars, its stone floors worn down by centuries of foot traffic, it was shabby and decrepit, and reminded me of old
King Louis. I was silent on the matter, of course, as he was the queen's
dear departed father.

As we passed the chapel, she paused and turned reverently toward
its open doors and the crucifix hanging over the altar, closed her eyes,
and crossed herself. Of course I had forgotten the sacred gesture and
quickly copied her. Claude's piousness seemed always so natural and
sincere. As we continued on our way, I chanced to speak without being
spoken to first.

"Your Majesty . . . ," I began. Clearly there was more to come, but
my poorly formed thoughts remained unuttered.

"What is it?" she said gently.

"How did you come to have such strong faith?" The question was
clumsy, I knew, but I had no other way to say it. "I mean, I sometimes . . ." I wished I had not begun.

"Do you doubt your faith?" she asked.

"Not exactly," I said. "But when we were on the ship coming here,
there was a frightful storm." I'd begun, and was now bound to finish.
"We were all of us on board afraid for our lives. And I could not help
but wonder . . . about God."

Claude stopped and stayed me with a hand on my arm. She turned
me to her and I was struck again at how young she really was.

"What did you wonder about him?" The passionate interest in my
thoughts gave me new confidence, and the words began to tumble out
with all honesty, and no fear of recrimination.

"I wondered if he was the same God we prayed to in chapel, the one
we thanked for our many blessings. There would come a huge wave"—
I began trembling at the memory—"and I *did* question whether the
Savior would smash our tiny vessel into splinters and send us all to the
bottom of the sea."

"So you doubted whether your benevolent God could be one and the same as that furious one?"

"I did," I answered, unable to meet her eye.

She lifted my chin. "Can I tell you a secret?" said Claude.

"Of course." I was hardly breathing. This great lady was taking me into her confidence.

"When I was delivered of my first child, the pain in my hips was so great. . . ." She stopped, remembering. "I felt as though I were being tortured. I thought, 'After all this horror I will die, and my child, if it even lives, will be motherless.' And for a time"—her voice lowered to a whisper—"I doubted God. In my screams of agony I may have even . . . *cursed* him."

I expelled a great long breath. "And then?"

"And then I lived. My baby lived. The pain was over. My doubts about God faded." She smiled at me. "But I was left with a wonderful gift."

"What gift?"

"Compassion and understanding for those who do question God's will. I've come to think that those who, for good reason, feel doubt are stronger than those who live their lives in blind faith."

"Really?"

"Really." She smiled happily at me, as though she was glad to be counted among the enlightened.

I was so grateful I almost cried. But I choked back the tears to show my strength.

"Is your sister, Mary, as thoughtful about these matters as you are?" Claude asked as we continued down the hall.

"She loves God as much as any good Christian does," I said, surprised at the question. "She does not displease you, does she?" I asked, all of a sudden concerned that Mary had in some way offended the queen.

"Not at all." Claude put a gentle hand on my shoulder as we entered the nursery. "She has a sweet heart. . . ." Her voice trailed away as though there was more to be said but no way to properly say it. "Ah!" she cried suddenly. "My lovely girls!"

★   ★   ★

There, in that overly warm but cheerful chamber, we found the royal infant sucking at the breast of her wet nurse, as well as the four-year-old Princess Renée—old Louis' younger daughter—who, even at her tender age, was dressed in a tiny silk gown, the stays and stomacher cinching her minuscule waist into the adult shape and fashion. Renée, who was nearly as plain as her sister, Claude, broke into a huge grin to see us and came limping over, as she also shared the queen's deformities of hip and foot.

As further proof of her goodness—though Lord knew no more was needed—Claude lavished every bit as much tenderness on her sister as on her own child, with kisses and embraces, having little Renée sing along to the nursery songs and patty-cakes, till the little ones were giggling with glee. I was so enjoying the feast of affection myself that I'd well and truly forgotten the dance lesson until Claude reminded me of it.

"Go on," she said. "You must come back later and show me the steps of the new dance."

How Claude could stay so cheerful, knowing she would never herself do the steps of the new dance, or any dance, for her gimp was too severe, I couldn't fathom. And even if it had not been so, the woman was pregnant again, and would have been forbidden all but the slowest and stateliest of pavanes.

I curtsied, kissing the queen's hand, and she put her lips to my forehead.

"Sweet Anna," she whispered. "You are a blessing in my household."

Her words brought instant tears to my eyes, for in all my life I'd not heard such heartfelt words from my own mother, and certainly never from my father. I swore a silent vow of loyalty to this woman, hardly more than a girl herself.

It was she who was a blessing in *my* life.

I hurried down the long echoing corridors of the palace and slid open the door of the ballroom. Two dozen of the ladies and gentlemen of the court, having gathered in a most cheerful and companionable state, were in the midst of practicing a *cascada,* the dancing master, Monsieur Brevard, tapping out the beat with a gold stick on the wooden floor. He was a thin man with bony shoulders, and so pale his veins showed blue through his skin. His hair was straight and golden as corn silk. His nose and cheeks were razor sharp, and the angles of his chin were square and perfectly symmetrical.

He was, perhaps, twenty. I thought him handsome, as did all the ladies who flirted shamelessly with him as they twirled by, or asked to have their foot placement corrected, leaning into him back first, and peering over their shoulders with upturned eyes.

I was too young for Monsieur Brevard to pay any attention to me in that way, but he did single me out from the other girls for what he called my "singular feet." I was graceful and could leap higher and spin more prettily than ladies of the court who had been practicing for years.

"Ah, *la Petite Boullan!*" he cried when he saw me enter. François' pet name for me had stuck and now, for better or worse, that was my moniker at the French court. "You are late, but not too late to show these lead-footed coquettes how this dance is done. Nothing I say convinces them that when they come down with both feet together, it looks like a sack of grain has been dumped on the ground!"

My sister, Mary, shot me a withering look at my being singled out, for if truth be told, she was, of all the ladies, most smitten with our dancing master. When we lay abed together at night in our tiny cell adjoining Queen Claude's chamber, we spoke of many things, but mostly of Mary's various flirtations. *For what of any interest did a nine-year-old have to gossip about?*

Mary was particularly fascinated by Monsieur Brevard's "bulge," as she called it. She thought it unusually large in so slender a man and he, like many Frenchmen, did not try to hide it with a codpiece. Mary said she could not take her eyes off the thing, which made me giggle uncontrollably, but the truth, which I kept to myself, was that Monsieur Brevard's bulge induced in me the same feeling between my legs that the sound of Mary Tudor and Charles Brandon's rutting had caused.

But I felt no affection for the dance master. *How could the sight of a*

*stocking-covered lump of flesh, with not a hint of love or even liking for the
fellow to which it was appended, cause that twitch of lust?*

So taking the dance master's hand and keeping my eyes well above
"the bulge," I moved to the center of the floor and, to the tap of his
golden stick, began my light-footed performance.

Afterward—when the ladies and gentlemen had been released from
the ballroom—was the time when the greatest flirting of the week occurred. All the dancers were warm and damp with perspiration, cheeks
flushed with happy exertion. Girls lingered in the corridor, leaning
up against the walls, chins lowered but eyes lifted to their suitors, who
towered above them, one arm on the wall behind the coquette's head.
They spoke in hushed whispers, but they laughed, too, the girls with a
variety of tinkling bells and throaty chuckles, all sounding to me like
promises of naughty favors.

It fascinated me.

I watched my sister, Mary, who, by virtue of her very great beauty,
was courted not by one man but by many. She was surrounded, in fact.
Something that caused the other ladies to skewer her with filthy looks.
She seemed oblivious to the women's hatred and reveled in the men's
adoration.

I moved closer to the gaggle of courtiers surrounding Mary, whose
laughter seemed different from the French girls'. The commotion
around her was all in fun, for Mary still had learned not much of the
language, and the men were attempting to teach her a few words and
phrases, which she botched—I was certain, on purpose—with the effect of great hilarity all round.

But what they were saying I found most interesting.

King François was going to war just a few months after being
crowned king. France, it seemed, was of all the countries of Europe the
foremost in gun and artillery making. He was even now stockpiling his
weapons, mustering and training his soldiers. Why these courtiers were
speaking of such things to a lady was that "war games" were every day
being held just outside Paris, and day-trips, complete with picnics, were
being arranged as entertainments.

Everyone—all the men at least—wanted Mary Boleyn to go along.

"*Robinette,*" I heard a gentleman enunciate carefully to Mary, as a schoolmaster might.

"*Robinette,*" she parroted back. This was a simple word for her.

"*Le robinette, c'est un petit arquebus.*"

"Ark-ee-buse?" Mary said, and giggled, as though the sound tickled her.

"*Et un grand canon,* BOOM BOOM!" the gentleman said.

"BOOM BOOM!" Mary echoed. That was understandable in any language.

Monsieur Levant, another man hovering about her, bent down to me and asked if I might convey to my sister the invitation to the war games.

"I shall be happy to," I replied in French, "though her agreement to go may not be sufficient. Queen Claude may not approve of her waiting ladies attending so violent a sport."

"But it is not a sport," he replied. "It is *war.* Her husband's war. He is very proud of his troops and weapons. I shall speak to the king about your sister's viewing of these martial exercises." He smiled at me. "And I shall ask him to allow *you* to attend as well. Would you like to see them, little sister?"

"*Mais oui!*" I replied with perhaps a sight more enthusiasm than appropriate, for Monsieur Levant laughed very heartily, and told his comrades that *La Petite Boullan* had a taste for bloodsport.

They all turned to me with approving smiles and laughter.

I blushed madly at that, and Mary looked at me askance. She understood nothing of what had been said, only that the attention a moment before being lavished on her was now directed at her skinny little sister.

What the courtiers said to François, and he to Claude, I will never know, but the effect was all that mattered. Mary, myself, and several other of the queen's waiting ladies were given leave for a whole day's outing.

We were going to view François' preparations for war.

CHAPTER 8

*O*n the first warm day of spring, just after dawn, a caravan of carriages, some loaded with ladies, others with liveried servants, and still others with food and wine and silken pillows, set clopping down the Paris pavements. In our coach were myself and Mary and the queen's most companionable lady, Mademoiselle Serene Minette. This was, I thought, next to the Channel crossing, to be the most exciting adventure of my life. But happily, whilst I would be witnessing men at war, neither they nor I should be in any danger of death.

As Serene and my sister chatted amiably, they hardly bothering to look out the windows, we passed onto a bridge over the Seine to the *cité,* which was what the Parisians called the island in its center. I had only ever seen country bridges before, and was astonished to see that this one was lined on either side with shops, and very fine shops at that. Goldsmiths and silversmiths and jewelers—all had their shimmering wares displayed behind glass windows.

My excitement, which I kept to myself, grew ever greater as we crossed onto the island. Everything here—unlike the Right Bank, where Tournelles was—seemed very grand, bustling with wealth and stateliness. There was the cathedral of Notre Dame with its looming towers to our left. The old *palais,* now the Parlement, to the right. And all manner of commerce in between them. The streets were crowded with finely dressed merchants, their wives and daughters, clergymen—

high and low—and city officials who could be recognized by their thick gold chains and pompous expressions.

Then I saw a disturbing sight—biers of men and women being carried inside a large stone building. I quit my silence to ask Serene what this was. She said it was the *hôtel-Dieu*—a "hospital," where the sick who had no money were cared for. I had never heard of such a thing. When our tenants were ill, my mother would go and tend to them in their cottages. But that, I supposed, was the difference tween country and city.

Crossing to the Left Bank, I searched for the famous *université* that Charles had spoken of, but found little in the way of an edifice, just a lot of poor, starved-looking young men whom Serene identified, quite disparagingly, as students.

But if the *université* was hard to find here, the booksellers were not. The street was lined with small but distinguished shops, all proclaiming their goods with handsome signs. There were permanent stalls, too, their sturdy tables piled with books. Every sort of Parisian, from poor students to fine gentlemen, browsed the stalls and passed in through the shop doors, coming out with his prize wrapped in brown paper.

Then the rows of businesses and storied houses thinned. Small gardens between cottages grew more frequent. Suddenly the city was no more.

We were in the countryside.

It was a longish ride on deeply rutted roads through rolling farm and pastureland, with many peasants at work tilling the newly sprouted crops or tending their herds. We could see in the distance several castles of François' highest noblemen.

Each was pointed out and described in some detail by Serene.

In one country home, she told us, she had been zealously courted by the son of the owner. In another she'd had a secret tryst by the lake with her most ardent lover. In yet another château she had been chased through a hedge maze by a roguish Burgundian. By the time the carriages pulled to a stop on a tree-dotted hillside above a wide green valley, I envisaged the whole of the French countryside as a huge tapestry of lust.

The footmen helped us ladies down, our bones still rattling from the bumpy ride, and set about laying down blankets and, upon them, piles of colorful pillows in every shade of the rainbow. Most were under shady trees, but a few were put in the bright spring sunlight, for it was here closest to the precipice where one could best see the "battlefield" below.

As the other ladies stood chattering together, waiting to be seated, I wandered among the servants. I could see the liverymen as they laid the bedding with the best views, and though they did not speak to one another—as servants were meant to be silent at their work—I could see that they were lingering, subtly, and sneaking glances at the army and cavalry drilling below, seeming to be watching François' army with more than passing interest.

It was *longing*, I decided. They did not wish just then to be attending a gaggle of gaily dressed, privileged, and demanding young ladies of the court. They wished to be soldiers down on that field, brandishing weapons astride their horses, or pikemen or archers engaged in manly pursuits—anything but prissy liverymen laying down silk pillows far above the action.

I was wrenched from my reverie by my sister, Mary, grabbing my arm and steering me toward the lush shade of a thick-trunked oak.

"I do wish they'd hurry with our lunch," she said. "Or at least the wine. I'm very parched, and my arse is sore from that jouncing carriage."

"Can we not sit closer to the edge?" I said. "How can we see the maneuvers from here?"

Her look was indignant. "I swear you are the most *ungrateful* child. I have secured for us the most beautifully shaded seat on this whole hillside, farthest from the bushes where we ladies are expected"—she pursed her lips in disgust—"to relieve ourselves, and all you can think of is 'maneuvers.'" She uttered this last word as if it were a stinking stool.

"But is that not why we've come?" I insisted. "To watch the military—"

"We've come for an outing in the open air on a pretty spring day. A blessed day away from the stultifying queen and her stitchery. Sometimes I should like to stitch Claude's pious little mouth shut."

"Mary!" I cried, then whispered, "That is so unkind. I *love* Queen Claude, and so should you. She has never uttered a harsh word to one of her ladies, even if they've been silly or cruel."

"She's so *boring*. All she does is pray and pop out babies."

"Shhh!" I hissed at Mary.

Serene and Mademoiselle Annette Malveux were approaching our blanket, followed by two liverymen with goblets of wine on silver trays. As the ladies sat and the three of them received their refreshments, I moved away, back toward the blanket closest to the precipice.

It was altogether deserted.

I sat down to watch what was going on below. The violent action. The pop of small arms. The boom of cannon. And the smell! I had never before encountered so much smoke, the acrid odor of gunpowder, the musk of huge battalions of horses.

A volley of deep rumbling cannon seemed to rock the air. From the sound alone I tried to find its source. It seemed to come from a line of heavy artillery, their attendants standing amidst the smoke of the big guns' recent explosions. Men on foot marched round in several different geometric formations—squares, circles, spirals, and something that looked like the letter *D*.

Other groups practiced drills or shooting. There was one great square of twenty lines of twenty men. One line would move with precision to the fore, kneel, and, at the commander's shouted order, all fire at once. They'd retreat and another line would take their place and fire their weapons. On and on till they had all fired.

"Wine?" I heard a liveryman say.

I looked up to see one of the servants I'd noticed staring longingly at the war games. He was nameless to me, as most of the male servants were, and he was holding out a tray with several goblets.

"*Non, merci,*" I replied, "*je ne veux pas du vin, mais avez-vous quelque chose à manger?*"

He smiled a friendly smile and told me he would bring some cold chicken, bread, cheese, and grapes, *tout de suite.*

But truly, I wished not so much for food as for conversation with someone other than the boring ladies on their silken cushions.

"That is a very large army," I said to the servant, knowing how simple I must sound. But he seemed keen to talk as well.

"My brother, Pierre, is down there," he said, never taking his eyes off the thousands of troops. "A cavalryman. I am Robairre," he added almost shyly, for although I was only a child, I was still a highborn lady to him.

"Who is France fighting, and why?" I asked, drawing him into a conversation he knew he should not be having with one of his betters.

"Milan, or at least its ruling family, the Sforzas. Two of the other Italian states—Genoa and Venice—are fighting on *our* side against the Duke of Milan. Italy is not one united country like France. It is composed of various independent territories, of which the Roman Papal States are another."

I thought to myself, *This man who serves wine and cold chicken is more knowledgeable and well-spoken than some fine gentlemen I have met.* I was encouraged that he would speak to me so, and asked, "Why does François go to war *now*? He has only just taken the throne."

"François was lucky," Robairre said, happy to talk of things military. "He was handed this war on a silver platter. The Duchy of Milan—it lies just over the Alps—is a bone well chewed on, one end by France, and the other by Italy. It is won and lost, lost and won . . . endlessly. And the Swiss—fierce mercenaries all of them—will fight for whoever pays them the most. Now they fight against *us*. For a while old King Louis controlled Milan, but before his death he lost it again. So François is simply picking up where his father-in-law left off. Avenging a recent military defeat."

I was riveted to his every word, trying hard to keep things straight and memorize them correctly.

"You can see," Robairre pointed out, putting down his tray, "there are 'men-at-arms.' They wear heavy armor. But the 'Scottish archers' "—he pointed to another part of the field—"they are protected only by leather jerkins and light helmets. And there, see. . . ." He pointed to a unit on foot armed with what looked like long jousting weapons. "Their units are called 'lancers.' The ones in the greatest finery on the beautifully armored horses are aristocratic volunteers called '*aventuriers*.' "

"What part does your brother play?" I asked.

The liveryman's eyes glowed with pride. "He is a cavalryman. Fought in Louis' war. After it was over, horse soldiers were mostly all France had left in the *gendarmerie*. It has been left to François to now build a strong infantry—that is, foot soldiers."

"He seems to have succeeded very well," I observed. Looking down, there were countless soldiers—thousands and thousands of them—in organized units engaged in formations and drills and mock battles with lances and pikes, crossbows and arquebuses.

Robairre was becoming more and more animated as he continued. I had not the heart to ask him why he was not among the fighting force.

"French artillery is the finest in the world," he said. "Our cannon are more accurate and more portable than anyone else's. They are light—cast in bronze—and drawn by horses. They are able, like in no other force in the world, to keep up with the army's marching speed. In fact—"

"Robairre!" It was the rotund Madame Gaspard, the oldest and severest of Queen Claude's ladies, who had been sent as chaperone to the younger ladies on this outing. "What are you doing?" she demanded. "Certainly you are not working. Make yourself *useful*."

"Yes, Madame Gaspard," said my new friend, Robairre, who retrieved his silver tray and bowed low to the older woman. All at once he became in his tone and posture not simply a servant, but *subservient*.

"It is my fault," I said to the older lady, who looked about to split the seams of her dress. It was a fantastic satin creation of peacock blues and greens, its bodice sewn with tiny jewels in the shape of that bird's fanned tail. Her duckies overhung her square, low-cut bodice. They were large white mounds that jiggled like two huge bowls of aspic.

This woman had several times gone out of her way to harry me. Small things. My sewing basket messy. My hems dragging too low. How long it had taken me to fetch the queen's sleeves. That I had stayed too long gossiping in the laundry with Lynette. Mayhap I had. But I did not like Madame Gaspard telling me whom I might talk to, or for how long. And here she was again, sticking her fat nose into my business.

Of course I went on in the politest of tones. "My fault completely. I insisted Robairre stop and explain to me what I was seeing below. Is it not all terribly exciting—the guns and the horses?"

Madame Gaspard instantly forgot the insubordinate servant and gazed down at the field below. A kind of pride glowed on her pudgy face. "My husband is the captain general of five hundred arquebusiers and four cannon," she bragged. "Of course he fought with Louis—" The lady's expression suddenly changed. She looked surprised and worried, as though she were sliding into a pit of deep sand. Louis and his commanders had *lost* Milan. An ignominious defeat. *Should she be bragging so loudly?*

"My husband shall bring great glory to our family and to France," she finally announced. Then, appearing to have decided she was wasting her time speaking to a child, and an *English* child at that, she turned and waddled away.

Not one lady joined me on my picnic blanket overlooking the war games, and I discovered how well I enjoyed my solitude, especially in the open air, with something so unique to gaze upon and wonder about. The life of a waiting lady was so unprivate. One was never, *ever* alone, except whilst sitting on the closestool. The times we were not praying or embroidering were filled with constantly chattering females, and the chatter was almost always of no consequence.

★   ★   ★

"This is madness!" I heard a woman say. "Why François will listen to me on every matter except going to war I will never know."

"Because he is king," another woman with a softer voice answered. "A fish swims. A bird flies. A king makes war. Think of all the pressure being brought to bear on him. . . ."

I had been so engrossed in the sights below that I had altogether failed to notice the arrival of a new party of ladies. Now two of them were standing just within earshot, staring down at the military exercises. If I concentrated, I found that I could hear their conversation.

This duo, in particular, stood out from the other newcomers, not solely by virtue of their magisterial bearing and royal *habillement*. I knew them by sight, having observed them at François' coronation. The older of the two was Louise of Savoy, the king's mother, and the younger—a woman who looked to be a few years older than François—his sister, Marguerite, Duchess of Alençon. Not only was she close in age to François; Marguerite was similar to her brother in her height—quite tall for a woman—the length and shape of her nose, a general attractiveness despite her extreme features, and the forwardness of her presence. Like her brother there was nothing shy or retiring about Marguerite. She spoke clearly and loudly—though not repulsively so. There was a cheerfulness in her voice, and command, as though she knew exactly of that which she spoke.

"Madame," as Louise was now called, had always been at court, even before Louis' death, but she had kept herself discreetly in the background, so much so that I was unaware of her until her son's accession.

I remember standing near Mary Tudor at François' coronation, and her whispering to her ladies that Louise was a woman to closely watch. That she had married at eleven—and schemed indefatigably on behalf of her son and daughter. Whenever Louis' first wife gave birth, Louise of Savoy would pray to God that any sons would be born dead. God or the Fates had answered her prayers, and Louis had only two lame daughters to show for his dynastic efforts.

Madame, letting nothing waylay her ambition, betrothed her only son, François, to the elder French princess, Claude, when the boy was seven. Then Madame sat back, content to wait for Louis' death, certain that François would, in the fullness of time, succeed him as King of France.

Now Madame was always at the king's side, his closest and most trusted adviser. He had few male counselors to speak of—no Cardinal Wolsey, as Henry in England did. Mostly courtiers with whom he gambled and drank and whored. François, I had heard Claude's ladies say, listened with sincere respect—even on matters of foreign policy—to his mother.

But Marguerite, the king's sister and a married woman, had lived away from court with her husband, the Duke of Alençon. Until now. I had seen her holding hands with Madame at the crowning, both their faces tear-streaked with the joyous fulfillment of François' destiny. "The Trinity," Mary Tudor had whispered rather sacrilegiously, watching mother and sister and king in their moment of glory.

It was believed by some that Marguerite possessed a love of her brother that crossed the bounds of decency. Now, only six months since his accession, the Duchess of Alençon was moving her household into François' court. Her husband, gossip told, was rarely with her.

Now on this precipice Marguerite was calmly defending her brother's desire to make war. "Think of all the old commanders whose reputations were destroyed by Louis' defeat, *Maman*. And the young upstarts who will have their first chance at proving their valor. I think there is hardly a man alive in France who does not wish to take part in this invasion."

"Because men are *stupid* when it comes to guns and battles," Madame added with more than a touch of ire. "They are like little boys who learn to fight with wooden swords. They do not believe they can be injured or maimed or killed. Even the old men who have been to war, seen the mayhem, seem to forget and wish to do it again and again." Madame sighed. "All I did to see him crowned . . ."

"There is no use in upsetting yourself. He is going, and we can only pray that no harm comes to him. Look!" said Marguerite, brightening. "Here he is now. Oh, even you cannot deny François looks magnificent in armor."

Careful not to move quickly myself, for I had stayed still as a post during my eavesdropping, I peeked out the corner of my eye to see that the duchess and Madame's attention had been drawn away from the battlefield. Only then did I turn.

There, indeed, was a spectacular sight. 'Twas the king and a dozen of his commanders, highborn noblemen—*aventuriers*, I thought, pleased that I was not now entirely ignorant of all warlike things.

François, by far the tallest of his men, appeared as a silver statue, sunlight glittering off his breastplate. His pure white horse was in matching armor and feather-plumed helmet. He chose the moment that we all turned to see him to spur his mount to rear up on its hind legs in a grand, whinnying salute.

I heard Madame sigh again.

"Don't, *Maman*. It is his moment of glory. Be happy for him."

"I shall be happy if he comes home in one piece." Madame took in a fortifying breath and plastered a smile on her face. "Come, we'll greet him. I'll be the proud mother."

Marguerite took Louise's arm and together they approached the king and his company. They were all dismounting in a loud clattering and clanking of metal on metal. Visors were thrown back to reveal which noble had been favored by the king to greet his mother, his sister, and the ladies of the court at the overlook.

As I approached from my solitary position, I could hear the women exclaiming with delight to see their husbands and lovers and brothers in that exalted party. Now the liverymen came with their trays of libations. 'Twas a sight to see—the fine ladies in their fashionable satins like a flock of exotic birds fluttering amidst a company of metal men, who very carefully brought the delicate Venetian glass goblets to their lips.

When François tried to embrace Madame, his heavy armor made him clumsy, and his hearty laughter boomed across the hilltop.

I watched as men and ladies went off together in small groups, the court fops suddenly all manly and strutting, holding the women rapt with their "battlefield" exploits.

I hung back, half-hidden behind a tree, wishing not to be seen so that I could observe more clearly. My eyes followed the king, not for his grandiosity, but because I saw him—despite the greetings he was forced to make to this lady or that, a courtly kiss on the hand of his current mistress—being drawn inexorably toward his sister, Marguerite.

She had never once taken her eyes off him and stood a distance from the small gatherings, a smile I thought most mysterious playing on her prettily bowed lips.

She was like honey to him, I thought, he a helpless bear able to taste its sweetness in the air.

Finally they faced each other.

François removed his helmet as though he was getting down to business. He had reached his destination. He smiled broadly and very, very warmly. Marguerite's reply was a wry grin.

"Consider yourself embraced," she said with affection that belied her chilly words. "I can do without cold steel on my skin."

"So," he said, not in the least put out. "Have you moved into your apartments?"

"I have," she said. "You've made them very beautiful for me. Thank you, brother."

"My court will be a better place with you in it."

Marguerite could no longer contain herself. She moved close to François and, standing on her tiptoes, put her arms around his armored neck and kissed him first on one cheek, then the other.

"I do love you so," she said.

"And I you. Come," said François, placing Marguerite's arm in the crook of his armored one, "let us pay *Maman* some attention, since we two are the only people on earth who she cares are alive."

CHAPTER 9

I sat and pondered what I had seen—a brother and sister who loved each other passionately, though I could not say, as some did, carnally. I myself had a brother, George Boleyn. He was several years older than myself, but we had only the most superficial intercourse. When, growing up, we'd lived together at Hever House, I'd seen little of him, he—the only boy in the family—learning the manly arts from my father. George was close in age to Mary—only one year apart—yet I did not think their love for each other any greater than ours.

Even from a distance I knew that George's disposition tended sweet rather than sour, like my father's was. He was handsome, with dark hair and features more like my own than like Mary's. And he was a kind and adoring son to our mother.

How did a brother and sister become such dear friends as François and Marguerite? I wondered. I truly had no idea how such a thing would happen, but in that moment I determined that I would in future make it so with my brother, George, and me. Mayhap I would start with a letter, telling him of all I had seen today. The mock battlefield, the war games, the smell of gunpowder and horses. News about France's new, lighter cannon that could keep up with a marching army. I'd describe François' silver suit of armor with his mount's plumed helmet matching the king's. Mayhap George would write me back. And then I to him again. A proper correspondence.

Suddenly I saw the king and his sister coming directly toward me. My surprise sent my heart racing and rendered me speechless. I did remember to curtsy low, first to the king and then to Marguerite.

"This is Anna, *la Petite Boullan*," he told her. "She is a clever little girl. Her French is impeccable. She is so full of grace one would never know she was English. You will like her."

I could feel myself blushing madly, and now that I had been given so brilliant an introduction by the king, I was desperate to deserve it. But no words came.

"François," said the Duchess of Alençon, "you've embarrassed the poor child. Anna . . . ," she said, taking my arm, "you come with me, away from these clanking, gunpowder-reeking *men*." She said this last word with as much amused disdain as affection. I had never heard a woman speak so boldly or carelessly to a man, a king no less.

Marguerite and I strolled along the precipice, well away from the courtiers and ladies, but I knew—for I took peeks from the corner of my eye—that many of the women were watching us, wondering that of all of them, I had been singled out for attention by the king's beloved sister.

I'd still not found my voice, but strangely, our silence together was companionable.

"I noticed you sitting alone watching the military exercises," she finally said. "Did you find them interesting?"

"I did, Your Grace." My answer came quickly and naturally in French, and suddenly the floodgates opened. "I was fortunate, when I first arrived, to speak to a liveryman, Robairre, who explained much of them to me. His brother is in the cavalry, and I think Robairre wishes, above all things, to be a man-at-arms himself."

This had all been blurted in a rush, and suddenly I wondered with horror if my revelations about the kind servingman would be used against him.

"Of course he is very happy to be in service to the king," I added. "Very, *very* happy indeed." I was sinking deeper into the hole I'd dug for myself, and Robairre, the liveryman, as well. "He never actually mentioned his desire to be a soldier. It was something I just guessed at. In fact—"

"Anna . . ." Marguerite fairly crooned my name. Her voice was so soothing. "I will tell no one about Robairre's desires. His secret is safe with me." She smiled the warmest smile then. I thought her very pretty. "What are you reading at present?" she asked, rescuing me from my own discomfiture.

"Well, the Scriptures, of course," I said.

"Not surprising, being a lady of my sister-in-law's household." This was spoken mildly, without a hint of rebuke. "May I suggest you read Christine de Pizan's—"

"*The Book of the City of Ladies?*" I interrupted her. Again, I was hor-rified at my overly familiar behavior with so high a royal. But Margue-rite only laughed.

"So you know the work?"

"I know *of* it, but have not been able to find one to read."

"I shall lend you my copy."

"Your Grace!" I was overwhelmed at such favor being shown me.

"And if you are so inclined," said the duchess, "perhaps you will read some of *my* writings."

Again I was lost for words. Christine de Pizan had written her pop-ular book in the defense of women one hundred years before, and she was thought a great oddity in her time—a female author. Few had fol-lowed in her footsteps. Now here was a highborn lady who not only called herself an author, in my very presence, but offered to let me read her works!

"Yes, yes, Your Grace!" I finally cried. "I would be most honored."

"Well, I am just now setting up my household at court, and I will see to it that Queen Claude allows you to spend some of your time with me . . . if that suits you," she added with a twinkle in her eye, for any fool could see that I was like a dog drooling over a meaty bone being held out in front of it.

I suddenly thought of my sister. "May I beg one indulgence, Your Grace?"

Marguerite looked surprised, but amused, by my impertinence.

"My sister, Mary Boleyn, is here with me at court . . . or I with her—she is older than me by three years, and also serving in Queen Claude's household. When I come to"—I could hardly contain my excitement—"visit you, might I bring my sister along?"

"Is she as precocious as you? As curious?"

I opened my mouth to speak and knew I would be telling a lie if I described Mary so, but I wished desperately to share Duchess Marguerite's favor with my only sister. "She is very beautiful," I said, avoiding an outright lie, but fooling no one. "And she has a sweet temperament. And she is going to learn the French language very soon."

The duchess, I could see, was biting the inside of her lip so as not to laugh. But she succeeded, and then smiled. "I will be happy to receive your beautiful, sweet-tempered sister as well as yourself. Now I should go and say good-bye to my brother before he goes back to his exercises."

Indeed, François and his courtiers had moved to their horses.

"You have done me the greatest honor, Your Grace," I said, curtsying low. "I hope in the future you will think I deserved it."

Her smile was wry but not unkind. "I am an excellent judge of character, Anna. I'll thank my brother for this introduction. We shall be great friends, you and I."

As she turned and moved to François, who was donning his helmet, I was stunned by my exchange with Duchess Marguerite—yet another piece of good fortune since my coming to France.

As I watched, she and the king exchanged a few words, gazed into each other's eyes in a way I had never seen a brother and sister do, and, as though it were the most natural thing in the world, kissed each other lightly on the lips before François clanked shut his visor.

I looked quickly round and saw that mine had not been the only curious eyes set upon the pair. No one dared cluck their disapproval. But this, then, was how stories of impropriety might begin.

It would be weeks before the sight of that small kiss ceased haunting me.

What, I wondered, *was really behind it?*

★   ★   ★

Marguerite of Alençon was to be my next tutor, and from the day of my first invitation to her apartments, just a week after François and his *gendarmerie* left for the Italian invasion, I felt myself blessed. Marguerite had not exaggerated the beauty of the rooms her brother had set aside for her, her household, and her husband, Charles, the Duke of Alençon. They were elegant, although, by her own choice, lacking all pretension and filled more with books than with anything else. A large writing table was always piled with parchment, quills, and inkpots.

I had hoped, as we'd clattered out of Paris at dawn on the morning of the military maneuvers, that the day would be an adventure. But never did I dream that the greatest moment of that adventure would have been securing the favor of *a woman*. In less than six months, life in the French court had surprised me again and again.

Card games. Sexual games. War games. But no human combat thrilled me quite as much as *mental games*.

The world of intellect. Politics. Power. From the moment I'd over-heard Marguerite's conversation with Madame at the precipice over-looking the military maneuvers, my head had spun with the possibilities. I knew I would need to stay on my toes. Keep a sharp mind. A keen ear. And when spoken to, choose my words carefully.

The company in Marguerite's household was as scintillating as Claude's was stultifying, for the duchess chose her lady companions for their perfection of character. At least in the privacy of her quarters they were liberal, though not licentious. Intelligent, though not intellectual. Well behaved, though never pious.

There was reading and discussion of Scripture, but in Marguerite's household, quite shockingly the Holy Bible had been translated into French! In England such a thing was unheard of. Laypeople, unless they were very learned and had Latin, always depended upon the clergy for reading the Old and the New Testaments. The duchess said that *everyone* should be able to read the Bible in their own tongue, but I was sure my parents—as our Catholic king, Henry—would find this notion very scandalous indeed.

We read romances and adventures. Translated tragedies and comedies of Greece and ancient Rome. Mulled over humanist primers. Studied books on the hunt, and chess. As the ladies passed these volumes round to one another, they would do something I found extraordinary. They would *talk* about them. Pleasantly debate an idea. Recall favorite parts of their favorite stories. The lover who rides off to a holy Crusade. The trials of the lady he left behind. The inevitable cuckolded husband catching his adulterous wife and the cruel punishment that ensued. The knights in the stories were always handsome and performed acts of chivalric love that Marguerite's ladies swore the Frenchmen *they* knew would never dream of doing.

Of her own writings I knew little, for she did not, as she had promised, share them with me. I learned from her that when she wrote, she would send everyone away and lock herself up with enough food and wine and candles that she might live comfortably for several days without the interruption of even a servant knocking on her door.

I was desperately curious at the thought of this. But there were worldly pursuits in Marguerite's household, too. Dancing and playing musical instruments. These were not confined to practice sessions with tutors as they were in Claude's, but enjoyed in Marguerite's rooms at all hours of the day and night.

Then there was card playing—rampant and, with these ladies and accompanied by the drinking of wine, quite boisterous. The stakes were high, for these were well-to-do women who could vie for jeweled brooches, or horses, or purses of gold coins.

The duchess's apartments were, in a word, *convivial*, with easiness about them, and in their inhabitants was a fondness for harmless pleasure.

Of course, on the whole, the French court was woefully quiet in these days of war, as the "Sun" and so many of "his stars" were absent from the firmament. Indeed, until he was gone, I had not understood how greatly François illuminated Paris and the halls of Tournelles, seeming even more dilapidated now, and how his nobles—smaller points of light that complemented that fiery orb—decorated our existence.

Aside from a few old or infirm men, young boys, servants, and some soldiers left to guard the palace, all that was left was the women.

Though we shone with our own light—like the planets, I liked to think—the question repeatedly occurred to me. *What were ladies without gentlemen?* By ourselves we formed a kind of universe, but there was no one there to observe it.

Marguerite's husband, Charles, duc d'Alençon, as gossip had told, had almost never been at court even before he rode off to war with François as high commander of the cavalry. Indeed, he was hardly missed, and one sensed that Marguerite simply *endured* the marriage Madame had arranged for her with her usual equanimity and good grace. Charles apparently let his wife live as she wished, never beat her, and controlled what jealousies he owned. A wise choice, I heard one lady tell another, as the king's sister had only to whisper a hint of abuse to François for the duke to find himself assigned to the farthest ambassadorial outpost . . . alone.

Perhaps the most frequent visitor of import and interest to Marguerite's household was the king's mother. François had, to some men's disgruntlement, named Louise of Savoy the country's regent in his absence. All the grumblers had had the good sense to keep their views to themselves, for no one wished to find himself in Madame's bad graces if he managed to come home from the war alive.

It surprised me that, aside from the great courtesy and deference shown Louise by Marguerite's women, they were, by and large, disinterested in the talks that were held between mother and daughter. After the necessary obeisance, the ladies would go back to their pastimes, leaving Madame and Marguerite in two chairs before the hearth, sipping spiced wine, warming their hands and feet in the ever more chilly evenings.

I made sure to seat myself closest to them during these visits, and even made excuses to be near them. Might I offer them more wine in their goblets? Should I lay another log on the fire? Occasionally I would be included for a few moments in their conversations, but generally family matters and affairs of state excluded me.

But there was much I *did* hear. For one, I learned before anyone else that François, previous to leaving for Italy, had planted another royal seed in Claude's fertile ground. Her last pregnancy had ended in miscarriage. Now all the queen's prayers, except for the safe return of her husband, were directed to Sainte Anne, who oversaw Christian women's fertility. Of course Claude and her mother-in-law were praying desperately for a boy, an heir to the French throne.

"She may be lame and unattractive," I heard Madame say one evening, "but the blessed child is fertile as a hare." She regarded Marguerite with a steady gaze. "At this rate I shan't get any grandsons out of *you*."

"Be honest, *Maman*," her daughter said without a hint of rancor. "My children are of no interest to you. If my son cannot wear the French crown, why even bother having one? In the meantime, I am content with a childless life."

Madame sniffed indignantly at the outrageous thought, but let it pass and drained her goblet.

"More wine," she said.

Whilst we waited for news from Italy, the company of Marguerite's ladies played and sang and danced and read. And of course we talked. Conversation was an art, and all subjects were fair game, and most frankly observed. But for all their intelligence, I learned, the women were largely untroubled by politics. News of the war was pertinent only if the battle spoken of was one in which their husbands, lovers, sons, or brothers were participants. They did not dwell morbidly on the subject of their loved ones' possible deaths, even as Louis' war the previous year had already made several widows.

One of them, Madame Claudette, became the target of the whole group's teasing one day as we sat in a communal tub in the Amboise bathhouse.

The bath keeper had just laid a silver tray of savory beef chunks on a board straddling the tub. The meat smelled so divine I thought that each one of us, if we were not so ladylike, would have been the first to pluck one up and eat it.

"It has been eighteen months, and you do not have a new husband yet," said Claudette's friend Juliette.

"Why would I marry again?" said Claudette, sitting up straighter in the richly adorned tub, her eye on the silver dish. "Why not a succession of lovers?"

Her breasts now bobbed above the water, and I had a hard time keeping my eyes off them. It was the French custom—different from the English-country custom—to bathe together, and bathe naked except for a linen shirt down to the knees that left bosom, neck, and shoulders altogether exposed. Sometimes ladies wore their jewels in the tub, but this was a more reserved group.

"Why not forget sex altogether?" Mimi La Salle suggested wryly.

"The abuse you suffer," Marguerite said. "You are probably hoping Bernard takes one between the eyes."

Everyone howled at that, and I tried not to look shocked.

"More chamomile and mallow, Nadine," the duchess instructed the bath keeper, who quickly obliged, sprinkling the herbs liberally on the surface of the water between the women.

"I'm a very happy widow," Claudette insisted. It was not difficult to believe her, as she was always gay and smiling. "There is no one hanging over me, telling me how to spend my money. And no cuckolded husband lurking around in the hedges." She finally gave in to her urges and took a bit of beef between her fingers, then sat back against the wall of the tub. "I do hope Alain is happy in heaven, because I am *delirious* without him." She popped it in her mouth as though to punctuate her declaration.

At that, Mimi grabbed the biggest piece off the tray, bit off half of it, and chomped down with exaggerated ferocity.

Everyone roared again, for there was not one lady in the tub who, at that moment, was not envisioning Bernard La Salle's head.

CHAPTER 10

I nagged Mary incessantly about taking French lessons, and she finally begrudgingly acquiesced. Her progress took a slightly better turn when the decrepit old tutor she'd been assigned died and was replaced by a handsome young Parisian named Michel, who could barely disguise his passion for his beautiful English pupil. Mary was more than flattered by his attention. She was just as besotted with Michel as he was with her, and claimed to have dreams about the man every night.

Claude's newest pregnancy had rendered her household even duller than before, but whilst I pined for the days my sister and I would be summoned to Marguerite's apartments, Mary was suddenly content at Claude's, using her embroidery time to stitch Michel a fancy shirt.

Mary and I had taken the stools closest to the fire, whilst Claude and her other ladies sat round a huge hoop, all working on the same tapestry—an intricate scene of Saint George slaying the dragon.

"Of course I'd never give away my virginity now," Mary said. "That would surely be the end of me." She looked dreamy, her needle poised halfway through the linen. "Though he *is* beautiful, my Michel. Do you not think so, Anne?"

"He is very fine to look at," I said. *How could I say otherwise?*

"And he is from a very fine family. Or at least *good*. Perhaps not as good as Father would wish." Her self-argument was already making me weary, so I enlivened it with a question.

"Do you kiss him?"

"Of course I kiss him."

"Do you let him . . . touch your duckies?" I was ever more curious about such things.

"Sometimes. But when I do, he insists on more. And more I will not give. So I think I shall withhold my pretty duckies from now on." She smiled to herself, no doubt thinking of the next time he might try to fondle her. Then her face darkened. "How shall I go *backward*? Once he has touched, the toucher believes he possesses the right to touch again."

"But you wish to go on kissing Michel?"

"Of course."

I thought a moment, trying to remember the chatter of Marguerite's ladies on just such a subject. "Is that not 'prick teasing'?" I said to Mary. She was taken aback. "I have not heard of going backward with a man," I went on. "Only forward . . . to 'completion.'"

Mary was suddenly very cross. "What do you know about men and women? And 'completion'?" she snapped. "Your head is always stuck up in a stuffy book. You're nothing but a naive little toad."

"Mayhap I am naive, sister, but 'tis *you* who are a toad!"

I laid down my embroidery and walked away.

"Anne!" I heard my sister whisper after me, but I ignored her and found a place in the circle of Claude's women.

Mary was very vain and, though I hated to say it, somewhat ignorant as well. Those traits I could bear, but cruelty to me in the smallest amounts I found intolerable. I was always kind to her and listened respectfully to the advice she gave me—much of which was harebrained—on every subject on which she chose to pontificate.

In a sermon once I heard it said that a family is like a ship, captained by its father, and that the vessel is only as seaworthy as its crew—the wife and their children. If they all pull together, it will sail swiftly and easily, even in the roughest of waters. But if even *one* of the crew should grow lax and allow a breach in the hull or a tear in the sail, the boat will founder and in the worst of cases sink.

Here we were, I thought, Mary and I, separated from the Boleyn family ship, two young English girls adrift, alone on a raft in a turbulent French sea. *Should we not eke out all the comfort, one from the other, that we were able? And could she not try harder to use her mind for something other than coquetry?*

She was kinder after that day, I must admit. The next time the two of us were hurrying from Claude's rooms, like some prison escapees, to Marguerite's apartments, she stopped suddenly and took my arm. "Thank you, Anne," she said, holding my gaze. "Thank you for asking the duchess to have me visit her with you."

"You are my sister," I said. " 'Tis what sisters do."

Later that day, as rain beat against the windows, a fire blazing in the hearth, eight of us ladies sat at two card tables playing primero. I sat across from the duchess and had just been shown an eye-opening display of the art of bluffing.

When you play, there is so much to consider. Memory of cards already played is essential. But just as vital is a sharp reading of the faces of your opponents. How calm, how surprised, or how intent their expressions are tells much of what you must know to win. But there are *tricks* to be played with facial expressions—subtleties and opposites.

In the hand just past, Marguerite, who had been vying quite reservedly but refusing to fold, looked perplexed to me one moment, biting the inside of her cheek, starting to lay down a card, then retracting it. In the next moment she sighed and appeared defeated. On the next deal she brightened. On the next even more. One by one we all folded, surprised at how large the pot had grown. When Marguerite finally laid down her cards, all she had in her hand was a pair of twos! Everyone laughed good-naturedly and complimented the duchess on her cleverness in bluffing. She had confused us with her changeable expressions and unerring calm.

Another hand was played, and this time Marguerite's gaze fell on me as I was staring hard at my cards—I had two kings. I was trying to decide how to play them.

"Anne, do you know the significance of kings in the deck?" said the duchess, almost preternaturally. *Or was I so transparent? Did I have "two kings" written in red and black on my forehead?*

"No, Your Grace," I said, trying with a bland expression to save my privacy. "I hope you'll tell me."

It was her play. "I'll have three cards," she told the dealer, supremely confident. When *I* asked for three cards, I was generally scrambling with desperation to stay in the game.

"They stand for the great monarchs of Europe," Marguerite continued. "So they would be . . . ?" She paused, allowing me to finish for her.

"François," I said, and all the ladies smiled.

"Very politic of you to mention him first," said Marguerite.

"And Henry VIII. And . . ." I had to think for a moment. ". . . Maximilian, the Holy Roman Emperor."

"And who is the fourth?" the duchess asked.

"I'm not sure," I said, racking my brain. *Someone in Spain?* I thought. Then I tried to remember what Robairre had told me about the Italian city-states. "The Duke of Milan?" I suggested. "A Medici perhaps?" Even with my limited understanding of politics, I had heard that the Medici family—bankers from Florence—were the wealthiest men in Europe.

"Ah, you have stumbled on a *part* of the answer," said Marguerite. "The fourth monarch is a Medici today . . . but may not be tomorrow."

I thought and thought. "The pope!" I finally cried. "Leo X is a Medici. But when he dies . . ." My voiced trailed off, for I had no idea who might be the next Holy Father.

"The fourth power in Europe is *always* the pope," Marguerite continued in the serious tone of a tutor. "François and Henry, in their youthfulness and strength, shall certainly hold much power in the coming years. But Maximilian is old and in ill health. The title of Holy Roman Emperor may or may not be passed down to his grandson, Charles."

I realized suddenly that Marguerite was speaking of my schoolmate in Malines. *Charles always claimed he would hold that title.*

"Why are there no queens in the deck?" I asked rather suddenly. "It seems odd."

Suzanne Brantôme, on my left, and Mimi La Salle, on my right, smiled knowingly, and I felt foolish. But Marguerite did not smile. "You have by now read *The Book of the City of Ladies,* have you not, Anna?"

"I have."

"Then *you* should tell us why the deck has no queens."

"Because . . . ," I began, but I hesitated, for my mind was racing far ahead of my voice. I wished so very much to please the duchess with my answer. "There has been so little recognition of the contributions of women in every walk of life?" I finally offered, with a woeful lack of confidence in my answer.

But Marguerite bade me go on with a subtle nod.

"Men have looked down upon our sex," I said. "They have withheld education and caused us great suffering. They do not see women as fit rulers and . . ." I stopped and thought about my summary of Christine de Pizan's work. When I began again, it was slowly, as if the words were falling together into an idea as they were spoken. "So why would men place queens in a deck of cards? It might signify their importance in the world."

Marguerite looked at me with affection and approval. "I have thought the same thoughts many times, as have my ladies at these tables. We all know very well there *are* no kingdoms without queens."

We sat silent for a moment as we pondered the wisdom of that idea.

"Mayhap someday soon there *will* be queens in the playing cards," I said hopefully.

"If it is left to the men to decide, we shall first see the Second Coming of Christ!" Lady Brantôme declared.

Everyone laughed at that.

Mimi, the dealer, looked to me, querying the number of cards I wanted dealt to my hand.

"I'll have two," I said. When I turned them up, my shock was so great that I gasped, and the blood rushed to my face. *I'd been dealt two kings. I now had all four in my hand!* All hope of finessing this hand or bluffing was impossible. I just grinned, fragments of thoughts skittering across my mind. *Kings were involved. And queens. And my future . . .* But it was all so quick and ephemeral that it was gone before I could make any sense of it.

Mimi was offering cards to Suzanne when the door opened and Madame entered. She seemed puffed up with excitement, and she did not keep us in suspense for long.

"I've had a letter from François!" she said. "It is one that I think he would not mind my reading to you all."

I had earlier learned from my quiet "overhearings" of Marguerite and Madame that the French had scored an early victory when the Duke of Bourbon and his lance had been the first to cross into Italy. They had taken the whole of the Swiss cavalry by surprise at a town called Villafranca, dealing a blow to our enemy, the Duke of Milan, who had hired these mercenaries.

We ladies all put down our cards and attended Madame with great interest. Marguerite went to her mother's side and read silently over her shoulder.

"François has written me from the Alps," said Madame. "He is taking the army across into Italy." Then she began to read.

" 'We are in the strangest country that any of us has ever seen, but I hope to reach the plain of Piedmont with my troops tomorrow. This will be a great relief to us, as we are finding it irksome to wear armor in these mountains. Most of the time we have to go on foot, leading our horses by the bridle. On the Italian side, the descent was so precipitous that horses and mules slipped and fell into ravines.' "

I heard a lady moan at that, and saw her friend take her hand worriedly. These two were happily married ladies, and their husbands were in Italy with François. The thought of such hazards terrified them.

" 'Guns had to be dismantled and lowered on ropes,' "

Madame continued reading.

" 'Nothing comparable has happened, Maman, since Hannibal's crossing of the Alps on elephants!' "

This last elicited clapping and exclamations—the thought of their very own François in league with one of history's greatest warriors.

Madame, glowing with pride, raised a finger for silence and continued reading. Even she, in the glow of her son's glory, had forgotten about her dislike of warfare.

" 'Our next stop is Turin, where all who wish will view the Holy Shroud of our Lord.' "

I thought in that moment I saw Marguerite rolling her eyes. *But was that possible? And why would she do such a thing at hearing about the famous Holy Shroud?* Suddenly I wondered if the whisperings—nay, *open gossip*—about the duchess's religious beliefs, which bordered on heresy, were true.

" 'And tell Marguerite,' "

Madame went on,

" 'that Charles has made us all proud. He is very popular with his men, who would follow him to the brink of hell.' "

Marguerite smiled at that, but I noticed that the look was something less than ecstatic. *Should not news of her heroic husband have elicited something more in a wife?*

There was so much to learn from this fabulous lady, I thought. So many secrets.

I was determined to learn them all.

CHAPTER II

The war was over and France had won.

Madame and the ladies of both Claude's and Marguerite's households, all wearing white, were once again at the front gate of Tournelles, as they had been every day for a month, to receive the coffins of the dead. They came together with the clergy, and the noblemen who, by virtue of their age or infirmity, had missed the war.

It was a somber task, and sometimes gruesome, as many boxes were not marked with their inhabitants' names. Mangled and putrefying corpses had to be viewed for identification, the only proof of the soldiers' nobility their fine uniforms.

There was none of the levity I had heard with Marguerite's women, at the sight of anyone's dead husband.

Two old courtiers had just instructed a carriage driver to carry the body of Captain Dresseau to his family's estate for burial. One of the gentlemen mentioned "Marignano," and remembered hearing that this was the great battle of François' war.

"The fiercest fighting anyone has ever seen," said one man, heavyset, who used two canes to walk.

"The Swiss overwhelmed our artillery, my son wrote me," said the other, one of his eyes and several of his fingers missing. "We were only saved at the last moment by our Venetian allies, who arrived shouting, 'San Marco! San Marco!' "

"A battle of giants, Marignano," said the portly man, his eyes aglow. "Twenty thousand buried there alone."

"But Milan is *ours* again. The Swiss our allies. We should thank God for our mighty cannon."

"And for François. He has proved himself a great Caesar on the battlefield."

"May God protect him."

"Well, we know the *pope* will."

They laughed conspiratorially.

"Worried he backed the wrong horse, is he?"

"Enough to make a papal treaty with France to fight the Turks."

"Marignano," said the heavy man wistfully. "I would have given anything to have fought there."

Another coffin was brought before the men by servants and the lid pried open.

"I, too," said his friend. "I, too."

Now we of the French court were en route to meet François in the south of France. He had ignored his mother's and sister's letters begging him to come home immediately, for he wished the progress to *lengthen* his celebration of victory, not to shorten it.

After some grumbling from Madame, a great party gathered to ride in progress out of Paris, mostly royalty, clergy, noblewomen, and old men.

I was sharing a carriage with Marguerite and Madame on the day we passed through the lush, rolling countryside of the Loire River valley and paused to gaze at the Château d'Amboise, one of François' palaces then under enlargement and construction. Despite the scaffolding and hordes of workmen—masons and carpenters and gardeners—it was a magnificent sight to behold, a sprawling fairy-tale castle four stories high, all of gleaming white stone and pointed round turrets.

We would not be spending the night there, Marguerite told me, but instead in the town nearby, as the château was filled with dirt and stone dust, and was largely unfurnished. All round it stood crates and boxes, some that were open, revealing what appeared to be full-sized statues of naked men and women.

"Too uncomfortable for habitation now," she explained. "We *will* be living much of the time here. It is my brother's favorite palace—the place of our youth." She gazed at the massive structure. "He is spending a considerable amount of money on its renovation."

"Too much money," Madame insisted as she glared at some work-men eating their midday meal on the scaffolding. "He is determined to create the most fantastical palaces in all the world, my son is," she said, disapproval coloring her words.

"He needs a showplace for the spoils of his victories, *Maman*. What good is a war with Italy if you cannot cart away its treasures?"

Marguerite had already explained to me about the "Renaissance," a term only recently come into use to describe the reigniting of passion for the classical world in art and philosophy and architecture. It had begun during the last century in Italy, and now François was determined that France was to be the next country to undergo such a "rebirth." The riches he was bringing home from the Italian peninsula—ancient Greek and Roman statuary, and paintings by the "masters"—would be a starting point.

"It will be magnificent," Marguerite insisted.

"Better than Margaret's at Malines?" Madame demanded of her daughter, possibilities beginning to unfold.

"A hundred times."

Louise of Savoy sat back in the cushions of her coach. Rare con-tentment began softening her features.

Marguerite smiled to herself.

"Drive on!" she cried, and the carriage lurched away.

Outside the town of Nevers an unnaturally violent storm came up quite suddenly, and the entire pilgrimage was forced into tents set up in the countryside. The rains were stubborn, lasting for five days. We were miserably confined under the canvases, I even more miserably, since I was kept away from Marguerite's tents, instead relegated to attend the queen.

I knew that pilgrimages were not meant to be gay affairs, but this was cramped and dreary beyond comprehension. There were no dancing or music lessons to escape to. All there was, was praying and going early to bed, as soon as the sun went down.

Worse still, Claude was at a stage in her pregnancy distinguished by continual and rather spectacular flatulence. Her farting in so confined a space was at once revolting and comical. More than once I had to chew the inside of my cheek to keep from laughing aloud when such an utterance spluttered on and on and on. This was followed by a further self-discipline, as I was forced to keep a pleasant face despite a stench so foul it could have struck a horse dead. I actually found myself wishing for something to *embroider*, for it might have passed the time more pleasantly than the incessant droning of prayers, the interminable nights, and the ghastly farts.

Too, I was jealous. Marguerite's tent was next to ours, and I could see out the door flap that both men and ladies did come and go from there. Whilst there was neither music nor laughter, there was *talk*. Much of it. Endless, lively conversation. And when night fell, candles were lit and the talking went on into the wee hours of the morning. I wished desperately to know what was being spoken of on those rainy days and nights. Desperately to be a part of Marguerite's entourage.

When the storm finally passed, I almost shouted with joy and henceforth stayed as close to my mistress Marguerite as was possible. She seemed jolly after this confinement, rather too jolly, and when I asked her how she had passed the time, she replied that it had been a great inspiration for her writings, but would say no more.

Our rendezvous with François in the port town of Marseille was quite the most splendiferous affair I had ever witnessed. First, there were the kisses and embraces both public and private between François and his mother, his sister, and his wife. Then the city's official welcome began, with a procession of two thousand children dressed in white. Guns were fired—a salvo from along the city walls and another by the dozens of galleys anchored in the harbor. There were living tableaux along the route, and performances by dancers dressed as savages from the New World and Africa, Sirens, pilgrims, Moors, and even giraffes.

Together with the king we traveled on from city to city—Aix, Salon-de-Provence, Arles, and Avignon. In the southeast was the Duchy of Savoy. It sat astride the Alps, separating France from Italy. A landscape of sweeping valleys and glittering blue lakes, great snowcapped mountains looming above.

But the strangest and most wonderful sight came as we entered Lyon, the climax of this victory march. Here, besides the pageantry, was *a life-sized mechanical lion who came walking toward us*! The creature stopped and for a moment, not a sound was heard. We all thought the thing had broken down. Then suddenly the lion's chest *opened*, disclosing against a blue background a bank of royal fleurs-de-lis. 'Twas altogether astonishing.

François, transported with delight, clapped his hands, shouting, "Bravo! Bravo! Leonardo!"

After we'd found shelter in the city, we were made to strip off all our finery and don the simple garment fitting a pilgrim. Wearing only black, tawny, and white, the king and his huge entourage went, on foot, to Chambéry—all except Claude, who was carried in a bier, too large with child to walk. We must have been a sight to see, and the whole of Lyon gathered on the bridge across the Rhône River to watch the holy procession.

As we approached the Château of the Dukes of Savoy, a massive structure of pale stone with a high, square, pointed-roofed tower, we filed into the palace that Madame's ancestors had built and inhabited for two centuries.

I had never been on a pilgrimage before and so stayed close to Marguerite, Madame, the king, and the queen, always following their lead. We were, however, not meant to stay long in the château itself, but were herded outside again into the courtyard, and then toward its church, named Sainte Chapelle.

It was in this place that, for the time being, resided that holy relic—the shroud that was said to have wrapped Jesus, and to bear his image. The one at whose mention Marguerite had, I was sure of it, rolled her eyes. It had lately come from the Italian city of Turin, where thousands of pilgrims had flocked to see and prostrate themselves before it.

As we passed in through the chapel doors, we each placed a coin into the hand of a monk with downcast eyes. I wondered if he looked down out of piety, or to be sure that the pilgrim was paying with a real coin or a fake. For everyone knew that fortunes were made by the families who owned such relics, by the pilgrims who handed over their money for the privilege of a glimpse of a finger bone of a saint, a bloody rag that had wiped Christ's face as he crawled down the streets of Jerusalem to his death, or a nail from the very cross on which he'd been crucified.

"These relics are just as outrageous as the sale of indulgences," I heard Marguerite say in a whisper to François. She referred to the printed papers a person could purchase from the church to reduce punishment in hell from an earthly sin.

"Holy relics, indulgences. They're harmless, sister," François replied quietly. "And they make the people happy. Give them hope. Provide them with a little mystery in their lives."

"Keep them mired in superstition," she hissed. "And *false* hope."

"Come, now, I told you the reason for this pilgrimage. Just be patient. I promise, you will not be disappointed."

Once inside the chapel I found myself staring up at its high, star-shaped vault, but except for the lancet-shaped windows, many of the church's other features were obscured by the crowd of pilgrims who had piled in behind the royal family.

I was surprised to see Madame awaiting us at the altar, looking very severe and very regal. I had not noticed her slip away from the horde of pilgrims on our arrival at the château. When everyone had quieted, Louise of Savoy drew back a heavy curtain.

I realized then that I had no clue as to what was appropriate behavior in such a situation. So I watched. The royal family—François, Claude, and Marguerite—were first to move forward.

The king, even *before* setting eyes on what I could see was a very long, horizontally fixed cloth lit by hundred of candles, dropped to his knees and prostrated himself before the relic on the stone floor. After a moment he rose and viewed, for perhaps five minutes, the shroud, sometimes moving closer, then moving back, tilting his head one way and then the other, as I had seen him view a beautiful work of art. Finally he stepped aside for Claude to take her place in front of it.

Her great belly made movement difficult, but devout as she was, there was no question that she would make the public prostration. A lady on either side of her helped the queen to her knees and, holding her shoulders, lowered her upper body so her forehead could meet the floor. Then with great effort and care they lifted her to standing. She gazed at the linen with awe, clasping her hands together and murmuring a fervent prayer. I could not hear it all, but I did hear the word "son" very clearly. She wiped away tears with her fingers until her lady provided her with a handkerchief. After a while her shoulders heaved with deep emotion, and finally she allowed herself to be drawn away from the relic to stand with her husband. François himself had, even from a distance, never taken his eyes from the thing, gazing at it intently.

I moved about subtly in line so that I could catch a glimpse of Marguerite's face before she came before the shroud. I was not surprised to see her lips pursed in displeasure. And in the moment before she prostrated herself, her jaw clenched tight, as though she were about to endure a beating. She had whispered her impatience with relics and indulgences, but it was altogether unseemly for the "Most Catholic King's" own sister to be anything but pious before the icon, and in front of a hundred other pilgrims.

My turn before the shroud was nearly upon me, but as I moved forward, I saw François, Madame, and Marguerite move through a doorway near the altar. Behind it I caught a glimpse of a man nearly as tall as the king, but much older. He was long-haired and long-bearded, and as the door closed, I heard the word "maestro" and saw François embracing him warmly.

Then I was standing before it—the Holy Shroud. I quickly made my obeisance, wondering how long was long enough to lie facedown on the cold stone. When I stood, I stared at the linen, trying to make sense of the image before me. On the right I could see the ghostly, skeletal form of an outstretched man, his arms folded across his groin. The face was dark, especially where his beard and mustache would have been, but the eye sockets seemed dead white holes. In his hair and on his forehead were the darkest marks, bloody wounds from the crown of thorns.

My head swam and my heart began to pound. *Was I looking at Jesus Christ's very winding cloth? Stains of the same blood of our Savior that we drank at every Mass?* The chapel throbbed with piety—low moans and quiet weeping—and the many candles threw an eerie, flickering glow on the shroud that seemed to make it move . . . ever so slightly.

Lost in the sight and sound of it all, I was startled when I felt the gentle push of the next pilgrim in line. I moved on in a daze, only regaining my senses when I'd stepped from the church into the shock of fresh air.

For the rest of the day, as we of the court were hosted by the family Savoy, the king, his sister, and his mother were nowhere to be seen. That evening at the simple pilgrims' supper of bread and wine, they finally appeared, and the man François called "Maestro" accompanied them.

He was the famous Italian painter Leonardo da Vinci, who was, I learned, the creator of the fantastic mechanical lion we had seen earlier that day. It was clear that this once-imposing old man had become frail. One arm hung limp at his side, and his broad shoulders hunched inward. But his eyes were still clear, his facial bones strong and sym- metrical. I thought that as a youth he must have been beautiful.

François doted on him, throwing his arms around the withered shoulders. Marguerite seemed taken with him as well, she smiling more than I had seen since coming into her household.

François was leading the maestro around the dining hall introducing him to his courtiers and ladies, and as they approached my sister and me, I found myself nervous, for the man was a legend and now, for all to see, a beloved of the King of France.

"*Les soeurs Boullan*, Marie *et* Anna," he introduced us.

We curtsied, and when I rose, I was startled to see the old man staring at me. It surprised me that if such a man would stare at one of us, it should not be Mary. She was certainly the prettier of the pair of us. But I was not mistaken.

He was staring at *me*.

"*Bonjour*, mademoiselles." He asked us in French how we had liked the shroud. I had never before heard the language spoken with an Italian accent, but the man was fluent nevertheless.

Mary had not quite mastered her French, so she stuttered stupidly for a moment, and in that awkward pause I spoke up, saying how magnificent it was to see the face of Our Lord, and how it had brought tears to my eyes. I had not actually wept, but I had no words to describe the jumble of my feelings.

The maestro nodded sagely and, bowing in a most gentlemanly fashion to Mary and me, turned with François to go. I heard fragments of da Vinci's comment in Italian. "Anna *ha occhi incantevole*."

He had commented to the king about me!

When later I was able to speak with Marguerite, she greeted me warmly with a kiss on both cheeks. As pilgrims in a holy place, we spoke in low, subdued tones.

"Your Grace," I began. I wished to tell her of my pounding heart and swimming head at the sight of the shroud, and wanted to know why she had rolled her eyes at the mention of it. But of course I could not.

"What is it, Anna?"

"This was my first pilgrimage," I said, feeling stupid.

She indulged my inanity. "Yes, I know. Are you glad you came?"

"Oh, yes! The progress was magnificent. France is such a beautiful country."

She gave me an odd look. "Have you nothing to say of the holy shroud you just saw?"

Oh, I wanted so to please her! To say what would have made her think well of me. But confusion reigned in my head. I *had* believed the relic was the image of Jesus.

"I will never forget it as long as I live." *It was the best I could do.*

Marguerite smiled enigmatically. "We'll be taking a different route back to Paris, so you shall see even more of our beautiful country." She turned, as if to move away.

"Duchess Marguerite!"

"Yes, my dear?" she said, turning back.

"Do you know Italian?"

"I do, a little."

"What do the words '*occhi incantevole*' mean?" I asked.

"Beautiful eyes," she said. "Beautiful eyes."

CHAPTER 12

We arrived back in Paris not a moment too soon. Claude was brought to bed for the second time, hardly able to control her terror of the ordeal. Although she was young, her deformed hips made the pain of birthing contortions excruciating. It was her further misfortune that Madame, always a rock on these occasions, was herself deathly ill with an ague.

But come the baby did, on a freezing winter night, with the wind howling as loudly as Claude was.

The father—it was the same in England—was nowhere to be seen. It was expected that François was in the cathedral, on his knees, praying desperately for the child to be born a male. Claude's ladies were nervous to be attending the birth without Madame, and I was nearly beside myself.

Two midwives arrived, haggard old women—sisters by the look of them—followed in by two maids struggling with a strange piece of furniture, its back rounded and a narrow horseshoe of wood for the seat, the front completely open. This, I presumed, was the birthing chair.

The crones opened their satchels and began emptying them. First there were jars and covered pots, their cloying odors filling the room in moments. Then they laid out an array of terrifying instruments that looked more like devices of torture than birthing tools.

Indeed, on seeing the women and their paraphernalia, the queen seemed to moan even louder, and she called for me to come hold her hand. I thought, *Dear God, spare me from witnessing this thing too closely.* But God was not listening to me; else my prayers were being drowned out by Claude's screams.

With no finesse or propriety, the sheet was thrown up and the queen's knees were raised and pushed apart. The old crone standing at her side poked Claude's belly, and the other woman, between her legs, stuck an unceremonious finger up the royal cunny, murmuring, "Saint Augustine said we are born between feces and urine."

"Ah," said the other, "the wisdom of men."

"And *celibate* men, at that."

They both chuckled, their laughs identical.

"Soon," said the probing midwife to the queen. "It won't be long, though I cannot promise it will not be painful. Your daughter gave us quite a time, if I'm remembering correctly. But you're a brave girl," she added a bit more gently as her sister anointed Claude's belly and nether regions with a sweet-smelling unguent from one of their jars.

"I'm hoping for a son this time," said Claude, the first real words I had heard her utter in several hours.

"We'll see what we can do about it," said the other sister, "but will we be forgiven if it comes a girl?"

"Of course. I love my children, sons or daughters." Then Claude shrieked, an agonizing sound that sent her waiting ladies scurrying into the next room. I wished so to be leaving with them, but Claude squeezed my hand even harder.

"Stay with me, Anna," she said, her voice a hoarse whisper. She must have seen the look of horror on my face and added, "This is not a command. Only a request."

It suddenly felt as if the heart in my chest were leaping forward in Claude's direction. "I will not leave you, Your Majesty," I said, my eyes filling with tears. "Not ever. Just squeeze my hand as hard as you like."

"That's a good girl," said one of the midwives, nodding at me, and all at once I felt important. The other ladies had fled, but I would hold the hand of the Queen of France as she gave birth. I would be steadfast and brave, and give Claude all the reason in the world to be glad of her choice of myself to see her through her labor.

The sisters and I helped Claude into the birthing chair, and beneath her they spread thick piles of clean sheets.

But all hopes of courage and strength of will abandoned me as Claude burst forth a hemorrhage of blood so wild and profuse that the midwife between her legs was suddenly covered in gore. Though it seemed not to rile the sister in the least, it so terrified the queen that she began to wail loudly that she and the babe were going to die.

"We are going to Jesus!" she cried, again and again, and the lament, as well as the blood—more than I had ever seen or wished to see again—convinced me that she and the unborn child were utterly doomed.

I began to weep, kissing Claude's hand, crooning, "I will pray for your souls, sweet lady, I will pray for your souls."

"Nobody's going to Jesus," said the midwife, handing her sister a towel to soak up the blood.

With practiced precision they stood, one sister straddling the queen, pulling her hips forward in the chair, whilst the other placed a pillow behind Claude's back. Then they knelt side by side in front of her.

"Look there, young miss," said a midwife to me. "Here comes the royal head."

She took my arm and brought me round the front, though I must have been pulling back away, for the next day I had her finger marks on my arm. But round I went and kneeling down, I saw a most riveting sight—the pale, heavy thighs parted, the knees in a wide V, the hairy-lipped mouth gaping open to a size I thought impossible, and a huge knob of flesh pushing out, tearing the skin below. The queen's cries had grown so fierce it sounded as if she were being rent in half.

Then a slime-and-blood-coated creature emerged from her, slipping so quickly into the hands of the midwife that I thought it would slide away. A double cry from the two sisters at the same moment—"A girl!"

And a groan—nay, a great sigh of relief—from Claude that brought me back to her side, clutching her hand, kissing her hand, kissing her face.

"A living daughter, a living daughter . . . ," was all she could say.

"Thank you, Jesus," I said, remembering the shadowy image of his face on the shroud, the white sockets of his eyes, and wondered why all our beseechments in front of that holy relic had brought only another princess. *Would François be angry?*

Then I went cold.

I grasped the arm of the standing midwife, busy pushing rhythmically down on Claude's belly as her sister took the babe to clean him.

"Will the queen live?" I whispered.

"Ach, the queen, for all her ills, is a solid cow when it comes to birthing. She'll live, all right, and if I'm not mistaken, that big, handsome husband of hers will keep her pregnant the rest of her life. He's got a second daughter. Now he will try until he gets a son."

"And another," her sister said, returning with the swaddled babe. "Here," she grunted at me, "you give the babe to the queen. You were a brave soldier. Go on, now, hand the future Princess of France to her mother."

'Twas the first time I had held a tiny infant in my arms. She looked shriveled and ugly to me, her bud lips puckering and unpuckering as if looking for the teat. I wondered briefly if she'd grow up to have a big nose, like François had, and then I bent and laid the girl in Claude's outstretched arms.

"Louise," she said to her, "*la Petite* Louise," and began kissing her everywhere not encased in the swaddling blanket. "Anna," she said to me, gratitude so apparent in her gaze that no words were needed, "go and find the king. Tell him he has a daughter."

I kissed Claude's hand again, guilty that I had hated the boredom of her household. Nothing in my life had ever been as thrilling as the queen's "great hour."

"It would be my honor," I said, and, curtsying low, hurried away to find François.

The English Maze

CHAPTER 13

"*P*rayers, everyone! Morning prayers!"

François was striding through the halls of Amboise after an early ride, calling the faithful to chapel with him. Monsieur Montbrison and comte d'Enghien flanking him, he was in his usual handsome good health and high spirits, and, after three years on the throne, bursting with confidence that bordered on arrogance. It was only his charm, my sister, Mary, insisted, that kept the king from utter obnoxiousness.

She and I were now three-year veterans of the French court and, like two dry sponges, had absorbed its customs and colors, its fashions, nuanced humor, and worldliness. Mary had finally succumbed and learned the language, though her use of it was nowhere near as broad or subtle as my own.

"Marie! Anna!" François called out to us. Delighted to be personally summoned, we fell in behind his growing party of courtiers and ladies, all laughing and chatting. We were the height of fashion, sophistication, glamour.

François had finally moved the court from Paris to the Château d'Amboise, which I liked very well indeed.

How could I not? It was a heavenly castle.

As Marguerite had said, François had created a fantastical residence—spacious and light-filled and elegant. It brimmed with classical and Renaissance masterpieces.

Every corridor was lined with paintings. Wonderful country landscapes. Depictions of famous cities like Rome and Venice and Florence,
which I could hardly tear my eyes from. There was religious art the
likes of which I had never seen. Voluptuous, creamy-skinned Virgins,
barely draped Magdalenes oozing passion and tragedy, and horrifyingly
lifelike crucifixion scenes. The strangest thing, though, was the *faces* of
the people in the paintings, and how they looked so real they might
have been standing in front of me.

There were several great ballrooms, my favorite of which boasted an
immense white marble fireplace carven with fleurs-de-lis and kneeling
angels, and arches of the same white stone that soared cathedral-high
above our heads. Even the windows were pretty, their frames decorated
with stained-glass *As*—for "Amboise."

There were endless outdoor places to walk in beauty. The best was
a formal garden, precisely set out, rioting with flowers and fruit trees
and hedges in shapes. Those nude statues of men and women I'd seen
in crates now adorned the garden paths. All of this was enclosed with
white painted latticework and little pavilions where courtiers could sit
and woo their ladies. All round *that* had been built a long gallery, so that
others could watch the wooing going on.

But nothing inspired so much awe in me as the huge round tower
called Minimes that rose like a great fortress from the Loire riverbank
and met the north wing of the château at its ground level. Inside was
a wide, empty spiral ramp that in times of war or attack had allowed
French soldiers to ride their horses in and out of the palace quickly and
safely. Now it was used only by François' ladies and gentlemen going or
coming home from a hunt. But it thrilled me nonetheless every time
we clattered en masse down the resounding tower.

This day, François and his favorites barely quieted as we passed
through the doors of Amboise's Chapel of Saint Florentin, our voices
suddenly amplified and echoing round the high vaulted ceiling. The
church seemed the only place in the château that the king had not
bothered to restore. The pews and altar were carelessly carven, the
stained-glass windows lifeless blues and reds.

I saw that Duchess Marguerite was already seated in the front on the left, several of her ladies surrounding her on the sides and behind. She graced me with a warm smile and a nod, indicating that rather than attending her, Mary and I might stay in the king's company, now settling on the right side of the aisle.

François and the men took seats in the second row and pointed the women toward the first.

This being a weekday, Archbishop de Lenoncourt was nowhere to be seen, probably sleeping late with his mistress again. A lesser clergyman moved serenely to the pulpit and began his droning prayers, *"Introibo ad altara Dei. . . ."*

That was the king's cue to commence his daily ritual.

"You begin, Enghien. First of all, who was she? Not one of ours?"

"No, Majesty. She came with her father, Monsieur Follet, the wine merchant from Rouen. Eighteen years old."

François and Enghien tried not at all to keep their voices down. Indeed, they spoke loud enough, not only for us women in the row before them to hear every word, but to drown out the priest's prayers.

"A virgin?" François inquired.

"Well," Enghien began with a smug laugh, "had it not been for the smear of blood, I would never have believed it. She was a wild creature, grinding and bucking and using her tongue like a practiced whore."

François' full attention was suddenly concentrated on his companion.

"You are saying a virgin sucked your cock?"

"That is what I am saying."

"Did she let you come in her mouth?"

I could just imagine Enghien smiling roguishly. "She did not have a choice," I heard him say.

"What else did you do?" François asked.

"Cunt and ass," Enghien said.

My ears were beginning to burn, but I kept my eyes fixed on the unruffled priest.

"And you came every time?" François demanded.

"I withheld in the cunt, but her ass was so tight and sweet I could not help myself, and exploded."

"Well-done!" the king cried.

I chanced a peek at Marguerite, who was shaking her head, but smiling indulgently. I myself was somewhat chagrined, as I knew quite well by now the myriad terms for the male and female organs, but I was still unclear about these references to "coming" and "exploding," though it seemed obvious that it had something to do with satisfaction.

When I had questioned Mary about it, she had only mocked me for my ignorance, but I suspected that for all her sophistication, my sister knew little more about the sexual act itself than I did. Lynette had got no further with her sisters on this subject, though my friend informed me that sheets were routinely soiled by male fluids during the "culminating moment." It was all very confusing.

"All right, Montbrison," the king said, turning to the courtier on his other side. "Let us hear about *your* evening."

"I will just bore you, Your Majesty. Madame Dussault and I have been lovers for two weeks now. Surely you know everything there is to know."

I could hear the lady in question rustling her skirts on the other side of Mary. In the past two weeks François' "inner circle" had indeed been privy to the most intimate details of this couple's bedroom habits. Madame Dussault was aroused most easily by Montbrison suckling on her nipples like a baby. He came to fastest erection when she slapped his buttocks so hard she made handprints. And she had angrily withheld her favors for several days after he had called out his wife's name at the "climax."

It never failed to amaze me that Madame Dussault showed no mortification whatsoever during her lover's reports to the king at morning prayers.

"We could perhaps have a rendition of your lady's utterances when you are fucking her," François suggested.

"You wish me to . . . ?" Montbrison sounded helpless.

"Yes, go on. Do the best you can."

The nobleman took a long breath and began. "Oh, oooooh! Good, good, harder, my love. Oh, oh, your cock is so hard. So big and red and *angry*!"

"I never said such things!" Madame Dussault suddenly cried, turning round to face her lover and the king.

Everyone began to laugh.

"Parce domine, parce populo tuo, ne in eternum irascarie nobis," the priest intoned in a loud voice, trying to drown out the argument.

"Why do you not ask me what *he* sounds like, Your Majesty?" said Madame Dussault. Without waiting, the lady began to grunt and snort like a rutting pig, which caused even more hilarity. No one was more delighted by the performance than the king, who doubled over with laughter.

"François!" Marguerite called from across the aisle. "Do control yourself."

"Yes, sister," he called back, and, trying with some difficulty to rein himself in, said to his favorites, "That is enough for today, my friends. We must leave something for tomorrow."

CHAPTER 14

"Excited? About seeing Father? I'd say not." Mary tucked the last stray hairs into my peaked velvet French hood and pushed it farther back on my head.

"Not even a little? After three years?" I asked.

"If Father were three years *kinder*, I might be happy," my sister said to her reflection, seeing to the last of her own powder and paint.

We were jostling for space in front of the looking glass in our tiny cubicle next to Queen Claude's apartments at Amboise. She'd been pretty before, but since we'd come to France, she had positively blossomed. Now it was commonly agreed that Mary Boleyn was the most ravishing creature at court.

"Though," she added thoughtfully, "there might be some benefit to me in his new post as Henry's ambassador to France."

"Does absolutely *everything* revolve around you?" I said, taking the pot of crimson cochineal from her and rubbing it into my lips.

"Not so much!" she cried, pulling the pot away. "You're not even thirteen."

"True, but *I* am the new French ambassador's daughter, and a young lady," I said with a hauteur she knew was a tease.

"Perhaps you should learn how to take more benefit for yourself," she said, pouting prettily, looking this way and that at her reflection.

"I have all the benefit I need, Mary."

"With the duchess? She's gone quite boring, if you ask me. All she talks about is *religion*. She's almost as bad as the queen."

"It's not the same thing," I said. "One is papist nonsense, and the other . . ."

"Anne!" Mary took me by both shoulders and turned me to face her. "You listen to me. Marguerite is playing a very dangerous game with her Martin Luther. But *she* can afford to be a heretic. *She* is the king's adored sister. *You* are a twelve-year-old guest at a very Catholic court. If you're not careful, you'll get us both burnt at the stake." She fluffed out the skirt of her yellow silk gown, and a delicate scent of lavender rose up around us. "Whatever you do, don't breathe a word of that Protestant business to Father."

"Do you think I'm stupid?" I said, the irritation in my voice unmistakable.

"No, of course not," Mary said, already contrite. "I'm just looking out for my little sister. Here." She brushed my cheeks with a bit of the cochineal. "You look very pretty."

"So do you. Come, we're going to be late. The last thing we want is to be late for Father."

It was a heady thing to walk into the astonishing great hall of Amboise and see the magnificent feast laid with gold and silver plate, the walls hung with François' finest tapestries, garlands of fresh flowers, musicians beating out their tunes, the ladies and gentlemen in their glittering best—all for welcoming and celebrating the new French ambassador's first visit in that capacity to the French court.

It had taken official business to bring Thomas Boleyn back to France. A visit with his only daughters had never crossed his mind.

Mary squeezed my hand excitedly, for our "entrance," and the evening the king had planned for our father, had been something she'd been imagining from the minute she'd heard of his coming. Claude, Marguerite, and Madame had, in fact, come in *first* to the usual fanfare in order to allow Mary and me our moment of glory.

But we were both startled when the music stopped altogether and a crier called out, "*Les soeurs Boullan,* Marie *et* Anna!"

This was even more than Mary had anticipated, for as we glided through the doors, every single eye was fixed upon us. I spotted my father across the hall, standing with François, Claude, and Marguerite. For a moment I felt paralyzed, and the smile froze on my face. But Mary seemed to ignite like a hundred candles lit at once.

She cried, "Papa!" as though she adored him, and hurried across the floor, all grace and beauty and shimmering yellow silk.

As I followed my sister across the hall, I watched her perfect performance; she curtsied first to our father, then, as though remembering etiquette, made flustered, fluttering obeisance to the queen, the king, and his sister. Then she reached up on tiptoes and kissed Father on both cheeks, in the French manner.

By this time I had arrived in rather less of a flurry, quite subdued after Mary's dramatics. I curtsied all round and, not wishing to seem less enthusiastic than she about seeing our father, gave him the obligatory double kiss.

"You're both looking well," he said to us with an appraising eye. And then, just like that, as though Mary and I had been pesky flies to be swatted away, he turned back to his conversation with François—something about old Maximilian's death, and the choosing of the next Holy Roman Emperor.

There was no way that Thomas Boleyn could conceal the ice that flowed, instead of blood, through his veins. The abrupt dismissal was apparent to others close at hand. I saw Claude flinch, but of course she would never dream of interfering with a father and his children. In her world—in most of the world we knew—that hierarchy was sacrosanct. The father was the undisputed king of his own family, nearly a god.

But Marguerite, bless her courageous soul, spoke up.

"Your daughters are two of the most charming young ladies in our court, Monsieur *Boullan*."

Father was forced by protocol to attend the duchess, and turned back to us.

"There is hardly a gentleman who does not desire Marie," Marguerite went on, "and yet she comports herself with great dignity and reserve." I knew Marguerite was not particularly fond of Mary, finding her too vapid for her tastes, but she was not going to allow Father to so publicly disrespect her.

He was irked by Marguerite's forwardness, though I was sure he was aware of her reputation. Ambassadors from all over Europe, after speaking to the king, would go and lay their business before the Duchess of Alençon, knowing the depth of her influence with François.

"It is kind of you to say so," my father said, and made a feeble attempt at affection, placing an arm around Mary's waist.

"But it is Anna—my young protégé—who might most surprise you," Marguerite went on.

I blushed. I had never heard the duchess speak of me as her protégé.

"Oh?" my father said, an edge on his voice. He must also have heard that Marguerite was known for her radical thought and religious perversity.

"She reads the classics with great ardor, and has an extremely clever turn of mind." The words of her compliment were so well chosen that she had elevated me, whilst saving me from suspicion.

"She was always a bright child," my father said, begrudgingly, I thought. He wished desperately to resume his more important talk with the king, not continue on with trivialities about his daughters. Then, as an afterthought, he turned to Mary and me and said, "There's a surprise for you." He lifted his chin toward the far side of the room.

Mary and I followed the gesture. Was it possible? It was! Our brother, George, suddenly looking like a grown man, stood amidst a gaggle of tittering mademoiselles. With perfunctory curtsies to our father and the royal family we hurried cross the hall and heaped on George many kisses and embraces.

"Look at you two!" he finally said, laughter in his voice. "You are, without doubt, the two most magnificent creatures in the room."

Mary, sure the compliment was meant only for her, twirled in a circle so George might see her beauty from every angle. But I caught him looking at me with no less interest, mayhap more. Or at least different.

I knew why. My idea to create an affectionate bond between my brother and me not unlike François and Marguerite's had not been an idle one. I had, after all, begun writing to George more than two years before.

He'd been happily surprised at my first rather long epistle, filled with my observations of the French king's war games, and had written back more quickly than I'd expected. His letter was chock-full of juicy gossip from the English court, he a newly made "Groom of the Body" to King Henry, placing him at the very center of everything intimate in that king's household: what fashions Henry followed, his minor illnesses, his temperament, which, as Queen Katherine produced more and more dead babies and only one living girl, was changing from jolly—"Good King Hal"—to something darker and more unpredictable. In fact, George wrote, Henry had taken a mistress, a pretty-as-a-milkmaid lady called Bessie Blount.

I had not mentioned my correspondence with George to Mary, wanting it to be something of my own, and not wishing for it to be spoiled.

But now she could see there was something secret between us, just in the way we smiled at each other.

"What's this?" Mary demanded. "What don't I know?"

" 'Tis nothing, sister," George said, hugging her to him. "Anne and I have been writing."

"Writing *what*?" she said.

Sometimes she was so obtuse.

"Letters, Mary," I said. "Just letters to each other."

You would have thought we'd slapped her; so shocked was the look on her face.

"And you never told *me*?" she said accusingly in my direction. She was truly furious, her moment of glory now doubly ruined by her father's indifference and her brother and sister's clandestine correspondence. She poked a hard finger in my chest. "You little twat," she said, altogether vexed, and, turning on her heels, fluttered away.

George squelched a chuckle, though in all honesty I felt badly. I'd

not meant to hurt Mary by our secret letter writing. But I was uncon-
scionably happy to see my brother.

"You look so handsome," I said to him. "The girls must be wild
about you."

"I have my share of attention," he said modestly. "There's a lady in
Queen Katherine's household I would die to have."

"And . . . ?"

"She would die to have me, too."

"Who is she? You haven't written me about her."

George's face twisted in sudden misery. He sighed. "Nothing will
come of it."

"Why?"

"Because I'm betrothed."

"Betrothed?!"

The music of a galliard had been struck, and couples were flowing
in pairs onto the dance floor.

"Do you know it?" George said of the dance, quickly changing the
subject.

"Do I know it?" I repeated saucily. "I am 'Queen of the Galliard.' "

I gave him my hand and we joined the others. This was a sprightly
triple-meter dance performed by a couple, embellished with turns and
high jumps in *solo*.

I had never bragged to George in my letters, but the truth was, I had
come to be known, in all of François' court, as the very best dancer. I
leaped the highest, twirled with the most grace, kicked twice when all
the other ladies kicked once. Young as I still was—or mayhap because
I *was* still young and lithe—whatever the dance, slow and stately or
wildly abandoned, my body was always at one with the music.

Older girls, and even older ladies, asked me to show them the steps,
and many of them had improved with my tutelage. I was therefore well
liked by those of my own sex, and admired for my skill by the other. I
was still too immature to elicit interest of a more sexual nature, but that
was fine with me. I cannot say I did not enjoy the attention.

George was an adept partner, very good in fact, and before we knew it, the dancers on the floor had thinned till we were the only ones dancing. Even over the music I could hear whispers of, "They are brother and sister," and as I twirled once more, I caught sight of my father, François, and the royal ladies, their eyes fastened on George and me. All but Father were clapping to the rhythm of the galliard, the tempo of which was intensifying.

But we stepped lively, the pair of us, keeping up with the beat, he twirling me higher, then leaping, staglike, in his own turns. The music built and built and I thought it would never stop and I would dance myself to collapse . . . till all at once it crashed to an end.

The applause and shouting deafened us, and we were instantly surrounded by a throng of revelers, congratulating our performance, clapping George on the back, men kissing my hand.

It was, I think, the finest moment in my life, the applause not just for me but for my dear brother. I had, I realized, begun to attain that state of grace enjoyed by Marguerite and François, and I knew George and I would forever in this life be joined in that special way.

"I think we should sit this one out, sister," I heard him say quietly in my ear.

He was right, of course, to leave whilst the adulation was the highest. I let him lead me from the dance floor, where couples were already taking their places for a slow, and I thought quite boring, *passamezzo*.

"Let me show you a little garden where we can find some quiet," I said, smiling at more well-wishers as we left the great hall. "I want you to tell me about your betrothal."

CHAPTER 15

*F*ather was busy all the time conducting state affairs with the "Trinity," François, Madame, and Marguerite. He'd been sent by Henry to France to wrestle with the problems of the void left after Maximilian's death, with his venerated title of Holy Roman Emperor supposedly open to all comers. It was not like any other European title—an inherited one. This was *voted upon* by eight heads of state called "Electors." But bribery, corruption, and open threats of violence against the candidates as well as the Electors had already narrowed the field to only two—Charles of Burgundy and François of France.

I remembered Charles bragging to me that when his elders died, he would inherit Spain, as well as the lion's share of the continent. Now it had happened and François, it was being whispered everywhere, was terrified that if he lost the coveted emperorship, Charles—still really a boy at eighteen—would have secured himself a very stranglehold on Europe. Even worse, Charles would use his new "Christian powers" in Rome to challenge François' recently won and much-coveted Italian interests and territories—a mortal blow, as everyone knew that Italy was the *true* seat of power in the world.

This furor over the emperorship seemed strange to me, for the ladies and gentlemen of court had rarely discussed politics. But with Father's arrival, talk of the Electors, Charles, and the unscrupulous tactics and outrageous sums of money he and his aunt Margaret were using to win the title was on everybody's lips—at dinners, on hunts, and even, it was said, between the sheets.

Thankfully, Father's heavy schedule gave Mary, George, and me unlimited time for entertaining ourselves. Claude, sweet soul that she was, wished the Boleyn sisters and brother all the togetherness possible during this visit, and gave us leave from her household whenever we wanted. The freedom was exhilarating. We rode every fine day, hawked, and practiced with our bows and arrows. Strolled through riotous Amboise gardens, and chased one another through convoluted hedge mazes.

Everything made us laugh. Madame Gaspard's jiggling bosoms, François' big nose. Queen Claude's farts. George regaled us with stories from the English court. How Queen Katherine—who'd become a religious fanatic—had broken out in a terrible rash, only to find that her new "hair shirt" was infested with lice. He even made light of his coming marriage to Jane Parker, a pinch-faced, foul-tempered woman whom father had chosen for him strictly for fortune's sake. In general, George explained, the more appalling the girl, the larger her dowry. Jane's potential bride-price was so enormous even our greedy father was satisfied.

"You poor thing," I said, passing him a bowl of grapes. Claude had organized a picnic for George, Mary, and me on a lovely day, but our sister was absent, bedridden with her monthly courses.

"I honestly don't care," George said of his upcoming marriage. "I haven't one friend who is well matched with his wife. 'Tis the way of the world. I thought you knew it by now."

"I do, I suppose, but . . ."

"There are no buts about it. And don't tell me again about Charles Brandon and Mary Tudor. They don't count. Besides, I heard tell that these days he treats her very badly. Even beats her. It might have been a 'marriage for love' on her part, but Henry has never felt the same about his childhood friend since Brandon conspired behind his back, and for this, he will never forgive his wife, 'French queen' or not." George stuffed a piece of bread in his mouth and chewed thoughtfully. He really did enjoy the art of gossiping. Finally he went on. "The king's new boon companion is a man named Wyatt. Thomas Wyatt. He's the court poet—you know Henry fancies himself a versifier. And Wyatt beats the king at tennis almost half the time. They're well matched."

"And Cardinal Wolsey?" I asked.

"Still running the country, cleverly humble in the king's presence, but growing richer and more powerful every day. Anne . . ." George looked at me strangely. "Why do you worry yourself so much with these things? You're not even—"

"Thirteen. Yes, I know how old I am, George. But I have ears, and a brain in my head between them. And I find such dealings a sight more fascinating than who was chased out of whose bed by which cuck-olded husband, and what noises Mademoiselle Surette made whilst under the covers with Monsieur Varengeville."

"What are you talking about?"

I sighed. "Isn't it apparent, George?"

"No, not really. *What* is apparent?" He was losing patience with me, but too titillated to change the subject.

"Well, it is said that François is 'clothed' in women. You know that he has an official mistress."

"All kings have mistresses. His is that red-haired beauty named Christine."

"He also keeps a trio of brunettes, whom he sleeps with all at once."

"Three at *once*?" Even George was impressed. "And he keeps them all . . . ?"

"Satisfied?" I said, answering his unfinished sentence. "That is the rumor."

"I swear, this is not the kind of education I thought my little sister was getting in the French court."

"That's not a fraction of it," I said, and went silent, with a mysterious smile on my lips.

"Well, come on! Out with it! Tell me everything. Don't leave *any-thing* out. And why have you said nothing of this in your letters?"

"I was afraid Father might intercept them, and then he'd bring me home from court."

"I'd say he would. But go on. Does François have any more mistresses but the redhead and the three brunettes?"

"Not at the moment. But he flaunts his adventures quite openly. Poor Claude. She pretends not to care, saying, 'He always comes back to my bed at night,' which he does in fact."

"To make royal babies, no doubt."

I thought for a long moment. "Certainly that, but I believe François loves Claude in his way. Certainly she adores *him*. How she puts up with the mistresses and all the other . . ." I was hard put to find the words.

"All the other *what*?" George demanded.

I popped several grapes in my mouth and chewed slowly, not only to give me time to gather my thoughts, but to tease George a bit more.

"Lasciviousness," I finally said. "Debauchery. Lechery. It permeates the court." My brother hung on my every word. "We are forced to eat some nights on platters painted with nude men and women. And there is one set of goblets that appear normal on the outside, but as you drain the wine"—I took a deep breath—"etchings come into view on the bottom of the cup. Etchings of people . . . and animals . . . and satyrs . . . and angels, all . . . copulating."

George's eyes were wide as saucers.

"The ladies pretend to be shocked at first, but then they brag to each other in front of the men and compare which of the scenes they had in their cups."

"Can I see some of these goblets?"

"George!" I cried in mock horror.

"Come, tell me more."

"Well, François not only himself keeps multiple mistresses," I went on slowly, "but he insists that his courtiers take them, too. If they do not, they are considered by the king as 'strutting fops.' "

"Go on. There *is* more, Anne. I can see it in your eyes."

"Well," I said, leaning close to George, although no one could possibly have heard us, "François demands that his gentlemen give him detailed descriptions of their 'amorous combats'—that's what he calls lovemaking. Everything, from the various postures they take"—I blushed—"from the front or behind, top or bottom, original or acrobatic. How vigorous or lazy the movements . . ."

"Are you *serious*?"

"I could not have made this up, brother. But there is more."

"Out with it!"

"François requires his friends to tell him precisely what noises the women make during their intercourse, and the expression on their faces as they . . ." I hesitated. ". . . come." I contemplated asking my brother about that business, but then thought better of it.

"This is *astonishing*," he said. "It makes Henry's court seem dull as a dirt yard." Then his expression became concerned.

"What of Mary?" George asked. "Has *she* fallen into this debauchery?"

"She is still a maid, thank Jesus, though she is sought by all the men at court for her beauty. I think *fear* keeps her virginity intact. What Father would do to her if he found her 'used.'"

"Does Father know this is the culture of the court where his daughters are growing up?"

"I think he cannot," I said, just as mystified as my brother.

We both remained silent, humbled by my revelations. Then I added, "Since Father's arrival here, François has kept his hands off his women, and I've not seen the offending plates or goblets. The state dinners are just . . . stately."

"But behind closed doors . . . ," George began with a wicked gleam in his eye.

"George! Look at you. You're drooling."

"I am not," he cried, but he laughed and pinched my arm.

"Ow!"

"Come, take me to where they keep the dishes." He had pulled up our picnic and our blanket. "I must see them."

"Well, my friend Lynette has a sister in the pantry."

Without warning, George planted a kiss on my cheek. His smile was broad. "I had no idea my little sister was such a vixen."

"There's much you do not know about me, George," I said in my most coquettish and mysterious voice.

We started back to the palace, naked men and women cavorting, François and three brunettes rutting, guttural grunts, and ecstatic moans crowding our thoughts. But truly, George did not know the half of it.

Mary, George, and I had been happily surprised to receive an invitation from Father for a private supper in his apartments a few evenings later. The ambassadorial suite was beautifully appointed with a massive carven fireplace, in which the servants had this night set a great, crackling blaze.

A table for four had been set before it and now we three children, all in our best finery, were seated with him, Mary and I flanking Father, George across, heads bowed before the steaming covered dishes.

"We thank you for the abundance, in the name of Jesus Christ, amen." This was our father's usual grace, offered most perfunctorily, as if even these few words were a waste of his time. Still, we felt honored to be sitting here with him, entirely alone, for he had sent all the servants away once the dishes had been set before us and the wine poured.

" 'Tis been lovely having you here with us, Father," Mary said. Her tone was so practiced and modulated that one might almost have believed the sentiment true.

"Yes, well, it might be some time before I return," he said. His voice was clipped and missing any sort of inflection. Monotone would best describe it. "I therefore wish to set forth to you girls my instructions for the next little while."

I sat up straighter in my chair, feeling suddenly important, warmed that my father thought enough of me that I should have a job to fulfill at François' court.

"You spend much time with the Duchess of Alençon," he said to me.

"I do, Father. She is a very fine lady, and I have learned . . ."

"I care nothing of what you have learned so far, Anne. It is what you will learn in the future that concerns me."

"I don't understand." But I *did* understand. I knew what his next words would be. The sweet warmth I had felt turned to uncomfortable heat, and I suddenly wished I were not sitting so close to the fireplace.

"You will keep your eyes and ears open. Whatever is said between Marguerite and François, Marguerite and her mother, or any combination of the three, you will report to me by letter. Your missives to George have improved dramatically over the last three years. Even your penmanship is readable."

"You . . . read my letters to George?" I stammered. A glance out the corner of my eye found my brother pale and shaken by this news.

"Of course I read them, silly girl. Do you really suppose that any correspondence coming in or going out of my household"—he smiled a snakelike smile at George—"does not come under my scrutiny?"

I wished to say something about privacy, but a kind of terror was creeping up my neck and rendered me mute.

"So you will make special note of any intelligence pertaining to François' dealings with Charles or Margaret of Burgundy, or with the pope, the Borgias, Medicis, or any of the Electors. I assume you know who the Electors are."

"Yes, Father."

"Well," he said, "what is it? You look like you've swallowed your tongue."

"Are you asking me to spy on my mistress and her brother and their mother?"

He put his face close to mine and, making a face meant to mimic my own, replied, "No, I am not asking you to spy, Anne. I am *ordering* you to spy."

The room was so quiet that I could hear only my brother and sister breathing, and the crackle of the great logs burning in the hearth.

"Now, Mary," he said, turning his attention to my sister.

She sat still as a statue, all smiles wiped off her face. Her creamy bosom rose and fell above her low-cut bodice.

"You are to give yourself to François."

Mary's peachy skin went suddenly the color of milk. The muscles round her mouth were twitching with the words she had not the courage to utter.

"He has lost interest in his current mistress and is ready for a new one. I've seen the way he looks at you. He desires you. I think he fancies a virgin."

That final word opened Mary's floodgates. "But I am a virgin and *stayed* a virgin so that you could make me a good marriage, Father! Now you are saying—"

My father slapped Mary hard, very hard across the cheek. She was so stunned she did not even bring a hand to her face to hold the place that had turned bright, stinging red.

"Now I am saying," he continued in a clipped, icy cadence, "you will go to the king's bed and keep him happy until I tell you to stop."

I did not dare look at George, but all at once I felt a hand on my knee under the table, searching for my hand. I slid it into his and as my father continued, we clutched each other as though we were two people drowning, with only the small comfort of each other's company in death.

"I will provide you with the clothing and jewelry, cosmetics, and artifice necessary to seduce a great king. It would be unseemly for him to be bedding an insubstantial woman. Of course he knows your lineage—the Howard blood." When he said this, I saw fury in him, that the great blood in our family was not his but his wife's.

'Father, please . . . ," Mary said, tears coursing down her face. "I don't want to be his mistress. I want a husband."

"Do you honestly believe I care what you *want*?"

With that, George let go a heavy sigh, as though Father's words were a long-sought-after confession finally vented. Here was the meat of it. Thomas Boleyn cared not one jot about the feelings of *any* of his children. They were all just soulless possessions, like horses or jewels or properties, each of his or her own value, to be traded in the international marketplace for Father's own enrichment.

He thrust a handkerchief at Mary. "Wipe your face. You look pathetic. The mistress of the King of France must never look pathetic. She must be perfectly groomed and coiffed, sparkling with jewels at the throat and on every finger. She will rustle about in the finest silks and lace. Every man in the world will be jealous that the king possesses such an unearthly beauty as Mary Boleyn."

Mary was dabbing at the cochineal that had dripped down her cheeks as she listened to our father speak of her future. Her tears dried. She sat up a little straighter.

"Now let me look at you." He pushed her face away to appraise her profile. "Be sure not to overeat, my dear," Father said to her. "I can see where you could easily go to fat."

During the rest of Father's ambassadorial visit, George was befriended by François. They rode and played tennis nearly every day. And several times a week, as he always did in fine weather, the king disappeared into the countryside with his favorite male companions to hunt and hawk until dark.

Mary and I, meanwhile, spent the time in a kind of daze. Thankfully, Marguerite and Madame were occupied in negotiations with their new ambassador, so I had no way to fulfill my marching orders.

One day I came upon Mary in a garden, alone and weeping. Not great heaving sobs, but silent miserable tears. Both her cheeks were wet, as though she'd just washed her face. Her nose ran, and her eyes were puffy red and brimming over like two waterfalls. Her normally beautiful features were twisted grotesquely.

Mary was a wholly alarming sight.

I didn't have to ask her what the matter was. I just took her hand in mine and held it. After a while she looked at me.

"I so wanted a husband," she said, sniffing back tears. "It has been fun, all this flirting and carrying on. But I expected a real marriage after all was said and done. And children."

"But you *will* have that. Eventually." I paused, for I was uncertain of my words. "Will you not?"

"I suppose. Most of François' mistresses are other men's wives. Or after they're discarded . . ." She started crying again.

"Oh, Mary . . ."

"I *hate* Father," she said with more venom than I ever suspected she possessed.

"I hate him, too."

For the first time in our lives Mary regarded me with envy. "All you have to do is a little spying."

Though I wished to say the task our father had foisted upon me was repugnant, I knew it did not compare with the forced sacrifice of Mary's virginity. My lips must have been moving without my knowledge as I sought unsuccessfully to find even the smallest words of comfort.

Suddenly my sister lashed out in her pain, and no one was there to receive it but me. "Just go away!" she cried. "You look like a dying flounder, gasping for air!"

I was stung. "I'm sorry. I'll go." Walking away, I was half-angry, half-hurt.

I'd only been trying to help.

Father spent all of his spare moments procuring for Mary the finery he had promised her. First, he sought out the head *fourrier*, whose job it was to issue lodging permits, and bribed him to secure for Mary a small private room of her own in each of the palaces in which we would be living. This was rare for the queen's ladies unless they were very high noblewomen indeed. The one at Amboise, where we were still ensconced, he furnished with lovely accoutrements and a large, comfortable bed.

Then, to our amazement, Father went to an Italian aristocrat living at court who had obtained from his famous mother a number of dolls, beautifully dressed in the highest Italianate fashions, to have these gowns copied for Mary. He insisted I be there for the fittings, which he himself supervised, instructing the seamstress to tighten a waistline or lower the cut of a bodice for the most sensual effect. And he suggested—rather, *ordered*—that Mary sleep with raw beef on her face to prevent wrinkles from forming.

As her wardrobe began to fill and her jewelry casket overflow with pretty trinkets—not expensive ones, for our father was far from rich—my sister, slowly, began to warm to the idea of her seduction of the king.

Never had I been so confused, not only by the tangle of virtue—respecting one's father—and vice—playing prostitute to the king—but by the admission to myself that the whole affair was as exciting to me as it was dismaying.

So it was that by the time my father and brother left France, I had seen too much of one, and too little of the other.

The leave-taking at the Amboise dock on the Loire was for me very bitter. The last remnants of my childhood and happy naïveté had been stripped away by my father's calumny. Of course I had made him the deepest curtsies and shown the utmost respect, knowing if I did any less, I might be severely beaten.

I tried to smile as I bade him good-bye, but my face felt like a piece of wood. When George embraced me, he whispered urgently in my ear, "Send all your private letters to me through Thomas Wyatt. I'll arrange to get them from him. Send some innocuous ones the usual way. Father will never know. My heart is with you, Anne."

They stepped onto the barge and within moments it had disappeared round a curve in the river. I looked at Mary, whose jaw was set and posture rigid. But neither of us spoke a word. We just turned and walked silently back to the palace and the "tasks" that awaited us.

CHAPTER 16

Several months later the queen finally, joyfully, gave birth to the long-awaited dauphin.

"*Le Petit* François" was strapping and chubby-cheeked, and Claude, weak and pained as she was, heaped even more than her usual mother love on the boy, knowing how happy the child—heir to the throne—made her husband. All of France had erupted into wild celebration at his birth, with bonfires as far as the eye could see, and Te Deums and bells ringing from every chapel and cathedral.

In the same month of the birth, several Protestants had run afoul of the church, and local officials had announced the burning of these heretics in the Amboise town square. François and the royal family were invited to join in the solemn occasion. The king, in turn, commanded all the ladies and gentlemen of the court to attend the event. The thought made me so squeamish that I'd begged to stay home with the excuse of waiting on Claude.

The morning of the executions I watched the smoke from an upper window of the château, but turned away when it drifted closer and I detected the horrible odor of burning flesh and hair.

Within the hour the royal entourage returned, and for that, I was ready and waiting at the main entrance.

Most of the party seemed already to have forgotten they'd just witnessed three horrendous deaths, for they were laughing and joking and almost carefree. I spotted Mary among them, and there coming after her was her new shadow, the king himself. She wore a dove gray and gold satin gown and was fanning herself with an exquisitely painted fan, a gift from François—one of so many he had recently heaped upon her. But Mary was paying no attention to the king. Indeed, she was ignoring him, chuckling with a handsome young gentleman, their heads tilted together like conspirators.

I looked closely at François' face. It was, as my father so rightly observed, a mask of desire. That desire had grown more and more heated in the past months as Mary Boleyn had presented the King of France with a challenge the likes of which he had never known.

Whilst my sister knew very well she must follow my father's orders and sleep with François, he had not insisted on the timing for the event, and so Mary, wielding the only control still allowed her, had created her own.

"He will have to wait," she'd told me one evening soon after Father and George had left for England. "And he will have to work to have me. All his other mistresses flung themselves at his feet. And very soon he tired of them and threw them away."

"Or threw them back at their husbands," I'd added. I was sitting on the bed in her private room whilst her hairdresser, a girl hired and paid for by our father, set some of Mary's prettiest paste rubies in an intricate coif of curls and ribbons.

"I shall be different. I'll pretend indifference. Truly, I shall not have to *pretend* indifference. I do not fancy him." She sighed deeply. "At least if I can make it a proper chase, he will want me more. He does love a hunt, does he not?"

"More than anything," I'd agreed.

Now in the Amboise entrance hall, watching François watching Mary the way he eyed a fallow deer from the back of his horse, I could see that she had been right. He was smitten with this prickly English rose, this beguiling creature, this unattainable virgin. He had been sending her gifts regularly for months. The first ones—costly bracelets and brooches and pendants—she'd sent back, claiming she could not accept such expensive gifts from a married man.

This was outrageous. No one sent gifts back to François.

He'd changed his tactics and sent parasols, painted fans, tiny birds in gilt cages. These she demurely accepted, and with each present she had not sent back, François reeled with delight.

Now I could see the king moving up behind Mary, where he would likely plant a kiss on the back of her neck, a public intimacy she was finally allowing. All the court was agog with the audacious game Mary Boleyn was playing with François. *Would she? Wouldn't she? When would it happen? Where would it happen? Would the king give up his other women for her?*

But before the royal lips could meet my sister's silky neck, Marguerite stepped up beside her brother and snaked her arm through his, leading him away from the chattering entourage.

It was my cue.

Guessing at their destination, I hurried to the duchess's empty apartments. I settled myself in a window seat behind a heavy velvet curtain, making sure I had a weighty book on my lap. If I was caught eavesdropping, I could always pretend that I'd drifted off whilst reading in the sunlight.

The heavy door opened moments later. I heard Marguerite's angry voice first.

"Do not *ever* force me to attend such an abomination again, do you hear me?"

"I hear you, sister," François replied like a chastised schoolboy.

"And why can you not *stop* this nonsense? It is your country to rule. If you do not wish heretics to burn, then heretics should not burn!"

"France is still a Catholic state, Marguerite, and I am still 'the Most Catholic King.' How can I defy the church so blatantly? Charles would be delighted if I did," he added sarcastically.

To François' great chagrin, despite all the French and English machinations and skulduggery, my childhood friend Charles of Burgundy had finally outmaneuvered the French king and been elected as Holy Roman Emperor.

"Wouldn't he just love to see me drift toward Protestantism, especially now that Henry has written out against Luther's doctrines?"

"*Henry* hasn't written anything, François," Marguerite replied with annoyance. "If anyone authored *In Defense of the Seven Sacraments*, it was probably Erasmus."

"It doesn't matter! Henry signed his name to the damn thing, and because of it, the pope named *him* 'Defender of the Faith'! I cannot be seen to look any less pious than either of them. And Charles is growing stronger every day."

"Then unite with Henry. France and England, allies. Why not? Wolsey wants it. Henry hangs on the cardinal's every word. There's your solution. Marry your son to Henry's daughter."

"My son is seven weeks old," François argued. "Too much can happen before he and an English five-year-old can be wed."

"That's right. Like hundreds more burnings at the stake of innocent Frenchmen. And women. François, your hypocrisy makes my head spin. You don't *believe* all that papist rubbish any more than I do!"

I literally felt my ears begin to burn at that last revelation. I'd known Marguerite had Lutheran sympathies, but I never realized that the King of France hated Rome.

"Won't you be ashamed when Leonardo comes to live with you?" Marguerite refused to let up on her brother.

But what did she mean about Leonardo?

"You are so desperate for him to love you," she accused. "And he is an *atheist*!"

"The maestro is a world unto himself," François argued. "And he knows what really lies in my heart."

"Maybe he does. But *I* do not. If you allow one more Protestant to burn, I swear, I will leave your court and never come back."

"Marguerite!"

"Don't touch me," I heard her say. She was furious. "Martin Luther is a genius. He is changing the world, François, and it will never, ever be the same. Go and be 'the Most Catholic King.' But for God's sake, show a little tolerance!"

Just then I heard the door open. The argument ceased abruptly as Marguerite's ladies entered in a flurry of conversation and rustling gowns. Soon I would find a chance to slip from my hiding place and pretend I had entered with them.

I listened as François greeted them all and took his leave. When I parted the curtains and saw that no one was looking, I backed out, rump first, as though I were looking for something in the window seat. Then I emerged, book in hand.

"Anna," I heard Marguerite say, and froze, horror-struck at the thought of being caught. I quickly composed myself, readying my excuse.

"Your Grace," I said, curtsying to her. I wondered if my guilty face was betraying me. "I found the book I left here," I said.

She smiled. "Which one is it?"

"Vigneulles's *Nouvelles.*"

"Very good. We'll discuss the stories when you've finished. Now run along. I've heard the queen is looking for you."

"Yes, Your Grace," I said, relief jellying my knees. "We will. And I will . . . run along now. Thank you. Thank you."

I tried to leave the room gracefully, smiling at her women as though I were a decent young lady and not a horrible eavesdropper, a spy, a betrayer of the woman I loved most in the world.

I hurried away to Queen Claude's apartments, praying to God for the wisdom to do what was right, and not simply what would save my miserable neck.

'Twas not till two days later that I found time to slip away from my duties with Claude and settle myself at a table away from all court hubbub to write my father. I'd slept badly since my episode of spying on François and Marguerite, indeed had slept hardly at all. Round and round in my head ran thoughts, like little demons. Guilty. Angry. Fearful thoughts all muddled by confusion and inflamed by frustration.

Whether a girl loved or hated her father, he was still her father and her highest lord until she married. And I was English, Henry's loyal subject. Father was in Henry's service and so by my father's instructions to me, *I* was in Henry's service as well. Yet I loved my mistresses

Marguerite and Claude, who loved François, and they France. England and France were ancient enemies, though now forces conspired to join them together as allies. Alliances, however, were fleeting. Today's friend was tomorrow's foe, and a friend again the day after. *Would something I reported or did not report provoke a person's death? Provoke a war?*

With a deep sigh I dipped my quill in the inkpot and carefully wiped off the excess, knowing my father would be cross receiving an ink-spotted letter.

To my right good and dearest father,

I wrote this, hating myself already for the lies within that salutation. He was neither right nor good nor at all dear to me. I thought of crumpling the parchment and starting again, but besides the waste, I knew that any less respect shown in the greeting would be unseemly, and might cause suspicion of me. I think my father had not a clue as to all that went on in my head. I was just a silly, docile girl, mayhap a good dancer, mayhap well liked by my betters, but a servant still, whom he could use at will for his various purposes.

If that was so, I suddenly reasoned, then he should have no cause to suspect that anything I wrote would be less than perfectly honest and perfectly complete.

I have found the opportunity to listen in on a conversation between Duchess Marguerite and King François.

I had to stop then, for fear gripped me and I turned, looking all round me. What would happen if such a letter was to fall into French hands? *Just quickly finish,* I instructed myself, and continued, trying to write neatly, but wasting no time.

François was concerned that he should look no less pious and Catholic than the Holy Roman Emperor or King Henry. Marguerite quite rudely suggested that King Henry had not really written In Defense of the Seven

Sacraments, *but that it had been penned by Erasmus. She also suggested that France more closely align itself with England by the marriage of the baby dauphin and little Princess Mary. Also, it appears that the Italian artist Leonardo da Vinci will soon be living under the protection of François at court. This is all that I heard, Father, and I pray it is useful to you.*

Hoping to finish quickly, your dutiful and loving daughter, from Amboise, this 12th day of July 1518.

Anne

I was pleased with my effort, for I had, I hoped, told some of the truth, but none that would harm Marguerite. I had, of course, omitted news of François' secret antipathy toward Rome and his love of the known atheist and heretic Maestro Leonardo. But that felt to me the most dangerous of intelligence, and too, I did not fully understand its implications. Indeed, I reasoned, *what would have happened if Marguerite's ladies had returned to her chambers a moment earlier?* I would never have heard "the Most Catholic King's" secret.

Who was I fooling? I suddenly thought. This was a lame excuse for lying to my father. But I didn't care. What I had written was all I wished him to know, and duty be damned!

I read my letter over for errors, of which there were thankfully none, and quickly folded the parchment and sealed it with red wax. I hurried to *l'Office du Courrier*, near the stables.

The last of several riders with heavy leather pouches over his shoulder was heading for his horse as I approached the office, a small separate building near the river Loire. I stuck my head in the door and saw Monsieur Filbert sorting through piles of rolled parchments and folded letters. He was a friendly gentleman who oversaw the coming and going of all correspondence at the French court. I had come to know him from the many letters I had sent to George from the time I was a girl. I believed Monsieur Filbert still thought of me that way, childish and sweet, and certainly not an English spy.

He looked up and saw me. *"Allô, Petite Boullan!"* he called out. "What have you today?"

"Bonjour, Monsieur Filbert," I replied, and gave him my prettiest smile. "A letter for my father in London. I understand my betrothed has gone into the service of Cardinal Wolsey."

"The Irish boy?" he said. "Into the cardinal's household?" Filbert loved any gossip, but the higher the personage being gossiped about, the happier he was.

I plucked a single ecu from the purse hung round my waist and placed it in his hand. He smiled broadly. It was enough to cover the courier's expense plus a substantial gratuity for Monsieur Filbert himself.

We enjoyed some more gossip and then I excused myself, eager to be alone with my thoughts. I walked out to the river and watched the barges coming and going, the greatest of my fears quickly fading. I believed the letter would reach my father untampered with. I had dutifully supplied him with some intelligence he would have had no other means of obtaining, yet I had not revealed that which might have betrayed my much-loved hosts in France.

Freed for the time being from the hated task inflicted on me by Father, I had a moment to consider the most fascinating of the facts I had learned. The maestro Leonardo da Vinci was going to live in France, with François as his patron. He was an old man with a withered arm, but there was something wonderful in the idea of his coming. I did not know how, but the French court would become a more exciting place. I was sure of it. I found myself smiling as I turned to go back to the palace.

He had said I had beautiful eyes.

CHAPTER 17

*F*rançois was always full of playful mischief and pranks. There were snowball fights and practical jokes. Once he had nearly brained himself during a mock assault on one of his own castles, leaving a nasty scar on his forehead. There were mornings when all the talk was of the king having gone out with his friends the night before. In masks they rode down the streets of Amboise, pelting passersby with eggs and rotten tomatoes.

We knew the rumors to be true, as Madame would be cross with her son all that day, and even Marguerite refused to speak with him, rolling her eyes at his stupidity and childishness. He would apologize and pretend humility, but everyone knew he did not really mean it, for it would happen again and again. Only Claude pretended it had not occurred, so on those days after such a night, he would cling to her, basking in her blind good graces.

It was, therefore, not much of a surprise when François impishly announced a "mysterious journey" on which only the royal family and the inner circle of its court would be taken on a summer's night. We were told to dress informally, the ladies to wear narrow, rather than full, skirts, and riding boots.

When we met, as we'd been instructed, at the top of a stairway leading to the palace's basement, it was clear to us—a party of perhaps thirty-five—that Marguerite was a conspirator with her brother in this mystery tour, as she and François were both handing out to each of us a good-sized torch. Queen Claude was nowhere to be seen. A servant came round and lit the torches, so now we were standing in a brilliant circle of flickering light, all of us twittering with nervous excitement and anticipation, which François delighted in drawing out to its extreme.

"*Bonsoir,*" the king finally said to the assembled with a wicked smile, and we quieted instantly. He was magnificently attired in a doublet I had never seen him wear before—a deep blue silk, its full sleeves and padded breast embroidered in gold with suns and moons and five-pointed stars, and with symbols I knew to be Egyptian, others Greek. He wore round his neck a heavy gold pendant sculpted into the shape of a bull's head.

Just then my sister, Mary, arrived, late, as she now usually was, spending far too many hours on her toilette, changing her gowns endlessly and choosing "just the right slippers or sleeves" that she believed would most titillate the king. Her face was a smooth glaze from the raw egg whites she'd spread over it for a sensual effect.

Acknowledging Mary's arrival with a warm smile, François nodded to a single piper. The musician began to play a most eerie tune, one that evoked exotic landscapes and pagan temples.

"You will watch your step," the king instructed them. Handing his torch to the servant, he led us to the sound of the pipe down the stair to the lower floor. There was a long hallway where, I was sure, few of the highest ladies and gentlemen had ever been. For here were the storage rooms, the locksmith's cubicle, and the laundry.

The Amboise basement was a sight more welcoming than the one in Tournelles had been. In his renovations, François had thought to make the belowstairs facilities more modern. I knew it well enough, as it was here that for the last several years I had stood with Lynette and traded the best of the day's gossip: whose sheets were the most sullied with bodily fluids from a night's lovemaking. Which clothing had been ripped off a lady or gentleman in the throes of passion. Who had bloodied the sheets in her lost virginity. Indeed, the laundresses knew more intimate details of the court than even the physicians.

But François could not seriously mean to take the crème de la crème of France on a tour of his laundry. Halfway down that corridor—we could see at the end the lit washroom, steam rising from the huge stone tubs—the king stopped and the piper ceased playing. Turning to the assembled, François put his forefinger to his lips to quiet us again, as we had begun whispering and laughing.

He pushed aside a faded, nondescript hanging—a rough textile curtain that I'd seen a hundred times and dismissed as no more than a protector against drafts. It had never occurred to me that a cellar would have *had* no window over which a curtain would be necessary. Instead, François now revealed a *door*, a very plain wood door but one with a great metal lock, the key to which he was now holding up before his face with a boyish grin. It was a long, odd-shaped key of a reddish color. Without another word he inserted the key in the lock and turned it. He pushed open the door. All was dark beyond, but echoing hollowly and smelling of must and decay.

"Behold," he said in the voice of a mad preacher, "we descend into the bowels of the earth itself. Ladies, hike up your skirts so you do not stumble."

"Are we going to hell, Your Majesty?" someone called out.

Everyone laughed, everyone except François, who had taken on a most ominous tone. "I will not say, but if anyone wishes to leave this expedition, they had best do it now, for once we proceed through this door"—he paused for the greatest effect—"there is no turning back."

In the glittering light I saw Marguerite suppressing a smile, so I knew that no real danger awaited us. No one left the "expedition." In fact, Monsieur Montbrison cried out, "Can we not hurry? I'm getting chilblains standing in the draft!"

With that, François disappeared in through the door, his torch held high, and we one by one followed.

It was another stone stairway, but this one was circular, its steps narrow and steep, with damp moldy walls and no handholds. The piper had ceased his playing, himself needing both hands for balance, I assumed, and all that could be heard was thirty-five souls breathing, magnified by the round, echoing stone chamber.

I had knotted the bottom of my gown around my hand and pulled it high, knowing that everyone—even the most lecherous man in our party—was far more interested in staying upright than peering at a lady's legs. For a summer's evening the stair was cold and getting colder as we descended.

Finally at bottom François was waiting, Marguerite behind him. They stood quietly till we were all on level ground, and with a nod to the piper to begin his oddly melodious droning, the king led us down what appeared to be a straight but very long, narrow passageway, and, if not for the procession of torches, dark as Hades.

Droplets of what I prayed was water dripped onto my head, face, and shoulders. Underfoot were puddles of foul-smelling mud, and I could hear Mary at the rear of the parade cursing the filth. I smiled to myself. She had either ignored or forgotten François' instructions about the boots, probably thinking them the least seductive of footwear, and now she was paying for her vanity with the ruination of a pair of expensive slippers paid for by our father, or mayhap François himself.

I heard something skitter over my foot and gasped. A moment later a woman behind me shrieked, and another behind *her*, as a rat ran backward through his passage, certainly wondering at this parade of giants. I prayed he was a lone rodent, as the thought of being overrun by a pack of the horrible beasts in the mold and mud made my heart thump hard in my chest.

But suddenly there was a kind of light at the end of the tunnel—*an open door?* The group of us hurried the final distance.

Soon we were all spilling out into what looked like a basement chamber, our laughter returning as we tromped in single file up a wooden staircase that seemed wonderfully ordinary. At the top was a final, beautifully carven door, and there standing before us was Leonardo da Vinci in a long, broad-shouldered gown of the same blue silk of François' doublet, all matching golden moons and stars and ancient symbols. Around the old man's neck was a pendant—a bull's head, brother to the king's, indeed a twin.

Leonardo held an ornate candelabra in his good arm and was smiling with welcome. "Come in," he said to us in his Italianate French. "Come into my home." I saw him bestow on François a look of profound gratitude as he ushered everyone inside.

"Mademoiselle Boleyn," he said as I came forward.

I looked up, surprised. "You remembered me, Maestro."

He nodded slowly, with the look of a sage. "Because you are memorable," he said matter-of-factly.

Then I was pushed ahead as others surged in behind me.

We were all now in the main chamber of a pretty manor house with many beams in a high ceiling, and tall arched windows. Two gentlemen stood to greet us, one about forty and still, at his age, achingly handsome. The other was closer to sixty with a sober yet pleasant expression. They were introduced by the maestro as his "students," the younger only as "Salai," and the elder as Signor Melzi.

A long table had been set with a lavish feast upon it, but it held little fascination for Leonardo's visitors, because they were all at once aware that though the room was laid out for dining, it was anything but a dining room.

It was an artist's studio.

The door through which we had entered was disguised as a window, the painting of a distant, mountainous landscape within its "frame." Every inch of the walls was covered in the maestro's sketches. There were drawings of the human body without the covering of skin, a parchment with fifty different renderings of the same hand from fifty different angles. "Cartoons" of what would one day become paintings. There were sketches of cities and canal works and aqueducts, and one of a magnificent double staircase. On pedestals were all manner of unusual objects of wood and leather and metal—a giant screw, a crossbow, a miniature bridge.

"Please, honored guests, look, touch gently, ask questions. All will be answered."

The ladies and gentlemen seemed to quiet and slow their speech. Even the most vapid coquettes were enraptured by what was before them—naked forms intimately rendered. Faces of immense grotesque-rie. *The inside of an eye!* Some began to squirm. Some even averted their gaze from images that were clearly blasphemous.

I found myself drawn to a wooden model of a great castle. I had never in my life seen anything like it. Its detail was minute, down to tiny pieces of glass embedded in the walls for windows.

I wondered if Mary was as intrigued by the sights as I, and I looked to find her. My sister might as well have been in a stable for all her interest in her surroundings. François stood behind her, leaning down to nuzzle her neck. She was smiling, pleased for his attention in a place where Claude could not witness it. For all her unkind words about the queen's dullness and the boredom in her household, Mary was wretched at having to seduce her husband, especially under the poor woman's nose.

Tonight she was free to play all the roles she'd desired for herself—the temptress, the Madonna, the woman in love. And François—having taken his licentious court through a secret tunnel a mere two hundred feet from Amboise to an altogether exotic, mysterious world—seemed freer and happier than I had ever observed. Looking at my sister and the king now, one would have thought they were young, innocent lovers with no past, no attachments. Certainly no countries to rule, no fathers to whom they were enslaved.

"I see you have found my model of Chambord."

I was startled by the sound of the maestro's deep, comfortable voice at my side, and the feel of him towering over me. He could see very well I was not looking at his miniature castle but staring at François and Mary. With his words he had very kindly allowed a graceful escape from my embarrassment—interest in his work.

"It is so exquisitely detailed," I said, quickly tilting my head to the side, as though examining the little structure from a new angle. "Did you say 'Chambord'? I have not heard of such a castle."

"That is because it is still a gleam in François' eye, and a pile of wood chips and shards of glass on a table in my house."

"But will he build it?"

"Oh, yes. Our young king will build many fine châteaus in his lifetime."

"So this is *your* house?" I asked, sweeping my eyes around the chamber.

Leonardo smiled. His teeth had begun to turn the color of old ivory, but they were still straight and strong. His hair, though mostly white, was thick and curled round about his shoulders. I thought it quite beautiful.

"The king has gifted me this manor—Cloux—for the rest of my life," he replied, "however long that may be. Old age is not for cowards," he added frankly, without a trace of self-pity. With his left hand he picked up his right and cradled the limp appendage. "Like a dead fish," he said. "It is fortunate I am ambidextrous."

"I do not know that word, Maestro."

He smiled again. "I like a person who is not afraid to admit what she does not understand. But I also like a person who will study to find the answers that are evading her. Do you have Latin?" he asked.

"I do not," I said, suddenly ashamed. My education was that of a highborn girl, but not a royal one. Even then it was a rare woman—like Duchess Marguerite—who read and wrote Greek and Latin.

"When next I see you, perhaps you will have learned the meaning of 'ambidextrous.' Now if you will excuse me, I should see to my other guests. Some of them look as though they have entered Dante's seventh circle."

"Thank you, Maestro!" I blurted. "Thank you for . . ." I could not finish, for I feared my words would have sounded groveling and pathetic.

"The pleasure has been mine." Leonardo had saved me with his graciousness. "I hope you will visit me again." He smiled and his face became a crinkled parchment. "Now you know the way."

He turned from me and from the folds of his mystical blue robe wafted the scent of frankincense. I was left openmouthed at his invitation, stunned by his kindness, overwhelmed by his very presence.

"François!" The moment I heard his name uttered I knew its source.

I looked up to see Mary throwing her arms around the king's neck, and him bending down to kiss her full on the lips. People were clapping and crowding round them. I slid through the throng till I could see them. See her.

A small fortune in diamonds now hung from her neck.

The seducer, I could see from my sister's face, had, in a shimmering moment, become the seduced. There was no doubt Mary Boleyn was about to see the underside of François' sheets. *What would become of her? I thought. What would become of her now?*

And what, in heaven's name, would become of me?

CHAPTER 18

I stood fidgeting nervously outside Mary's bedchamber door. 'Twas morning. The morning *after*, court gossip had it, François had finally "plucked" his English rose. Indeed, my sister, Mary, had not attended Queen Claude in her early toilette. She was so conspicuously absent that even the ladies of that demure household whispered urgently on the way to chapel and passed outraged glances over the tapestry they were embroidering with less than their normal care.

I was a near pariah. Only Claude herself spoke to me with her usual kindness. And terrified that the rumor was true, I could hardly muster the courage to reply to the queen. Could not look her in the eye.

The moment I was free of my duties and the other ladies were occupied, I chanced a visit to Mary's room. But when I raised my hand to knock, I pulled it away again, as though the door were red-hot metal. *What would I say to her? How should I act? Would she seem different?* I stood there stupidly until I heard a sound within. Something, furniture, was being moved about. I gathered my courage and cleared my throat before I knocked.

I heard a cheery, "Who's there?!"

"Anne," I called back, my voice nevertheless cracking.

"Come in, come in!" The door opened and there she stood, looking as she always did—simply lovely and smiling. She grabbed my hand. "What are you standing out there for? Come *inside.*"

The door closed behind us and I looked round. Everything in the tiny room was the same. Everything except a chair that had sat beside a small table. It was now under one of the windows, and an intricately embroidered Oriental tapestry, one that I'd not seen before, was now hanging haphazardly over one of them.

"You can help me," said Mary. She was very chirpy. "I want to decide where to put it. Do you like it at the window as a covering? Or should I just hang it as a tapestry? Isn't it pretty? François gave it to me."

I went to look at the thing more closely. It was, indeed, a miracle of handiwork, patterns of fabulous colorful birds and dragons, all in the finest of silk threads and the tiniest stitches.

" 'Tis very rare," I said, then blurted, "Mary, is it true?"

She was straightening her already straightened bed, absently rearranging the pillows. It was only then that I saw her sheets piled in a corner. She turned and looked at me, smiling.

"I pleased him, Anne. Really pleased him. He cried out in so much ecstasy, I thought he would wake the palace. He said he *adores* me. He wants me to have a nicer room. A larger room than this. I think he wishes me to be his only mistress. He said he would be sending Christine back to her husband." Now I could see an unnaturally bright sparkle in Mary's eyes.

"Did it . . . did he . . . hurt you?"

She did not answer at once. It was as though she was choosing her words very carefully.

"He didn't mean to. But he is quite, well, *substantial*." Her smile was now obviously forced.

I wanted to reach out and touch her, but I sensed at that moment that the last thing she wished for was to be touched.

"Did you tell him to stop?"

"I could not."

"Why, Mary?"

"Well, he is the king."

"He's not *your* king."

"I know. But I *had* to please him." She looked hard at me. "You know that." All semblance of the smile was now gone. Her chin quivered. "It was awful," she said. "I bled, but it just excited him more. He kept pounding and stabbing, and I thought I would rip apart."

I stood silently, having nothing to say, no questions I dared ask. But she went on, remembering.

"I was moaning, but he thought—or chose to think—it was for pleasure. And then . . ." She stopped and averted her gaze from me.

"And then *what*?" I could not imagine what came after pain and François' feigned ignorance of it.

"He . . . turned me over."

"What do you mean?" I was mystified.

"On my belly." Tears were brimming in her eyes now.

"I don't understand," I said. "What could have possibly happened if you were . . . ?" I felt my mouth drop open to form a small *o* as my mind formed a terrible picture.

"Mary! Oh, sister . . ."

I took her into my arms and she, who was not one for family embraces, held me tight to her.

"I'm sorry, I'm so sorry he hurt you."

"I still feel pain"—she nodded back over her shoulder—"*there*. But I cannot show it. To anyone. They'll expect me to be ecstatic. The happiest woman on earth. Mistress of the King of France." Then she stiffened and pushed me to arm's length. "I *shall* be happy. It cannot always be as it was last night. It must get better, more pleasurable. Mustn't it?" She looked at me in a panic.

"Of course it will," I said quickly, and forced a smile. "How could it not when everyone enjoys it so? Craves it."

A sharp knock made us both jump. Mary closed her eyes and steeled herself. She put back on her prettiest smile and pulled open the door. She sagged with relief to see it was just a page. He held forward a small box.

"For Mistress Marie, from the king."

Mary took the box and closed the door. She stared at it for a long while. Finally she opened it and we both gasped. There on a bed of cloth of gold was a diamond bracelet, one that perfectly matched the necklace she had received at Leonardo da Vinci's manor a few nights before. It was spectacularly beautiful and glinted in the morning sun. Mary stared at the bracelet for the longest moment, then looked up at me.

And without another word, she burst into heartrending tears.

I'd offered to take my sister's "virgin sheets" to the laundry so that no other ladies or gentlemen could get their hands on them and parade them round to make lewd jokes at Mary's expense. I tried to be discreet and unobtrusive moving through the corridors, but some people saw me with my bundle. There were various smirks and titters. I met no one's eye.

All I felt was gloom as I walked the long basement corridor at whose end was the laundry. I heard female laughter coming from within and knew I would find there Lynette, her mother, and at least several of her sisters. But I was in no mood for their boisterous conversation.

I peeked my head round the heavy door. Lynette was blessedly close, and with a loud "Pssst!" I'd caught her attention. I darted out and waited for her. A moment later she was there. She had grown from a scrawny child into a plump, healthy, and rose-cheeked girl—pretty in a straightforward way, like so many young women from the country were.

She looked down at the bundle I carried, and I was reminded of the first time we'd met—another pile of bloody linen between us.

"Is that it?" she said.

I sighed. "Does *everyone* know?"

"I would say so." She regarded me closely. "Why so glum? Now your sister is one of the highest ladies of the court. Is she not celebrating?"

"She is hurting."

Lynette was blasé. "That will pass."

"And how would a virgin like you know such a thing?" I said, suddenly annoyed with my friend.

"From a family of married sisters."

I knew this was true. Lynette and her kin were a font of venereal intelligence. I'd learned much in the last several years. Everything from the odors that should and should not emanate from a certain female cavity, to which lumps in the duckies were to be feared, and which were merely an annoyance. The treatments for itching, burning, vermin, and "white" infections of the cunny. And alarming conditions—"wandering" and "suffocated" uteruses that could afflict women who did not menstruate. And I heard of the best cure for women whose monthly courses had ceased—a decoction of myrrh and apples that could be either drunk or put in the shoes and walked upon.

Now I hoped for Mary's sake Lynette was right about the pain in her arse being temporary.

She saw I was still troubled. "Anna, it is the way of the world. At least *this* world. Believe me, everything is fine. Better than fine. Your sister's life . . . your life . . . both will be better now. You'll see."

I wondered how—we unwilling servants of our father, and Mary now a gilded slave to the French king's every desire—life would be better.

It was still a mystery to me.

Despite Lynette's assurances I was gloomy all that day, through my dancing lessons and the session with my lute master, who said my singing was sour. It was sour, for I *felt* sour. Angry at my father and François and the society that had forced Mary into a bed in which she did not wish to lie. If I knew her, she would make the best of it, as all women were taught to do. *What was the sense of complaining?* There was no changing how men used women for their various purposes—fathers to enlarge their fortunes through dowries, husbands through making heirs, royal families for making alliances. And the entire male sex for the getting of erotic pleasure.

The women of the French court seemed, unlike the English, to equally enjoy the sexual act. Were they pretending, or was there something more than the stabbing and pounding and ripping that Mary had endured? I was quite sure that after this morning's rare display of sisterly intimacy, Mary would speak no more of the subject to me. The tears would cease. François' gifts would soothe the aching arse. The diamonds would blind her to all indignity. The exotic hangings and satin slippers and painted fans would make bearable the shame she felt in her heart that her virginity had not been given freely to her rightful husband, but taken by an arrogant king with a big nose and an even bigger prick, who used her in any way he chose, and closed his eyes to her pain.

It all seemed so unfair.

I'd joined Claude and her ladies for afternoon prayers and had averted my eyes from her for as long as I could, but finally, once back in her apartments for supper, there was simply no avoiding the queen.

From across the room she regarded me with the mildest of smiles. I smiled back but knew that the expression was more of a grimace.

"Anna, come here."

I did as I was told and instead of merely curtsying, I knelt at her knee and bowed my head. She touched my shoulder, then lifted my chin.

"You can look at me, Anna."

I felt the tears coming, and again I was tongue-tied.

"It is not your fault. Not your affair." She was quiet for a time, breathing slowly and evenly. "I am queen," she finally continued, "and that is the rarest of privileges in this life. All the people of France are my subjects, and they are bound to bow down and serve me. I have the softest beds, the finest clothes, the best food, musicians and entertainments whenever I please. I have no worries in the world. I am married to a tall, handsome young king whom I adore. We were betrothed for so much of our childhood that before we married, we had become good friends. He has always been kind to me and gentle with my deformed body."

I wondered, thinking of his roughness with Mary, if François' gentleness with Claude stemmed from their friendship, or knowledge that he might kill the poor woman with splayed hips who was the mother of his heirs.

"Queenship has its luxuries and its advantages," she went on. "It comes, too, with its heartaches. My husband is the law of the land and, other than God, my highest lord." Now Claude looked away, past me, and I was reminded of Mary in the moment before she admitted an act of François' that she considered beastly. "But he is a philanderer. He has always had his women. He took Madame Disomme as his mistress on the very eve of our wedding."

I saw Claude's courage crack then, almost imperceptibly, like the fine crazing of ice on a spring pond.

"You are not blind, Anna. You've seen how many women there have been, all the money he has spent on these playthings."

I bit my lip, embarrassed to think that my sister was now among the king's long line of "playthings." Then Claude's features softened, and what I believed was a sincere smile spread from her mouth to her eyes.

"But I, and I alone, am the mother of François' children. They are France's children as well, of purely royal blood. They are future kings, Anna, future queens. It is my *privilege* to give birth to them."

I felt I suddenly understood this singular young lady, so plain, so ill made, yet so immensely blessed. Of all the women in the world, how very few were given the gift of royal childbearing. 'Twas a gift I would never be given.

I kissed Claude's hand and held it to my cheek.

"Why are you crying, Anna?" She wiped the dampness from my face.

"She is my sister." It was almost a wail. "How can you be so kind to me? You will probably continue being kind to *her*."

"I will see to it that the chamber François gives Marie is far from my apartments. I have asked Marguerite to take her permanently into her household, and she has agreed." Claude forced me to look at her again. "Your sister is not a bad woman. She is simply a *woman*, and women have very few choices in this world. I would not be at all surprised if the seduction of François was not of her own volition."

I was quite taken aback at the queen's words. Then she shocked me once again.

"Are we not all our fathers' daughters?" she said.

CHAPTER 19

I was a guest at a private dinner in the king's chambers. There were an even dozen of us, he and Mary at the center of the table, the two of them holding joyful court over their favorites. Fascinated, I watched her every move.

My sister had been happy for the past year. As promised, François had sent Christine into retirement and ensconced Mary in the residence set aside for the royal mistress. She had become the belle of French society, often paraded before diplomats and ambassadors—certainly after the queen, Madame, and Marguerite, but paraded nevertheless. Shown off like a particularly beautiful horse.

Though she and I would never discuss it, I had to assume the sex act had become more enjoyable for Mary, for unless she had suddenly become a mistress of deception, there was none of the hurt or fear I'd seen in her eyes that first morning.

Watching her at that table, I saw a glow about her. François, looking handsome and happy, loomed over her, his puff-sleeved arm draped protectively round her delicate shoulders. Marie *Boullan*, François had been heard to say, was the perfect royal mistress.

How could she not be? She was docile, fantastically beautiful, and wholly appreciative of her master.

He'd whispered something, then nibbled her ear, making her laugh gaily.

"I love that laugh!" he cried and, turning to his friends at the end of the table, demanded, "Do you not love that laugh?" Not waiting for their answers, he turned back to Mary and tickled her waist, eliciting a peal of giggles. "I could listen to it all day."

The morning after the private dinner, a note from her was delivered to me insisting I come to her room as soon as I was able. 'Twas late in the afternoon before I could get away from my duties—the day split between Queen Claude and Duchess Marguerite. This, I'd learnt, was the best time to find my sister in her chamber, as she would surely be dressing for the evening's entertainment.

I knocked—a special signal that told her it was me—and she bade me enter.

The bedchamber of the Official Mistress of the King of France never failed to astonish me. It was a glory of ostentation, a thrill of opulence. The king had spent a fortune on the furnishings and tapestries, all of which tended toward the East—intricately carven wood doors and screens, exotic fabrics, wild with reds and blues, screaming oranges, yellows, and golds. The embroidery spoke of India and the Ottoman Empire. Smelled of incense and frankincense and patchouli. The grand bed was not only heavily carven, but gilded and painted as well, its clothes a welter of satins, brocades, fur rugs, and dozens of soft cushions. The chamber's ceiling could not even be seen, as gossamer silks hung in soft folds from the corners, and were pulled into the center with an enormous round "button." Every corner of the room was strewn with more goose-down pillows. Huge, long-handled ostrich-feather fans adorned the walls. All that was needed was Nubian slaves fanning Mary to complete the fantasy of a harem.

Proud of all François' fantastic gifts of jewelry and lace fans, ermine wraps and Indian silk saris, she had displayed them, every one, on the walls. It was a veritable gallery of treasures for all who entered to see. Many times when I visited my sister, she would, as we moved slowly about the room, prattle away, gazing at the display of François' adoration, absently fingering the delicate embroidery on a pearl-encrusted glove, even putting on some ruby earbobs to admire them and herself in a silver-framed looking glass.

And there she was now, her back to me, standing hands on hips before three spectacular new gowns of the latest fashion, worn by headless manikins.

"You must help me decide," she said, not bothering to turn or greet me. "I love the green silk, but the crimson . . ." I imagined that her features were creased with indecision.

Mary fluttered round behind the red dress with a bodice so deeply cut I thought it might be indecent, even for the likes of the French court. She stuck her head where the manikin was missing hers, and pouted prettily.

"What do you think of the color?" she asked. "Does it make me look too olive?"

That was a not-too-subtle jab at me. Mary knew my complexion was olive, which was never as highly regarded as pink alabaster skin, like hers.

"I cannot actually see how your face will look next to the gown," I said evenly, "as there's no material to speak of in the front."

We both enjoyed a little sisterly competition. With an impatient "Tsk!" she picked up the full skirt and lifted it all the way up to her chin.

"Is that better?"

"Turn, so I can see you in the light," I ordered her.

She did, and the golden rays streaming through Mary's large window fell on her and picked up minute flecks of metallic thread in the red dress.

"It's wonderful, Mary. You'll look lovely in it," I said, altogether sincere.

"Oh! I nearly forgot . . . ," she said, darting away from the trio of dummies. "The reason I asked you here." She grabbed my hands in hers. "Close your eyes."

I did as I was told.

"Now come with me." She began to pull me round the room. "Pick up your feet, clumsy girl, or you'll have us both flat on our faces."

"Where are you taking me?"

"Quiet!"

I felt as if I were being led in circles.

"All right," Mary said finally. "Turn round and sit down."

"Sit?"

"Just *do* it."

I sat and instantly, by the feel of it, knew I was on Mary's bed.

"Now put your feet up and lie down."

There was no sense arguing with her. As I lowered myself into her pillows, the scent of her perfumed bedclothes engulfed me.

"Wait . . . wait . . . ," she instructed breathlessly. "All right, open your eyes."

I obeyed the command and saw, quite unexpectedly, a full-length reflection of myself, with Mary lying stretched out beside me.

"Good Lord!"

A great mirror covered the whole of the bed canopy's underside.

"Do you like it? François had it installed so we could watch ourselves making love."

"It's . . . stunning," I said, not wishing to offend Mary, but not at all sure what I really thought. Then I grinned.

"What?" she demanded.

"You must see a good deal of the king's arse," I said.

This made her laugh.

"Not to mention his hairy bollocks," she added.

"Mary!" I cried in mock horror, and jabbed her in the ribs.

She screamed with laughter and poked me back. Soon we were in stitches, rolling round like children on her bed, making grotesque faces into her mirrored canopy. Life had taken yet another odd turn for two English girls at the French court.

And I, for one, was not about to question the Fates.

★　　★　　★

In the year of Mary's rise to glory, Maestro Leonardo and I had become friends of sorts. We would always meet in the company of others—most often a party arranged by François to visit the old man at Cloux, as the two had become great companions, even, it was said, seeing each other every day.

Sometimes the maestro would come to court for an entertainment, accompanied by Salai or Signor Melzi as companion and helper. He was not one for balls, for he could not—because of his infirmity—dance anymore. Nor did he appreciate loud, strident music or the sound of too many voices. He did on occasion bring with him an oddity—one of his inventions to delight François' ladies and gentlemen. The mechanical "walking lion" we'd seen on our pilgrimage at Lyon. A depiction of a white-clouded heaven suspended high in the arches of Amboise's great hall, complete with hovering angels. He had even masterminded an enormous display of paper doves that, by the use of mirrors and smoke, made the birds appear to be flying unaided.

But every time the maestro and I were in each other's presence, we managed a few quiet moments alone. He was eager to hear of my life in the court. If I was happy or gloomy. What I was studying. What I was *thinking*. It was this, above everything, that made him so dear to my heart.

One day when we were at Cloux, Leonardo had surprised me with a gift. It was nothing more than a single flower—a buttercup—but he had kept it fresh in a tiny Venetian glass vase. I was touched at the gesture, though my face must have reflected bemusement. A flower given from a man to a woman was an act of romance, and I did not think it was the case here.

He soon confirmed it. "Have you ever looked at a flower?" Leonardo had asked. "I mean *really looked*? In a bright light, at the texture of its petals? Its veins? At its insides, the cluster of tiny stems upon which adhere even tinier particles of orange dust that in a breeze are taken and dispersed into the world? Have you discerned that perhaps the fragrance is not so prominent if breathed in quickly? If it is taken in on the slowest and most delicate of inhalations, the sweetness of the odor explodes the senses."

Of course I had done none of those things. They had never occurred to me to do.

"The simplest articles of the natural world, each and every one, are small miracles," he said, his eyes glowing with passion. "Inventions of perfection."

"Do you not believe that *God* created the whole world?" I asked him, realizing how bold I had become. "That he alone fashioned every human, animal, vegetable, and mineral into its perfect, natural state?"

"No," Leonardo replied very simply. "I believe that Nature *is* God. At least she is *my* God."

Nature God? And God a *she*? I wished to say, *And what of the Bible's teaching of the Creation? And what of Jesus?* This man had just uttered blasphemy so atrocious that if spoken publicly, it would have seen him dragged to the stake and burned as a heretic!

He must have noticed my alarmed expression, the color rising in my cheeks, but he crowned his statements with a final outrage. "I contend it is better to be a philosopher than a Christian."

I was speechless.

Taking pity on me then, the maestro sought to relieve my discomfiture, saying, "Perhaps if you *drew* a flower, you would understand it better."

"Me? Draw?" I laughed. "My tutors have only just stopped slapping me for my penmanship."

He smiled. "Just try. It is an exercise not in art but in learning."

After that, if I knew we would be meeting, I began bringing *him* gifts. Tiny tokens, but ones I believed he would think thoughtful, even meaningful. A pair of fur-lined gloves I had made him, a cloisonné box. A small but beautiful gilt birdcage with no bird inside. The story had oft been told how the maestro would buy caged birds at the marketplace just so he could set them free—their natural state. But the gift he liked the most was my rather pathetic rendition in ink on parchment of the inside of a snapdragon.

It had been difficult to absent myself from both Claude's and Marguerite's households on the day I'd decided to attempt the drawing. Indeed, I'd had to choose my day carefully for one of warmth and bright sunlight. Then I lied to my dance master, saying I was too ill with my monthly courses to practice. I found a little-used corner of a garden and plucked the most interesting flower I could find. Then pulling out a quill, tightly capped inkwell, and rolled-up sheet of parchment from my skirt pocket, I sat down on the ground before a sun-drenched stone bench and gently opened the snapdragon's petals to reveal the delicate fascination within.

I began.

Every quill stroke had been torture, for once made, it could not be unmade. What I created looked hardly like what I was seeing, the tiny dots of pollen too large, and the stamen upon which they were stuck like little sticks in no way graceful, curved, or *alive*. The inner sides of the petals surrounding this artless rendition were similarly wooden.

When I had stayed as long as I was able, I'd put away my implements and rolled up my feeble attempt at drawing. I thought then that I should never give it to the maestro, as it was so very poor. But I remembered what he had said—that it was learning, not art that I was practicing. I simply wished to please him by taking his advice, showing my interest in the things that interested him. And he would be kind toward my efforts.

He was, of course.

When we saw each other next—a walk in the gardens at Amboise with François and Mary and a few members of the court—I beckoned him aside and presented my drawing. He beamed with pleasure.

" 'Tis awful, is it not?" I said matter-of-factly. I was beyond embarrassment.

"It is a first try," he said. "One never gets things right on the first try." He looked me deeply in the eyes. "But you made the attempt. I am proud of you."

I thought I would collapse at those last words. *Had anyone ever told me he or she was proud of anything I had done?*

He was still staring at my scratches on the parchment. "Have you heard the term 'perspective'?"

I had not, and so Maestro Leonardo began explaining it to me. When my expression screamed "Confusion!" he told me to hold his good arm, which I did, and he knelt on the ground on one knee. There in the dirt he drew with his forefinger a rectangle. In its middle he poked a single dot. Then drawing four lines from each corner to that dot, the maestro began elucidating the principle of "perspective." It was a way in which to render objects and landscapes as they appeared in life—larger in the foreground and smaller in the background. It finally started coming clear to me.

"This," he told me as I brought him back to standing, "will help you with all your drawings."

"I'm not sure I have the courage to do any more."

"You followed my instruction too closely, and started with the most difficult subject—a living thing. Try a house next time." He smiled a crooked smile. "A *small* house."

We laughed together at that.

Suddenly his face darkened, and I saw him gazing at Mary, who, to the applause of their friends, was allowing François to pull a lace handkerchief out from her bodice between her breasts . . . with his teeth.

In the presence of this great man I found myself mortified at my sister's behavior and could not meet Leonardo's eyes. But then I heard him speaking very low and very urgently to me.

"Listen to me, Anna. You must at all costs protect your virginity. Please understand this is not for the purpose of denying yourself lust or love, which are as natural as breathing. It is only for the preservation of your reputation." He paused, seeming uncharacteristically troubled. "There is nothing to fear as much as a bad reputation."

François had finished his game with Mary and was bearing down on us.

"I'm going to steal my friend from you," he said to me, and threw his arm round Leonardo's shoulder, leading him away.

I was left to ponder the maestro's final words. Certainly I was well schooled in the importance of a spotless reputation—though it had certainly taken a strange twist here in François' court. I sensed that Leonardo was suffering with this notion most personally.

I wondered if I would ever learn the cause.

The next day a package arrived for me. 'Twas from the maestro. I opened it and found some sheets of woven paper and a small box. Inside was a note saying, "To make your drawing easier," and below it were some short, thin sticks of red chalk.

I was touched and deeply honored. I was, I suddenly decided, the luckiest and most privileged girl in the world.

CHAPTER 20

*M*arguerite had announced she was giving her ladies a special treat—the royal barge floating lazily downstream from Amboise on a glorious warm day, *no gentlemen allowed*! Even the king, who begged his sister to let him come along, had been told in no uncertain terms that his presence would spoil what she termed a "Summer Celebration of Womanhood." She had even bemoaned the need for male oarsmen, but they would remain discreetly out of sight.

We were boarding just after dawn. Our ladies' maids, female servants from the kitchen, and even the laundry had been pressed into service to meet our every need. Now they were carrying across the gangplanks rugs and pillows and feather beds, and a specially prepared picnic for no more than ten of us.

Where normally several thrones would be set on the broad front deck, the rugs and feather beds were being laid over the boards. Piles of cushions were placed on top of them so each of us might have a space to sit or even recline in comfort. And they were spaced, to Marguerite's specifications, not too close together, but as far from one another as possible. The duchess had instructed each of her ladies to bring aboard a book, or writing implements, or even a sewing project—anything that would help her pass the time quietly and pleasantly.

We were, every one of us, happily anticipating this unique adventure. I was helped up the plank by a happy, smiling Lynette, who, by my suggestion, had been invited to serve. The day promised to be as unique and pleasurable for the servants as for the noblewomen.

"There is only one space on the rear deck," she whispered to me. "The view might not be so grand as the foredeck, but if you want the greatest privacy, that would be the place."

"You do know me so well," I said.

Lynette had heard me complain of the lack of privacy for a woman of my circumstances. We were so rarely afforded any time to be alone with ourselves.

I saw that each of the ladies was finding a pile of pillows on the front deck that suited her fancy. Many had indeed brought books with them. There were French romances. Some were humanist tomes. But not a Bible or an otherwise religious tract was among them. One lady brought embroidery, but I knew it to be a finely stitched vest for a gentleman she was hoping would soon be her lover.

Mary smiled excitedly as she came aboard. "What a wonderful gift," she said to me, looking round the deck at the women making themselves at home in their own little corners of the barge. I noticed she was carrying a handbasket overbrimming with cut flowers and greens, pretty pieces of ribbons, little trinkets and beads—all the makings of a love knot.

The last two ladies to come aboard the barge were Marguerite and Madame, daughter helping mother up the gangplank. Claude, alas, was again with child, in the early stages, and felt that in her nauseous condition, a day on the water would be disastrous.

Marguerite looked very pleased with herself as she watched her women taking in their new and unusual surroundings. She found me with her gaze and nodded with a smile. From her demeanor, all the ladies could see that this day was one meant not for chattering and gossip, but for contemplation and quiet pleasures.

I made my way along the narrow side deck of the barge to the back. There, as Lynette had promised, was a solitary sitting place. A fur rug had been set down next to the back wall of the cabin, and upon it were five silk and brocaded pillows of different sizes and shapes. The wall, I quickly determined, would allow me to sit up with support to my back if I liked, and better still, an overhang of the cabin gave me shade from the sun if I desired it.

I placed my handbasket down and, pulling my skirts aside, sat down in my little nest. I was further delighted to find that the rug had not been placed on the hard deck, but itself rested on something soft—one of the feather beds, I assumed. As I nestled into the pillows, rearranging them to my taste, I felt I could not have been more comfortable if I'd been sitting on a cloud in heaven.

Suddenly I felt a sharp stab of worry. *What if this singular place on the rear deck had been meant for Marguerite herself?* What if I had usurped my good mistress's throne? But then I felt the barge begin to move. There were shouts of boatmen from the dock, and in a moment we had caught the tide and were floating serenely down the Loire. Time passed and I reasoned that by then Marguerite would have assumed her own place on deck.

This, then, was my little kingdom for the day. As a warm breeze kissed my cheeks, I breathed in the fresh river air. Sun glinted off the water as if in a dream. We floated past Cloux first, and then pastures with cows grazing, copses of trees, and long manicured lawns and gardens, their fabulous châteaus set back behind them. Other vessels passed us, and every boatman tipped his cap at the barge and its noble occupants. Fishermen fished with nets, and women slapped and scrubbed their laundry on flat rocks, then rinsed them in the river water. A brown and white dog came down for a drink and his owner, a little shepherd boy, came down to fetch him.

All was idyllic and serene.

I began to unpack the contents of my basket, not at all sure what I wished to do first . . . or whether I should simply enjoy the slowly pass-ing sights and scenery. First I took out my book, the French translation of Boccaccio's *Lady Fiammetta*. Then I removed the paper and red chalk that Maestro Leonardo had given me.

Staring at the implements and the blank page, I began racking my brain to remember all he had taught me about perspective. I drew a rectangle that took up most of the page and then placed a dot at the center. I had just drawn lines from the corners to the dot when I heard a rustling from above.

I looked up to see Duchess Marguerite standing there smiling down at me. She held a sheaf of papers under her arm. I began to scramble to my feet, but she stayed me.

"May I sit down?" she asked.

Flustered, I swept my hand across my rug, moving my drawing tools and some pillows to make room for her. She sat quietly for a long while, staring out at the river.

"I rarely see things from this vantage point. We are either on the foredeck of the barge, or inside in bad weather."

I was not sure what to say. Marguerite had clearly come seeking me out. *And what were the papers in her hand?*

"How do you like an outing with no men?" she suddenly said.

"I . . . don't know." I laughed uncomfortably, wondering if there was a trick in the question, or if it was a riddle.

"Men are beasts," she said. "Most men, that is. There are exceptions. Your friend Leonardo is one."

"But surely, Your Grace . . . the late king, and your brother . . ."

"Both appalling lechers."

My eyes went wide and I was again rendered speechless.

"Of course I love them dearly. Louis, God rest his soul, died for his lusts. And men are unrelentingly unfaithful. They cheat and lie and steal and even murder. For the most part women are superior beings." She looked at me with a mild smile. "You should close your mouth, Anna. A fly could buzz in."

"Yes, Your Grace. It's just that . . ."

"You've never heard a woman speak so."

"Never."

"For one thing, women do not start wars," she went on.

"That is true."

"And they do not have people tortured or incinerated for their beliefs. Our *dear* cousin Isabella in Spain was the rare exception, she and her unholy Inquisition that raced across Europe like a plague. . . ." Marguerite paused and touched the fine jewels on each of her fingers.

"Women are far stronger than men would let them think they are. All but a few of us believe the lie of powerlessness." Then her eyes flashed with rare anger. "For the most part, despite our natural intelligence and book learning, despite our high status—even royalty—we women become the victim of men's whims, their violence and aggression. Fathers. Husbands. Lovers. Even sons take part with no thought of wrongdoing. And I speak not only of courtly men. Some of the worst offenders are men of the cloth, hiding their perversions under those coarse brown robes. At least a gentleman's desires are there for all to see. Even the largest codpiece hides very little."

"Your Grace," I finally said, finding my voice. "Why are you telling me this?"

"Because you are young. And alone. Your good mother is far away. Your sister is . . . lost." Marguerite looked sad to be saying so, but I knew that despite Mary's enjoyment of her high status and fine gifts, what the duchess said was true.

"Queen Claude has been very kind," I said, "and she has spoken to me about such things, though, how shall I say . . . ?"

"From a rather more virtuous viewpoint," Marguerite finished for me. "Poor Claude. She is the worst victim of all—as high a princess as she can be and, if not for a barbaric French law, the rightful ruler of France. Yet she was sold into marriage without her consent or even her opinion. Until she dies, she is wed to a man who uses her as a field to spill his precious seed, with no concern about what constant pregnancies will do to her malformed body."

"Yet she adores him," I said. "She told me so. She forgives him his infidelities. She believes his mistresses are his right."

"Do you?"

"*I*? You wish me to judge the behavior of a king?"

She skewered me with an intense stare. "I wish for you to become *opinionated*, Anna. You have a sound mind. A questioning mind. People of great value, value *you*. You will make something of yourself in the future, but only if you strike out beyond the near horizon set for you by those who see you only as their tool. Do you understand?"

I nodded.

"Good. I would like you to read this." She handed me the sheaf of papers she had brought with her. "When you are finished, we will have more to discuss." Marguerite stood and looked down at me in my nest. "I was hoping you would find this spot today."

Then she was gone.

My head spun as I tried to remember everything she had said, to set it firmly in my mind. *Was I really worthy of her belief in me? Did I have the courage to strike out beyond the near horizon?*

I tried to calm myself by breathing deeply, but found my hands trembling as I placed the thin sheaf of papers onto the rug so they would be illuminated by sunlight. Before I could pick up the first one, a breeze ruffled the pages and my hand darted over them. I placed a pillow, then another, on this immense treasure—for I knew the writings had to be Marguerite's own. I carefully pulled the top page out and began to read.

I was, from the first word, enthralled. This was like nothing I had ever read. In the story's prologue a group of highborn ladies and gentlemen, all of them members of the court of François I, Marguerite, and Madame, were traveling home to France from a pilgrimage in Spain when a sudden deluge made their way impassable. Finding themselves immobilized and waiting for the moment to resume their journey, these nobles gathered each day to tell stories to pass the time.

Of course my thoughts raced back to our journey to meet François in the south of France after his war, and our pilgrimage to Chambéry to see the Holy Shroud. How we had been stopped in our tracks by a terrific storm and forced into our tents for five days. But whilst I had had to content myself with the company of eight pious women and a flatulent queen, Marguerite had gathered her companions, men and women, round her in her tent, and there had been spun endless conversations and laughter till the whole party had all been able to continue on its way home. *Was this the inspiration for her story's setting?*

But as I read on, I realized the motif of the stranded storytellers was where the similarity between the pages before me and real life ended. The story became an adventure whereby the fictional party was broken up by swollen rivers that swept away hapless servants and horses, destroyed bridges, and washed out roads. Each man and woman had been forced to find his or her way through rugged and hostile terrain to safety in farm cottages, monasteries, or châteaus—wherever someone would take pity on his or her plight. And every one of them was beset by outrageous misfortune, some attacked by bandits, their hosts hacked to death by swords. Others were chased by bears!

Finally, through a combination of courage and good luck, they all found their way to the same abbey. But since they were on the wrong side of the river to reach Paris, and the only bridge for many miles was washed away, they were forced to wait ten days for a new one to be built. So on each of these ten days the group met under a shady tree, and each person was asked to tell a story. It had to be about the nature of men and women, their differences and difficulties. Any story could be told, no matter how terrible or frightening or outrageous.

As long as it was true.

I was riveted to the prologue, and after each page was read, I turned it over and placed it in a pile under a second pillow. When I saw where it was leading, I could not help myself and cheated by looking ahead, just to make sure some of the actual stories were there in the pile for me to read. I could see there was only *one*. I finished the prologue, which, while itself fascinating, could never, I imagined, be as exciting as the stories themselves.

Now I stared at a page at whose top was written "Story Four."

In Flanders there once lived a lady of high birth, of birth so high, indeed, that there was no one higher in the land. She had gone to live with her brother, who was very fond of her. He himself was a noble lord of high estate, married to the daughter of a king. This young prince was much given to his pleasures, being fond of the ladies, of hunting, and generally enjoying himself, just as one would expect of a young man. His wife, however, was rather difficult, and did not enjoy the same things he did, so he always used to take his sister along as well, because she, while being a sensible and virtuous woman, was also the most cheerful and lively companion one could imagine.

Good Lord, I thought, *this story is the Duchess Marguerite's own!* She could not have described herself, François, and Claude better. I found my heart pounding. What story of men and women would she tell? I took a deep breath and began reading again.

When I was finished, my mind was whirling, though not unhappily, but mightily unsettled. "Story Four" had told of a highborn lady of Flanders—clearly Marguerite—and her brother—certainly François—who were invited as houseguests into the home of a "Great Lord," though not as great in station as the brother and sister. They never suspected that the lord of the manor lusted desperately after the lady. Knowing his suit for her affections was hopeless because of his lower status, he decided the only solution was rape. The lord placed the object of his affection, together with her old serving lady, in a room above his own and, by use of a trapdoor in the middle of the night, climbed up into the lady's room and jumped on her in bed.

He had not counted upon this good lady's strength and courage, nor upon the loyalty of her serving lady. Between the two women they made mincemeat of the man, who, scratched and bloodied, retreated in shocked disbelief back down his trapdoor and into his own room.

But the story did not end there. Following the account of the attempted rape, there was a dialogue between the lady and her old waiting woman, the latter being of some great intelligence and worldliness. A person who, though not highborn, was listened to with respect by the lady of higher station. Of course the lady was righteously upset by the attempted assault and was ready to go to her brother, the prince, to report it so the perpetrator could be duly punished.

But the old woman sat her mistress down and convinced her that reporting this crime would be a terrible *mistake*. People would assume that a man would never try to carry out such an assault unless he was given "a certain amount of encouragement" by the lady concerned. That no matter how virtuous, she herself could not be without some blame. Her honor would be put in doubt, and that would be the greatest tragedy of all.

It was finally agreed that the lady would shut her mouth about the abuse at her host's hands, though she would take other, milder measures to avenge herself.

If that were not enough of a rousing tale, I was soon to learn the story was *still* not ended, and the rest of it shocked me more than the attempted rape and the argument for keeping silent about it *combined*. At the end of the Flanders lady's narrative, one of the other storytellers—a man—interjected his opinion of the actions of the characters involved. He believed that the lord of the manor "lacked nerve." He should never have been content to eat or sleep until he had *succeeded*, the man insisted. He said the lord's love for the lady could not have been very great if it had failed so miserably. What he should have done was to *kill* the old waiting woman and then, using all his force, rape the lady! *This would be the only way to save his own honor!*

None of the other storytellers were particularly surprised by either the woman's account of the assault or the male storyteller's outrageous response to it. The next person in the party—a woman—simply began to tell "Story Five."

There were no more pages for me to read. But I could not imagine that any other tale told of in the world could ever be as intriguing as this had been. And Marguerite, by giving it to me to read, had shown me the greatest of honors.

For a moment, thinking on that honor, I allowed guilt to stalk me. *How could I have spied for my father on this venerable lady? Where was my honor? As a female child of a domineering father, could I never hope to have integrity or independence of mind?* Surely, I was one of the women who believed the lie of our powerlessness. I was able to comfort and forgive myself only by remembering that I'd delivered Father no intelligence of value about Marguerite, and would henceforth refuse, even under threat of beating, to do such filthy bidding for him again.

My thoughts and imagination thus inflamed, I could neither continue my efforts at drawing with chalk on paper nor read *Lady Fiammetta*, which would surely have paled in comparison with Marguerite's manuscript. Instead I lay back on my rug and pillows and as the countryside floated on behind me, I let my mind wander as it wished, pondering the endless comments and questions about the duchess's story that I would later discuss with her. I was so happily alone with myself that it was a shock when I felt a thump—the barge bumping gently into what, of course, would be the quay.

By the shouts of the dockmen I knew we were ashore. I gathered my things and put them back in my handbasket, and carefully placing Marguerite's manuscript pages on top, facedown, I made my way to the front of the barge.

I saw Madame, the duchess, and her ladies being helped down the gangplank, not by the dockhands, but by King François and his favorite gentlemen, their horses stamping and snorting behind them. Farther back I could see one of François' hunting lodges, a large, rambling, and rustic house surrounded on three sides by a great wood.

There was surprise within our party of women, as we had not been told that our "ladies' day" would be ending in the company of men. I looked to Marguerite and saw she stood with her brother apart from the others, speaking, gesticulating, and though I could not hear her words, I could see she was unhappy, herself taken aback by our unexpected "male escort." But François was smiling and cajoling, dismissive of her objections and bad temper.

The ladies were joining with the men now and as I approached, they seemed a very flock of colorful exotic birds, all doing that mating dance one sometimes sees in springtime gardens, fluffing and preening, with bowing and tilting of heads this way and that.

Now François was hovering over Mary, whispering in her ear. He was holding the pretty love knot she had made this day, woven with flowers and fragrant herbs and trinkets. She batted her eyelids at him, curving her pretty smile for the dimples in her cheeks to be seen to their greatest effect. I thought in that moment that Mary had taken coquetry to its supreme limits.

I was coming carefully down the plank and had just moved to my sister's side when I saw her expression change from one of delight to one of abject horror.

"But François . . . ," she whispered in a pleading voice.

" 'François' . . . ?" he said in a manner in which I was unsure whether he meant to sound playful or stern. "What has happened to 'Your Majesty'?"

Mary grew flustered. "Your Majesty . . . ," she said, and looked deeply into his eyes. She spoke softly, but not so softly that I could not hear. "You cannot mean this."

"Oh, but I do, Marie. I most definitely do." Now the king grinned wickedly at Monsieur Hortense, a thin, dark-haired, sharp-nosed dandy whose demeanor was as icy as his hands.

Hortense fairly slithered to Mary's side, and his arm slid round her waist. Tears had sprung suddenly to her eyes as she looked imploringly at François.

"But I do not *want* to share his bed tonight."

"Why ever not?" the king asked, as though he could not fathom her objection.

Now everyone's attention was drawn to the scene. I heard a lady titter and saw a gentleman hush her, but he was unsuccessful in squelching his own smile.

Suddenly Mary grew indignant. Her year as the king's official mistress had, I thought in that moment, stiffened not only François' cock but Mary's spine as well.

"No," she said. "I will not. I am not a whore. I am your mistress!"

Now there were open "ooh's" and "aah's" from the gathered. I glanced at Marguerite and saw her expression was even darker and angrier than it had been a few moments before.

"I think, Marie," François said, still retaining a light demeanor, "that you are whatever *I* say you are. You do whatever *I* say you do. And *I* say you pleasure my friend Monsieur Hortense tonight."

Mary looked ready to bolt and her eyes were wild, as a horse's would be trapped in a fenced yard during a storm of lightning and thunder.

I was paralyzed, helpless as my sister suffered the most abject humiliation . . . and something worse. Much worse. As we all watched, Mary Boleyn slipped a farther circle down into Dante's Inferno. She'd been sold once into sexual slavery by a father who cared not a whit for her, and now again by a man who claimed to adore her.

"Don't be a naughty girl," François added, his voice growing colder, "or I will withhold your allowance and your gifts." He chucked her under her chin and smiled at everyone listening. "And we all know how much you love your allowance and gifts."

He'd begun losing interest in the scene or, I thought, he had not counted on so much resistance from his docile little doll. In any case, he turned his back on Mary and headed for his sister. But Marguerite gave François a withering stare and turned her back on him, walking quickly to join Madame, who, hurrying to the lodge, had missed the whole ugly affair.

"Come," he said pleasantly to his guests, "I've had Cook prepare the wild boar we hunted today. Even *it* was in a better temper than my mistress and my sister."

With that, François and his court started for the lodge, no one daring to look back at Mary, who stood trembling with fury and fear. I'd stayed behind and, now moving to her side, took her hand. She did not pull away, and neither of us had a single sensible word between us.

We stood, a pair of mutes, silenced by François' hideous cruelty.

I wished to tell her that she had a friend in Duchess Marguerite. That the woman commiserated. That men were beasts. But it was all too hard to explain, and I doubted if in this moment Mary would have listened or, if she had listened, would have understood.

In any event, even Marguerite's support would not have mattered. François was the king. A god on earth.

And Mary, after all, was nothing but a woman.

CHAPTER 21

This was the kind of night that everyone at court relished. My favorite great room had been emptied of everything but card tables and chairs, and other tables for dice. Still others were reserved for trictrac, which some called by its Eastern name—"backgammon." A fire roared in the marble fireplace, and from the high arches were hanging candelabras, so that we could see our playing by their lights. On a gaming night like this, musicians were dispensed with, and only light wine was served—sparingly—as everyone was intense with concentration.

Fortunes were being won and lost. Mistresses traded away. Even titles awarded at the king's pleasure.

"I will call and raise you," I said, staring comte d'Enghien in the eye. He was sitting across from me at a card table. My expression was flawlessly noncommittal, though I had just tripled the pot in this hand of primero. I could see the count trying desperately to read me for signs of bluffing, but I had in the last year become inscrutable when it came to card playing. My chess had improved as well. These were defenses I'd acquired for games of chance, but more importantly for living life at the French court.

I had learnt too well that it was naught but a war waged between men and women, and if one lacked defensive plays as well as offensive ones, a courtier or lady could lose more than a purse of gold. He or she could lose all that was most precious—the favor of the king, the means for making a living. A beloved wife. Virginity.

François was in fine form at the dice table, even though by the sound of his curses and laughter he was losing substantially. At one point earlier I'd seen the king bouncing a die off the forehead of a man who had bested him, and great merriment had ensued.

Madame, who was playing on my left, folded, unable to match my bet. I felt her gaze boring into me, but I refused to engage her. Now it was comte d'Enghien's play. He'd never taken his eyes from me, but I was calmly rearranging my hand, biting the inside of my lip, then showing the hint of a smile, but only a hint. For I *was* bluffing. I had in my hand only a pair of sevens, and I knew from having watched every card played, and especially each and every card comte d'Enghien had picked up, that he had *at least* a pair of eights. He might have had much more than that, but early in the game when he'd asked for three cards, I'd read the infinitely subtle disappointment in his expression, one that he'd quickly shifted to pleasure.

He was a fine card player, as was Madame, but these days she was less interested in my skills at gaming than she was that I was a Boleyn. Intensive negotiations and espionage between England and France were never ending, and Madame—especially in her correspondence with Cardinal Wolsey—was an important part of them. I was the English ambassador's daughter, and Mary, also his daughter, was still, after a fashion, the French king's mistress.

So we were to be carefully watched.

Diplomacy, of late, had been taken to absurd ends. François sent Henry a living lion as a gift, and not to be outdone in extravagance— but certainly trumped in originality—Henry sent a different lion to François. The once-terrifying creature arrived in Paris lethargic and pitiful from its long sea journey from Africa, and its bumpy overland journey from Calais.

The King of France, looking to go one better than the King of England, put on an apron and himself baked a massive pie from the largest boar ever killed on French soil. He had it shipped across the Channel to Henry with the warmest greetings.

Soon after, it was rumored that a great mirror had been placed atop Dover Castle, the invention to be used to see across the water to spy on France.

I once heard Madame say to Marguerite of Henry that no matter his pretensions, he could never match the regal powers and royal breeding of François or Charles—that he was a "little king."

Well, little king or no, Madame was fully engaged with England, and she had her eye on me whether I was playing at cards or riding in a hunt or dancing for François.

Her interest in my sister, which at the beginning of the affair with her son was searing, had waned from the moment he had begun sharing Mary with his courtiers. Monsieur Hortense had been only the first. After that, whilst she retained her status as official mistress and kept her pretty room, she was passed from man to man, forced to endure all of their sexual proclivities and perversities. Mary had become known as the "English Mare," as so many men had ridden her.

Once, in an act so cruel that even some of the gentlemen of the court were stunned, François had had the dead body of a hanged criminal placed in Mary's bed whilst she was sleeping off a night of drunkenness. In the morning her shrieks of horror could be heard even in Queen Claude's apartments.

When reprimanded by his mother, François had tut-tutted and told her he was an inveterate rapscallion who lived for his practical jokes. To "beg her forgiveness," he'd given Mary a beautiful white horse, but as it had been a mare, there was still laughter at her expense.

It was a tragedy for Mary, but that her reputation—all of value that a woman really had in life—had been wholly and irreparably destroyed, no one in the French court cared. Marguerite was angry at her brother for his caddishness and cruelty, but he was, after all, a man doing what men did, and being that he was her brother and the king, she had no choice but to forgive him.

My heart broke for Mary, but selfishly it was quelled, for I wondered, if her fate could be so offhandedly and savagely devised by first our father and then the King of France, what were my chances of coming out whole? So far I'd been lucky, as my betrothal to James Butler was still of financial interest to the Boleyn family, and of import to English and Irish policy. But these things were as changeable as the weather, and many nights I lay awake wondering if I, too, would be forced into noble prostitution.

Comte d'Enghien, after the longest of deliberations, called and raised. The lady on my right, who was dealing, folded. Feeling quite reckless, I pushed every coin I had left into the center of the table. A panicked look crossed my opponent's face. He had already placed most of his night's winnings in this pot.

With a grimace that was meant to pass for a smile he slapped his cards facedown. "I am out, mademoiselle," he said to me. "Let us see your cards."

I laid them down, revealing the best I had, the two sevens. Knowing he had folded with at least two eights, he pounded the table so hard that some of my winnings clattered to the floor.

Madame glared at him. "Mind your manners, monsieur. In this court we are as gracious in defeat as we are in victory."

Surely she was being facetious, as she could not have missed her son bouncing a die off his competitor's head earlier that evening. Then she looked at me unsmilingly.

"You play cards like a man, Anna."

"May I take that as a compliment, madame?"

Her eyes narrowed. "You may take that as a warning." Then she smiled ever so sweetly and pushed all the coins toward me. "It is late. This old woman is going to bed."

By the time I had gathered my things and stood to go, I was surprised to see that the great room had nearly emptied of players, the fire having burned down to embers. I'd been so completely engaged in my playing, all else had disappeared around me, including time itself.

As I left the room, a servant approached me. It was Robairre.

"Mademoiselle," he said, and bowed. Then he held out a lace shawl. "Your sister, Marie, dropped it on her way out. The king asked me to have you return it to her."

I told him I would, and after handing it to me, he bowed and backed away. As I started for the east wing and Mary's room, my thoughts veered from my recent winnings and what I might buy with them, to Madame's strange comment to me about "a warning." And to Mary, also, who underneath a desperate gaiety seemed to be almost despondent. I would, I decided, write of it all to George, who was himself concerned about our sister's sad reversal of fortune.

Our letter writing had, as a result of his visit to France, and by virtue of my growing from a girl to a young woman, become a lifeline for me, communication with the one person in my family whose motives were pure and whose love for me I knew was true.

Besides being able to vent my fears and frustrations and woes of my own and Mary's, and having a venue for my telling stories of the French court, I was rewarded by return letters from George that were a source of, not only comfort, but enjoyment and elucidation. For my brother was moving swiftly up the ranks in King Henry's court, from Royal Cupbearer, to Master of the Chamber, to Master of the Horse.

Now he spent many hours of the day, not only dressing and grooming Henry, but playing at his side in many sports, gaming, and jousts. He was invited to every entertainment unless it was a strictly family gathering, and it seemed, from what George had been writing, that the king found him a happy companion.

George's affection for and loyalty to Henry seemed genuine, but it did not stop him from writing me in great and not-always-flattering detail of the goings-on of the English court and its high master. There was little in his letters about politics, which, he said, were kept well within the conferences between King Henry and his highest adviser, Cardinal Wolsey.

Instead I heard much about Henry's character and tempers. That he had become a moody king who sighed frequently. He was prone to outbursts of anger that bordered at times on hysteria, particularly at any mention of François' name. There were tears and tantrums, and his courtiers had come to fear him. But he and his incubus, Wolsey, were still a force to be reckoned with. Henry was canny. He attempted nothing except that which would have a happy outcome. Far from reckless, he wagered only on a sure thing. It seemed to upset him that François let his mother and sister rule the French court. This was, George believed, a less-than-fond remembrance of how, with a fist of iron, Henry's own grandmother—the "dragon lady" Margaret Beaufort—had ruled the English court of Henry's father. And how she had, in the months after young Henry took the throne at eighteen, ruled him as well, choosing his entire Privy Council before herself passing away.

I had, without realizing it, reached Mary's door. So lost in thought was I that my arrival took me quite by surprise. It was quiet, no male or female sounds of ecstasy—either real or feigned—coming from within. When I went to knock, however, I found the door unlocked, indeed cracked open. I saw the flicker of candlelight.

"Mary," I said quietly. "Are you there?" I pushed open the door and stepped inside.

What I saw before me I can still hardly bear to describe.

Mary's great canopied bed was, every inch of it, covered with writhing, naked female flesh. Mayhap six ladies of the French court, my sister among them, and six known whores hungrily kissed, touched, sucked, and probed one another's bodies. Breasts and buttocks sticky with honey were licked clean by darting tongues. One woman was thrusting a fat candle into the moist pink cleft of another. Many were staring ceilingward, no doubt watching their mirrored selves in that naked bacchanal.

For all the lust or passion, or whatever it could be called, going on in Mary Boleyn's bed, there was hardly a sound. Or what there was of it was muted by the heavy curtains and canopies and the folds of cloth draped, haremlike, at her ceiling. The next thing I heard, therefore, when it rose from a wall behind the open door, froze me in my place.

It was the sound of a man groaning in raw animal pleasure.

I swear I did not wish to know the face of that noise's maker. I began to back out the door, keeping my eyes ahead, but then came a voice. Deep. Softened almost to a grunt with its sensuality.

"Mademoiselle *Boullan*."

I knew at once whose voice it was. I knew I had to turn and address him. I did so slowly, swiveling and sweeping into a deep curtsy in one move.

"Your Majesty," I barely managed to utter.

François was slouched low in a wide, high-backed chair, his long spindly legs splayed out in front of him. Though he had just addressed me, his eyes were yet fixed on the Caligulan scene on the bed. His right hand—God help me—was moving slowly and rhythmically beneath his codpiece. Finally he turned and smiled at me, a leering, invitational grin.

Two quick shuddering breaths escaped me before I turned and fled, tripping over my own skirts so that I hit the doorjamb with my shoulder. I could hear François' laughter as I ran full speed down the corridor. I did not stop running until I had reached my shared cubicle in the queen's apartments.

I fell on my bed fully clothed, facedown to best shut out the world. But I could not shut off the visions in my head. The flicking tongues on honey-glistened arses. A church candle disappearing into a woman's most intimate cavity. The king's hand moving blissfully under his breeches.

There was no sleep for me that night. Or peace.

I wondered if they would ever be mine again.

CHAPTER 22

*I*n the next days I stayed close to Queen Claude, leaving her quarters as little as possible. Yet even as we dark-clad pious ladies strolled through the gardens, my eyes would inevitably be drawn, as they had never been before, to the finely cut muscles and the sheathed cock of a naked Greek statue. Or as we crossed the courtyard on our way to an afternoon of scriptural study, I glimpsed, then *stared* at, a stableboy playfully grabbing the backside of a giggling kitchen maid. Another time, idly gazing at an iris, I pushed open the petals to find that its soft insides were nothing short of erotic.

Everything was making my cunny twitch, and I had no way to make it stop.

I thought of speaking to Lynette, but I was too ashamed. Ashamed of what I had seen in Mary's bed. Of the king's bald-faced lechery. I had even come to believe that he had choreographed the entire episode. Made sure that Mary had left her shawl in the gaming room, ordered Robairre to give it to me with instructions to return it to my sister. Left Mary's door ajar. I wondered if he had even ordered the women in bed to be silent so that I would not be alarmed by the sounds from within, and turn away without entering.

Most of all I was ashamed of what I was feeling between my own legs. The place was meant to be, I had always been taught, a most private, most precious and guarded breach, one that brought pain on deflowering and in childbirth. The one for which kingdoms were won and lost, by which fortunes were transferred from family to family.

Now this dark, secret cavern I saw as one made for all manner of pleasuring—with *women* as well as men—for licking and sucking and even *watching*. I could not bring myself to say these things, even to Lynette, and certainly not in my prayers to Jesus.

So I suffered in rising agony that *itself* felt like pleasure, which made it all the worse.

I believed the ladies and whores and my sister in her bed had been too engrossed to have noticed my brief entry into that orgy room. She and they—the ones of the court whom I recognized from the jumble—treated me no differently from before. There was no laughter behind a fan, or smirking whispers with narrowed eyes directed at me.

But I avoided the king like a plague dog. If I knew he was coming to visit with Claude and their children in her rooms, I would conveniently absent myself. When an entertainment was presented at which the entire court would be assembled, I would claim illness. I never stayed in the corridors unless accompanied by Claude's ladies. And if I saw François coming toward us, I would hide myself behind them as our paths crossed.

Once I made the mistake of peeking back after he'd gone by. He had turned and was looking straight at me. Smiling that same languorous smile he'd worn while he was stroking himself. I cursed myself as my lower parts involuntarily convulsed. My face reddened with rising heat, and I wanted to weep.

I was in fiery hell with no escape. Nothing, *nothing* could save me.

The night of my "meeting" the king in the hallway I could not find a way into sleep. My pallet felt hard and lumpy, my pillows suddenly smelled of mildew. No way I turned or held my arms or curled my knees to my chest comforted me. Finally I lay defeated on my back, arms at my sides, legs splayed the width of the bed, my nightdress tangled about me.

Without warning, the memory of the perverse voyeur François

filled my vision. This time when the inevitable clenching began, my hands flew to that dark mound, as if to stay it. I knew I should pull my hands away at once. 'Twas a sin, touching oneself. Everyone knew as much. But suddenly a thought provoked me, then overtook me.

If parts of my body were acting on their own accord, *defying* me, then mayhap it was my duty to rein them in, bring them under control, like a rider would a wild, unmanageable horse.

A fine idea, I thought then, berating myself.

This nether region was a foreign country to me. Except to quickly dry myself after making water, I was a stranger in strange territory. Yet it *was* a part of me. A part that was every day now forcibly making itself known, calling out with its sudden twitches and tinglings.

I felt the soft down of my maiden hair. Stroked it gently. This felt comforting, like petting a small dog. That thought made me giggle, but I quieted myself, not wishing to wake my cubicle mates. I ventured lower with my fingers and felt the surprise of flesh—*moist* flesh.

And with that touch I was, all of my body, flooded with sensation. It was something like the unasked-for contractions I'd been experiencing, but much sweeter, for I'd brought the sensation on of my own accord.

I grew bolder. Found more of the wet, unspeakably soft skin that dwelled in delicate folds. And finally the cleft itself. It felt to be the mouth of some fathomless cave, but my fingers were at such an angle that I could not venture too deeply. Now the lovely sensations were sweeping from there, in some mysterious fashion, to my ducks, the nipples most particularly. So with the other hand I touched one, very softly, and lo, the feeling ran straight down from breast to cunny again! *How could this be? Were they connected by some vein or nerve or invisible humor?*

Then seemingly without my conscious will, my finger strayed to the center of it all, just above the cleft.

With that one touch all others were forgotten.

A gasp escaped me and without thinking, I began to move my finger over a tiny bud of the tenderest flesh. My finger was gliding smoothly over it, for now I was well and truly *wet*. Soft and slippery. I seemed to know precisely how to touch and probe, flick and slide, then pull back and hold all movement.

Pleasure—though that word does not express what beauty of feeling was there between my thighs—grew and grew, and the deliciousness began to shape itself into a distant point, one to which I was heading, not unlike the dot of perspective into which four lines coalesce. I seemed with every tiny stroke of my finger on that nub to be rushing from everywhere toward that point. Closer and closer and closer . . . oh God!

I could hear myself shouting "Ahhhh, ahhh!" like I'd been shot, and was vaguely aware that I'd woken the other ladies in beds next to mine. But I could not quiet myself, though the shouts turned to moans of helpless delight.

I came back to myself, my breath ragged, as though I'd run a distance, and my heart pounded fiercely in my chest. I could hear Claude's waiting women giggling softly. *They knew of this! Each and every one!* Even these pious ladies of the most pious queen were no strangers to solitary pleasures.

Too embarrassed to speak to them, I turned on my side and faced the wall. Soon all their whispering and laughter ceased. The cubicle fell quiet.

Was what had happened . . . could it be . . . what "coming" meant?

"Culmination" would certainly describe it. I had no partner save my own hand, I reasoned, but surely there could be no satisfaction greater than this! It did leave me to wonder how a man's presence would change the thing—his organ moving within my moist cleft. . . .

Another twinge at the thought of this! I had to *stop*. I turned on my back, sucked in a deep breath, and folded my arms safely over my chest. Suddenly the pallet felt as soft as a feather bed, and my pillow smelled sweet as new rushes.

My eyes closed and happily exhausted, sleep took me into her arms and bore me away.

★   ★   ★

I did manage to stay out of François' way for near two months. After my discovery of ecstasy, and knowing it was a vision of the king that had first sparked it—though the sight of him no longer caused those spasms—I grew flushed with shame in his presence.

But my avoidance could not go on forever. Marguerite took notice first of my absences from everyday entertainments that I had previously enjoyed. She asked repeatedly after my health, insisting that I looked too well to be ill so often. She threatened to send her personal physician to visit me, and the thought of his bleeding me, his leeches—or, worse, probing my womanly parts—brought me immediately to "perfect health," with no excuses left.

Therefore when the duchess announced that the ladies of her household would be joining a hunt to the hounds with the king and his men in the forest outside of Amboise, I had no choice but to join in. I did love a hard ride, and who could not enjoy the magic and excitement of the greenwood?

We all met at the top of the Minimes Tower, where stableboys had led the finest hunting horses François owned, and we took to our saddles. Then came the moment I most craved. All of us at once spurred our mounts and began the thundering descent down the spiral ramp, sun streaming in through the high windows, with visions of soldiers past riding out to meet the invaders.

There was always a shock of silence as we exited the tower at the river's edge, at least until the hounds bounded out to meet us, yapping with the joyful racket of the hunt. We were off before I knew it, racing after the dogs down the well-worn woodland trails.

My horse was very spirited that day and seemed to revel in the chase. Without my prodding he sped to the fore where I could suddenly see François and Marguerite's husband, Charles, racing side by side like young brothers, low on their horses' necks, shouting joyfully.

Then François rose in his saddle to point ahead, from where came the sound of the pack yelping excitedly, having cornered the stag. But in rising, François had missed seeing a thick branch fallen slightly over the path. At full speed he rode into it with his forehead!

I heard a sickening crash and saw the king propelled backward off his horse, crashing in a tangle of his own long arms and legs onto the ground.

He lay horribly still.

Charles circled back and flew off his mount to his brother-in-law's side. Those of us coming up on the scene also dismounted and rushed to the fallen king. A moment later Marguerite burst through the circle that had formed, and shouted, "François, François! Oh, my brother!"

She knelt and, seeing his limp and bloodied condition, began weeping and clutching him to her. He did look dead, and all who had heard that crack as his head met the branch believed it could mean nothing less than the end of François' life and reign. Others began weeping as well, but several of the courtiers had fashioned a rude bier, and the king's unmoving body was gently lifted upon it and borne back to Amboise.

I shall never forget the two days next, when François lay in a coma so close to death. There could be no three more miserable nor desperate souls than Madame, Marguerite, and Claude, who was, again, huge with child. Such cries and sobbing, so many fervid prayers to God, so many promises made to him if only François could be brought back whole to this life.

Maestro Leonardo was sent for. He came out from the king's room somber as I'd ever seen him. He could manage only the barest greeting to me. With his knowledge of the brain's anatomy he had schooled the royal physicians of François' condition. But there was nothing more he could do. He was no doctor, he'd told them, only a craftsman with more than his share of understanding of the human body. Whether the king would live or die he could not say. He simply sat outside the sickroom with paper and red chalk and, with his good hand, made sketch after sketch of the man who'd become so important in his life.

And then, on the third day, François opened his eyes and spoke, saying, "May I have some broth?"

His family's joyful weeping and wailing that then ensued was louder and more potent than the cries when he had fallen. Soon he was sitting up, smiling, and eating his soup.

The weeks that followed found François generally weak, though more on one side—that opposite the injury on his head—than the other. And whilst he smiled much and was very pleasant with us all, he seemed not altogether as he'd been before. Not the François we'd known.

Mary told me he never came to her bed anymore, nor sent other men—and I thought, *nor women*—to have their way with her. She seemed grateful and relieved to be left alone, and spent hours in her room admiring her baubles or reading a French romance.

François could almost always be found with Marguerite or Madame, or with Claude and his children. He doted, of course, on his son François, who, at less than two, was coming to resemble his father, long nose and all.

Policy he left to his mother and sister, and he met infrequently with other counsel or clergy, though Claude did have him praying at her private altar when she could.

He began again to visit Leonardo every day, though in his weakened condition he used not the secret passage with its steep and dangerous stairway, but would either walk the distance to Cloux if the weather was fine, or be rowed if it was foul. Indeed, their friendship was a great source of discussion and mystery among his courtiers and ladies. Marguerite would say only that the maestro gave her brother a philosophy he could find nowhere else.

"A philosophy?!" everyone cried in wonder. Leonardo da Vinci was a painter. An inventor. An architect. *But a philosopher?* I said nothing, for what little I knew of his beliefs seemed antithetical to papists—who would be *everyone* at court, except perhaps Marguerite—and therefore unhealthy for the old gentleman if they were made public.

It came, therefore, as a great shock to me when as I walked alone in a hedge maze, I looked up to see François walking beside me. His slight limp had disappeared, and I could tell he'd slowed his long-legged gait to move in concert with me.

I stopped for a quick curtsy and the proper obeisance, but he tut-tutted and bade me continue walking with him, as though the protocol was unnecessary. I surely did not know what to make of this display of friendship. I saw no leering licentiousness in his expression, and I found myself able to look at him, even speak to him, without blushing scarlet.

We talked of several things, stopping once to sit on a stone bench in the sun. He seemed to know of Leonardo's fondness for me, and I thought perhaps this influence was at work, as François did not wish to offend the friend of a friend. But we engaged interestingly on several subjects. He inquired whether I had read William Caxton's *The Game and Playe of Chess,* which I had, and then asked my opinion of it. He told me that we would soon be acquiring a stableful of fine Irish horses bred by the family of my betrothed, James Butler. And he commented about the beauty of the Netherlands lace on the sleeve of my gown.

Never could I have asked for a more gentlemanly conversation as I had with the king that day. As for what he had surely led me in to see that night in Mary's mirrored bed, there was no hint. Not the slightest. It might never have happened. I was grateful, feeling as though I'd finally wakened from a long nightmare. The world was as it should be, the French court no longer a seething cauldron of lust and reckless abandon.

One day soon after our walk and talk I found on my pallet a volume I'd heard Marguerite speak of, *The Prince* by Niccolò Machiavelli. 'Twas newly translated from the Italian to French, and she'd recently complained that she could not get her hands on one. I believed the book to be a sweet gift from her until I opened it and out fell a note ... from François.

It was nothing but polite, he claiming to know of my interest in the subject, and since he had acquired two copies and had gifted his sister with one, he wished to gift me with the other.

Very thoughtful, it seemed to me. Marguerite had said that people of value valued me. Here was the King of France—to be sure, a new man after his accident—befriending myself. I was chuffed, warmed by the thought.

I began reading *The Prince* that very day, excited by the idea that I could soon discuss it with Marguerite, and mayhap the king himself.

François had been behaving himself so well and for so long that when I received a written invitation to join him in the east wing of Amboise in a chamber that we all knew was under construction for housing the royal library, I felt at ease to go. There had been more gifts of books from him, some of them the heretical ones that Marguerite so enjoyed. And there had been several debates with François and Marguerite about Luther and the corruption of the Roman church. These had stimulated my intellect so that I hardly wanted them to end. The king was a brilliant conversationalist who, it could not be denied, took great pleasure in hearing himself talk.

As I approached the library, I heard loud hammering from within, and the sounds of workmen shouting at one another for buckets of plaster or a larger hammer. When I entered and saw the scaffolding all round the tall arched space, and shelves still in the roughest stage of construction, I wondered why the king should want me to see such a thing.

"Mademoiselle *Boullan*."

I turned. There was François looking tall and splendid in a spectacular burnt orange doublet trimmed with gold, and a flat feathered cap sitting jauntily on his head. His hair appeared freshly washed and hung loosely about his wide shoulders.

"I fear I can no longer call you *la Petite Boullan*," he said with a warm smile. "You have become quite a grown lady."

Indeed, my body had finally sprouted curved hips and a pair of small, high duckies.

"I'm not yet sixteen, Your Majesty," I said, curtsying respectfully. François' recent behavior had all but quashed the loathsome memories I'd had of him. Mayhap, I'd told Mary, all that obnoxious men needed was a good clout on the head. This sent her into a fit of laughter, but in the end she'd agreed.

There was talk of François taking a new mistress, a very pretty young

French noblewoman named Châteaubriant, who'd recently come into court as Claude's waiting lady. It was said she would supplant Mary and take her room. By now my sister was more than ready to give up her role as royal concubine. In fact she was threatening to write to Father asking if she could come home. I cautioned her about such a letter, fearing that he would take offense—no matter how tactfully the letter was stated—at being "told what to do." "Let things unfold as they might," I urged Mary.

Look how the Fates mellowed the King of France.

"Do you like the chamber?" François asked, sweeping his hand around at the scaffolding.

"I can see it will be majestic once it's done," I said, "though some imagination *is* needed."

"Let me help your imagination along," he said, taking my elbow and helping me step over piles of wood beams and workmen's tools. He led me to a pretty carven door on the other side of the library, and opened it.

I could immediately see its contents. There were piles and piles of books. Crates of them. Pyramids of rolled parchments. Medieval manuscripts on heavy pedestals. I had never seen so many books in one place in all my life, even at the Palace of Malines.

"Your eyes are glowing, mademoiselle." François sounded pleased.

"But this is wonderful, Your Majesty! These are the volumes that will fill the library's shelves!" Without his permission I moved through the repository's mountain of books, picking them up to see the titles on the spines, barely daring to touch a manuscript that might be three hundred years old.

"Come here, Anna. There is more here than meets the eye."

He was standing over a wooden casket, which he opened. Inside were coins and medallions that appeared to be ancient. "From the Greeks and the Romans, dating back from before Christ," François said, confirming my guess.

He placed several in my left hand. I brought them closer to my eyes.

"Is that the head of Caesar?" I said to François, pointing to a gold piece.

"Let me see," he said, picking it up and holding it in the sunlight pouring in through a window. "That *is* Caesar. This coin was minted in the same century as Jesus lived."

The breath went out of me. He showed me another. "This is one from the eighth century. A denarius of Charles the Bald." He shot me a grin. "Why would a king allow himself to be known as 'the Bald'?"

I laughed. "In England we had 'Harold the Harefoot' and 'Ethelred the Unready.' Ethelred was my favorite."

With a smile François took the coins from me and, dumping them back in the casket, grabbed my hand and fairly dragged me cross the room. He was as excited as a little boy.

From the pile of large parchments he found one he was looking for and carefully unrolled it before me. "Look at this!" he cried. "A map of the world by a Turkish cartographer! Here is Europe. And here is Spain's 'New World.' And look down here." He pointed to a land mass near the bottom of the parchment. "An island the size of a continent in the far south! I think," he said, taking time to form his words, "that I should like to try something more than *warring* in my reign. I think, like the Spanish and the Portuguese, I should like to send men exploring. In ships. Claim some of the New World for France. Wouldn't that be exciting?"

"Indeed," I replied, my mind suddenly awhirl.

"And look at these," he said, pulling me into the main stack of books. Suddenly I was surrounded by them.

"King Charles VIII began the French royal library, but he had no real passion for books. Barely read them at all. Nor did Louis after him. But I have sent agents out to every country there is, employed only with the task of looking for rare books for *my* royal library. It is what Cosimo de' Medici did in the last century in Florence, and he created the greatest library in all of Europe! This, if I am lucky, will surpass it."

François ran his finger down the spine of an ancient volume.

"I've hired Guillaume Budé as my chief librarian. He's a brilliant man. Brilliant! He says I am not like the other kings, who merely collect books. I *read* them all. And I will open my library, Anna, open it to scholars from around the world. So that all the knowledge in this room can be spread everywhere! It is a time of peace in Europe after so much war. Erasmus says this may be the dawn of a 'New Age.'"

I thought François would burst his seams with his enthusiasm.

"Look at this." He pointed to a gorgeous manuscript, illuminated with fabulous beasts and flowers, and intricately filigreed gold borders. "It is the *Book of Hours* of Marguerite d'Orléans. And here is Petrarch's *The Triumphs*, also illustrated—his poems of Love and Chastity, Fame, Time, and Death."

François now turned from me and moved to a small locked cabinet, which, as I followed him over, he unlocked with a key on the same ring as hung the long red key to the underground passage to Cloux. Then he stood staring silently at the volumes before us.

"Here," he said with solemnity, "are the most valuable books in the collection."

He regarded them with so much awe that I refrained from any questions, aware that he would tell me as much or as little as he wished to. François seemed to be carefully choosing his words and, after what seemed to me a very long time, finally spoke.

"These books are those of the occult sciences."

Unlike with the others he had shown me, he did not handle them nor let me touch them.

"Except for their Italian translations of the last century—Ficino and Mirandola—they are very, very ancient. From Rome, Greece, the Holy Land, and a few dating back to Egyptian times. In those days the great magician Hermes Trismegistus was practicing and writing."

I chanced a look at the king's face. Now it was François' eyes that were sparkling. His expression was exceedingly reverential, the way the most pious Catholic would look upon a splinter of the True Cross on which the Savior died.

"In fact I have put in motion the plans that establish a new college to study classical languages. I have already invited Erasmus to head this college."

I was, to say the least, confused. Humanism I understood. The teachings of Erasmus were deeply respected in all of Europe. He had, in fact, tutored King Henry when he was a boy. *But magic? Alchemy? Astrology?*

"Your Majesty," I finally said, surely sounding tentative, "do these books not represent the height of . . . heresy?"

"Maybe they do, Anna. But they also hold the key to understanding the mysterious forces that rule the universe." François paused and his eyes grew unfocused. "The mind and memory of man are divine. . . ." Now he spoke as if these thoughts were not so much his own but parroted, as if from a tutor or book. "We have the powers to understand these forces through Hermetic teachings." He stopped suddenly, as though he thought better of speaking this out loud, and his eyes snapped back to their sharp intensity.

Before I could ask any further questions, he pulled me farther into the stacks, and opened a rather plain-looking volume bound in green leather, thrusting it into my hands.

"What is this one, Your Majesty?"

"*The Book of Melusine,*" he answered. He had come to stand behind me, towering over my shoulders. "It is a romance glorifying the Lusignan family from Poitou."

"It has lovely illustrations," I said, paging through the book, but wondering at the king's sudden change from interest in Hermeticism to domestic trifles.

"Very lovely," he agreed, and suddenly I was aware of his warm breath on my neck.

He must be leaning down, I thought, for I could feel the humid exhalations. I froze to the spot, feeling the toes in my slippers gripping the floor to keep me steady on my feet.

"This one," François said, reaching around me with his long arms to turn the pages till he'd stopped at another illustration, "shows the husband breaking a taboo by viewing his wife bathing."

I swallowed hard. There on the page was indeed a man watching a woman—altogether naked—standing in a tub of water.

All at once I felt François' hands on my breasts. His touch was oh-so-light, but *possessive*, as if it were his kingly right to touch me thus. Now his hot dry lips were on my neck.

Stupid girl, I screamed inwardly. *You've fallen for his trap! The Cabala, Erasmus. Petrarch!*

I had no time to think, only to act. I let the book slip from my hands.

"Oh!" I cried. "I'm so, so sorry, Your Majesty!" I squatted quickly in place, freeing myself from his grasp, and reached to retrieve the volume. "I've dropped your book. Your *precious* book." I turned to face the king, stepping back and holding out *The Book of Melusine* to him. "Can you forgive me? Oh, please forgive me, my lord!" I swept into a deep curtsy. From that posture I spoke in a whisper. "I am so ashamed. I cannot look at you. May I have leave to go?"

There was silence from above. I was afraid to breathe. After an eternity I felt the book removed from my hand.

"Yes, Anna. You have my leave to go."

"Thank you, thank you, Majesty. Forgive me, Majesty," I kept muttering as I backed out of the repository, careful not to knock over any piles of books. This would have been comical in a fool's sketch of a silly girl and the king she should have known had never been cured of his lechery from a single clout on the head.

Once past the carven door I ran, stepping nimbly over the boards and tools in a frantic dance to get away from the royal library, and the king who might be thinking to make me his next mistress.

What in heaven's name was I to do?

CHAPTER 23

I was frantic with no one to turn to. I could not say whether Father knew of the king's desire for me, if he approved or not. Mayhap my betrothal to James Butler had been nullified; else Father and Cardinal Wolsey had decided that, as with Mary, it was not necessary for me to go to my marriage bed a virgin. Or that being the mistress of a famous king would only enhance my suitability for the Irish match.

My confidants at court were similarly out of the question. Mary was in a world of her own—injured, then pampered, then abused. Finally free, but in François' debt. Queen Claude, though she was full aware of her husband's infidelities, would only be made miserable to think that I was now in François' sights. Even Marguerite, who knew how bestial he could be and disapproved of the level of his lewdness, had said that day on the barge, "He is my brother and he is the king. And I do love him." Mayhap in this world gone mad with sensuality, Marguerite and François were indeed lovers. I did not know, nor could I fully trust her.

Then I thought of Leonardo. I knew that the maestro himself would have certain loyalties to the king—they were friends who spoke every day. And of course François was the man's patron who would be providing him home and hearth for the rest of his life. But I sensed that Leonardo possessed the deepest wisdom and the most steadfast honor. That whilst he would do no wrong to the King of France, neither would he do wrong to me.

But how would I meet in private with the maestro?

We never visited by ourselves. We only stole moments together in the midst of court gatherings. It would not be seemly to be noticed hurrying by myself downriver to Cloux. If the king was to find out about a secret meeting, it might endanger their friendship and indeed Leonardo's peaceful retirement in France.

The only answer was the underground tunnel, and the only key I knew of to the Amboise basement door was in François' possession.

Then I thought of Lynette.

She had of late been complaining that the castle locksmith had been paying her some unwanted attention every time she left the laundry and passed his workshop cubicle. He was almost twice her age, and the things he called out to her as she hurried past lacked finesse, though, she made a point of saying, they stopped short of outright crudeness. There must, I reasoned, be a second key to that door, or a master key that could be used to unlock it. Lynette became my only hope.

The next time I was able—three days and many avoided meetings with the king later—I insisted upon taking the queen's soiled linen to the laundry just before going to bed. Launderers worked round the clock in shifts, and I knew this to be a late night for my friend. I found Lynette at the soap tubs, she rosy-cheeked and dripping with condensed steam. When she saw my expression, she became alarmed.

"What is it, Anna? You look like the devil's chasing you."

I thought of admitting that he was and his name was François, but I thought better of it. Why burden the girl with a problem to which she could have no solution, and a secret that—frightful gossip that she was—she would be burdened with keeping?

Instead I told her only half a lie, that I was having problems with my father and that I needed the maestro's private counsel. Did she think she could somehow, using her feminine wiles, get the locksmith to part with the key I needed? It was a great favor to ask, I said, but strangely she agreed in a hurry.

"Do you *fancy* him, Lynette?" I asked her, suddenly suspicious.

"Not in the least," she answered too quickly for me to believe she meant it. But I did not press her, instead described the key in François' possession, hoping she might see a duplicate on the locksmith's wall of keys or, if that failed, discover a master key for all of Amboise.

How she would take possession of the key I left to her discretion and ingenuity. But now Lynette seemed to have a plan in mind, for her eyes twinkled mischievously, as though this were a game she was keen to be playing. She told me to stand just inside the drying room door, almost opposite the locksmith's cubicle, and wait for a sign from her.

"What sign?" I asked nervously.

"How do I know?" she answered. "I am not inside yet. If the Fates mean for you to visit your friend at Cloux, I will be giving you a sign. And then you must act quickly."

"Good luck," I said, and kissed her.

She smiled and tousled her hair. "How do I look?"

"You *do* fancy him," I accused her.

"He has lovely eyes and a nice set of teeth."

"Nice teeth!" I cried, stifling a giggle.

"And he is not nearly as old as I thought."

"Lynette, you're a little tart."

"A tart who is doing you a favor. So no more teasing."

"All right. Go on, then. And Godspeed."

Accompanying me to the drying room and leaving me there, she darted across the corridor and tapped on the locksmith's door. It took only a moment for the man to open it, for the cubicle in which he worked and slept was very small. But I caught a glimpse of him as well as his expression when he saw who'd been knocking. Lynette was right. He did have nice eyes, and within the broad grin that split his face was a great white and very straight set of choppers. I could not hear the words that passed between them, but there were very few before he pulled her inside and closed the door.

The wait for my "sign" seemed interminable. I literally sweated, as the drying room's hot rocks and lines of damp sheets and intimate linen made for a moist heat. To pass the time I counted nightgowns and lawn shirts and ladies' shifts. Time and more time passed. Wiping my perspiring forehead, I even tried to identify whose undergarments were whose. I had just determined that a certain line of nightgowns was Queen Claude's when I heard the locksmith's door open, the scraping sound of metal on stone, and the door closing again.

I peeked out and saw lying on the floor in the middle of the corridor a twin of François' long red key to the secret passage. My heart leaped. I darted out and grabbed the thing, pocketing it before I resumed my position in the drying room.

Go quickly, I said to myself. *And boldly.*

With a few fortifying inhalations I stole out into the hall again, satisfied myself that no one was about, and made my move. Grabbing a wall torch, I shoved aside the hanging, put the key in the lock, and nearly cried out in relief when it opened smoothly. Careful not to set the tapestry afire, I entered the stair, closed the door partway, and with one hand pulled the hanging back over the outside as best I could. Then I shut the door all the way.

I was in and out of sight. The first leg of the mission had been accomplished. Only God knew what Lynette had had to do to liberate that key, though on the morrow I would surely hear all the details.

But as I turned from the door to face the spiral stone stair, pitch-black except for light thrown by a single torch, and me alone in that long, moldy, rat-infested tunnel, it seemed for a terrible moment an adventure I was unprepared to make.

My legs trembling, I hesitated on the top step, watching the torchlight flicker on the wall, asking myself if this was the act of a sensible young lady or a madwoman. But when I considered the consequences of doing nothing to stop François' assault on me, my legs suddenly steadied and my back straightened. I pulled my skirts high and took the first curved step down . . . very carefully. There were twenty-six of them till I hit the muddy bottom and the dark straightaway.

With only my small circle of light I felt it wise to keep one hand on a wall to guide me, but with the other holding the torch high, my skirts fell into the mud. No matter. The destination was the thing. And the destination *quickly*, with as few rats scurrying over my toes as possible.

Mud sucked at my riding boots, but I plodded on down the tunnel, ignoring the dripping water on my head and shoulders.

Ugh! The dead, rotting rodent underfoot needed not to be seen to be known. I gritted my teeth and moved ahead, only to have what felt like a whole tribe of the wretched squealing creatures run alongside my skirts and even between my legs. That so unnerved me that I thought for a moment I could go neither on nor back. That I would be forced to stand just as I was in that hellish tunnel, revulsion rising in my throat, rats skittering over my feet, for all eternity.

No! I was close now. I had to be. I tromped on, my wet skirts slapping my legs till lo, I saw before me the steps up to Cloux, and then the door! *Thank Christ!* I hesitated once more but not for long, for I heard unholy noises behind me in the dark. All ladylike behavior deserted me then. I rushed up the stairs and began pounding loudly on the maestro's door, calling his name.

It was flung open wide, but there stood, not Leonardo, but Salai. He just stared at me. Here was a young lady he knew by sight, but certainly not one who should be standing at this particular door at this particular time of night, covered halfway to her waist in mud, and altogether uninvited.

"Signor Salai," I said with all the calm I could muster. "I must speak to the maestro at once. The matter is quite urgent."

"It is not possible," said Leonardo's longtime apprentice. "He is in his bed. Sleeping."

"Wake him!" I cried, shocked at the demanding tone I had acquired.

"I will not wake him. You will come back tomorrow and come dressed more presentably."

"She looks presentable as she is. In fact, she looks quite beautiful."

The maestro, in his nightclothes and a fabulously embroidered velvet robe, had come into his studio, holding a three-pronged candelabra.

"Look at the way the torchlight plays on those black eyes of hers, Salai. And have you ever seen a neck so long and lovely? She could teach a swan a thing or two." He fixed Salai with a mildly disapproving look. "Have we any ladies' skirts in the house? Go and find them. She'll catch her death in those wet ones."

The younger man, lips pursed with displeasure, left, and the maestro, looking altogether pleased and not a bit surprised at my unplanned appearance, now took stock of me as he doused my torch and placed it on a sconce outside the door, closing it.

"Well," he said, pulling me inside, "either you have fallen in love, you've angered one of your royal friends, or the king has finally discovered your rare charms."

"But I *have* no rare charms, Maestro!" I cried, revealing in that one outburst the whole of my hand, but relieved that I would not have to torture myself with an embarrassing explanation. "I have lived in François' sight since I was nine," I said. "I have seen him daily, and he me. Why now? Have I unknowingly done something to deserve his sudden attention?"

"There is nothing sudden about his attraction to you, my dear," the maestro answered matter-of-factly. "It has been growing, growing as you have grown. François' court is like his personal garden, bursting with beautiful creatures, and flowers for his picking. He is the Mad Master Gardener. You were sent there to live as a girl. For a time you were a chrysalis in Claude's household. Then you unfurled into a butterfly under Marguerite's tutelage. Finally, and miraculously—for it was under no one's direction—you devised spots and whorls and colors of your own making, spectacular and original. How could a man such as François help but want to ensnare such a rare creature?"

"Maestro! I don't understand what you're saying. I'm just a *girl*."

Salai had returned with the simple wool skirt and petticoat of a maid. He directed me behind a three-paneled screen and I changed into them. When I emerged, Leonardo thanked Salai and bade him go. He did, with a jealous scowl on his handsome face.

"What exactly has François done?" Leonardo said when we were alone.

"He enticed me into his library. . . ."

"Ah, his famous book depository. 'The greatest library in the world,' " he said with a sardonic grin.

"That *is* what he said. Greater than the Medicis' in Florence."

Leonardo was quiet, but his eyes were blazing. "Not in a thousand years will François' collection come close to Lorenzo de' Medici's library."

"It was filled with heretical texts—of the occult, Hermeticism, the Cabala," I told Leonardo, remembering how odd it had seemed at the time.

"Does this surprise you?" he asked.

"Yes and no," I replied, choosing my words carefully. There was much about François' and Marguerite's religious leanings I was not meant to know, but did. "He is 'the Most Catholic King,' " I argued in François' defense.

"Would it surprise you to know, Anna, that *all* the princes of Europe—the Medicis, the Borgias, the Dukes of Milan, even Charles, the Holy Roman Emperor—are fully schooled in these ideas? All of them but your king, Henry. He is perhaps the most backward of monarchs in the philosophical quests."

"Please, Maestro," I said, desperation overcoming me. "I need your advice about *François*."

He looked hard at me. "I believe you do," he said, then turned and walked from the studio. I stood where I was. He looked back at me with an amused smile. "Are you coming?"

"I . . . yes, I'm coming."

He was already partway up his stairs.

"It is too drafty in my studio," he said. "We will go to my chamber. Salai has laid a fire. We will drink a little wine. Talk."

He walked up ever so slowly and I followed behind. He grunted with every step and his infirmity—a weakness of the whole left side—was more pronounced than ever. The wall to the right on the stairs was, like those of his studio, hung with sketch after sketch of every imagining in the world. With the maestro's dragging feet, there was time to view the drawings, many of them red chalk on paper, some that seemed quite obsessive. A page of cats—dozens of them—in every conceivable posture, interspersed occasionally with dragons. Others made no earthly sense to me—circles with straight lines radiating out from them. And many of the anatomical sketches for which he was famous—to many, *infamous*. There were twisted bowels, hearts laced with bulbous veins, the private parts of men and women. Hands, backs, chests, brains, eyes—all rendered in such exacting detail I shuddered at the sight of them.

What most intrigued me, though, were his studies of knots, both lovely and bizarre. There were elaborate intertwinings of everything from circles and squares filled with the intricate patterns, to studies of the braids of a woman's hair, to fancifully woven branches of trees, and waves of water.

I was unaware that I'd slowed to look at them.

Leonardo stopped and turned back to me. "So you like *miei molti disegni di groppi* . . . knots?"

"They are extraordinary."

"I come from a little village where, along the river, a certain kind of willow grows in profusion. In old Italian it is called '*vinco*.' The river is the Vincio, and of course the village is Vinci. From a little boy, I watched the women soak the willow in the water and weave the shoots into beautiful wickerwork baskets. The men used the *vinco* for strong bindings." Leonardo smiled wistfully. "Of course Dante called the sweet bonds of love '*dolci vinci*.'

"For me they are small fantasies, at first appearance a riddle for which there is no answer. But one can see the *groppi* as life itself. Each problem, each challenge, each enemy, a knot." He looked at me directly. "Be patient, Anna. Learn to unravel each one, and you will find satisfaction and success in your life." He began climbing again.

There was a final grunt of triumph. "Here we are, then."

At the top of the stairs was a longish corridor. At its end was an arched antechamber, through which I followed him to his bedroom. It was a lovely chamber, not overlarge, with a good-sized bed on a raised platform, its four posters in tall spirals. The scalloped canopy and corner drapes of the bed were royal red velvet, and once again very little could be seen of the bedroom walls for all the sketches covering them.

As we moved to the crackling fire that Salai had laid, I saw along the floor of one wall a line of bird cages, all of them empty. Among them was the pretty little gilt cage that I had given Leonardo.

I smiled with pride to think that my gift to the great man was part of his collection.

He had already lowered himself into one of the chairs in front of the fire. He saw me staring and said, "I know that you know the significance of the empty cages, or you would not have made me a present of one."

"Is freedom so very important to you?" I said, turning to him.

"I prefer death rather than the loss of liberty," he answered matter-of-factly.

"Were you a *prisoner* in Italy?" I asked, confused.

"Not in body, though that was becoming more a distinct possibility with every month that passed after Leo—the Medici pope—died. Freedom of *thought* was being denied me, and that is every bit as valuable as freedom of movement."

With a nod he invited me to sit opposite him in front of the fire. As I arranged my rough skirts under me, I felt myself a very great lady to be seated thus, in private with so venerable a person.

"So François wishes to bed you," he said, more a statement than a question.

I nodded.

"My poor, dear misguided friend. He is in so many ways a prince above all others. But he is also an ambitious tyrant . . . and your *groppo*." Leonardo rubbed his wrinkled forehead with his fingers. "I should not be speaking so about him." He shook his head slowly. "But you giving in to the king would be a tragedy beyond all proportions."

Tears began to cloud my vision. I bit my lip to keep from crying. I did not wish to appear weak in the maestro's presence.

"But what can I do?"

He stopped to collect his thoughts and, only after a desperately long silence that made me squirm, continued.

"In these cases," he said, "one must find a means of *offense* or *defense* in order to preserve that chief gift of nature, which is liberty. Your poor sister was denied hers when she was thrust into François' arms."

I hung on his every word, each feeling like a precious gem being tossed in my lap, for he was speaking with such dangerous candor with me about his only patron and benefactor.

"What I want you to understand about François, who is now your personal tyrant, is that he is dealing with a tyrant of his *own*. His penis."

So unexpected and outrageous was this statement that I barked out a laugh. Leonardo, not unaware of his words' effect, strove to keep a straight face as he continued, for he was as amused as he was serious.

"The thing displays an intelligence of its own. Sometimes it moves on its own without permission, or any thought by its owner. Whether one is awake or asleep, it does what it pleases. Often the man is asleep, and it is awake. Often the man is awake, and it is asleep. Or the man would like it to be in action, but it refuses. Often it desires action, and the man forbids it."

Leonardo paused and, leaning forward, holding on to his limp arm with the good, warmed them both before the fire.

I was, of course, at a complete loss for words.

"François, unlike any man I have ever known, *never* forbids it. It is, in my opinion, the king's most dire failing. But then, who am I to pass judgment?" He sat back in his chair and sighed, his eyes losing their focus, as if he was remembering the past. "I am not like other men. I see the act of coupling and the members engaged so ugly that if it were not for the faces and adornments of the actors and the impulses sustained, I believe the human race would surely die out."

"Maestro!" I cried. "Surely you don't mean that."

"But I do. And think of the inequality between the sexes! The one who sows the seed does it only with pleasure, but the one who awaits the seed may *receive* it with pleasure, but nine months later brings forth with the most terrible pain. Perhaps that is why I have renounced the tenderness of human relationship. Now I live only for things of the mind. But that is my choice, Anna." He gazed at me with affection. "You are young and lovely, and you are gifted with a fine intellect. There is no doubt that you will marry." Now Leonardo leaned forward and took my hand in his. Though the skin was wrinkled and spotted with age, I felt its strength.

"My beloved mother," he began, but did not immediately finish. It seemed he *could* not. He went altogether quiet then, and more emotion—joy, pain, pride, misery—played upon that old face than I had ever seen displayed by man or woman in my whole life. Finally he said, "Through no fault of her own I was born illegitimate, and though she did not wish it, I was brought up in my *father's* house as his acknowledged son. But as a *bastard* son—a terrible state of affairs for an Italian boy. Even though I was entirely blameless and without vices, my reputation—from infancy onward—was in ruins. My mother"— Leonardo's eyes closed as he spoke the next words—"fought her whole life to protect and love me. That love was my only shield against the miseries the world was so eager to inflict upon an illegitimate child.

"You, my dear, deserve to find requited passion with a man in this life. Just . . . let that lover be your lawful husband."

I gazed into this dear man's eyes, which by now were moist with emotion.

"When I become a mother," I said, "I can only hope to inspire such love from my child as yours has from you." I felt my shoulders slump. "As for keeping my reputation and finding a way into my marriage bed a virgin, I have less hope. François is used to having his way."

Leonardo sat back in his chair and stroked his long beard. I could see he was thinking hard on my problem and I thought, *How extraordinary to have this genius pondering on the plight of a girl of so little account.*

He finally said, "You must be the sole creator of this work, Anna. You will form the concept in your mind, outline the cartoon, mix your colors, and paint in the brushstrokes. I cannot help you with these details, but one overarching principle is as clear to me as winter light over a mountain lake. It is this: For there to be a happy outcome for yourself in your problem, François must save face. I know the man well. If he is humiliated or shamed, even in private, you will become a detested enemy and in danger of your very life. But he is a great player of games. He may occasionally cheat, simply to prove that he is the king and can get away with it. But in a fair fight, if he is bested by superior skill, he will respect his opponent."

"You have too much confidence in me, Maestro." I felt my heart sink, for I'd hoped for more of a solution than this.

"It is true that François has never been bested by a woman he desires," he said. "Few kings have."

I stared ruefully down at my own hands. "Mayhap that is why there are no queens in the deck of playing cards."

"So you have noticed that as well?" He smiled a small smile. "I have always seen it as a gross inequity." He looked up and gazed out the window. "Ah, there is that venerable snail, the sun. It is rising. You should go."

I stood, and as he rose, he took both my hands in his. "I believe one ought not to desire the impossible . . ."

I faltered at those words, and he had to have seen my expression change.

". . . but with you, *cara mia*," he finished, "*all* is possible."

CHAPTER 24

*I*n the following days my nerves suffered, and I could tell that every day I was becoming more high-strung. The pitch of my voice increased. I found it easier to lose my temper. I did not relish what I was going to be forced to do, nor did I know for sure that my plan would unfold in the way I wished it to. I could wait, hoping that François would lose interest in me and turn to another woman. But if the maestro was right, that the King of France had been for a long while setting his sights on me, it would only be delaying the inevitable.

I also knew that if what I tried failed, I would sooner than later be another in a long line of François' whores, with no reputation left, and the course of my life changed forever.

I was alone in my thoughts and worries, and the details of my "solution." Neither Mary nor Marguerite nor Claude could be consulted. Lynette—who had found a very happy and requited lust with the locksmith—could also not be trusted with the secret. And I had no loyal old waiting lady, like the one in the duchess's story, to help me fight off the king's assault.

I prepared myself mentally in the only way I knew how. By repeating over and over to myself the wisdom Marguerite had spoken—that women were stronger than men would let them think they could be. That I had a sound mind and would make something of myself in the future. Too, I endlessly recounted the conversation with Leonardo, remembering the astonishing confidence *he* had in me, the belief that I could accomplish anything I desired. If the great man thought so well of me, spent his precious time in considering *my* problem, then I must needs be worthy of that belief. He respected me, so I must respect myself.

No one could be sure of the outcome, but a concerted attempt at saving my virginity and reputation had to be made.

Once I had decided and chosen the date, I delivered a note directly into François' hand as he came out of the chapel, much the same as my sister had done to arrange for Mary Tudor's secret meeting with him after Louis had died.

François looked surprised, but delighted, when he found the folded paper in his hand and gave me a sly wink. I replied with a most ladylike curtsy, as his wife was not far behind.

On the appointed evening, I made appropriate excuses so that I'd got leave to sleep in both Claude's and Marguerite's households, therefore confusing my whereabouts. Then I made my way carefully, so as not to be seen, to a little-used private game room in the east wing of Amboise.

It was unlocked, a signal that François was at one with the rendez-vous, and I slipped inside. Indeed, the smallish chamber was already candlelit, with a fire blazing in the hearth. A table with two chairs was set for cards, and a deck lay in the center of the table. There were two piles of gold coins, and a flask of wine and two Venetian glass goblets sat nearby.

My heart in my throat, I walked to the table and stared down at the cards. They were backs up, and I saw in the flickering light that the king had chosen a deck with the design of a man and woman engaged in mutual oral satisfaction.

I almost lost my nerve at that, and thought I would still have time to flee the room if I left immediately. Then the door opened and François, never looking larger or more handsome or more hungry, stepped inside. The click of the lock was so delicate but so definite that the sound registered with a tiny jolt between my legs. I groaned inwardly, for if any inkling of the lust inspired by the sight of François watching that orgy of women in Mary's room haunted me *this* night, all would be lost. The best of my intelligence told me that the past spasms inspired by the king had nothing to do with love, nor even desire for the man himself. It had been my misfortune that the spark igniting my infant eroticism had been François.

"Good evening, Anna."

I curtsied low, knowing that the deep décolleté of my bodice would show off my small, high breasts to perfection.

"Your Majesty," I said, modulating my voice to its lowest and most sensual pitch. Then I lifted my eyes and, with the greatest effort, held his gaze.

"Need I say you look ravishing tonight?" he said as I stood.

"Compliments are always welcome, my lord." I saw him take a step toward me, his arms beginning to rise in my direction. I stepped back but smiled prettily. "You have accepted my invitation here tonight, Majesty. Will you not abide by the rules I have set forth?"

His smile was rakish. "A series of card games with the loser of each hand forfeiting, not the pot, but a piece of clothing? I accept the challenge."

"Then if you will . . ." I gestured to one of the chairs, and only when he was seated did I take mine. "May I deal first?"

"Of course."

I picked up the deck and pretended to see the image on the backs of the cards for the first time. I offered a little smile, as if the sight pleased me.

"What shall we play?" he asked.

"*Piqué*," I said with no hesitation.

"That is your strongest game, is it not, Anna?"

"May I have some wine?" I said in reply. One was always meant to answer the king's questions directly. I found it enjoyable to rebel against protocol in this tiny way.

Mildly amused, he filled my goblet, then his. He held up his glass. "A toast."

"No," I said simply, and began to deal. I could feel at once that he was intrigued with my subversive behavior. Did not know what to make of it. *Where was the wide-eyed girl, the one who'd been so flustered by his hands on her that she'd dropped his book?*

"Are you going to play, Your Majesty, or just sit there staring at my ducks?"

He laughed at that, and at once was happily engaged with both the card game . . . and my seduction of him.

The first hand I lost. I started removing my necklace.

"Jewelry is not allowed," he said. "Clothing only."

"So *you* are making the rules now."

"I am the king. I always make the rules."

I pouted prettily, then kicked off a slipper.

"No shoes, either," he added, "or we shall be here all night."

I gave him a crooked grin.

"Take off a sleeve," he said, his voice husky.

"I notice *you* did not wear sleeves tonight, my lord."

Indeed, he was wearing a simple satin vest over his shirt.

"Take it off, Anna."

I unlaced my right sleeve and let it drop to the floor. I pushed the cards to him and he dealt. It was a very good hand for me to begin with. I kept drawing high cards and before long had three kings and two knaves. I laid them down, winning the hand. I steeled my nerves and stared at François directly.

"Take off your vest," I ordered him.

How perverse it is, I thought, *to enjoy ordering a king about*. No matter how dangerous, the power of it made me feel magnificent.

He undid the garment and folded it before laying it aside.

"A new rule," he said.

"No new rules!" I cried.

"New rule," he intoned forcefully. "Once a piece of clothing is taken off, it may not be put back on again."

I thought for a moment, then graced him with my most coquettish smile. "Agreed," I said, and thought, *The sooner this is done, the better.*

In the ensuing hands I was shorn of my second sleeve, both stockings, and my petticoat. François lost his stockings, and made a great display of unlacing his large flowered codpiece. As he did this my heart felt as though it were tumbling all round my chest, but I held firm, pretending gaiety.

When I lost my bodice, I asked him to undo it in the back. He did so, savoring every button, and breathing hotly onto my neck. And though he kept his hands where he was meant to, he leaned up against me and I knew from the hard rod against my spine that his restraint was only inflaming him further.

We sat back down and I dealt. I lost my skirt, then he his breeches. I now wore only my shift, and he his long shirt. Both of us were naked beneath.

"Your deal, mademoiselle," he said with a smirk.

I could hold my smile no longer. I was trembling all over. The time was at hand.

I dived off my chair and fell to my knees before François. Clutching his feet, I began kissing them.

The shock was so great that he stood suddenly, towering over me.

"Your Majesty!" I cried. I was really weeping now, the pent-up anxiety of the last months, my anger and frustrations, all released in a sincere flood of tears and sobbed words. "It has been so horrible for me, all these years at court, for I have been in love with you!"

François was utterly silent, stunned by this unexpected outpouring.

"I've wanted so badly to give myself to you, but first I was too young for it to be seemly. Then there were the other women. The worst was *Mary*!" I fairly howled my sister's name. "That was the hardest to bear. Oh, God forgive me, I *love* you!"

I let myself moan more and more loudly and tore at my hair. I knew I was raving, and I could feel the king shifting on his feet, of which I would, under no circumstances, let go my hold.

"I want to have your children, François. Many, many children. We both know Claude cannot survive much longer, and I know—" I gave a truly grievous sob. "I know I cannot be your queen. But you can make me your mistress. Your *only* mistress. Oh please, please, I know you love me, too!"

I rose to standing then and *threw* myself into the king's arms. I clutched at him, digging my fingernails into his back so hard he cried out in pain. The next moment he pushed me to arm's length and stared at what must have been a terrible sight—a wild-eyed fifteen-year-old in a thin shift, teeth bared, hair all askew—and smiled.

"What a performance, *Petite Boullan*. Remind me to put you in my next entertainment. You play a very frightening madwoman. My prick has gone quite limp." He appraised me very closely. "It is one thing to chase a lady who is only pretending she does not wish to be caught. You are something else altogether." He sat back down in his chair. "Put on your clothes, Anna."

I began dressing in a daze—skirt, petticoat, slippers. When it came to my bodice, he waved for me to turn round so he could button me up.

"Besides," he said, "you are too much cut from the same cloth as my intellectual sister to put you in my bed. If I did, you would probably wish to talk politics . . . or religion. And you would beat me at cards far too often." He paused thoughtfully and said with a straight face, "No woman has ever kissed my feet like that."

I began to giggle.

"What are you laughing at?" he demanded.

"Your feet . . . ," I said, trying to get control of myself, ". . . are so *big*. Like two barges on the river!"

He began to laugh, and soon we were roaring at the ridiculousness of everything, tears running down our faces.

Finally he shook his head and sighed. "You are destined for greatness, Anna. But not as my mistress. Now get out of here before I change my mind."

"Yes, Majesty."

I hurried for the door.

"Anna!"

Hardly daring to breathe, I turned back to François.

Between his fingers the King of France was holding up my two silk stockings.

CHAPTER 25

I was happier than I had ever been.

My life at the French court, which, until that night of cards with François, had been a mass of raw excitement and confusion, suddenly assumed a straighter and more pleasant path. It was an odd thing, for I was now more self-respecting, believing I had a modicum of control over my own destiny.

To Leonardo I'd written a note, not even signing it, and had it delivered by a young page I paid well to keep silent. Cryptic to anyone but the maestro, it said only, "Face has been saved. All is well."

The king was a delight to be around. He flirted with me, but very lightly and so harmlessly that the flirting could be done right before Claude's eyes without embarrassment or discomfort. Once in a while he would grace me with a peculiar smile that I was sure indicated "our little secret."

My sister, Mary, was vaguely suspicious because she sensed so profound a change in me, but her only comment was that I had, all of a sudden, seemed to "grow up." This only confirmed my suspicions about *her*, that she was, despite her past reign as the royal mistress, still a naive girl who took things at face value and could not comprehend—and had no interest in seeking—a deeper or more complicated level of understanding or existence.

I wanted desperately to write of my adventure to George, but I did not like the odds of someone intercepting the letter. All that I had gained would be lost—and much more than that—if even a hint of gossip was revealed here or in England. So I kept my counsel and instead wrote to my brother of my improved mood and my enjoyment of growing up in France.

Happily, as we were living in a time of relative peace, with no dire political events at hand, there was little news of espionage I could write my father, except for François' occasional grumblings about another European monarch or the Ottoman threat, or some bellicose undercurrent that had been made up of my imaginative embroidery as much as the fabric of truth. More than ever I counted the King of France—as well as his sister and his wife—as my friends, and I was loath to do them any harm unless treason against England was involved.

I had made one annoying blunder, however. Growing more and more desperate about my upcoming marriage to James Butler, I'd written to my father asking if I might be allowed to see a portrait of my betrothed. I'd heard that sometimes looking upon an image of the enforced marriage partner caused the one looking to fall in love with the promise of the picture. And I could not help but be haunted by the vision of him as a poxy monster with beady eyes and a receding chin.

Father's response to my request was nothing short of outrage. *Who did I think I was to be asking to see a portrait of the heir to the Butler fortune?* This was something prospective *husbands* demanded, he wrote back, not their prospective brides!

It did give my father the idea that such a portrait, since he'd heard that I was indeed growing out of my gawkiness into an attractive young lady, was a wise investment—something to keep the Butler family interested in the Boleyn match. So he commissioned a minor French artist called Bessant, and every afternoon for two weeks I was forced to sit very still for this bad-tempered young man, in a staid black headdress and square-cut bodice, pearl and gold chains crisscrossed on a broad expanse of pale breast, and the Boleyn *B* proudly centered in it all, and hung with three teardrop pearls.

I resented every moment of that sitting. The portrait was meant to sell me to the Butlers like a prize horse. Somehow I could not imagine James even trying to fall in love with me through my picture. All I'd heard of him and his father was that they were Irish country louts who'd had to be talked into the marriage by Cardinal Wolsey.

One afternoon after my sitting, I came round a corner outside Claude's rooms and crashed full bore into a pile of linens as high as my headdress. As soon as I heard a profane oath coming from behind the pile, I knew who was carrying it.

Lynette had taken a step up. Up the *stairs*, that is. I'd convinced Marguerite and Claude that the young washerwoman was quite presentable and should be promoted to laundry maid, thus allowing her the privilege of delivering clean linens, sleeves, shirts, and shifts to the royal bedchambers and wardrobes.

Lynette was forever in my debt, she'd said, for she was no longer a lowly drudge but a proper servant required to wear a decent dress, and not a shapeless old sack stained with oils and lye. She could finally see, firsthand, the kings and queens and courtiers and ladies I spoke about, in all their glory, every day.

I took two folded sheets off the top of her pile.

"Thank Jesu it is you," Lynette said.

"Thank him, indeed. It might have been your crippled queen, and she would not have thanked you if she'd landed on her rump."

"Speaking of rumps . . . ," Lynette whispered conspiratorially. She was altogether unperturbed by the thought of knocking down the Queen of France.

"Oh, no no no," I said with mock horror. "No more lurid details about 'Longet of the Cellar,' " as she now referred to him.

She kept me in stitches with her naughty stories of how perfectly Longet's "key" fitted into her "lock," and how it was sometimes necessary to "oil the mechanism" so as not to get stuck together all night. In all honesty, the stories about her torrid affair with the locksmith were a great source of entertainment for me, as well as an education.

I was dubious, though, as to whether Lynette had felt that explosion of sensation that I had had in my bed, by accident. And the same as I had brought forth several more times, on purpose.

She always spoke of joy and warm excitement and, of course, love with Longet. But nothing she described sounded *ecstatic*. Never quite like "culmination." I did not press her on it, afraid to spoil her happiness.

And mayhap I was wrong.

Lynette was still in full dark about my encounter with François. Many times I had wished to tell her, feeling it only fair—friend to friend, tit for tat. But to her and her sisters, gossip was like a good meal—meant to be savored, but most importantly to be *shared*. I did not like the odds of tempting Lynette with so juicy a tidbit, and expecting her silence.

She had backed me up behind a column, and we were altogether out of everyone's sight and, I hoped, out of their hearing.

"He's asked me to marry him," she said, and gave a little squeal.

"That's wonderful!"

"Longet is frantic, trying to find a way to approach my father, who will instantly know in meeting my love that he has already deflowered his daughter." She grinned lopsidedly. "Oh well, it was the same for all my sisters. First Papa will shout and threaten to beat me . . . and kill Longet. Then he will weep for joy."

I sighed deeply. "Longet really does adore you."

She smiled dreamily. "And I him. Oh, Anna, everything is different when you are in love."

Lynette had always insisted her and Longet's liaison was not a simple case of lust, but true love—an idea that had first captured my imagination when Mary Tudor and Charles Brandon had defied the King of England for the same. My friend knew the chance for such a match in *my* life was near impossible. Now her speaking of this honest passion, and a marriage for love, evoked in me such longing for the same, it made my heart hurt. Lynette could read the pain in my expression.

"You know, you might fall in love with James Butler after you marry him," she suggested.

"My mother always tells me that," I said.

Lynette didn't know what she could say to make me feel better. "I'm sorry, Anna."

"You better go," I told her, placing the two sheets back on her pile and pushing her back into the hallway. "I don't want you to get in trouble." The truth was, I was close to tears, ashamed to be jealous of my friend's happiness.

I watched her leave. "Tell me what happens with Longet and your father!" I called out after her.

Marguerite was asking more frequently for my presence in her household, and so I was spared the routine of Queen Claude and her dull circle of stitchery.

I always believed that the duchess knew of my "tryst" with her brother, that François had confided in her. I found her even warmer and more respectful of me than before, and prone to off-color jests, as though I was no longer a girl but a full-fledged woman who understood such things.

She was more than ever involved in her religious progression away from the Roman Catholic Church, and toward the teachings of Martin Luther: external rituals rejected for inner faith; ecclesiastical authority eschewed for individual conscience; and the whole idea of celibacy boldly challenged. Priests' remaining unmarried, Marguerite would often say—reminding her ladies that she was in agreement with Erasmus on this—was *a criticism of marriage*, and therefore inferred the inferiority of women. No one in her inner circle argued with Marguerite about the great worth of the female sex and the generally pathetic nature of men, particularly corrupt and hypocritical clerics, who, she said, were the worst of all lechers in society.

But she was also concerned with the question of marriage, and the inequality of the sexual freedoms allowed men and those allowed women. One day as we sat companionably in her chamber—Marguerite, six of her ladies, and I—she put to us this question: "Who may marry whom, and upon whose authority?"

The argument was very lively, for though many of the duchess's women were liberal-minded like she was, several had more old-fashioned leanings when it came to the question of marriage, and believed, as most people did, that parents, particularly fathers, should be the only arbiters of nuptial partners. When it came to marriage, love was not only a silly pretension but a dangerous one as well. Most men were, after all, unfaithful—expected to be. And women who took lovers—except royal mistresses—almost always came to a horrible end.

"What about a marriage entered into without the family's consent?" Marguerite posed as a question.

"Clandestine?" Madame Brantôme inquired, sounding surprised.

"Yes, with only the two people knowing of it. I am considering writing one of my stories of such a couple."

There was silence in the chamber, for even the liberal-minded women were clearly thinking twice about such a risky undertaking.

"Is there no one here that would, if she were not already married, consider such a thing?"

"This scenario supposes that the two people have somehow secured time and a place to be alone, so that such difficult promises can be exchanged," Madame Duprée offered.

"Are they young and beautiful in your story, my lady?" asked Madame Elion.

"I am thinking *not*," said Marguerite. "I am thinking she is a girl disliked by her mistress, the queen, and uncared for by her father, so that no attempt at all is made for a suitable match. She is lonely, and meets a man of no more attractiveness than herself, perhaps lower in rank than she, a second son with little future or fortune. But they do have the sincerest affection for each other, and while no one is watching, they meet in a church, and under the eyes of God exchange rings and vows."

"I would do it!" I piped in.

All eyes turned to me.

"You would marry against the will of your father and your king?" Madame Brantôme asked me, very shocked indeed.

"Brave girl," Madame Duprée added.

"True and mutual love would have to be involved," I said.

"Could you bear the punishment inflicted when the marriage was discovered?" Marguerite asked.

"What punishment?" I said.

" 'What punishment?' you ask. I have met your father, Anna," the duchess said. "He is a harsh man in the best of circumstances. I think that if you defied him so blatantly, you'd be whipped within an inch of your life."

"Has your heroine lain with her husband?" Madame Brantôme asked, dismissing my suggestions as impossible, and more ready to play with the idea of Marguerite's story than my fantasy. "Is he a fabulous lover, or is the marriage never consummated? Without consummation it could be annulled," she said, "even against the couple's wishes."

"If she is clever, she might have *all* she desires," I insisted. "Vow, consummation, pleasure in bed. And her father will lose his control over her once she is married!"

"And then," Madame Duprée added, "one can only hope that her chosen husband is faithful and worthy of her sacrificed family, and perhaps fortune."

"Oh, he would be perfectly faithful," I said with confidence in this still-unwritten literary hero.

"What if he had no fortune of his own and would depend on the lady's inheritance?" Marguerite asked, amused at my idealism. "What if he were altogether penniless?"

"The Fates could always intervene," I replied. "A distant uncle could die and his favorite nephew—her beloved—could be gifted with a huge fortune and a château so far into the country that they would never be bothered by court gossip, and could live out their days in privacy and utter happiness."

"Perhaps *you* should write this," said Marguerite, smiling.

"I'm not a writer, Your Grace," I said, blushing, "but I hope you'll let us read the story when it's done."

Marguerite regarded me through playfully narrowed eyes. "You're not hiding anything from us, are you, Anna? A secret lover? Handsome but penniless?"

All the ladies began to titter at the teasing and I smiled mysteriously, enjoying the banter.

"I'll never tell," I said, "but if I someday suddenly disappear and never return, just imagine me in that distant château with my Adonis, deliriously and ferociously happy in my marriage bed."

"Mademoiselle *Boullan*, you shock us!" cried Madame Brantôme, and everyone laughed.

This seemed a fitting end to our storytelling, and it was decided that we'd play cards then. The two tables were pulled out, the chairs arranged around them.

"What shall we play?" someone asked. Everyone piped in with their suggestions. Then Marguerite caught and held my eye.

"*Piqué*," she said, smiling conspiratorially at me. "We shall play *Piqué*."

CHAPTER 26

*T*he time of peace came and went very quickly indeed. The courts of the three great rulers of Europe were suddenly awash with intrigue. Thankfully, François' ruminations on war were so overt that I was not called upon by my father to spy.

Thomas Boleyn had earned a name for himself as the foremost diplomat of England after Cardinal Wolsey, and the most active gentleman on the king's council, and in the Star Chamber as well. He'd gained King Henry's praise as the best and most experienced negotiator he had ever known.

This—according to George's letters to me, which were now coming fast and furious across the Channel via Thomas Wyatt—had *enraged* the good cardinal. To him it seemed that Henry liked our father too much. "A furious pig in a red hat" was how George described Wolsey on hearing he'd been beaten at his own game by Thomas Boleyn.

The story was that Wolsey, who controlled all appointments at the English court, in a fit of childish spite and jealousy denied Father the high post of comptroller that he sorely desired, and appointed instead a less qualified man. But our father was as canny as his reputation. He might have gone head-to-head with the cardinal, but knew this would have put Henry, who loved and trusted Wolsey, too, in a wretched position. So Father bowed humbly to the cleric's will. Then he bided his time. The ill-chosen comptroller had the good grace to die after less than a year, and Wolsey could find no further reasons to deny the post to Father.

François, meanwhile, was volubly thanking God that he'd not won the Holy Roman Emperorship. It would have caused him trouble, he insisted to anyone who would listen. However, *contesting* the election as he had done had been a brilliant ploy, for it had forced Charles to spend vast amounts of money that made the Burgundian much the poorer.

It occurred to me that this was a "face-saving device" on François' part, for I knew that his pride had been badly hurt by losing the election. Charles's triumph in coming to rule lands as far afield from one another as Germany, Spain, the Netherlands, and parts of France and Italy had tipped the whole balance of power in the world.

Ironically, Henry, "the little king," found himself in the enviable position of being courted by both François *and* the Holy Roman Emperor.

Mary and I had grown closer of late. As time healed the wounds that had been inflicted upon her at court, the sweet girl she had once been reemerged and I, for one, was happy to see her. François had, in fact, taken Madame Châteaubriant as his new mistress and installed her in the infamous mirrored bed. We sisters had breathed a simultaneous sigh of relief, and Mary was returned to Marguerite's household, where she was treated like a proper lady again.

We had taken to strolling together to *l'Office du Courrier* to send and receive letters to and from our home. Monsieur Filbert was very pleased to have the two loveliest women at court—as he called us—come to visit and pass the time with him. For Mary and me our visits were a breath of fresh air. There was no need to perform, be the perfect coquettes. My intellect was not on display as in Marguerite's household, nor my piety as in Claude's. We were just a pair of girls who liked to laugh and while away an hour with a pleasant man.

"Letters for you both today!" Filbert called out when he saw us coming. "For you from your brother, Anna. And your father for you, Marie."

"Why is Father writing to *me*?" Mary said as Filbert turned away to sort through the pile of documents that had arrived the night before.

"Because he loves you so dearly?" I said, and braced myself for the poke in the ribs I knew was coming . . . and did.

Filbert held out our letters and whilst I took mine with a delighted smile and asked the chief courier how he was this fine day, Mary had the look of Cleopatra putting her hand into a basket of poisonous snakes.

As was our custom, we would read our letters once over as we stood there, and visit with Filbert afterward. Then we would share the contents with each other whilst we walked back to the palace, and read them again back in our rooms.

Mine from George was news of Henry's mistress, Bessie Blount. Cardinal Wolsey had recently arranged for the girl, pregnant with Henry's bastard, to retire to the Priory of Saint Laurence for the rest of her confinement. Apparently she would not be coming back to court, though the king had been well pleased with her for the four years of their liaison. All Henry could talk about, George said, was his hope that the child, bastard or not, would be a son. Distraught that his queen had still been unable to give him a living boy, he would wander about clutching his head shouting, "Am I not a man like any other?!" over and over again. This pregnancy, should the Fates allow him a son, would be a triumph for Henry.

"My God, Anne. I'm going home!" I heard Mary cry.

I looked up to see her pretty face flushed all pink, her eyes sparkling.

"I'm going to be *married*," she said as she read the letter again. "A young man named William Carey. And mother has written a note to me on Father's letter to say that my William is handsome, and well made, and oh"—tears glistened in her eyes—"very kind."

I hugged her and she, trembling with the first true joy I had seen since our arrival in France, fiercely hugged me back.

"I'm very, very happy for you, sister," I said. "When do you leave?"

She started to read the letter but then looked at me with sweet helplessness. "I cannot see through my tears," she said, thrusting our parents' missive at me.

I read that arrangements had already been made for her Channel crossing in a month's time. I felt her clutch my arm again, and now when Mary spoke, there was fear in her voice.

"Do you think he'll hate me because . . . I've been used?"

"He will be the happiest man alive when he sees the beauty he's getting for a wife. And he must know what you've been through," I said. "Something like that is never a secret. Mayhap *he* is a virgin and you will teach him a thing or two."

"So you have good news from home?" Filbert asked.

"Oh yes!" Mary answered. "The best news. I'm going to be married."

"Lucky man," said the chief courier with the utmost sincerity. " '*La Belle Boullan.*' "

"You see?" I whispered to Mary.

She smiled happily. "Once he's finished his service to the king, perhaps we'll move to the country. I shall have a lovely home, and children. . . ."

"Many children," I agreed, then added, thinking of Claude, "though not *too* many."

With all the excitement we cut short our visit with Filbert and started back up the path to the palace. Mary began to giggle beside me. I asked her what it was.

"He is the king's 'Groom of the Stool.' "

"Why, that is the most"—I could not, hard as I tried, keep a straight face—"elegant of titles. Henry must think it a *waste* to use him otherwise."

Mary again jabbed me in the ribs, this time for my bad pun. But I was not finished.

"The Stool-Keeper's Wife. The butt of many jokes."

I had to dart quickly to escape her blows. The two of us ran laughing up the path to Amboise, silly as two jesters and twice as happy.

Spending so much time with Marguerite and her ladies, I sometimes found myself longing for the simple sweetness of Claude.

It was during one of these visits with the queen that François stormed into her chamber. I could see he was in tears, his eyes puffy and red-rimmed, as though he'd been weeping a long time. He waved all of Claude's ladies out of the room, but before I left, I saw him collapse into his wife's open arms and cry, "Dead! Oh, sweet God in heaven, how can it be?"

As we filed out, I could see many servants scurrying about. I thought of Madame, but she was young still, and altogether healthy. I stopped a page who was running past me.

"Who has died?" I pressed him.

"Leonardo da Vinci," he replied. "The king's dearest friend. They say the maestro died in François' arms."

I stood very still where I was, the chaos building around me. Marguerite came rushing to Claude's door and was instantly admitted. Then Madame arrived and from inside I could hear wailing—it was François—and the sound of women consoling him.

Bitter tears stung my eyes. *Who would console me?* I thought. Leonardo was my friend as well, though no one knew how close and dear he'd been. How he had comforted me, saved my very life.

I walked slowly back to Marguerite's apartments, speaking to no one, somewhat dazed. Already servants were draping the corridors in white gauze, and I heard whispers as I passed of the grand funeral that would be held to honor him.

Before the outer door to the duchess's room I stopped short. My head cleared some. I knew what I had to do.

I turned and hurried back through Amboise to a basement room in the north wing where the silkwomen worked. They knew me well, for much of my game winnings went to beautiful new gowns, and I gave them much credit for their talented fingers and keen eye for fashion.

Clearly they had not yet heard the news, for three of them sat stitching companionably, smiling at their work and the gossip they shared. They sensed my presence all at once, and stared at me standing in the doorway.

"Anna, what is it?"

"What has happened?"

"Come. Sit down. You look ill."

"I need a white dress," I said. "I have no mourning clothes." My cheeks were suddenly wet, and a moment later I began to sob uncontrollably. "Please make me a white dress."

I had never seen François' court as sad or solemn as in the next weeks. 'Twas not so much that everyone loved the maestro, but that the king—normally the most cheerful of men who lent the whole court that spirit—was so horribly aggrieved. He could not, for anyone, hide his raw pain, and I thought no one could mourn a father or mother as deeply as François mourned Leonardo.

I was surprised when a note was handed to me as I sat in Marguerite's apartment. Signor Melzi was apparently asking to see me. I met him in the hall. He looked like death, his color ashen.

"I hope you are not ill, signor."

"No, mademoiselle, only more miserable than I have ever been, or expect to be for the rest of my days."

"I'm so sorry for your loss," I said.

Melzi's face darkened with something akin to anger. "Salai knew he was dying. He left two weeks before the day. Left me to deal with it alone. All of the maestro's notebooks and sketches, thousands of pages of them." Melzi ground his teeth together. "There was no one like him. Ever in the world!"

"I know," I said, and placed my hand on his. That was when I noticed he was carrying a small package wrapped in the softest red doeskin, and tied in an extraordinary pattern of knotted string.

"This was bequeathed to you by Maestro Leonardo."

A lump grew instantly in my throat and I fought hard to hold back tears. I thanked him and took the package. The moment it was out of his hands, he turned and fled.

I hardly knew what to do with myself, or with that which I had been given. Surely it was meant to be opened, and I was desperate to know what was inside the wrapping. Not only were the *groppi* daunting, but I was uncertain as to whether the maestro meant for me to untie so artful an array to get my gift, and ruin one of Leonardo da Vinci's last works of art.

I sat staring at the thing for a good part of the afternoon, but when finally I realized that the knotted twine was the maestro's idea of a joke, I excused myself from Marguerite's presence and went down to my favorite writing room. There, with the afternoon sun shining on the unexpected treasure, I began to search for the solution. Finally, along the bottom edge of the package I found a row of *groppi* that looked slightly different from the rest. These knots I worked slowly, with infinite care, as though each were a small prayer, a meditation on the greatness of the man, his staggering genius, and each of the precious conversations he and I had shared.

It was delicate work, but finally the entire line of knots was unraveled.

"Success and satisfaction." That is what Leonardo had said I would feel in unraveling difficult *groppi*. Now, indeed, I did. I put the knotted casing aside and stared at the leather, so prettily dyed.

The wrapping was simple. As soon as I unfolded one flap of doeskin and then the other, the gift was revealed.

It was a deck of playing cards, faces up.

I was looking at an ace of hearts. The sight of the single pip in the center nearly stopped my own heart, for I knew without a doubt it had been painted by the maestro himself. The color red he had mixed and its purplish shades and shadows were achingly beautiful. And instead of the simple white background normally used and stenciled upon, it was a miniature landscape with trees and a glorious mountain lake, the surroundings reflected perfectly in the water.

I put the ace aside and looked at the two of hearts. The pips were the same, but the background was different, this one showing a river. The three had, between each of the hearts, three rivulets of a rocky waterfall. Four was a glorious pink and white clouded sky. Five had the hearts at the tips of a pentangle, with magic symbols like the ones on the maestro's and François' matching robes in all the spaces between.

And so it went, each card of the suit a different tiny masterpiece. Then I reached the knave of hearts. It startled me and I looked closer, placing it in the brightest spot of sun on the writing table. I was not mistaken.

It was a miniature full-length rendition of my father in his sober black tunic, hands held behind his back as though hiding his next horrible surprise. I could hardly believe what I was seeing.

Thomas Boleyn was the knave of hearts!

I laughed aloud. "Dear, dear Leonardo," I whispered to myself. *Had there ever been a gift so unimaginably wonderful as this?*

I was eager to see who Leonardo had used as his model for the chevalier, but I was surprised to see the *king* was next in the pack. Surely it would be François with the large nose and spindly calves, I thought, as I placed the card in the sunlight. I was therefore startled to see there, with the tiniest pale blue eyes, red gold hair flaring round his head, and calves bulging with muscles, the likeness of Buff King Hal of England! This was very odd. Was the *French* monarch not the ultimate breaker of hearts?

Studying Henry VIII, so lifelike even in miniature, I tried to imagine the man George wrote about in his letters. A large, handsome man who behaved like a little boy, with tantrums and disconsolate fits and worries about his masculinity. I would have lingered longer on the English king, surely a fascinating enigma, but I was too eager to see the rest of the deck.

I could always come back to Henry.

So I turned up the next card. There in a fabulous crimson gown, wearing a golden crown, left hand raised, holding up a heart at the end of a torch . . . was myself. There was no mistaking it. The black eyes. The silky black hair falling round the pale shoulders. The long slender neck.

I was dumbstruck. Leonardo had painted me as the queen of hearts against the somber background of craggy cliffs, a sodden gray sky, and haunting dark water.

I gathered all the cards together and rewrapped them in the red doeskin, brought the package to my heart, and held it there for a very long time. I did not know if the dead could hear you speak to them, but I spoke, silently, to my friend all the same. What could I do but thank him, and promise that I would, with every breath before I died, try to earn the lofty praise of his words, and the high esteem shown to me with this gift.

There were forty more cards. I had greedily devoured the sight of the first twelve. I determined that I would allow myself to view but one a day for the next forty days, thus extending the surprises the maestro had in store for me—my private world painted on a deck of playing cards.

A deck, I was now certain, that included all four queens.

The Queen of Hearts

CHAPTER 27

*a*n event—nay, a *spectacle*—devised by the great Cardinal Wolsey himself had been advertised through all of Europe as a "Feat of Arms." The call had invited all knights to show their brotherly goodwill and test their prowess, participating in jousts and mock battles before the two greatest kings in the world—François and Henry, as well as the ladies of their courts.

Now I stood on the dock at Calais, waiting impatiently amidst a horde of English servants and workmen who'd come half a year before to make ready for their visiting nobles. King Henry, his family, and his entire court were arriving momentarily from Dover, all to participate in Wolsey's extravaganza, this day come to fruition.

I'd been kindly given leave from François' court to meet the ships, my family on one of them.

Oddly, the native language being spoken around me by my countrymen sounded somehow foreign. I am sure that by the look of me, and if I had spoken, I would have been taken for a Frenchwoman. But I had no desire to speak, or to be friendly. I was simply too excited for pleasantries, for I was soon to be seeing my mother, brother, and sister. Of course my father would be coming as well.

There was yet no sign of the main fleet. I heard men muttering that it must be soon, as the day had been so fine and the Channel so quiet and calm. In weather like this the crossing could be made in four hours.

Four hours! I thought. It had taken Princess Mary and her ladies four nauseated, terror-filled *days* to do that crossing.

I sat myself on a barrel to wait, thinking how little I desired to see Father again.

If a colder man than he walked the face of the earth, I could not imagine it.

I knew it was a mortal sin to think on the death of a parent, but I had recently imagined my feelings if, on the day of his arrival, Father had *not* stepped through the door, but instead a messenger bearing news of his ship lost in a storm on the Channel. I wondered whether I could have mustered tears or if, had tears come that were for *secret joy*, I could have passed them off as grief. Such thoughts were so dire I had omitted them from my confession.

But I later suffered with my guilt much less than I thought I might.

Father had come seven months before to François' court on a twofold mission—first to be present at the christening of Claude and François' second son, whom they had named Henri, "after the English king, their dear friend." His other mission was the organization of passage from England to France for the six thousand laborers—stonemasons, carpenters, and artisans—needed to prepare the way for the Feat of Arms.

My father, with so much business on his mind during that visit to the Paris court at Tournelles, had had little energy to spend on his younger daughter. Mary had by this time gone home and even then—with Father in France—was marrying her kind and understanding William Carey.

On greeting him at the palace steps—pretending to be his dutiful daughter—I'd asked Father if he did not regret missing that wedding, for *I* sorely did. He dismissed it with a sneer and a wave of the hand.

No more than I had expected of him.

In any event, the day before he'd left Tournelles, Father had deigned to have a private dinner with me in his rooms. Despite himself, he could not help but be pleased with me as I was so well liked by all the people who mattered to him.

Mayhap relieved that his mission had been successful on all counts, he'd drunk more wine than was his wont. He was delighted, he bragged to me, his tongue loosening with the fine claret, with how brilliantly he had conveyed Henry's goodwill to François, as well as the English king's delight in having had the new French prince named after him.

Father had, even more importantly, reconfirmed that the five-year-old dauphin, François, was still firmly betrothed to little Princess Mary, Henry and Katherine's only child. And he had set in motion the plans for building the English living quarters for the first meeting of the two kings at the "feat" taking place the following summer.

It might have been that my father knew me so little that he believed my naive, worshipful wide eyes, or mayhap it was simply the wine. But he began to talk in the way George would do with me, though Father revealed things of far greater import. He spoke of a treaty in which the French town of Tournai, conquered and still held by Henry in his war several years before, was being *sold back* to François for the sum of sixty thousand ecus. My father downed another good swallow of wine, and his eyes lost their focus before he spoke again.

"Sixty thousand for Henry and all of England," he said. "Another twelve thousand livres for Cardinal Wolsey *himself*." I did not have to ask for an explanation, for it came slurring out the next moment. "All that money for the loss of his bloody church in that city. And Henry allows the man—son of a lowly butcher—to take such things for himself! You should see the palace he is building in his own glory at White-hall. It *disgusts* me. Well . . . ," he said, standing from his chair and pacing before the fire, forgetting to finish his sentence.

I was about to speak, thinking it was time for me to retire, when he burst forth again. I should have known that whilst my father's voice was silent, his mind was not. He did not address me. I might not have been there at all but as a receptacle for his tirade.

"Wolsey thinks he is all-powerful, that he is the puppet master behind Henry's king puppet. Well, let him go on thinking so. All who see Henry's tempers and tantrums, his love of dancing and music and fast horses, think he is shallow, inconsequential, and led by the nose by his cardinal. They are *wrong*. He is magnificent, our King Henry. A god on earth. Knows every detail, every article, every expense down to the last bolt of wool. Once learned, these things are not forgotten. His boyish charm is playacting."

Now my father, his face made red by the fire or some internal rage, turned to me, though needing to hold his chairback to steady himself.

"I tell you it is by Henry's *conscious grace* that Wolsey is allowed to think himself so grandiose. Allowed to grow so obscenely rich. How dare a butcher's son believe he is greater than the true heir of the houses of Lancaster and York! He shall fall, the fatted cardinal. *He shall fall!*"

'Twas then my father stumbled, and he himself almost fell. I did not wish to be witness to that humiliation, so I called for his servant and, curtsying as low before him as I would a king, asked his permission to retire. He waved me away as coldly as he had the mention of Mary's wedding, and I backed out the door, vowing silently that I would miss his leave-taking early the next morning. I knew full well that he would not miss my absence, nor remember all the state business he had revealed to me. If he did recall any part of it, it would not trouble him, for I was a cipher, a green girl, and not worth a second thought.

Now standing on the Calais dock I squinted to see a tiny white speck on the horizon and heard someone shout, "There! To the south!"

As it came closer and larger, more specks that made up England's fleet came visible.

Halfway from the horizon it seemed as though the sails of the largest ship were not white but *gold*, and that ship, compared with the hundreds of others, was immense, like a giant among dwarfs. I wondered what I was seeing.

The wind was fair, and now all the ships were coming fast and straight into Calais Harbor. All round me dockhands and servants were scurrying so wildly about making ready for the arrival, that for a few moments I lost sight of the fleet.

But when next I laid eyes on the largest of all the vessels, leading the rest into the harbor, I thought my eyes would pop out of my head. What I had thought was gold flashing in the sun *was* gold—a giant set of sails that were made of sumptuous cloth of gold! The flagship itself as it was towed to the center of the harbor was enormous, the size of a very castle.

Its name, *Great Harry*, was emblazoned on its polished wooden bow, with gaily colored pennants and banners snapping at every masthead. On the deck stood the royal family and its entourage and what, to my untrained and awestruck eyes, looked to be almost *a thousand* mariners. Some were climbing the vast rigging like monkeys to furl the sails, some manning the rudder and ropes. But most, in sparkling red and white uniforms, stood at strict attention as the dignified passengers prepared to disembark.

Even at close range the other ships, like the ones on which I'd made the Channel crossing, looked like toy boats. Suddenly I began to wonder where my family might be found—on what vessel.

If the dock had been frantic before, now it was utter chaos. Though I had never been to Henry's court, I did recognize many faces from that day on Dover beach, when so many of his highest nobles had come to see Princess Mary off for her wedding with Louis. The leading families of England were there in force—the Howards, the Dudleys, the Parrs, and the Seymours.

I caught sight of my uncle Norfolk, brother to my mother on the Howard side and, according to George, along with our father, in his ascendancy in Henry's government. He was tall, thin, and sharp-nosed, and had a pinched, bitter mouth.

I saw Mary Tudor hanging on the arm of Charles Brandon, the Duke of Suffolk, still darkly handsome, though a small paunch had developed under his doublet. Even now she was referred to by many as "the French queen." The greatest reason was to avoid confusion with *the other* Princess Mary Tudor, still a small girl. The elder was still lovely, though I did not see the pure happiness in her eyes that was there when she'd left France, having succeeded in marrying for love.

"Anne! Anne, is that you?" I spun round quickly, knowing my

mother's voice at once. A moment later I was in her arms receiving the warmest embrace I'd had in years.

The rest of my family was not far behind, all except Father, who was busy in the hubbub, ordering people about.

"George, Mary, neither of you told me how beautiful Anne has grown. A proper lady." Mother forced me to turn in place so she could admire my gown and headdress. "And what *style*. Is this what the women of fashion are wearing?" she asked, tucking a strand of hair back into my French hood.

"In some ways. I always like to do it a little differently." Then I grabbed my mother and kissed her face again and again, not caring if everyone in the world saw so untoward a display of emotion. Over her shoulder I caught my first sight of William Carey, my sister's new husband.

He was, as my mother had said, well made, if shorter than the male blood in our family. The look in his eyes was indeed kindly. Mary came forward to hug me and then made the introduction. William kissed my hand like a right gentleman, and graced me with a warm smile.

A tap on my shoulder was from no one else but George, dear George. This was the sweetest of all the reunions, for part of my heart resided with him, and his with me. I had no secrets from George, less those I feared would be intercepted in our letters, and I looked forward to the coming days in which I could bare my soul to him.

Mother said she would wait for Father, who was now supervising the transportation of the royal family to the site chosen for the Feat of Arms, on ungodly roads some fifteen miles south of Calais.

Mary, William, George, and I were sent on one of the first coaches out of town. It gave me a small thrill of pleasure to think that Father would have to deal with the headache of it all—ten *thousand* nobles and servants, *and* their horses. Knowing Father, though, I could not be sure if the task would actually delight him. Clearly, if handled well and it caused the king pleasure, it would only enhance Thomas Boleyn's status and raise his rank. But enough of that! I let all obsessions with my father fade and turned my attention to my handsome brothers and sister. The jolting carriage navigating the barren coastal road was no impediment to our cheerful party.

'Twas the first time Mary and William had traveled together, and I think they never once let go each other's hands. Both of them smiled frequently, and there was much open admiration in Master Carey's eyes for his beautiful bride, so flushed with excitement. Mary, I think, relished the idea of returning to the French court—a place of ignominy for her—as a proper married lady, one with no secrets about her past from her new husband. I prayed it would go as happily for her as she planned.

George, however, was eager to catch me up with the gossip he knew I craved, gleaned from his nearness to our king.

"I heard Henry say he was certain that François wished him worse than he did the devil himself," George said. "That he wants peace, but if the King of France attacks, he will fall into his own pit."

"From where I sit," I said, "I see no evidence of François wishing a war with Henry. He seems most concerned that Henry might give his affection and alliance to *Charles*."

"Well, he *should* be concerned," William broke in, turning away from Mary for the first time. "Just days before our fleet left from Dover, the Holy Roman Emperor arrived."

"Charles went to Dover!" I cried.

"For a visit with his aunt, Queen Katherine," William continued.

"He did that knowing the whole English court was on its way to see François?" I said, incredulous.

"*Because* the whole court was on its way to see François," my brother added. "Charles timed it perfectly, for of course the French king would be told, and his worry would grow. And the people of England—perhaps because they love Katherine so—have decided to love her nephew as well. Katherine and Charles—he's only twenty—had never met before. She was waiting to greet him on a first-floor landing at Dover Castle. He stood at the bottom, looking adoringly up at his mother's sister, then ran up the steps to her open arms."

"It was quite a scene. Copious tears of joy," William said. "And

Henry pretended he'd not made all those insulting jests about Charles's jutting jaw before he came, and embraced him like a friendly uncle."

My brother's eyes gleamed with admiration. "Charles. Henry. François. I think they are magnificent statesmen."

"Or a trio of idiots," Mary piped in, making us all laugh.

"Some are worried the mock battles at this 'Feat of Arms' will turn into *real* battles," William said.

"There was a rumor—someone called it 'definite evidence'—of a planned attack on the games by the French," George added.

"Queen Katherine has been nagging Henry about it for months," Mary added. She had become a lady-in-waiting to the English queen, and had seemingly opened her eyes and ears to more than petty gossip. "She thinks the whole endeavor is madness—'ill fated'—and prays constantly on her knees that no harm comes to Henry on the field."

"Nothing will happen to Henry," George said. "He's tough as a bull. He's been practicing on the lists . . . endlessly."

"So has François," I said.

"It should be a good fight," William added, unable to hide his excitement.

Mary tucked her arm through his, worry distorting her features. "William is scheduled for the jousts." She turned to face him. "I pray for *your* safety, husband."

He kissed her lightly. "Well, *there's* a guarantee I shall be killed."

Mary punched his arm and we all laughed again.

I do not think we had a moment's silence the whole way from the coast along the road inland from Calais. So engrossed were we in one another that we hardly felt the violent jouncing of the carriage, nor the stifling summer heat, nor even bothered to look out the windows. It therefore came as a surprise to hear voices all round us.

There were knocks and pounding on the still-moving coach. We heard the driver shouting at people to move out of the way.

Now there was music—pipes and drums and sackbuts. We all peered outside and saw we were surrounded by a near riot of humanity. Minstrels in their gaudy outfits danced and played behind farmers and laborers in their rough, stained work clothes. Some looked more to be villagers in simple but tidy garb, women trying to get a glimpse of some ladies of fashion in the carriages, fathers with their children perched upon their shoulders to watch the never-before-seen spectacle. There were old beggars and young, their hands thrusting through the windows for money, and men hawking paste baubles and fake gold chains. Women peddlers ran alongside selling meat pies that smelled like heaven, and wives of fishermen held out baskets of whole fried herrings.

William threw one such woman a coin and she handed in the still-hot, fragrant fish, which we devoured greedily, covering our fingers and faces in oil, then giggling as we had no way to clean ourselves. Mary very generously lifted her overskirt and allowed us to use her petticoat.

The hangers-on were left behind as they accosted the next carriage on the road, but we in the coach were suddenly at attention. Anticipating something wonderful. Unexpected. Exotic. For the place of our destination had an utterly romantic name—the "Val Doré," meaning the "Golden Valley."

But nothing could have prepared us for what lay ahead.

First our coach passed through the cobbled streets of Guines. The town was a wasteland of shattered walls, cottages, pubs, and shops. What trees there were, were burnt to stumps. The old castle, which might have once been a pretty thing, lay in ruins. The townspeople we saw looked poor and half-starved, yet they waved when we passed them.

"What happened here?" I said, all of a sudden sobered.

"This was a town Henry invaded," George explained, "the year you were in the Netherlands. There was a great slaughter here. It hasn't recovered. Neither has the village of Ardres, just to the east. It was burnt to the ground. The valley between them is our destination."

"Whose macabre idea was that—a party between two hells?" Mary said then. "I swear, François and Henry are equally insane."

I think we all felt relief to be gone from Guines, and now descended into the shallow valley George had described. Whilst Guines and Ardres might lie in rack and ruin, what we now saw before us—our heads stuck out the carriage windows—was far beyond all of our imaginings.

Just ahead and looming into the sky was a long rectangular palace of stone, that which Henry's six thousand workers had created on this barren plain in the half year past. It had been built in what could only be called the "Italianate style," and was magnificent to look at. There were high brick columns, battlements—which must, of course, have been for show—colorful ornamental tiles, and a huge fan-shaped stone cornice above the front entrance. Surmounting the whole second story was a grand expanse of tall arched windows that now, with the sun's reflection, set the whole castle gleaming with unearthly light.

The carriage stopped abruptly in front of a large fountain, which was spouting, of all things, red wine! The driver came round to open the door.

"All of ye, 'cept Mistress Anne," he said, tugging at the neck of his too-tight livery. "This'll be yer stop."

Mary looked at me and groaned with disappointment. "Can you not stay with us here?" she cried, hanging on to my hand.

"I'm needed in Claude's retinue," I told her, equally frustrated. "She speaks no English. I'm to be her interpreter for the whole event."

Mary looked ready to cry.

"It's all right," I said. "I shall see you *every day*. I'm sure of it." I looked at my handsome brother and my brother-in-law. "All of you. Either I'll seek you out, or you'll seek me out. This is to be *our* celebration, as much as the French and English royal families'."

"That's right," said George, kissing me. " 'Twill be the grandest time we have ever had." Now it was three smiling friends that stepped down from the coach, leaving me to go on alone with the driver.

As the carriage descended the minor slope, my head was again stuck out the window staring in wonder at the hundreds of tents that would hold the overflow from the English palace, and the large newly erected wooden buildings from which emanated the smells of roasting meat and baking bread. We passed thousands of sheep and cows, and their keepers, just as if they were herding them in any French or English countryside.

But there, across the broad field at the base of the hillside village that was Ardres, was a staggering sight, one that took me more by surprise than even Henry's castle had done. I suppose it could have been called a "tent," but the sheer size of it made it something much more—a kind of castle or pavilion, its whole enormous breadth covered, as Henry's sails had been, in *cloth of gold.*

I would have expected nothing less from François.

The deep blue canvas roof was decorated with suns and moons and the mystical signs of the zodiac, glittering in the afternoon light. At its tall peak was a human-sized gilt statue, a man in robes, whose identity I supposed was Saint Michael, as François had named him his patron saint. There were other tents behind—hundreds of them—much smaller ones in brocades and velvets, topped with metallic apples, and gay banners proclaiming the arms of their inhabitants beneath.

But the giant pavilion had an overwhelming and spectacular effect on its surroundings, so that as barren and wasted as the nearby towns and meadows might be, the place had, after all, been aptly named—"the Golden Valley," a field of cloth of gold!

My heart quickened when I realized François' blue and gold tent was my destination, for that was to be home to the royal family and their retainers for the next three weeks. I could just glimpse the tiltyard beyond, and its rows of high stands for the spectators, but I could hardly wait to enter the fantastic pavilion.

Finally the carriage stopped and the English driver delivered me there. As I stepped down, I could see that the French had, in their numbers, arrived. Noblemen and noblewomen, gorgeously attired, were strolling in and out of the richly draped front door, altogether nonchalant, as if the great behemoth were an everyday occurrence.

But as I passed in through the door, I heard some of them talking. One man said the tent was the most beautiful ever seen, and his companion agreed. It was, he said, more magnificent than the miracle of the Egyptian pyramid, or the amphitheater in Rome.

I was inside by then and could only gape in wonder. Lashed together for the central support were two intricately carven ship's masts, each so thick two men could not have wrapped their arms around it. The smell here was divine, as all the walls were alive with climbing ivy and fresh-cut branches of pine and oak, even boughs of apple and peach and orange trees, with ripe fruit hanging off them to be plucked and eaten. The cloth-of-gold walls that graced the outside of the great tent formed the inner walls as well. The strong summer sun did not altogether penetrate the fabric, but illuminated it with unearthly light.

The public half of the tent was a very hive, excited courtiers meeting one another and showing off their fine attire and, as the French always did, flirting and teasing—but now with even more abandon than usual.

The partition to the private quarters was hung with gold brocade, and a quartet of soldiers guarded the doorway in. I knew them all, and after I'd given a smile to each of them, they allowed me to pass in to see my mistresses.

CHAPTER 28

*I*t was not till the next day that Cardinal Wolsey and his enormous entourage graced us with the grandest of all entrances. So that the effect could be at its greatest, he and his minions had spent the night at the castle in Calais, and risen before dawn to mount their procession from the coast.

The French and English alike had come out to see it, though François and his family watched from a distance at the pavilion, for the meeting of the two kings was meant to be an event unto itself. Because Queen Claude had hung back with François, I was able to sneak away and as I had promised my family, I sought them out near Henry's castle, which was now peopled with our nobles, as though it were a proper English court.

Henry, Katherine, and the princesses Mary were seated on thrones front and center at the wine fountain, though due to the solemnity of the occasion, all refrained from tilting their cups to the spouts. Lesser nobles and dignitaries, including my father and Uncle Norfolk, stood up behind them. All the rest of us lined the way on both sides, waiting and whispering.

Then to the racket made by a hundred horn players and a hundred drummers marching, came the parade. The noise was so deafening Mary and I held our hands over our ears and tried not to giggle at those who suffered in dignity, their hands clutching their clothes.

Thankfully the musicians passed, allowing for the first of the cavalcade—fifty mounted gentlemen in crimson velvet, followed by fifty ushers, each of the latter carrying a solid-gold mace that George whispered to me was bigger than Cardinal Wolsey's head. Next was a large man who, strong as he was, staggered under the weight of an enormous gold and jewel-encrusted cross.

Directly behind the crossbearer came the butcher's son, splendidly humble on a mule, like Jesus riding into Jerusalem, though so fat and heavily robed, with gold chains thick enough to drag an anchor, that the poor creature beneath the man could barely lift his hooves off the ground. Wolsey's face was piglike above several jiggling chins, and his lips were puffed with pride and arrogance. His eyes were hard to see, nearly buried in flesh, and I wondered that a person of such revolting countenance could be so pleasing to our king.

He was followed by dozens of mounted bishops, each more smug than the next. The cardinal's secretaries and pages came then, very luxuriously attired, as they were sons of great lords, fortunate to have been taken into Wolsey's service. I scanned their young faces. One in particular caught my eye. He was tall and broad-shouldered, but very slender at the waist with shapely calves. His face, I thought, was that of an angel.

"Which one is James Butler?" I said to George, hoping my angel might be he. I was finally going to meet my betrothed, who served in the cardinal's household. My brother turned to me.

"Did Father not tell you?"

"Tell me what?"

"Your husband-to-be was brought home to Ireland by his father. Wolsey was unhappy to lose the lad, but Piers Butler's been made lord deputy of Ireland, and suddenly decided it was safer if his son was by his side."

I sighed, exasperated. I had been looking forward to meeting my betrothed, finally, so that I could more easily find ways of making myself love him. But to be honest, that he was absent from this gathering left me more relieved than disappointed. My always-simmering anger at Father came to a boil, however, thinking of how little he thought of me that he had not even mentioned James Butler's return to Ireland from the English court, and that he would not be coming to France.

By the time I looked back at the procession, I saw that it was ending with three hundred archers with their bows flexed. Their purpose I could not fathom. Was Wolsey trying to say to François that he and Henry had come in peace, but if that peace should be broken, the English were prepared?

"Come inside, Anne," Mary urged me, taking my hand and pulling me toward the palace. "You must see what a glory it is."

As we entered, I saw the Italian ambassador to François' court staring awestruck up at the front facade and heard him say to the Duke of Bourbon, "Even Leonardo could not have done it better." I smiled to myself, happy that my friend's memory had not been forgotten. And when Mary and I walked through the high doorway, I knew that the ambassador was right.

Although we were indoors, the feeling in the palace was of the *outdoors*. The inletting of nature was not accomplished, as it had been attempted in François' pavilion, by living plants at every turn, but by the device of the windows—so many of them and so tall that clear sunlight, that most prized of all elements in the maestro's reckoning, flooded everything and everyone. We seemed to glow like heavenly beings, and we walked about in a dazed state, smiling in wonder at the beauty of it all.

"Look at this!" Mary exclaimed, pointing to the wall ten feet above us. "Did you not think the whole palace was stone and brick?"

"Is it not?"

"Look closer," said Mary. "Above that line." She pointed to a place perhaps eight feet up where now I could see the real masonry ended. Higher than that was canvas painted perfectly to *look* like stone and brickwork.

"And that?" I said, pointing up beyond the massive dome at what appeared to be slanted lead and slate ceilings.

"Painted cloth," Mary answered, as proud as if it had been her own invention.

My jaw was agape, and I thought that, indeed, Leonardo would have been delighted with this illusion. But that was not all. The window frames themselves shone with an inlay of gold, and every inch of wall and floor was decorated with some fine tapestry or Turkey carpet, every column carved and painted, or gilded, with beasts and vines and Tudor roses.

There were four corridors leading to each of four corner blocks, three for living spaces and the fourth for the chapel. Each hallway was similarly decked out with Henry's finest treasures, culled, no doubt, from his many palaces. But some pieces had been specially made, Mary told me, like the statues of great English knights and generals lining the halls, brandishing weapons in their most warlike poses. These, like Wolsey's archers, I supposed, were clearly meant to speak a message to François of England's military superiority to France, even though it was more in Henry's mind than in truth.

Mary pulled me inside Cardinal Wolsey's chapel to see the ostentatious display of solid-gold chalices and candlesticks looted from Westminster Abbey, and the pearl-embroidered gold tissue that hung as an altar cloth. As if there were not enough glitter to satisfy the gaudiest of tastes, all along the sides of the chapel were standing the twelve apostles, cast in gold, each of them half the size of a grown man.

The tour finished, we strolled back into the central court and bathed ourselves in light.

"When and how do our kings meet?" Mary asked me, as though I should know the answer. Strangely, I did.

"On the morrow, though Claude will not attend. None of us, save Father, are invited. I've arranged to spend the day in Marguerite's party, so I can see it. You and George and William should climb to a high spot in the Guines hills. And take Mother. It should be a spectacle, even from afar."

The next day dawned cheerful and bright, an auspicious moment for the historic meeting of Henry and François.

I had climbed, huffing and puffing and holding my skirts high, with Marguerite and her ladies to the Ardres hillside where François and a contingent of his greatest knights were already mounted, all on pure white horses and, except for the king, clad in their most glorious suits of armor. He wore the most fabulous of outfits, a doublet of French blue, embroidered everywhere with golden fleurs-de-lis, and a matching blue cap with a spray of long white feathers.

There was little talking, but everyone strained to see the far hillside of Guines where a similar gathering of knights had congregated, they on their black horses. On the tallest of all the animals, Henry was, like François, armorless, arrayed in kingly crimson.

The roar of cannon fire behind us was so sudden and unexpected, we ladies clutched one another, laughing nervously. But none of the men were laughing. The blast had been the signal for them to start down toward the dead center of the Golden Valley, where a spear stuck in the ground, topped by French and English banners, marked the place of meeting. Nearby was a small white tent.

"My mother is in there, and your father," said Marguerite to me, indicating the tent. "And Wolsey and Monsieur Bonnivet. They will open the ceremonies after the kings meet."

I could see Henry and his knights descending the opposite slope, mirroring the movements of François and his guard. When both parties reached the valley floor, there came another booming cannon shot.

Now all but François and Henry hung back. Then the two kings, as if moving with a single mind between them, suddenly spurred their horses forward, the beasts attaining great speed and throwing up clouds of dust behind them as though they were racing toward a clashing combat. But there was no armor. No lances. No swords.

This was meant to be a meeting of peace.

I saw Henry's right arm rise off his rein in François' direction, a gesture of hopeful embrace. Then François' right arm lifted, and as they began to slow their horses, the warm greeting of two ancient foes seemed imminent. But at the last moment Henry's mount shied left.

The two great kings had ridden right past each other!

Undeterred, they simultaneously came off their horses, both young, vibrant, full of grace. They doffed their caps and their long arms went round each other in a manly embrace. Even from the distance at which we stood we could see them pushing back and looking upon each other for the first time ever. Then another embrace. Their laughter echoed up from the valley floor. And *another* embrace.

I looked at Marguerite out the corner of my eye. She had a pleasant smile plastered on her face, but I thought she looked skeptical, too, as if the display of affection we were watching was a sham, a useless moment of theatrics that had to be endured, and was ultimately meaningless.

When, arm in arm, Henry and François disappeared into the white tent, Marguerite turned to her ladies. "That is all we shall see," she said simply, and started down the hill toward the French pavilion.

But I knew her mind was racing, making plans. She may not have been in that tent with Madame and Wolsey, Father, and Bonnivet and the kings, but her *ideas* surely were. Her worries. Her hopes. Marguerite did not wish for a fight with the Holy Roman Emperor, but from the look I'd detected, she was not at all sure that a war with Henry Tudor was out of the question.

I said nothing, for here in this field of cloth of gold, my position of favorite to the French king and queen and king's sister was, for the first time, uncomfortable. And I wondered if Marguerite, despite the love she'd always shown, did not view me as an interloper from the camp of her enemy.

"I *knew* he would do it," said Marguerite as her mother buttoned up the back of the duchess's gown. Madame enjoyed doing such menial tasks for her daughter on certain occasions. With the prospect of the first banquet of the event a few hours away, Louise of Savoy needed time to confer with her daughter.

The quarters were cramped in the pavilion and the servants decreased by half, but I was among the few chosen to stay close at hand with the royal ladies. The waiting women had their separate quarters, cots lined up next to one another with no privacy whatsoever.

Only a gossamer curtain separated the queen from her sister-in-law's rooms, and as I lingered at a trunk to choose some baubles for

Claude's hair, I could hear every word Marguerite and Madame were saying, and see their gauzy outlines.

"Of course he did it. Of course Henry would call himself 'the King of France.' What else would a King of England say? They all still believe they *are* the Kings of France. Henry V conquered us at Agincourt, and nothing that has happened since has erased that memory. His titles were being read . . . and that was one of them."

"No, *Maman.* That is not what you told me happened in the tent," Marguerite said. "Henry's titles were being read, and he *interjected* that he was the King of France. Clearly it was staged for the sharpest effect. Wolsey's work, no doubt."

"It does smack of Wolsey. But, my dear"—Madame finished the buttoning and turned her daughter to face her—"if you allow it to annoy you or throw you off your stride, *they have won.* And we know very well who the King of France is."

They embraced then, Marguerite softening. I was eavesdropping again, I realized. For better or worse, it had become a habit. But I had tarried long enough at the queen's trunk, and turned to help her finish dressing.

Shortly thereafter it was I being buttoned up by my "maid," Lynette. I had been allowed, for the next three weeks, a servant to help me dress, and I had chosen my friend. Though the other hours of the day she was busy in the laundry tent, she—like the rest of the staff who had been chosen to work at the Feat of Arms—would happily be allotted time to view several of the tournaments, as long as their necessary work got done.

Lynette had been moaning since her arrival. Longet had not been asked to come to the Val Doré, for tents were without doors, and there was no need for a locksmith. She missed her husband already, the warmth of him in her bed at night. Someone to make her laugh and bear the backbreaking work she did.

"Sit down now," Lynette ordered me. I did as I was told and she began brushing my hair. It was, I think, my proudest feature—long, thick, and shiny black. "I think that tonight you shall speak to your future husband," she said in a mysterious tone. One of her sisters had, of late, begun telling fortunes, and now Lynette fancied herself a bit of a seer.

"I told you, James Butler is not here."

She snorted. "That means nothing. He is not the one meant to marry you."

"Then who is my husband-to-be?" I said indulgently. "How shall I recognize him?"

"You will know him when you see him," she said simply.

"The way you knew Longet when you saw *him* the first time?" I said, teasing her. She and her locksmith had worked on the same basement hallway for four years before they'd discovered their love.

"It is different for you," she said with utter confidence.

"And why is that?" I demanded.

She was quiet for a long moment, during which time she delicately arranged my hair round my bare shoulders for the most fetching effect.

"Because *you* are *different*," she said slowly, the confidence suddenly gone. She seemed as though she did not understand her own words. "You are just different."

I did not argue the point, but I wondered if what she'd said was true. *My future husband here, tonight.* Suddenly I was afraid.

Lynette had not mentioned a word about love.

CHAPTER 29

*T*he opening banquet of the Feat of Arms—though now it was being called by many the "Field of Cloth of Gold"—was held in the central court of Henry's great palace as the sun began its slow summer descent. Buttery light streamed in through the arched windows, falling on the feast tables, long planks draped with silks and brocades and set with Henry's gold plate and jewel-studded goblets. I had never seen so many people seated for a meal in all my life, nor had I known—even at François' most gala occasions—so inexhaustible a stream of dishes.

Some were simple, like the savory sides of beef and lamb. But the fowl were spectacularly prepared with all their feathers, appearing intact and not lying dead on a platter, but standing as if alive, even fighting one another. The fish were clearly deceased, but decorated beautifully with all manner of fruits and vegetables carved into flowers, lying on beds of gilded lettuces and black seaweed. The sweets were the most outrageous of all creations, for they'd been fashioned into castles with towers and turrets. It took six men to carry out "London Bridge," complete with tiny heads of traitors made of berries stuck up on pikes. There was a mountain range of marzipan, its peaks covered with clotted cream for snow.

My mouth was watering, even though I'd been made to eat before coming, as all the royals had done, so they could talk with one another throughout the meal and not be concerned with food. Though I coveted the delicacies being paraded before us, I was well aware of my privileged position that evening.

I stood in the middle behind the chairs of Queen Claude and Queen Katherine, listening above the din to what each was saying, and then translating it for the other. The two women, who had never before met, were very cordial and, it seemed to me, sincerely so. I sensed no unpleasant undercurrent, none of the competition that often marred the conversations of men.

Indeed, they spoke mainly of their offspring, and of childbirth, its fears and horrors. Once, when I had whispered in Katherine's ear the pure agony Claude had experienced with the delivery of her third child, the English queen laid a gentle hand on the arm of the French queen. And when I translated Katherine's pain of having borne a living son for Henry, only to watch him die two months later, Claude's eyes filled with tears.

We were saved from an entire evening of grieving by some astonishing contortionists who, nearly naked, twisted themselves into such outlandish knots that we laughed along with our applause. Next came a choir of Cardinal Wolsey's pages, dressed alike in rust and black, who stood before the two kings and their queens and sang a song they'd announced that *Henry* had written. 'Twas a love song, a plaintive one, about a lady named Greensleeves who had wronged the gentleman who adored her.

In one verse a young man stepped forward to sing solo. He was the one I'd seen in Wolsey's procession, he with the face of an angel. There was a voice to match, and he sang with such feeling, and an expression that made so real the emotions of the bereft lover, that now it was *me* with tears in her eyes.

I was discreetly dabbing one away when, of all things, the singer saw me in my moment of weakness. I straightened, pretending to be pulling a stray hair from my eye and tucking it behind my ear, but when he stepped back in line for the chorus, he *smiled* at me, most directly.

I thought I might die of mortification and wished to run, but what would have been the use? I'd been caught out, and could only hope to avoid him and my humiliation.

As the servants cleared the sweet course from the table, Cardinal Wolsey himself approached the monarchs. After making the proper obeisance to Henry, Katherine, and François, he bent toward Claude and kissed her hand.

He spoke perfect French and so my services were not needed. The cardinal heaped elaborate praise on the queen and her famous piety, her husband, and the country of France. It was well-known that Wolsey sought peace between François and Henry. It was he who had brokered the betrothal of the dauphin and little Princess Mary. But when he was done and had, according to protocol, backed away from the royal quartet, I heard Claude whisper in François' ear that Wolsey had the eyes of a wild boar. He needed close watching, for he was dangerous in the extreme. François, one of a tiny few who knew how keen were the shy queen's observations and opinions, smiled and kissed her on the cheek.

"Will you dance with me?" I heard from behind. The music had already started, and with ladies and gentlemen, mam'selles and monsieurs, hurrying to their places on the floor for the first dance, I thought it was my new brother-in-law, William Carey, asking me. When I turned, I was face-to-face with the singing angel.

I was flustered into speechlessness. I knew he could see my extreme discomfort, but he did not flinch from it, nor laugh at it. Never taking his eyes from my face, which he seemed to be studying quite carefully, he just waited patiently for my answer, which, finally, regaining my senses, I gave.

"I . . . I would," I said, trying for my usual gay voice.

But as I had delayed, and so many people had crowded onto the floor for the slow, stately pavane—steps that everyone with two legs could master—the young man and I found ourselves with nowhere to dance.

"Sorry," I said, feeling stupid. Where, I thought, had the witty, sophisticated Mademoiselle Boleyn got to?

"Maybe it's best this way," he said. "We haven't even met. I know who you are. I'm Henry Percy . . . of the Northumberland Percys." Suddenly shy himself, he searched for my right hand, which was lying like a dead fish at my side.

He grabbed it and kissed it so clumsily that in that moment we became equals in embarrassment.

"Shall we?" he finally said, nodding to the palace's front door. He made way for us through the crush until we were outside. We watched in the torchlight as men and ladies chatted happily, dipping their goblets in the fountain and catching the red streams that poured from the spouts.

"Would you like some wine?" Percy asked, an afterthought.

"You'd have to go back inside and get us cups," I said.

"Oh." He looked dismayed. "Will you have to get back to Queen Claude soon?"

Finally I smiled, feeling easier. Feeling myself again. "No. I've been dismissed for the evening. She retired early. She nearly always does . . . if she comes out of her rooms at all."

"Is she ill?"

"No. Pregnant. Again. I think she's been pregnant the entire time I've been in France." I discovered it was easy talking with young Henry Percy. "How long have you been in the cardinal's service?" I asked.

"I've only just begun. I'm the firstborn, and my father was desperate for me to have a place in Wolsey's household."

"Why desperate?" I knew enough of the great dynasties of England to realize that as a firstborn son, this young man was heir to the high Northumberland title and a vast family fortune.

Percy hesitated, as though he had suddenly noticed he'd wandered into a dangerous conversation with a stranger, someone who had been living in the heart of the enemy camp. Someone he was not sure he could trust. He examined my face for what seemed an eternity, and I became aware I'd for no apparent reason been restraining all the coquetry I had been perfecting for years. I forced myself to look him squarely in the eye and waited for his answer.

"My father believes the real power in England lies with Wolsey," he said very quietly. "He wants me near that, so I can learn."

Percy had not shied from the truth, I realized, so I did him an equal honor.

"*My* father believes everything the cardinal does is by Henry's grace alone. That the king is playacting his shallowness and tantrums."

Percy smiled then, as though I'd just handed him a gift. It was a wonderful smile, the same as he'd made catching me all teary at his song.

"Let's go inside and dance," he said. "I'm not very good, but you, Mistress Anne, you look to be very light on your feet."

"Oh, do I?" I said, my instinct to flirt returning with a vengeance. I half turned and looked back over my shoulder at him with saucily curled lips and flashing eyes.

His face lit instantly. Here was a young man—an *English* man—who was serious and lighthearted both. I liked him. I could tell he liked me.

We returned to the crowded dance floor and took our places. At the sound of the first chords my heart leaped. It was a *lavolta*, a spritely dance. The one I did best. All of us clapped our hands over our heads, twice.

And then the music took us.

'Tis fair to say that Percy and I danced the night away. Every dance. He'd been modest in saying he did not dance well, for he danced well enough, though not brilliantly. That was fine with me, for what he lacked in style and grace, he more than accounted for in strength and energy. Beyond that, he was clearly enchanted with me and seemed proud that he was on the floor with a woman who danced so well.

As the evening progressed, my gown grew damp with my exertions, and I could feel my face and neck and bosom glowing with heat. He shone with the same inner sun and grew even handsomer in my eyes.

I became aware that I looked forward to the dances wherein Percy was forced by the steps to touch more than my hands. I'd begun feeling a thrill when he gripped my waist prior to lifting me into the air, and I fairly swooned when he caught me in descents that followed, my body sliding down the front of his. Without speaking of it, we drew those descents out, so our bodies could press together as long as decency allowed.

But no one was watching.

Father was doing business all over the court, with French and English alike. Mary and William were in a happy world of their own. George was flirting madly with a petite redheaded coquette, and Percy's father, Lord Northumberland, was engrossed in his own conspiracies.

Then I saw my mother on the sidelines. She *was* watching me, though for how long I was not sure. With a pretty curtsy to Percy I excused myself and joined her. Mother smiled when she saw me approaching.

"Are you having fun?" she said.

"Oh yes. Very much," I answered, taking the first deep breath I'd had for hours.

"Do you not think," she said carefully, "that you should dance with someone other than young Lord Percy?"

I grinned at her. "I *would* if someone else asked me."

She looked at me sideways, not sure to believe my story.

"I suppose it might look untoward," I agreed with a contrite sigh. "I shall just have to be the one doing the asking." I gave her a peck on the cheek and escaped her well-meaning clutches. I felt a hand on my arm and turned, smiling, expecting Percy.

It was my father.

"Come over here, Anne. And straighten yourself up. I'm going to present you to the king."

I was suddenly nervous. I'd thought hardly at all about Henry since our arrival. I had seen him from afar this morning as he rode hell-bent across the valley toward the French king, and at dinner he had been but two seats away from where I stood behind Katherine and Claude. But he had been deep in conversation with François, or the many courtiers who'd come to pay their respects. Once I had set eyes on Percy, everyone else in the immense, teeming hall had faded into a blur.

Even, I thought, my own king.

I could see him now, standing with the dukes of Bourbon and Suffolk, sharing a bawdy laugh. Even amidst great men, Henry stood apart. Whether it was the size of him, the curly, golden halo of hair and beard, the broad, fair, and handsome face, or the overwhelming confidence that radiated forth from his being, he seemed now—as he had when I was eight and saw him at the Burgundian court—to be something more than a mere man.

Bourbon and Suffolk parted as Thomas Boleyn approached with his daughter. Now I could see Henry was not much taller than François, though his body was thicker, more muscular, his thighs and calves more shapely. Some said the French king, with his slanted eyes and long nose, looked like the devil. This king, whilst retaining all necessary grandeur, had an open friendliness about him.

And just now he was smiling at me with strong white teeth and sparkling blue eyes.

"So this is your *younger* daughter?" he said to my father as I swooped into the lowest and most graceful curtsy I could execute without falling on my face.

"I'm honored, Your Majesty," I said, allowing myself to look up at him from below.

"Stand up, Lady Anne. Let me look at you."

I did as I was told and felt myself blushing as the king's eyes took in the sight of me—from my perspiration-damp hair to my flushed face. My head felt suddenly as though it were perched atop a too-long neck, and the low décolleté of my gown exposed a sight more of my ducks than was suddenly comfortable.

"My wife says you are very good with your translations," he said, "that Queen Claude seemed to have understood and felt all that Katherine was saying."

"I could not have dreamed of a greater privilege than serving my queen."

"Is she your queen? Katherine, that is?" Henry's tone grew a bit less friendly, though his smile never faltered. "You have been in the service of Claude for so long I wonder if you do not see *her* as your queen."

"Your Majesty," my father quickly interjected. "My daughter has no—"

"Silence, Thomas. Let her speak for herself."

My heart was pounding. I knew what I said could make or break me, and my family as well.

"Queen Claude is the kindest of women, and I have been happy here, but England is my home, and it is you and Queen Katherine that I love and revere before all others." I was unsure if that had satisfied him. "Indeed, Your Majesty," I went on, striving for sincerity in my voice, "I have been very homesick."

"Have you?" He sounded skeptical, and I feared I'd gone too far with this line of thought, for it had become true only this very night, since I had met Percy and knew he lived across the Channel in England. *But had I erred? Did my words signify a rebellion against the life my father had chosen for me?* I felt the pulse pounding in my throat.

"Well," Henry said as though wrapping up a conversation that had begun to bore him, "perhaps we shall have to bring you home."

I smiled, trying hard not to catch Father's eye. "Thank you, Majesty," I said, though it came out barely a whisper.

Then Charles Brandon was at Henry's side, pulling him away. I braced myself for my father's wrath, but when I turned, I saw that he was more intent on the Duke of Suffolk's conversation with the king than the silly prattling of his younger daughter.

I sagged with relief.

"What did you think of him?"

I smiled to myself, realizing I already recognized Percy's voice. There he was behind me with a crooked grin.

"He is magnificent," I said.

"I shall be seeing him quite often in England," he said. "Well, not *I*, but Cardinal Wolsey. I am in his household. Cardinal Wolsey, that is. But you know that."

Henry Percy was flustered. *Was I having such an effect on him?* I wondered if I should soothe him or tease him. I decided to do both.

"I don't mind you repeating yourself," I said, looking him straight in the eye. "About your being in the cardinal's household. And seeing King Henry quite often. You may even tell me *again*"—I tilted my lips into a pretty bow—"for I like the sound of your voice."

"You do?"

"Very much."

He stood up a little straighter.

"Will you dance with me?"

"I have to dance with someone else," I said conspiratorially. "*Anyone* else. My mother noticed your monopoly on me."

"I don't *want* you to dance with anyone else," he said playfully.

"What if it's my brother?"

"All right."

"And my brother-in-law?"

"That would be fine."

"And after that . . . ?"

"After that, you dance with me again."

"My thought exactly."

He took up my hand and this time when he kissed it, he was not at all clumsy. In fact the feel of his warm lips on my skin brought a familiar twitching between my legs.

"Till then," I said.

"Till then." He turned to go.

"Percy . . ." He turned back again. "Who will *you* dance with?"

"No one," he said. "No one."

CHAPTER 30

I hardly slept at all that night, for I could think of nothing but Percy. I loathed to think of myself as a superstitious person, but Lynette's words about speaking to my future husband played over and over again in my mind like a tune I was practicing on the lute. *But how could that be?* I was already betrothed to James Butler, the match a fait accompli for our families, Cardinal Wolsey, and the king.

I was desperate to know whether my young Northumbrian lord was aware of that betrothal. He had only recently come into the cardinal's service. Indeed, he might have taken the spot vacated by James Butler. But though these marriage plans were of great import to me, I somehow doubted they were the topic of much conversation in Wolsey's household, and Percy was, after all, just a page.

Would he have come dashing so enthusiastically after me had he known I was set to marry someone else? He was a bright, highborn young man. He well knew how court society worked. If he knew of my bethrothal and was yet pursuing me, he was far more rash a person than he appeared.

I began worrying that it was my place to tell Percy the truth of the situation. *But why should I?* He had not declared himself. He had only danced with me and spoken a few words. Surely the French were not the only flirts in the world. He might be dallying with me. *Of course he was!* He was one of the wealthiest young heirs in all of Europe.

Would one day be a peer of England. Despite my father's ascendancy in Henry's court, Thomas Boleyn was hardly noble; except for his wife's connections, he was as common as sheep.

And yet I could not forget the way Percy looked at me, the feel of my body sliding down against his, the shock that went through me as his lips touched the back of my hand. I was not imagining this!

But what "this" was, I could not say.

By the time I felt sleep tugging at me, the sun was starting to rise and ladies around me were stirring. I prayed Lynette would be late coming to dress me, but she was not. She bustled in, too merry for my bleary head. My dullness was a boon in this case, an easy cover for the elation I was feeling about Percy. And Lynette seemed to have forgotten her prophecy of my meeting my future husband the night before.

She was all agog, for this was a day she would be allowed to view the tournaments. Jousts were something she had never in her life seen, nor might she, in her lowly position at court, ever see again.

"Longet made me promise I would remember every detail," she told me as she slipped a clean shift over my head.

"My sister's husband will be riding today," I said.

"Is he handsome, Mary's husband?" she asked.

"Handsome enough. And he adores her. You shall see them both today."

"And did you speak to the man you will marry last night?" Lynette said. She'd not forgotten at all.

"Pull the laces a bit tighter," I said lightly.

She stopped dressing me altogether.

"You met him," she accused me. "And you did not *tell* me? What is his name?"

"Henry. Henry Percy," I whispered, trying to encourage her discretion. I realized it was the first time I had spoken his name aloud. "But he cannot possibly be my husband." I peered around to make sure no one was listening. Everyone was elsewhere engaged with their own toilette.

"Why not?" Lynette demanded.

"Because I am already *betrothed*."

"That means nothing."

"Mayhap to you."

She looked at me slyly. "And yet when I asked you if you had met your love, you said, 'Henry Percy.'"

"Shhh!"

"Will he be there today?"

"I assume so."

"You will point him out. I will tell you if he is the one."

"So now you are the Oracle of Delphi?"

"Who?"

"Never mind. Finish me up and we can go over to the tiltyard together."

"Whatever you say, Lady Percy."

I huffed a deep sigh of exasperation, but I could not help loving the sound of that title.

The jousts, exciting as they should have been, were for me a full day of frustrations.

The morning was stifling hot from the start. Claude could simply not be made comfortable in her covered litter, no matter how many cushions we placed behind her back and under her legs. Seeing her in such misery was horrible, but she would not hear of missing the first day of the contests. Too grave a disappointment for François, she kept saying.

The palfrey I was given to ride behind her with her other ladies was an ornery beast who attempted to throw me, and nearly succeeded but for a quick-witted stableboy who broke my fall. He managed to quiet the horse and lead him, with me hanging on for dear life, all the way to the jousting field.

It was, I admit, a fantastical sight—the enormous rectangular en-closure all of wood, built equidistant from François' and Henry's en-campments, the tiered scaffolds already filled with thousands upon thousands of cheering spectators, vendors hawking wine and meat pies and succulent roasted ribs. At each end of the field were miniature "castles" where the knights and their horses would don their armor. Most boggling of all was the skeleton of a monstrously tall and ancient tree standing at the gates of the tiltyard—the "Tree of Nobility," it was called—upon which all the challengers had hung their shields.

But Claude managed to last only long enough to watch Henry and François' first joust, in which both kings were slightly injured, and both queens nearly died of fright. She retired after that, afraid to watch anymore. I offered to attend her back at the pavilion, but she insisted I stay. She took with her instead some of the older ladies—ones who had seen more than their share of men bashing one anothers' brains out on horseback.

It seemed like everyone who jousted was knocked about that morning. A splinter pierced the helmet slit of an Englishman, and nearly took out an eye. Dozens of lances were broken. There were snapped arms and legs, and hobbled horses.

By the time I found Mary in the crowd she was frantic, with all day to worry about William, who would not ride till the afternoon tilt. Lynette, who had found her before me, was having trouble comforting her.

"He'll be killed, I know he will!" Mary cried after I joined them in the risers. "I'm supposed to be thrilled that my husband is a 'brave knight,' but I am *not*. I think it's madness. If a man must go to war and is killed honorably in battle, it is one thing. But to die in a *game?*"

"No one is ever killed in the jousts, Mary," I said in my most convincing tone. "And they've blunted all the lances. I heard someone saying, too, that the English far outstrip the French in size and ferocity."

But she would not be comforted. I therefore held her hand the rest of the morning as the armored jousters on each side trotted out of their tiny castles and made grand entrances onto the jousting field, causing their horses to bow and prance for the audience and the royals. The roar of the crowd was deafening and grew even louder as their horses, at the sound of a firearm's blast, picked up speed and raced alongside the center rail. At the proper moment lances were lowered and the inevitable collision came, its own crash of metal on metal unheard over the crescendo of shouts from the stands at the moment of impact.

With each set, Mary's fingernails dug deeper into my palms. Lynette kept mouthing at me, "Where is he?" but I could only shake my head helplessly. I'd been searching the crowds as best I could, but there were no signs of Percy near us on our side. The tiers on the far side of the field—which was immense—were too far away for me to recognize him if he *was* there.

We had been spared further terror, as George was yet one year shy of being allowed entry in the lists, though he, like all other gentlemen, could hardly wait for his turn at glory making on the field of honor. He was even now in the English knights' "castle" helping the jousters on with their armor.

Till this day I had never thought of the madness of men trying to maim or kill one another outside of battle. Even François' war games had preceded a real war. But suddenly I thought of Percy in that saddle with thousands of people on the sidelines shrieking for the sight of his blood or broken bones for the sheer entertainment of it, and I shivered in the noonday sun.

Therefore when William's name was called and he emerged, silver-clad on his horse, I was near as terrified for his safety as Mary was. We clutched each other and watched in horrible fascination as William and his opponent, Monsieur Richeaux, rode at breakneck speed along the tiltyard rail toward seeming oblivion. At the collision Mary turned her head away, but I did not flinch from it. I was rewarded by the sight of William left sitting upright in his saddle, claiming victory for the round. The Frenchman, unhorsed, was lying on the ground flat on his back.

"Mary, look!" I cried. "He has won the round!"

As she turned she said, "Yes, but there are three more rounds to go."

"I think not. Monsieur Richeaux does not appear to be getting up."

By now the French knight's grooms were kneeling over him. The downed man was weakly waving one of his armored arms, in a sign to all that he was not dead. He did have to be carried from the field.

Mary quickly regained her spirits, clapping and cheering and calling William's name as he rode to the royal box to receive his accolades from both kings and Queen Katherine.

Then Mary insisted we leave, so she could see her beloved and hold him, and be sure that he was truly unharmed by his combat. I had already grown resigned to missing any sight of Henry Percy this day, and I did want to see for myself that my new brother-in-law was all right.

And if truth be told, there was some relief in leaving the scorching field and the sea of raucous, bloodthirsty humanity.

The plan that evening had been for François and a small group of courtiers to entertain Queen Katherine in the French pavilion, and for Henry and his inner circle to simultaneously fete Queen Claude in the English castle. As Claude's translator, I once again found myself, not only in the center of her world, but now surrounded by the King of England and his power mongers, including my father, and Cardinal Wolsey with his household.

Henry Percy was among the latter.

I could barely contain my joy upon entering the king's private rooms with Queen Claude, where the entertaining would be held. His huge and opulently appointed "Bed of State" had been disassembled in London, only to be rebuilt here in his temporary abode. With the finest of his tapestries and carpets adorning every inch of wall and floor, one would never have known the place had been built just months, not centuries, before.

A trio of musicians played very softly in a corner. An intimate U-shaped table had been set, with Claude in a seat of honor tween Henry and Wolsey. Whilst I had been brought along as a translator once again, my services were in fact unnecessary throughout the long meal, as both king and cardinal spoke perfect French. My father made sure he was close at Henry's other hand, and as for the rest of us, we were left to shift for ourselves.

Delighted by our good fortune, Percy and I, with no words spoken and pretending nonchalance, deftly maneuvered ourselves toward one of the table's far ends. On our other side was my uncle Norfolk, who had both ears pricked toward the power-laden dais, and could not have cared less what was being said on his other side by the two least important people at the gathering.

We fell instantly into a world of our own and found conversation easy as two old friends who had not met in a long while. There was, though, the excitement of conspirators, as we knew there was danger in this flirtation, one that should not become publicly known. We appeared to chat amiably but did not touch nor even dare to lean too close to each other. We counted on everyone's entire disinterest in what we were saying to provide us our privacy. And thus it was granted.

"I looked for you today at the games," Percy said. "But when I found you on the opposite riser and ran round to see you, you were gone."

"My sister came nearly undone when her husband rode, and we had to leave," I told him. In this quiet setting I was able to better examine his features. There was nothing coarse about them. His chin, cheeks, and nose were almost delicately sculptured. His lips were full, his hazel eyes large and bright. There was still a touch of the boy about him, but with a little age, I thought, he would be a perfectly handsome man.

"When I got to your place and found it empty, I was so angry I nearly throttled the pie vendor," he said in a jest of exaggeration.

It wrenched the hoped-for laugh from me, but I quickly stifled it, not wishing to draw attention to ourselves.

"You look beautiful tonight," he suddenly said. "You *always* look beautiful." Color rushed to Percy's cheeks with the words, and I realized he was inexperienced as a lover. Even flirting caused him to blush. But he was brave enough to never take his eyes from mine.

"I never even *found* you in the crowd at the tiltyard," I offered. "It ruined my day."

"It did?" he said happily. "I mean, I'm sorry your day was ruined but . . ."

"You're gratified it was not seeing you that ruined it."

He nodded. Then he grew serious. "I'm afraid we haven't much time, Anne. I want to . . . I want us to . . . how do I say this?"

I was silent, for I could not imagine what it was he wanted to reveal.

"I want us to tell each other our secrets."

"Secrets?"

He looked round to assure himself no one was watching us.

"Bare our souls. Swear to keep faith with one another. Swear on our hearts, for there's nothing we can trust more than that."

His declaration left me flummoxed, silent, and suddenly I saw his courage slipping away for want of encouragement.

"I agree," I blurted. "Trust me . . . and I will trust you."

He closed his eyes, relief flooding his face.

"All right. I will begin."

He took a long breath, then spoke very quietly. "I hate my father. He is a soulless, murdering thug posing as a gallant noble." Percy studied my expression and must have found it comfortable, for he went on then. "I loathe the martial arts and hope never to go to war, spill another man's blood. I've told Father, and of course, for that, he thinks me weak, girlish." He sighed very deeply, fixed me in his sights once again, and continued.

"The things I say to my confessor . . . they're mostly lies. For that, I shall certainly burn in hell." Suddenly he began to smile, as though his declarations were lightening a heavy load. Clearly he had never spoken such truths aloud before. "And I love my dogs, quite substantially more than I do most people. *All* people." He grinned at me. "Except you."

I was thrilled by his confessions. Emboldened. I thought I had never heard anyone speak more bravely. I grasped one of Percy's hands under the table.

"I hate *my* father," I began. "I think he has learnt the art of cruelty from the devil himself." That out, the rest came easily. "I, too, lie in confession, but I do not believe I will burn in hell. Nor will you." I took a long breath. "I love several people who are avowed enemies of England. And I have seen things, and done things, that should inspire the greatest guilt and shame in myself . . . but they do not."

I had to stop, for I'd suddenly lost my nerve. Then Percy squeezed my hand and with his sweet eyes bade me go on.

"I have dreamed of love, a marriage for love. But I have let myself be convinced that is impossible, and have allowed those dreams to wither. And all for the lack of faith . . ." I looked deep in his eyes. "Until now."

The breath rushed out of him and he fairly slumped with relief, as though he had run a long race, and won it.

Suddenly the musicians burst into a fanfare so unexpected that Percy and I in our little world both startled, he nearly jumping out of his seat. A team of jugglers for whom the fanfare had been played streamed into the room and began racing round inside the U in so comical a routine of their art, with everything from flaming pins to bowls of water, to live chickens, that everyone was soon doubled over in laughter.

It was the end of all intimacy tween Percy and me that night, but all the words that had needed to be spoken had been spoken. My services were finally called for with the queen only twice to translate for the few Englishmen who did not know French.

Percy and I managed to cross paths again just as Claude and our tiny party were leaving. He whispered that we should meet the next night at the blue and gold pavilion, where another feast for all men and ladies was being held. I quickly agreed.

Drunk on Henry Percy's words, I covered the distance back to our quarters in the blink of an eye. It startled me to have lost time like that. I was suddenly undressed and in my bed with no memory of the past hour. Surprisingly, I fell right asleep.

If I dreamed, I do not remember. If I had, the dreams could not have excelled that which I had lived in the waking world that day.

For I believed I was falling in love.

CHAPTER 31

*O*nce, twice, three times again, Percy and I were thwarted in our amorous ambitions.

The night after Henry's private dinner for Claude, Wolsey and all his men absented themselves from the festivities for intensive peace negotiations with Madame and Marguerite. Percy was kept close at the cardinal's side during the jousts the day after that, and then Claude fell ill, much worried about a miscarriage. I had to forgo all manner of entertainments and mummings, jousts and masques. But nothing could be done, as the poor woman needed her household at hand.

Early on the fourth morning of her confinement, François arrived in the queen's room all aflame. He kissed her where she lay abed, then kissed the hands of every one of her women, and even twirled one or two about him, causing laughter all round.

Claude insisted he tell us what had caused his high spirits. He said he had just come from Henry's chamber, where he had surprised the king in his bed—woken him, in fact, from a dead sleep.

By now Claude and her ladies were all smiles at François' antics, boyish in the extreme, but entertaining nevertheless.

"Then," he said proudly, "I announced myself his prisoner."

"His *prisoner*?" the queen exclaimed.

"Henry liked the game. Jumped up out of bed. I held up his shirt and helped him into it."

"François!" Claude smiled indulgently and the king, in a most expansive mood, lay down next to her, his arms under his head, his long legs crossed. He turned to her.

"Shall we have our breakfast in bed?"

"If you like." It was clear Claude was enjoying her husband's open attention.

"Ladies," she said, "if you will . . . ?"

We all scurried out to see to the royal couple's breakfast, smiling at the rare sound of Claude shrieking with laughter.

The very next morning, a Sunday, the women of the queen's household were awakened just at dawn by a great commotion coming from François' chamber. First there was his raucous laughter, then the unmistakable sound of King Henry's booming guffaws. We threw on our wraps and hurried down the curtained hall to see the guards to François' draped door standing back looking chagrined, and the figure of the English king striding round the French king's bedroom!

"Come in, come in, mam'selles!" François cried when he saw us peering in. But Madame Gaspard, who was scandalized by the whole affair, hustled us away back to our rooms to dress for church.

Later, as the royal entourage made its procession to church services, it was not the solemn and dignified pilgrimage to François' tented house of worship to hear the Mass sung by Archbishop de Lenoncourt. It was a gay march with bemused courtiers and ladies following the two kings—the French one having been dressed by his "faithful servant," the English, and the two of them striding arm in arm like boyhood friends to Wolsey's golden chapel.

François' good cheer had been infectious, and after their previous morning of breakfasting in bed, Claude's spirits had returned with her good health. Though this Sunday she was being carried to church on her litter, she waved at her subjects and smiled as she passed.

I caught up with Marguerite, whose expression was all but unreadable.

"It appears yours and Madame's peace negotiations with the cardinal are progressing nicely," I suggested.

"What you are seeing here should not necessarily be construed as success, Anna. I am sure if you asked your father, he would think rather cynically of these antics." She was referring to the "morning visits" the kings had made to each other's bedchambers. "This is not to say that no progress is being made." She shook her head. "I do wonder, though, what drives those men who can make bloody war upon each other, or live in peace, to choose war."

"Must we not hope for the best?"

"Always," she said. "And expect the worst."

A dusty wind had kicked up the next day, making the jousts a misery.

It was bad enough for the riders and horses, but they at least had eye shields on their helmets. The spectators had no protection from the sun and blowing grit high in the risers. Many of the noble guests had left, so in order for the stands to remain full for the honor of the contestants, servants were pulled from the bakehouses, laundry, stables, and foundry to cheer them on.

I had finally given up after my headdress had been blown clear off me. Blinded by the driving dust, I stepped down . . . right into Henry Percy's arms! He had a cloak with him that he held above our heads like a tent, and guided us down to the ground and away from the tilt-yard. Completely at his mercy, I let him take me, believing he would never lead me wrong. We walked for some time in silence, except for the howling wind, our bodies jostling together under the cloak.

Finally I felt a relative peace of surroundings. When the garment was removed, I found we were inside a small but richly appointed family tent, which, without asking, I knew must be the Duke of Northumberland's. No one was there.

Percy and I were still pressed together, our faces close. I experienced a small moment of panic. But he did not hesitate. He kissed me hard on the mouth. I had been dreaming of his kiss, but somehow thought the first would be more tender, soft. This was *better*, far better than my wildest dreams, lips and tongues in the sweetest battle, and hands everywhere roving—faces, necks, breasts, buttocks. Breath coming hard.

His cock a steel rod against my belly. Then our knees jellied and we tumbled onto his father's bed. . . .

That realization stopped us cold. We pulled apart, trembling, his face flushed as scarlet as mine felt. This was madness. We could not be caught groping each other in the Duke of Northumberland's bed. He stood and helped me up, tried to push my hair into a semblance of order. I straightened his doublet and laced one of my sleeves that had come undone.

I looked at him and smiled, trying for levity. "If we go out now, you'll need a larger codpiece."

He laughed. Then he pulled me to him once again.

"We cannot, Percy. Not here. It's broad daylight." I straightened my skirts. "See if anyone is looking."

He peeked out the tent door, shook his head.

"We'll go to the palace," he said, resigned.

"It won't be so windy there," I replied, trying to lead us into sensible conversation. That was where we *should* be heading.

But when he held open the tent flap to allow me through, his expression was so desperate, so *hungry*, that I nearly flung myself back down on the family bed.

Sadly, good sense prevailed and a moment later we were back in the wind and the sun, shielding our faces with our arms and heading for the stone and canvas castle.

There we dallied the rest of the day amidst hordes of French and English, seeking shelter from the storm. Much as we wished exclusively for each other's company, Percy and I thought it best to separate and make conversation with others.

I had seen very little of my brother, George, the whole time, and this day he sought me out.

"You seem to have made yourself quite indispensable to your hosts," he said.

"They like me well enough. You seem to like the Frenchwomen better than the English."

"I like how free they are with their favors. Now, what is going on with you and young Percy?" he said unexpectedly.

"What?"

"I saw you at the tiltyard ducking under a cloak with him without even a word spoken. Like you were the oldest of friends."

"Not old friends. *New* friends," I said with as much levity as I could muster.

"You are good at so many things," George said, his eyes following that pretty redheaded French girl, whose hair was gleaming extraordinarily in the sun that streamed in through the high arched windows, "but you're a shockingly bad liar."

"I'm not lying," I said, color flooding my cheeks.

He sighed heavily. "You're betrothed elsewhere, sister."

"I know."

"Try as *I* did, I was not able to shed myself of the grim and unlovely Jane Parker," George said.

"When will you marry?" I asked.

"In the next year or two, once our father can negotiate a higher dowry from her father." Then, "He's a nice fellow, Lord Percy."

"George!"

"But you really must not dally with him, Anne. You'll have Father raining down such horrors on your head. . . ."

"If I dally with him," I whispered fiercely to George, "I shall do so discreetly, and Father will never know."

"Ha!"

"You won't say a word," I ordered him, "not even to Mary."

"If you keep swanning around so obviously with him, I won't *have* to tell anyone."

"We're not 'swanning around.'"

"The night of the first ball you danced with him exclusively."

That sobered me. "I thought you hadn't noticed."

"I hadn't. Mother told me. See, there're two of us who know already."

"What shall I do?" I moaned. "I think we love each other."

"Then *stop* loving each other! Could you have chosen more stupidly? He serves in Cardinal Wolsey's household."

"I know that." I was starting to lose my temper.

"Is he aware of your betrothal?"

"No."

"Wonderful."

"There hasn't been time."

"Do you mean to tell him?"

"I don't know."

"Anne!"

"I'm leaving," I said, and turned away in anger.

"Leave *alone*!" he called after me.

I did leave alone, and I went very wretchedly back to the French pavilion, wind-whipped hair stinging my face. Hundreds of men were frantically shoring up the great tent as if it might blow away.

Fully clothed, I laid myself down on my cot and raged at my predicament.

George was right, of course. It was madness to think I could defy my parents, Wolsey, and the king. I was just a girl, not yet seventeen. Fathers had killed their daughters for slighter infractions than the one I was considering. And I hardly knew this boy. Had danced with him one night, conversed with him another, and wrestled with him in his father's tent today. *For this was I prepared to risk my father's wrath? And what of Percy?* He was yet unaware that the lady he trusted with his deepest secrets was hiding news of her betrothal to another man.

Did he even love me?

I racked my brains remembering every word spoken between us. Every sigh. Every murmur. The truth was bitter. He had never once uttered the word. How he talked—the sweet desperation, the urgent desire for sharing our confidences—had led me to believe . . . nay, I had led *myself* to believe he had professed that emotion. 'Twas *I* who had admitted to wishing to have a marriage for love. Not he.

Oh, I'd been such a fool!

I began to weep then, for the dream of Henry Percy and me as happily wedded man and wife seemed all at once ridiculous. This was my punishment for listening to a laundry maid's prophecy and wishing for the impossible.

Slowly the pavilion began filling with the royal family and their entourage. The ladies coming into their quarters were undressed and lay down for a nap before being redressed and coiffed for the next event. After dinner there was to be a fireworks display. I pretended I'd already been asleep on my cot, so no one bothered me. Ladies gossiped as they helped one another out of their gowns down to their shifts. Then they whispered awhile and one by one fell asleep.

I stayed wide-awake brooding on my misfortune.

Before long their servants arrived to rouse them. As the ladies bustled about, Lynette came and stood staring down at myself, still fully dressed from the day, pretending sleep.

"What is this? Why are you trying to fool me? You do not fool me. What is wrong? Open your eyes!"

I did as I was told.

"So you saw him again," Lynette accused me.

"Shhhh!" I warned her.

"Young Henry Percy."

"Yes, Henry Percy. But he is *not* my future husband," I said quietly.

"But you love him," she insisted.

"Lynette, I'm not feeling well," I said. "I'm not going out tonight."

"Not going out?" I might as well have said I was going to cleave off my right hand.

"That is *insane*. It is François' fireworks display, the one your friend Leonardo designed. It is the most exciting, the most fabulous of all the nights of this—"

"I'm not going."

"You are a coward."

I began to object, then decided Lynette was right. It was a cowardly escape from Percy, but it was just the sad fact. There was no chance for us. I had not even told him about James Butler, so I was a liar *and* a coward. I simply could not face him again.

"You are getting dressed," Lynette said, searching my trunk for the gown I was meant to be wearing this night. She held it up before me. It was a truly spectacular creation, in black velvet with scarlet embroidery in tight figures of knots that boggled the eye, and covered every inch of skirt and bodice. The sleeves were opposite, of the same color red velvet with black embroidered knots. I'd spent most of my winnings from cards to have my dressmakers re-create the patterns of Leonardo's *groppi*.

"I'm sorry. I really am." I stood. "Help me out of this dress," I ordered her. Sulking, she obeyed and began unbuttoning my daytime gown. The other ladies had donned their gayest gowns and, one by one, were leaving the pavilion.

Finally when I was stripped down to my linen shift I sent Lynette on her way. Lying back down on my cot and pathetically clutching my beautiful black and red gown to me, I cried myself to sleep.

I was awakened by a hand on my bare shoulder.

"Lynette," I said, my eyes still closed. "For the last time, I'm not going out."

"Then I must watch the fireworks alone, I suppose."

I nearly jumped out of my skin, sitting up and pulling the dress to cover my breasts and neck.

Henry Percy was sitting on the end of my cot in the otherwise deserted women's quarters.

"How did you get in?" I stammered, feeling utterly stupid.

"There is not a soul in either camp who is not gathered to watch the spectacle François has advertised as the greatest fireworks display in the history of mankind."

I stared at him, unable to speak.

"Why are you not with them?" he said, smoothing my cheek with the back of his hand. "Why are you not with *me*?"

I could not look at him, and felt tears welling in my eyes.

"I cannot be with you, Percy. I'm betrothed to another man."

"I know."

"You know?!" I stared up at him, incredulous.

"Do you not think that I would have made a few inquiries about you before . . . ?" Now he fell silent.

"Before what? Before pursuing me? For that's what you've done. You have pursued a virtuous girl who is spoken for."

He looked a little ashamed. "I know. But I could not help myself." Now he cast his eyes all the way to his feet. "I've fallen in love with you."

The sound that escaped me was half a sigh and half a groan of delight. In any event, it was loud enough to be heard.

"Can I take that to mean you feel the same for me?" he said.

"Yes." I was trying not to weep.

I saw him peering round the deserted quarters, then at me in my thin shift, clutching my gown.

"I haven't decided yet what to do," he said. "How to tell my father."

"You mean to tell your father?" I said. "I don't think I can tell *my* father. This marriage of mine solves a long feud with the Butlers."

"I know all that. But the Northumberland Percys are far more powerful than the Irish Butlers."

I could hardly believe what I was hearing. Henry Percy was trying to clear a way to marry me!

"But for right now, Anne"—he looked round again—"I think you should get dressed."

I smiled, wiping my eyes.

"Stand up," he said. "I'll help you."

I loved how he commanded me, sternly but gently. Was that not how all men should treat their women?

I stood and thrust the gown at him. He turned it over in his hands with the greatest consternation, as though it were an intricate puzzle to be solved. I took it back and held it in such a way that any fool could see how to put it over my head. I raised my arms and he slid it down. Then I turned my back to him.

"There are a hundred buttons here," he said. "And they're very small."

"Then we shall be here awhile," I said, thinking that I would savor every moment. But I had no idea that the feel of his fingers playing along my back, from its small between my buttocks, to its middle between my shoulders, would make me shiver with so much delight. He kept up a quiet conversation as he worked, sometimes talking to me, sometimes addressing a pesky button that defied his too-large fingers. Else he was quiet, and mayhap those were the best times, for his warm, moist breath on my neck was by far the most intimate of all the sensations.

Part of me wished that his hands would stray from his task and find my soft ducks. That we'd fall on my cot as we'd done on his father's bed and continue making love. The other part clung to Percy's words about him speaking to his father about me. He meant marriage, of course, and the upright part of me wished him to finish dressing me to prevent any untoward behavior.

"Done!" he finally said, very self-satisfied.

"Now the sleeves," I reminded him.

"Sleeves!" he cried.

"Am I to go without sleeves?" I teased him. "They're easy. Just like you lace up your saddlebags."

I handed him the black and red embroidered sleeves. Just as he finished lacing the second one he leaned over and kissed me under the ear. That was all it took. We came crashing together—lips, hands, grinding loins. I thought my heart would fly out of my chest.

And then the first explosion came.

Through the translucent pavilion walls we could see the sky alight, and heard fifteen thousand voices roaring their approval.

I must say it sobered us instantly, not simply the thought that we should rein in our passions, but a desire to see the spectacle. Percy pushed me to arm's length for a final appraisal.

"You are so beautiful, Anne." His eyes were moist with sincerity.

I stood on tiptoe and kissed him sweetly.

"We should go," I said.

"Not together." He was so odd a combination of wildness and caution.

"Right. You first. I'll meet you at the fountain," I suggested.

He turned and hurried away. I closed my eyes and stood in place, smiling.

No longer was it a silly girl's fantasy of love. Once a dream, it had found a place in the light of day.

CHAPTER 32

*T*he night proved magical for Percy and me. We'd found each other in the crowd and managed, for the whole of the evening, to never let go of each other's hands, though this time I was sure no one was the wiser. All eyes were tipped skyward, as the fireworks display seemed a celestial conversation with the maestro from beyond the grave. There were spinning suns and moons, and twinkling constellations, and the appearance of whole armies marching across the sky. But when in a burst of red, blue, green, and gold, *a dragon breathing fire* appeared above our heads, it moved past delighting the crowd to *terrifying* them. Some ladies shrieked and fainted at the sight. Clerics knelt and crossed themselves.

Even the two great kings on their viewing platforms seemed cowed by what they well knew was naught but a clever arrangement of gunpowder and sulfur. Mayhap, I thought, they were not so sophisticated as they were superstitious. Not so learned as they were fearful of God's wrath for their many sins, both past and yet to come.

But as the colors faded from the sky and the great fire-spewing dragon dissolved into puffs of harmless smoke, all were relieved, as well as sorry that the show was over.

"Thank you for making me come out," I said to Percy. "I would have missed one of the great wonders of the world."

"*You* are a wonder of the world, Anne Boleyn."

I saw his father coming toward us in the crowd.

"Till tomorrow," I said, finally dropping his hand. From the look on his face, that separation was, for him, more like a severing.

"Tomorrow, my love," he said, and turned away.

Never had I heard three more welcome words.

That "tomorrow" became the day and the night that, of all from the Field of Cloth of Gold, I most remember, revere, and despise.

It started well enough. The winds had died down and the weather had cooled to something bearable. Everyone, still overawed by Leonardo's lightworks the night before, had assembled in the tiltyard for a different "feat of arms" from the jousts.

This was combat on foot where teams of knights, French against English, fought with puncheon spears and two-handed swords, as they would—except for blunted weapons—on a battlefield. It was nevertheless very fierce and frightening to watch—at least it was so for the women. The men in the risers shouted for harder fighting and even for blood.

It made mine run cold, and I thanked Jesus that Percy was not yet old enough for such mayhem. George and William Carey were due to fight that afternoon, and I hadn't yet decided if I could bear to watch.

I stood under the royal canopy behind Claude, who sat near Queen Katherine, their two husbands side by side, cheering on their respective "troops."

My father arrived late with my mother and Mary, and as they took their seats nearby, close to the refreshments tent, I saw King Henry clap eyes on my sister. It was not as though he'd never seen her before. After all, she served his wife. But she did look exquisite this day, her fair curls framing the palest cheeks, brushed lightly with peaches. Her creamy bosoms wobbled daintily above her low-cut bodice. There was something so unself-conscious about Mary, now that she was happily married and respectable.

But Henry was staring at her as though she were a cut of the finest, most succulent roast. I swear I saw him lick his lips. François caught him staring, and I saw a strange look cross the face of the French king. Henry spoke, and François looked strangely at him.

I carefully sidestepped toward them so I could better hear what they were saying. Indeed, I was rewarded by intelligence, but it was such that I wished I had never heard.

"Marie is *always* 'luscious to look at,' " François said to Henry. "Do you fancy her?"

"She does make my cock hard."

"Have you had her?"

"Not yet."

"Ah, you should," said the French king. "She's soft and sweet inside . . . though my men and I have loosened what was once a very tight little cunt."

I saw Henry's posture straighten, as though he'd just received a stinging insult, but François either was unaware or precisely meant to egg Henry on.

"Marie *de Boullan.*" François said the name as a wistful sigh. "She is a great prostitute. Infamous above all others. I think while she is here I shall ride 'the English mare' one more time for good measure."

Henry stood suddenly, his face a shocking red. He said nothing, but stomped down the platform's steps toward Mary and our parents. He looked hard at my sister for a long moment, then entered the refreshments tent.

I watched as François stood and followed him. He smiled seductively at Mary, who seemed utterly confused. Our father watched the drama that was unfolding with a hawk's eyes, staying very, very still. Mary, sensing danger, tried to bolt, but Father snatched up her arm and held it viselike, making her wince.

A moment later Henry and François seemed to *erupt* from the tent, each holding a full goblet, neither speaking nor meeting each other's eyes. They stopped before Mary. My father let go his grip on her and pulled my mother back with him into the shadows. Mary looked like a lamb at the slaughterhouse.

She stood trembling and silent as both kings held out their goblets to her to choose.

I chanced a look at Claude and Katherine, but the queens were pointedly looking away from the incident.

With Mary paralyzed and unable or unwilling to choose either goblet, the gauntlet had suddenly been thrown down. At the same moment both cups were dropped, and with a growl, Henry grabbed François by the throat. The French king, furious, wrapped his huge hand round Henry's neck. With their free arms, the men embraced violently.

Those around them stepped back and Mary, full of horror, picked up her skirts and rushed away. The kings were grappling now, as wrestlers did. Well matched in size, they swatted at each other's heads and pulled and twisted, hoping to unbalance the other. They ripped apart then, and with knees bent, arms outstretched, circled round like two animals stalking. Suddenly with a raw grunt, François lunged and, in a lightning move, tripped Henry up. The look on the English king's face as he hit the ground with a *thud* was terrible to behold. He lay staring up at François from his back, shock and shame tearing his features apart.

François himself seemed surprised he had thrown down this bear of a man. He offered his hand, almost sheepishly.

Henry suddenly became aware that those around the tent and the platform had witnessed this unspeakable humiliation.

"What are you staring at!" he roared.

Everyone instantly averted their gaze.

I turned away quickly and caught sight of the two queens. They were still watching the games on the field and, even without benefit of an interpreter, were sharing a quiet laugh.

That is how it is done, I suddenly thought to myself. *That is how a woman spares herself. She looks the other way.* I hardly knew why I should think such a thing. I was in love with a young man who loved me. A man who wanted to marry me. He'd never betray me with another woman. I would never be forced to turn my gaze away from watching so awful a public humbling as Claude and Katherine had had to do.

The morning was ruined. Both kings retired to their chambers. Their absence from the royal platform soured the will of both the French and the English players, and all the vitality went out of the fight. It was a relief to break for the midday meal, and then it was announced that the afternoon combat had been canceled.

Later I made my way to William Carey's small tent. He was elsewhere, but Mary was there. Her eyes were red-rimmed, and her creamy skin was blotched with anger.

"Father just left," she said, sniffing back tears.

I felt suddenly afraid. I wanted to run from the place, never hear what he had said to my sweet sister.

"When we return to England . . ." She could not go on for her trembling.

"When you return to England . . . ," I prompted her, closing my eyes as if that would shut out the worst of it.

"I am to become Henry's mistress."

I opened my eyes and looked at her. She was altogether stricken. I wanted to shout out, "What if you do not wish this?! What about William?!" But I knew the words were futile. Kings had insulted my sister. Fought over my sister. Claimed her like a piece of turf, or a walled city. She had no say in the matter. Our father had certainly not fought with Henry for her honor. Her honor had long ago been forfeited by Thomas Boleyn for his own gain.

So I simply took Mary in my arms and hugged her, let her weep for the loss of her short-lived happiness, and her uncertain future as another king's whore.

In that moment something of my resolve to stay pure in a putrid world began to fall away. *Rush to joy wherever it shows itself,* I thought. *Nothing is guaranteed. Everything of value will be fouled with night soil.*

I walked slowly back to the French pavilion, my heart sore, and a view of my new world starting to take shape.

Much of it, mayhap *all* of it, was entirely out of my control.

That night I dressed in a daze. For the first time I allowed Lynette to pluck my eyebrows and forehead, paint my cheeks and lips with vermilion, and rim my already black eyes with kohl. She rouged my nipples, dabbed me high and low with perfume. I cannot say what I was feeling or planning, only that there was a desperate air about the whole business.

Lynette kept speaking of true love found, but all I could think of was Mary's fate. She was no better or worse than I. We were sisters. *What, beyond my marriage to James Butler,* I wondered, *did our father have in store for his younger girl? How would my disgraces benefit his purse?*

When I found my love at the banquet in the English castle that night, I tried to seem gay. He mentioned nothing of what had transpired with the two kings and my sister, though by then it must have been common knowledge in both camps.

Displaying his expected contempt and cruelty, Father had insisted that Mary be present this night, and not keep to her bed as she wished. Her expression was hard as a marble statue, but William, sitting next to her, was in sheer agony. All pride in his lovely wife had been shattered, and he was cast as a helpless fool. François and Henry were shameless, fawning all over their wives. Henry pretended love for the French king, and François was utterly deferential, as if to pretend that throwing the English king on his back in public had not even happened.

Worst of all I caught François staring at *me*, time and again. *What did I have to do with the farce that had played itself out today?*

When the tables had been cleared off the floor and the dancing began, I was in no mood for it.

"Take me out of here," I said to Percy, and without a word he did.

We sought the shadows behind the bakehouse and were at each other the moment we felt ourselves hidden. There was nothing hindering me. Nothing to lose. He was swept away by passion, mine as much as his. All thoughts of a proper progression—fighting for my hand, betrothal, and a marriage bed—were forgotten in the dark.

His hands lifted my skirts, his deft fingers seeking the wet, hot place we both wanted them to go. I moaned so loudly when he found it, he had to cover my mouth with his other hand. Our eyes met, and there was less terror than I imagined there would be, and more love than I ever believed possible. He was groping with his breeches when we heard a sound.

My skirts were dropped; his hands returned to his sides. We turned.

Standing there was, of all people, François! With only the moonlight on his face I could see he was grinning, as though he had discovered a lost treasure. I was at once relieved and horrified.

"Your Majesty," I said, and curtsied, but my knees were so jellied from the previous frenzy I started to tip forward.

Percy caught my arm and steadied me. He bowed to the French king.

"I am going to stop you, Anna," François said. "Stop you from disgracing yourself. Here you are rutting in the shadows with a young man, not your betrothed." He turned to Percy. "What is your name?"

"Henry Percy," he said with more dignity than I thought possible in the circumstances. "Of the Northumberland Percys."

"Ah. Well . . . ," he said, then paused.

I was trembling. *What would he do to us? To me? I had spurned his advances, and here I was with a green boy.*

"Let me make a suggestion," François finally said.

"Anything you say, Majesty," I intoned in a voice of resignation.

"Follow me," said the king, and we did, Percy holding my hand and steadying me on the uneven ground as we weaved in the dark between the English bake- and slaughterhouses, the forge, and finally the family tents. Onward past the deserted tiltyard and its huge, black-limbed tree, its noble shields clanging about in the wind, to the first of the French tents. Here there were more torches, and the footing was easier. Guards were stationed at intervals, and to each, François nodded pleasantly, they saluting him smartly but dispassionately.

Finally we came to a tent, nondescript canvas, like the several that were nearest it. But when the king opened the door flap, all pretense of the ordinary vanished. Inside was a lush, candlelit paradise. Almost the entire space was occupied by a bed, opulently thrown with ermine rugs and royal red and purple silks. Down cushions were thrown carelessly about, and a tall Turkish hookah stood at one side as though guarding the sacred mattress. On a small inlaid table were a flask of wine and two Venetian glass goblets. It smelled heavily of patchouli, sweet smoke, and sex.

"My little love nest," said François. "I would be happy to lend it to you for the evening. After the spectacle I made of myself today, I shall be sleeping only with my wife. No one will bother you here." He looked directly at me. "No one will *catch* you here."

He turned to go, but I caught up his arm.

"Why are you doing this?"

He smiled a rakish smile and with the candlelight flickering in his eyes, I could suddenly see how some could think François looked like the devil.

"I have been watching you, Anna. I watched you grow from a girl to a woman in my court. And I have been watching you with your young lord these past weeks."

Someone *else* had noticed! *Had we been so obvious?*

"I simply believe that everyone deserves, at least once in their lives, a moment of wild, unsullied passion." François took up my hand and brushed it gently with his lips. He looked at Percy. "This is yours."

Then he was gone.

When I turned, I saw Percy standing by the side of the bed. His body was straight, almost rigid in posture, but his features were soft as a cherub's, the eyes liquid, those lovely full lips parted, urgent. There was a confusion about him, one that I full understood. Here we were, both of us hungry and, for the first time, with no hindrance to our having each other in full. There was no need for groping in the shadows. For fear of discovery, shame, or punishment. For a terrible moment I wondered, if those terrors vanished, would desire vanish, too?

The answer came with Percy's rush toward me. I was swept suddenly into his arms, his warm mouth everywhere seeking my flesh, delightfully helpless against his onslaught. He might have been a man weeks without food or water, having found a feast laid out on the shore of a green oasis.

We paused just long enough to savor lying down together amidst the luscious silks and furs and cushions. Percy gently turned me around. I felt his fingers at my back.

"Thank you," he whispered softly into my neck, and I knew it was gratitude for the laces I had worn this evening, and not a hundred buttons. I was hardly breathing as he loosened my bodice and started on my sleeves. Still looking away from him, I undid my own skirts and pulled away the upper garments till I was shod of all but my shift. I finally turned to face Percy, expecting him to be wearing no more than his thin shirt.

He was wearing nothing.

Kneeling there on the bed, his body was slender but rock hard. His manhood stood erect, nearly touching his belly. All fear had gone from his face, and that emboldened me. I went down on my hands and knees and, never taking my eyes from his, stalked him slowly, like a cat her prey.

He liked the game and himself dropped to a crouch. I darted out and licked his shoulder. He lunged and gently bit my neck. Then he fell on me, our limbs entwining, and we devoured each other with kisses. Then his hands found the hem of my shift and with a slowness that was sweet torture, he began to lift it.

I had always believed that at the moment of my first nakedness with a man I would feel shame and worry that my body was too thin, my ducks not full enough, or my black bush offensive. But as the thin linen gown revealed more and more of me, I felt nothing but strength and beauty and passion.

When we both were reduced to our natural state, we paused and pushed away to arm's length, allowing us to feast our eyes on each other. There was such glory in the moment, such triumph. We two—

young and hitherto weak children against our fathers, the church, and the state—had somehow seized our destinies, chosen a joint path. One with love and lust that would no doubt last a lifetime.

But as Percy pulled me to him for that ultimate embrace, I was seized suddenly by a rogue emotion. It jolted me. Caused my limbs to stiffen. 'Twas not fear, I knew with certainty, nor was it doubt.

It was *power*, a sense that a choice was here, *mine to make*. I might let myself be driven by passion, but I could yet choose against it. I had already defied the Fates. Must I now take the obvious road? Conform to the foregone conclusion?

All of a sudden I thought *not*.

Percy was covering me with kisses, either unaware of my hardening or choosing to ignore it. Even as he took my rouged nipple in his mouth, I felt no quickening below, for *above*, my mind was alive, ruminating, filling itself with logic. I thought of Queen Claude, who reveled, not in her beauty, but in her hard-won ability to give birth to her husband's lawful heirs. I remembered Maestro Leonardo, whose own bastardy had forever fouled his life. And there was Duchess Marguerite, blessed lady, who had taught me nothing if not that a strong-minded woman could hold power in a man's world.

Then a vision of my father filled my head, vile and heartless. The loss or retaining of his daughter's virginity was of equal value to him, depending on the circumstance or the size of the purse.

If I lose that virginity now to Percy, I said slowly and silently to myself, *Father has won! All that I have learnt in France these past years will have been wasted. My reputation will be ruined, my ability to move through society with any semblance of dignity lost.*

"Percy," I whispered in his ear. "Listen to me, sweetheart."

He faced me, his eyes glazed, his breath coming in short gasps. I pushed back a damp strand of hair from his dear brow.

"We cannot do this here tonight. Not any night. Not till we are married."

He looked at me distressed, as if I had suddenly gone mad. But I was growing more determined with every moment.

"You and I must convince our parents and Cardinal Wolsey that my betrothal to James Butler is foolish. That the most propitious alliance is Boleyn with Northumberland."

Percy was nodding slowly, agreeing with me more readily than I imagined he would.

"I don't know how we'll do it," I continued. "But we'll force ourselves to think straight, make a plan."

I kissed him then, full on the mouth, and he kissed me back. There'd been no lessening of our passion for each other. Just a necessary dose of common sense.

"Come," I said, "help me dress. You know how to do it."

He found my shift in the twisted bedclothes.

"Wait, Percy. You put on your breeches first." I smiled sadly. "The sight of you naked is already softening my resolve."

He dressed himself first. Then me, tenderly, with bittersweet sighs. He planted kisses on every part of my body before covering it or lacing it out of his sight. By the time he was finished, I was weeping with quiet frustration.

We stood holding each other inside the tent door.

"We'll find a way, Anne," he said. In the short time since my announcement of this wretched "plan," he had embraced it and, by agreeing with its wisdom, thus honored me. I could only love him more for that.

He left first for the English camp, and though the night was still young, I made for the French pavilion. I had no stomach for music or dancing, for empty flirtations or wicked, grasping fathers.

But I was not unhappy. On the contrary, I felt tall and light and strong like a young reed on a riverbank. The wind was coming up again and though it blew my skirts and my hair wildly about me, I knew I was rooted firm in the earth. Though I might bend, I would never be broken. For—by the grace of my beloved teachers—I had found who I was. I would choose my destiny and stand before my enemies. Of course, only time would prove my true worth.

But I was young, and more than content to wait.

The devil wind refused to abate and indeed grew into a gale. Further tournaments were canceled, and on a day in the third week of the Field of Cloth of Gold, François' magical pavilion was lifted up and blown entirely away. Several men and one lady died, and the festivities were called abruptly to a close.

Holding on to his red hat, Cardinal Wolsey staged a final mass on the tiltyard. François and Henry afterward embraced like loving brothers, promising to build a chapel—"Our Lady of Friendship"—on the very spot, to commemorate this glorious celebration of peace.

I had gone to see my family off. It was a mad scene with a thousand English nobles packing up their trunks on wagons and carriages. Behind them the faux castle was being dismantled piece by piece—canvas, timber, stone, and glass. The wine fountain was bone-dry and stained red. All that had been so fantastically real was now revealed for the mere illusion it was.

The royals, and also Wolsey's household, were this day leaving, so as I stood with my mother, George, and William, seeing to their cases and bedding and chairs, I had several occasions to lock eyes with Percy, who was seeing to the cardinal's mule. No one was watching. We smiled broadly at each other.

My father appeared with Mary beside him. He was in his usual foul temper reserved for his family.

"Say good-bye to your sister," he ordered me.

Mary and I hugged very fiercely, and both of us began to cry.

"No need for hysterics," Father snapped. "You'll be seeing each other in no time."

I noticed he was staring at François, who had come to say his last good-byes to Henry. The two kings were making a great show of good-natured bear hugs. Tears glistened in their eyes.

"This so-called peace is fragile as a quail's egg," my father muttered. "We'll be at war with France by the end of the year."

Shortly thereafter my family climbed into a carriage and were off. They were quickly out of sight, a wind-driven cloud of dust obscuring them like a puff of magic smoke.

I tarried in the English camp, though, for Cardinal Wolsey's entourage had yet to go. I walked boldly up to Henry Percy and said his name. He turned with a smile.

"My father may be a rat's bag," I whispered, "but he knows his politics. He says we shall soon be at war with France, and so I shall be coming home to England."

Percy's face lit like the sun emerging from behind a cloud. "That's wonderful news!"

"So," I said, "we shall write every week till then."

"We should write every *day*."

"We cannot draw attention to ourselves," I warned him, though I loved his sentiment. "And you will do what you can to convince your father of our match."

"I will do *everything*." His eyes darted round him. "I want to kiss you."

"Sweet love." I put out my hand to him like a proper lady, though all I could see was him kneeling naked on François' bed, looking ready to devour me whole. I was starting to falter. "Kiss my *hand*, Percy."

He took it to his lips and, with a defiance that made me adore him all the more, held it there for far, far longer than was seemly.

The moment he let it go I turned away, fearing tears—a deadly mistake, that.

I left behind my love, Cardinal Wolsey, and the King and Queen of England. Then I made for the French court on what remained of the Field of Cloth of Gold.

I had never felt or learned so much in so short a time, and the course of my life had never seemed so clear. If Father was right, my remaining time in France would be short-lived.

I determined to make the best use of it.

*a*s Father had predicted, the brittle shell of peace had cracked immediately.

Henry left the "Field of Cloth of Gold" and several days later met with the Holy Roman Emperor at Calais, he and Charles promising, both of them, to *never* make a treaty with François. Conspiracies were hatched on all sides, invasions were launched, and promises betrayed.

When it could no longer be hidden that war between France and England was imminent, word was sent that all English scholars should return home from Paris. Father wrote from England that I should pack my trunks and wait for transport.

I was so torn in my emotions, for I had come up very far in the French court. I had friends there, high and low, and good-byes had to be said.

I did the hardest one first.

Queen Claude was pregnant yet again. This time, from the earliest days, all could see it was not going well with her. She was quieter than ever, clearly subdued, and, I thought, fearful of her life. But Claude was never one for complaining or wallowing in self-pity.

When I came into her room, she was sitting by the fire, even though it was a warm day. She turned her head slowly, as though she was very, very tired, and indeed she was frighteningly pale, lines of pain creasing her forehead and the corners of her eyes. But she smiled when she saw it was me, and put out her hand. I went and sat at her knee.

I'd thought we would say the things that friends did when they took their leave of one another. "I will miss you." "Thank you for your kindness." "You have been so dear to me." "Please write." But we said none of it.

Claude simply and silently stroked my hair, my shoulder, my cheek.

And I wept. Silent tears, silent sobs, for I knew I would never see this great lady again. We both understood she could survive few more pregnancies. That she had sacrificed her own life at the altar of childbearing.

Finally I kissed her hand, over and over again. She patted my face dry with her handkerchief and smiled that sweet crooked-toothed smile.

"Adieu, Anna. Go with God."

I nodded and fled her chamber, not wishing to drown the world with my tears.

My next farewell was a sight happier.

I had enlisted the help of Robairre to carry to the basement a wardrobe box wherein hung four of my gowns. Lynette, on her way upstairs, squealed with delight when she saw them and dropped her pile of clean linen on the floor. She hugged me and kissed me and squealed even louder as she fingered the fine silks and brocades that were now hers. I was much relieved that this good-bye would not be so wrenching an affair as that with Claude had been.

Indeed, Lynette was happy for me going home. She would miss me, of course, but she knew I'd be reuniting with my love, and nothing, she always said, was better in the world than the daily presence of one's true mate in life.

There was one last thing, however, that I had to know.

"Lynette, when you are making love with Longet . . ." I paused for a very long time, still unsure of the way to say this.

"When I am making love with Longet," she prompted, curious now.

"At the end . . . or just before the end . . . ," I finally went on.

"When he explodes, you mean?"

Yes! She had given me the words I needed.

"Do you explode as well?"

"Me?" She looked dubious. *"Explode?"* She thought for a long moment. "I would not use that word in particular. But I feel lovely and warm and so close to my love. . . ." She saw my expression, which must have just then looked impish. "Why do you ask such a thing? And what would *you* know of it? You said that you and Percy did not . . ." She glared at me indignantly. *"Did* you? Did you do it and not tell me?!"

"No," I said quickly. "We did not. But *I* have exploded."

She eyed me with suspicion.

"I believe that all women are meant to explode," I said.

"Then why haven't I?" she demanded.

"I don't know, Lynette, but"—I drew her closer and lowered my voice—"if you like, I shall tell you how it can be done."

By the time I left the Amboise laundry for the last time, I had given her a parting gift a hundred times better than four pretty dresses.

But Lynette had given me one in return—a promise that in all the world she could never have had a better friend than me.

Of all my good-byes there were none so fraught with varying emotions as the one with the king and his sister.

On my last day Marguerite summoned me to her rooms. There I found her and François alone, all her ladies having been sent away.

"We will miss you very much, *la Petite Boullan,*" François said, invoking the name he'd not used for many years.

"And I you," I said, grasping Marguerite's hand and holding it to my cheek.

Then from the folds of my skirt I retrieved a small red doeskin package. I held it out and pulled open the flaps of leather to reveal the top card. It was François as the king of diamonds. He broke into a broad grin. It was instantly clear to them both what they were seeing, and by whose hand it had been executed.

"Below you will find yourself, Your Grace," I said to Marguerite. "You are the queen of clubs."

Her eyebrows arched in surprise.

"There are *queens* in this deck?"

"Four," I said proudly.

"Well-done, my dear," she said, and pulled me into a warm embrace.

"The deck is yours," I said to them both.

"You cannot mean that, Anna," François said.

I had argued endlessly with myself about relinquishing the maestro's deck, the most precious gift ever given me. Whilst I had kept the knotted covering as a memento of Leonardo, I had decided I had no other way of making known my inestimable debt to this brother and sister who had given me the things most important in life—friendship and education.

"But I do mean it." I smiled. "Mayhap when I return to France someday, the three of us will play a round of *Piqué* with it."

François kissed my hand and refused to let me curtsy to him. For all we'd been through, for all he had put Mary through, even though he was King of France, I felt this a fair gesture, and instead nodded respectfully.

I turned to Marguerite. From her I had learnt what I believed to be my most valuable lesson in life. *That intellect was wholly unexpected in females, but that wise men enjoyed it.*

For her I reserved my most humble obeisance. I swept into the lowest, most worshipful female bow I could manage, staying in that posture altogether silent for a very long time. Long enough, I hoped, that she would understand the depth of my love and appreciation. Long enough to express that I thought her a woman above all others. One whom I could only hope to emulate.

Then I took my leave.

The next day I was driven to Calais, and with a shipful of English scholars, I crossed the Channel, the waters nearly as angry as they had been eight years before.

*N*ow I am bobbing in a dinghy, making for Dover beach. Our foolhardy captain has decided the chop has lessened enough for his passengers to make for land. Finally the little boat bumps the shallow sand, and with shouts from the crew the passengers are carried ashore.

I can see the sand dotted with English nobility coming to meet us. It is not quite the spectacle it was when Princess Mary left for her French marriage, but King Henry and Queen Katherine are here, Wolsey and his entourage. My family.

The trunks are carted across the beach. I see that Katherine, fatter and more dowdy than ever, hangs back and avoids watching Henry with his arm round my sister, dripping in jewels and finery—the royal concubine. I avoid meeting Mary's eyes, which are half-dead again. William Carey is nowhere in sight.

Then I see Percy, who, through our weekly letters, is more a friend and a lover than when we parted in France. He is so full of joy at seeing me, I can only hope my own expression conveys as much to him.

I dip in greeting to my father, and Cardinal Wolsey behind him. When I rise I am struck by an odd sight.

King Henry is staring at me. Quite brazenly. Mary can see it. So can Father. It is unnerving, but he is my sovereign and I his subject. I execute a low and graceful curtsy.

"Welcome back to England, Mistress Boleyn," he says, staring at me with an almost puzzled expression. He is, perhaps, wondering for the first time if I am something more than a pretty face.

I hold steady and refuse to avert my gaze.

"Your Majesty," I say, and flash him a charming coquette's smile. "It is good to be home."

NOTES FROM THE AUTHOR

Anne Boleyn clearly made her mark in the French court. François, in a letter to Henry VIII, before outright hostilities between their countries began, wrote, "I think it is very strange that the English scholars of Paris have returned home, and also the daughter of Mr Boullan."

Queen Claude, having given birth to seven royal children, died of exhaustion at the age of twenty-five.

In 1532, after a six-year courtship with Henry, in which Anne retained her virginity, they sailed to Calais and there were entertained in style by the only monarchs in Europe who supported their marriage—François I and Duchess Marguerite.

Marguerite, by then the Queen of Navarre, published a collection of stories of sexual and moral conduct in French society called the *Heptaméron*. Groundbreaking and shocking, it was an instant bestseller, and is still in print today.

Anne Boleyn's progressive religious education in Marguerite's household influenced her deeply. In the years after her return to England she was the only person with enough power over the still-Catholic Henry to bring him Lutheran texts, and she did much to further the "New Religion" in her country. She was a prime mover in the schism with Rome, the Protestant Reformation, and the fall of Cardinal Wolsey.

In 1536, Henry Percy was one of the twenty-six peers of England to declare Anne and George Boleyn guilty of adultery and treason, and call for their executions.

From the time of the reign of François I, the deck of playing cards has always included four kings and four queens.

ACKNOWLEDGMENTS

My first thanks must go to Anne Boleyn herself. It was her unique, courageous life and tragic death that imbued and sustained in me for so many years a passion that spawned not only two novels about her, but the foundation of my entire career in historical fiction.

I've had the amazing good fortune to be represented by two extraordinary literary agents, Kimberly Witherspoon and David Forrer. From my first book to my last, I've always been able to count on their unflagging support, their impeccable taste, and their many wonderful ideas that led me to new and unexplored places in my writing.

Kara Cesare is quite simply the editor of my dreams—razor sharp, but as kind as a person can be. Wonderfully imaginative, but committed to authenticity and excellence. No one could have shepherded this book more perfectly.

For the writing of *Mademoiselle Boleyn*, I was lucky enough to have many "bibles," written by some of the great historians of the period: R. J. Knecht's definitive *Renaissance Warrior and Patron: The Reign of Francis I*; Marie Louise Bruce's *Anne Boleyn*; Carolly Erickson's *Mistress Anne* and *Great Harry*; Retha M. Warnicke's *The Rise and Fall of Anne Boleyn*; Lacey Baldwin Smith's *Henry VIII: The Mask of Royalty*; Edward MacCurdy's edition of *The Notebooks of Leonardo Da Vinci*; and Lynn Picknett and Clive Prince, who introduced me in so unusual and fascinating a manner to the Maestro in *The Templar Revelation* and *The Turin Shroud*.

When I was up against a rare but frustrating "wall" in my research about France, Kathryn Cesare came to my timely rescue, and for that I thank her.

I am grateful to my dear friend Betty Hammett for her longtime literary guidance and the love that one expects only from a mother.

I think of my aunt, Sylvia Saxon, as not only a fond relation, but as a lover of the arts and the foremost patron of my writing career.

My much-loved mother, Skippy Ruter, did not live to see *Mademoiselle Boleyn* published, but she was the earliest fan and collector of my writings, and the creator of the infamous practice of "bookstore terrorism"—haranguing booksellers so that my novels were always re-ordered and prominently displayed at eye level on the shelves and at the middle of front tables. I truly believe I would not have had the gumption to pursue my path as a writer had she not instilled in me an unshakeable sense of self-worth.

There are simply not enough words of love or gratitude for my husband, Max, who saw me through the most devastating year of my life and kept me sane enough to write a book. There is not another person in the world I would trust to follow through fire. He makes every day worth living.

Mademoiselle
Boleyn

ROBIN
MAXWELL

A CONVERSATION WITH ROBIN MAXWELL

Anne Boleyn is one of the most denigrated characters in English history and on the pages of recent works of historical fiction. Why did you choose to write not one but two novels about her, and why do you perceive her in such a sympathetic light?

I'm always suspicious when a figure in history is consistently portrayed either too scathingly or too well, which makes me want to do deep research and learn the other side of the story. Once I became aware of Anne Boleyn, I found her utterly fascinating, but so much of what was written about her was downright hostile. Even the best biographies had a faintly disapproving edge to them, and almost all of them described her as shrill, ambitious, and scheming.

But I persisted, reading every word I could lay my hands on, and then trying to read between the lines. When studying history, you must always consider the sources, as virtually all of them are biased, especially the ones who were alive during the period written about. You have to understand what benefit or trouble they would derive from speaking well or ill of a certain person. Whom they worked for. Who was paying their salary. In those days, "getting axed" from your job had far graver implications than it does today.

During the early years of her relationship with King Henry in England, and regarding the subject of Anne Boleyn's much-requited love for Henry Percy, the only contemporary source who spoke of them was a person named George Cavendish. He was extremely disdainful about both Anne and Percy, and didn't think much of Henry's passion for "that foolish girl yonder in the court." It didn't take much digging to discover that Cavendish was a loyal manservant to the monstrously powerful Cardinal Wolsey, who had every reason to oppose that young love affair. Neither he nor Cavendish could ever have imagined that "that foolish girl" would, less than ten years later, bring about the cardinal's downfall.

So it was necessary for me, when reading the words of this source, to go inside Cavendish's head and look for his motives for saying them. And many times I would decide that if he said "black," I would be well served to think "white." That he was almost certainly saying what he knew his master would want him to say. It was a kind of "job security" we still see in politics and business today.

Then there were the small passages and anecdotes about Anne within the histories that were seemingly innocuous, but spoke volumes to me about a woman who was always characterized as cold and unfeeling and a rotten mother to Princess Elizabeth as well. Elizabeth had, after all, refused even to utter Anne's name for the first twenty-five years of her life.

One day during my reading I came upon a passage in a very respectable biography saying that when Elizabeth was a tiny infant, Queen Anne insisted upon keeping her on a silken pillow by her side whenever possible. That was the first eye-opener for me. I thought, *Are those the actions of a cold, unfeeling mother?*

I read on, and there was an account from the same period, on the occasion of Henry's deciding to send the tiny princess far away from court to her own household. Anne, who had already fallen far out of favor with King Henry and was in deep trouble for not giving him male children, *argued passionately* with the king about sending the baby away. There were even quotes from Henry, who was furious with Anne, shouting that the decisions about sending his children to distant palaces was "the prerogative of kings, the prerogative of *kings!*" And *still* Anne persisted. Again I thought, *Why would Anne further antagonize Henry and jeopardize her already dangerous position in order to keep Elizabeth near her, if she was such a heartless mother?*

But there were more clues about Anne's true character that I turned up while doing research for my first novel, *The Secret Diary of Anne Boleyn*, which, in fact, gave me the premise for that book. I learned that in the first year of Elizabeth Tudor's reign, something turned her mind around about her mother. *Completely* around. Whereas Elizabeth originally believed all the horrible rumors about Anne—her infidelities; the charges of incest with her brother, George; her deadly ambition—suddenly she was viewed by Elizabeth, who was as hardheaded a woman as ever lived, with extreme favor.

Indeed, Elizabeth began wearing a silver locket with Anne's miniature inside it. Within a couple of years she had heaped honors, titles, and fortunes on the few and badly-thought-of Boleyn relatives at court that Henry had left alive. Here was proof from her own daughter that Anne was a person deserving respect, and not scorn.

These were all excellent lessons for me to learn early in my career as an author of historical fiction.

As for the claims that Anne was wildly ambitious and would stop at nothing to attain her goals, I always kept in mind that she began as an innocent, if highly intelligent girl, a romantic idealist who had the backbone to defy her father, her king, and Cardinal Wolsey, in order to pursue a marriage for love with Henry Percy. It was not until *after* she'd had that love taken away and been virtually forced into a relationship with Henry that she seized her destiny and began watching out for her own interests, pushing her own agendas.

It is true that she was audacious and had the temerity to refuse being taken advantage of. Almost unbelievably, she held out as a virgin with Henry for *six years,* so that any child she had with him would be born legitimate. For these qualities I do not judge her harshly. I admire and applaud her.

One learns much about a person by studying their friends *and* their enemies. In Anne's youth, during the years at Margaret of Burgundy's and François' courts, she had only admirers, and they were individuals of distinction. It wasn't until she returned to England and, as a woman, dared to assert herself in a world of domineering men, that she gained a host of powerful enemies. These were among the cruelest and most grasping men and women at the English court.

I've always believed it was her steady hold over Henry's affections for so many years, and her insistence on treating him like an equal and not her better, while everyone else groveled at his feet, that caused her so much trouble. They were *jealous* of Anne Boleyn. The jealousy engendered hatred. And the hatred inspired the conspiracy that led to her downfall and execution.

There have been novels about Anne and her sister, Mary Boleyn, that have not only kept the slanderous rumors and unsavory reputation alive, but have gone several steps further in character assassination. One book actually claimed that a male child born to Mary, fathered by Henry while she was his mistress, was *stolen* by Anne and brought up by her at court as her own.

That Anne brought up her sister's son at court, claiming it as Henry's and hers, is, as far as I know, entirely fictitious. There would surely have been a great deal said about it in history books, as the king was desperate for his lawful wife, Anne, to give him a male heir. Too, if that had been the case, Anne's many enemies would have had a heyday with such information. There is not a whisper of it anywhere.

What was Anne's importance in the sweep of sixteenth-century history?

Of course her having given birth to Elizabeth I is significant. But what I most respect is that Anne Boleyn was a pivotal player in the Protestant Reformation. It's true that it was Henry VIII who moved heaven, earth, and the Catholic church to divorce his very Catholic first wife, Katherine of Aragon, in order to marry Anne. But it was Anne, having inherited her Protestant learning from Duchess Marguerite of Alençon, who first brought the Protestant (and ultraheretical) books and pamphlets to Henry's attention. Anne who urged him to take heed of those writings, as they would help him in attaining his desired goals. And Anne who, despite England's deadly attitudes against reformers, continued to practice and push the "New Religion."

An even more closely guarded fact about Anne—one that is made mention of in only one history book (Anthony Martienssen's *Queen Katherine Parr*)—is that Henry actually appointed Anne to spearhead a small coterie of the most powerful figures at court, who met weekly at Durham House in London and whose sole purpose was freeing England from Rome's influence in order to land Henry his divorce. The still publicly Catholic king ("Defender of the Faith") could not allow himself to be seen engaging in such dangerous activities. Clearly, he trusted Anne's intelligence and judgment enough for the job. The image of this woman, still in her twenties, *as the leader of men* in what was, without question, the greatest religious and political battle of the sixteenth century—a battle that was *won* by Henry and Anne against the pope, creating the "schism"—is mindboggling.

Yet hardly a soul knows about the Durham House gatherings. It takes up less than half a page in a scholarly but rather obscure history book. No mention of it is made in any of the biographies of Anne Boleyn. She simply remains to most one of the "bimbos of history," the second wife of Henry VIII, who had her head whacked off for behaving badly.

I think it's finally time to rehabilitate Anne's reputation and elevate her to the place of respect among historical figures that she justly deserves.

Describe your method of story development.

As in all my books, I have had to piece the characters, places, and events together in what sometimes feels like a linear jigsaw puzzle. I use the tools of "deep reading," extrapolation and expansion from history, a good bit of psychoanalyzing, speculating, and imagining. I stay as close to the facts as possible, never veering from those that are well documented, but taking joyful liberties in the filling of many gaping voids in the historical record with what is "probable" and "possible."

The most magical moments in my writing life happen when I come across a tiny fact in a book or online that has been written nowhere else, that perfectly closes one of the holes in my story, explains a mystery or a character's motivation. One of the most exciting of these moments was the discovery that during the time Anne was an insider at François' court at Amboise, Leonardo da Vinci came to live there, and became the French king's dearest friend. When I went back to my many biographies of Anne, there Leonardo was! Every book asserted that the two were at court together and that she had to have at least met him.

That Leonardo became Anne's friend and mentor is my invention, though. I must admit it is one of my very favorites. This is a perfect literary amalgam of a period that is chock-full of holes, an extrapolation of known facts, and a leap of imagination. I reasoned that the friendship *could* have happened, and there is no evidence against it.

Another wonderful historical tidbit became the foundation of two chapters in *Mademoiselle Boleyn*. While I knew that the Loire châteaux of Amboise and Cloux stood close to each other along the river's bank, I discovered on a Web site that in the early sixteenth century there was a secret underground passage from one residence to the other, and that François, who visited Leonardo nearly every day in the manor house he'd gifted him, would often use the tunnel for their meetings.

My thinking went like this: *A secret underground passage! François often visiting his dear friend, using the tunnel to get to Cloux . . . François, a playful prankster of a young man who enjoyed entertaining his inner circle at court . . . There had to be a first time he introduced his friends to the maestro. . . . Could there be any more dramatic and magical a way to make that introduction than through a dark, moldering tunnel lit only by the flickering torches of the king's delightfully terrified courtiers and ladies?*

There was another subject in *Mademoiselle Boleyn* that the history books mention only in passing that I fleshed out into several important chapters—indeed, one of the major threads of the novel's narrative. I think it's an important aspect of what I consider the "job" of authors of historical fiction.

All histories and biographies of the period will tell you that while the Boleyn sisters were living in François I's court, the more beautiful of the two girls, Mary, became François' mistress, and was later passed around to so many of the king's courtiers that she became known as the "English mare," as so many men had ridden her. Later on, François really did publicly refer to her as an "infamous prostitute."

Yet you will never find more than those bare facts about why Mary ended up living a promiscuous life at the French court. Whether she chose it, or whether it was chosen for her. Whether she was content with her reputation or humiliated by it. Whether she enjoyed sex or hated it.

And there is always "the morning after" a girl loses her virginity. I thought it would be fascinating to be a fly on the wall of Mary's private bedchamber when Anne confronted her that fateful morning. I wanted to know what Anne thought about Mary's situation, and whether it had any effect or influence on the younger girl's life. That became one of my favorite chapters because we learn so much not just about Mary's character and feelings but about Anne's.

How do you do your research?

When I began writing historical fiction a dozen years ago, aside from material collected on several trips to England and Ireland, and a handful of purchased books, the major source of my research was the public library system. In most of the libraries at that time they still had "card catalogs." I'd have to stand poring over small, typed-out cards, trying to guess at the best way to cross-reference a historical figure, place, or event, then search through the stacks for what sounded like just the perfect book, many times to discover that it was checked out or stolen.

I was always lucky enough to find a couple of books that became my "bibles," like Marie Louis Bruce's *Anne Boleyn.* I was able to check it out for three weeks and renew it for another three, but then I was forced by library rules to return the book and leave it overnight before checking it out again. I'd find myself praying on those nights that no one else would check it out. I'd rush back the next morning and take greedy possession for another six weeks. For those first novels, the strange "library dance" would go on for the whole time I was researching and writing, as long as a year and a half. It was frustrating and difficult and, of course, I could never mark up the library books, forcing me to do extensive note-taking and massive paper file creation. I'm not the neatest person in the world, and during those periods my house looked like a war zone.

Then came the advent of online bookstores, such as Amazon, Powell's, and Alibris. Suddenly I was able to find both in-print and fabulous older and out-of-print used books, as well as collector's editions. I started *buying* all the books I needed. Today, with seven books researched, my fifteenth- and sixteenth-century history collection overflows two large bookcases. An added benefit of buying books is being able to mark up the texts any way I please, making my work easier.

On the last three books I've written, I've used the Internet more and more extensively for research. In order to get a feel for locations I've never visited, I can call up dozens of photographs and descriptions. I can cross-reference subjects and characters using popular as well as scholarly links. For *Mademoiselle Boleyn* I found some wonderful sites on Charles, the Holy Roman Emperor; Margaret of Burgundy; and Marguerite, the Duchess of Alençon—much of which I could not find in any book. While I was able to order from online bookstores several volumes on sixteenth-century playing cards, the Web provided invaluable material about the rules of specific card games of the period, and even the language used while playing them.

All in all, the modern world is a much happier place for me to be doing historical research.

If you could ask Anne Boleyn any question, what would it be?

I'd love to know what it was about Henry Percy that caused Anne to fall so madly in love with him. So in love that she managed to bring the entire male establishment of England down on their heads. I'd also ask her if she ever was in love with Henry VIII, or whether, after she was torn away from Percy and pursued by the king, she was ever able to open her heart again.

QUESTIONS FOR DISCUSSION

1. There were numerous influences in Anne Boleyn's life, for better and for worse. Who do you feel most influenced her character? Her education? In order of importance to Anne's life, how would you rate the following individuals: Charles of Burgundy, Archduchess Margaret of Burgundy, Duchess Marguerite, François I, Queen Claude, Leonardo da Vinci, Thomas Boleyn, and Mary Boleyn? Which of these historical figures would *you* like to have known better?

2. Arranged marriages have been accepted as normal among English royalty and noble families, even as recently as that of Prince Charles and Lady Diana Spencer. How extraordinary was it that Anne, at the age of sixteen, pursued a "marriage for love" with Henry Percy, against the wishes of her parents, Cardinal Wolsey, and King Henry?

3. What other antiauthoritarian tendencies did Anne display in her youth? Did these serve her well or ill?

4. If you had been a teenager or young person in the court of François I during the period in question, would you have been attracted to a friendship with Anne, or turned off by her? Would you have preferred a friendship with Mary Boleyn?

5. The name Anne Boleyn is almost synonymous with the image of beheading. For most people it is almost the only thing they know about her. Were there any surprises in this book about Anne? If someone were to engage you in a conversation about her, what would you like to share with that person?

6. What do you think Thomas Boleyn had in mind for his younger daughter, Anne, when he sent her alone, at the age of nine, to the court of Margaret of Burgundy?

7. Do you think that during the period of time portrayed in *Mademoiselle Boleyn* Anne had an inkling that she would end up married to Henry VIII and becoming Queen of England?

8. Do you think that in her youth Anne could be described as "ambitious"? What other words would you use to describe her best?

9. The "Field of Cloth of Gold" was one of the greatest and most fantastical gatherings of any age. If you had been in attendance, what part of it would have attracted you most?

10. Though it may seem absurd, one of the major reasons Lady Diana was chosen as a wife for Prince Charles was her unimpeachable virginity. For all the noblewomen in *Mademoiselle Boleyn*, virginity was a burning question. What do you think was the underlying reason that it has, for so long, been demanded of highborn females to be "intact"?

11. In this novel, we observed the sexual awakening of Anne Boleyn (and to a lesser degree Mary Boleyn). Do you think much has changed with that issue since the early sixteenth century?

Praise for Robin Maxwell's historical novels

"History doesn't come more fascinating—or lurid—than the wife-felling reign of Henry VIII."   —*Entertainment Weekly*

"Breathes extraordinary life into the scandals, political intrigue, and gut-wrenching battles that typified Queen Elizabeth's reign. . . . The powerfully lascivious intersections of sexual and international politics . . . combined with Maxwell's electrifying prose here make for enthralling historical fiction."   —*Publishers Weekly* (starred review)

"An energetic, full-dress period novel."   —*Kirkus Reviews*

"Filled with fascinating descriptions of court life and references to historical figures and events, this novel is highly recommended for fiction collections."   —*Library Journal*

"Maxwell is one of the most popular—and one of the best—historical novelists currently mining the rich vein of Tudor history."   —*Booklist*

Turn the page for a preview of Robin's next rich historical novel, about a very important woman in Leonardo da Vinci's life. . . .

THE DA VINCI WOMAN

*T*he sweet, sickening stench of roasting human flesh assaulted the old man's nostrils, yet he could not bring himself to turn away from the sight of the two burning figures, now unrecognizable save for bits of heavy brown cloth still clinging to their charred bodies. He took no pleasure in the suffering of his fellow humans and was thankful that the pair, chained atop a platform in the center of the Piazza della Signoria, had had the life choked out of them before their incineration.

Glancing around him, he could see that some onlookers in the crowded square seemed to derive satisfaction from these deaths. If he had to guess, though, many more Florentines were watching with grim and fearful expressions.

Now from the town hall came a flurry of motion. A handful of city fathers, somber in their long tunics, were followed out by two *Signoria* guards, who were dragging by the armpits a man in the coarse brown robe of a Dominican monk toward a third, still-unlit pyre piled thickly with pitch-covered logs and branches. The man who was to die was small, his eyes closely spaced, his lips large and fleshy. He was an ugly man by most standards, but clearly made more so by his sweat- and blood-matted black hair and the purple bruised swellings on his face, no doubt inflicted during torture in the previous days. While conscious, the monk appeared almost boneless, his arms hanging limp from the shoulders, the tops of his bare feet dragging across the stone piazza.

"*Strappado,*" the old man heard whispered behind him, and turned. There stood a more-than-familiar figure—a friend, though one he had not seen in many years—his expression unreadable. "They say when they drop a man from a height, his arms bound above his head, the bones and sinews of his shoulders break and snap." Now there was the faintest hint of a smile. "How have you been, Cato?"

"Welcoming the return of my good spirits," the old man replied, keeping his voice low. "And you, Pico?"

"We have missed your company."

"*We?*"

"Some of us recently . . . have begun to gather again. Very quietly."

The monk moaned loudly and called out the name of his savior. Cato's eyes were drawn back to the platform as the man was hoisted, his broken legs bumping up the platform steps, and tied to the hardwood stake. Conspicuous in his absence was a priest to give the convicted man his final blessing, and the hooded executioner allowed his charge no time for final words, unceremoniously wrapping a knotted rope around the monk's neck.

"Is it not fitting that he should die in this way?" said Pico.

"He will no doubt burn in the hell of which he so eloquently spoke."

As the garrote tightened and the beady eyes began to bulge, Cato turned away.

"Are you leaving now? Before he burns?"

"Knowing he burns is enough." Cato clapped a hand on Pico's shoulder. "It's good to see you, my friend."

The old man made his way against the crush of Florentines who, whether ghoulishly pleased or mournfully beating their breasts, were now surging forward to witness the final moments of the monk's agony. Cato had paid a boy a florin in advance to watch his carriage and team, with promise of a second if he was there on his return. He found the boy standing on tiptoe in the driver's seat, straining over the crowd to view the spectacle. He glanced down at Cato only briefly.

"They'll soon light the fire!"

"Come down. Here's your other coin."

Reluctantly the boy climbed from his perch and snatched the florin from Cato's hand. He wasted no time plowing into the seething mass and would no doubt be at the front when the torch touched the tar-soaked pyre.

Suddenly weary, Cato climbed up into the driver's seat. The merest movement of the reins was enough to start the horses, skittish on even the outskirts of so large and unruly a crowd. The team clip-clopped out of the piazza, but before the carriage had reached Via Largo, a great cry went up from the assembled, and a blast of heat at his back signaled to Cato the destruction into ashes of the one who had called himself the "Mouthpiece of God."

His stomach turned at the thought of what must now be occurring, but as he crossed the Santa Trinita Bridge and headed toward the softly greening hills, Cato allowed himself to smile.

By the time he drew the carriage into the stable, the noonday sun had washed all color from the sprawling Tuscan villa's golden granite walls. Avoiding the front door, the old man chose the back of the house and with aching bones climbed a crumbling, vine-covered exterior stairway to a second-floor balcony.

Closing the door behind him, Cato crossed the threshold into a bedchamber. As many times as he had come into this room, its appearance never failed to startle him. He might have been stepping into a sultan's harem, what with the lengths of vermilion silk draped and woven above, altogether tenting the ceiling. Brilliant-hued brocade cushions were piled around the room's perimeter on the intricately patterned Turkey rug. Crossed scimitars hung on one wall, an exotic stringed instrument inlaid with tortoise shell on another. The latticed window threw patterns onto the low, satin-draped bed, and a hookah to one side, its long tube of mouthpiece hanging down, seemed to await languid partaking.

The early summer day had grown warm, so Cato was relieved to kick off his velvet slippers and strip off the long brown mantle, which stank of evil-smelling smoke. The doublet he wore underneath was, without an extra pair of hands to help, more complicated to remove. He unbuttoned the sleeves, full at the shoulders tapering down to the wrists, then untied his hose from eyelets at the doublet's hem and stripped them off. Fortunately, fashion had lowered the cut of the doublet's high square collar, which, till recently, half-covered a man's face but retained the rounded, pigeon-breasted front.

Undoing several laces and freed from the padded garment, he felt a breeze through the window ruffle his thin lawn shirt, cooling him. But it was not until the voluminous roll-brimmed hat was removed and Cato's long graying hair fell loose to his shoulders that he at last felt unburdened of the morning.

He went to a prettily painted Chinese wardrobe and threw open its doors. Inside hung a single garment—an olive-colored dress, its low, rounded bodice finely pleated and trimmed with thin gold ribbon. Over one shoulder hung its separate sleeves, soft and tawny as a doe, and over the other a lighter olive cape. Cato stood staring at the clothing for an overlong moment, as though perhaps some mistake had been made.

Then, pulling the thin shirt over his head, he let it drop to the floor. With stiff fingers, the fine Italian gentleman began unwinding a long linen strip that encased his chest. Round and round he pulled till he'd loosed from the bindings slightly sagging but still womanly breasts, and, breathing freely for the first time that day, he reached for the olive dress.

"Signora Caterina!" The plump cook looked up from her vegetable chopping and grinned. "We did not expect you today. How is the fine city of Florence?"

"Somber for the moment, Beatrice. By this evening I would expect a disturbance or two." Caterina lingered in the large, sunny kitchen, drinking in its rich aromas like a soothing elixir. She lifted a floury cloth, revealing fat rounds of yeasty dough.

"Behind you," Beatrice said. "Some cheese and finished bread. Help yourself."

The old woman cut herself a wedge of ripe yellow cheese and tore a crust off a long loaf. She nibbled at them as she found herself drawn to a black pot bubbling over the fire in the kitchen hearth.

"The maestro's favorite minestrone," said Caterina, both a question and an answer.

"It is."

"But you've added something different today, haven't you?"

"That nose of yours." The cook chuckled. "You'll have to guess what it is."

Caterina closed her eyes and with slow, almost lazy sips, tasted the air over the pot. "Not basil, not pepper, nor onion nor garlic nor . . . parsley. Yet somehow parsleylike. Tell me, Beatrice."

"In the maestro's last shipment from the East, along with the saffron and indigo, they'd sent another herb, large round seeds, called . . . Well, I don't know what they were called, as the writing was in Araby, but I stole a few and planted them in my garden and, lo, what came up was something that *looked* like parsley—more like clover on tall stems—but smelled . . . of India. You'll have to stay for dinner and taste it for yourself."

"Thank you, I will." Caterina smiled. "Now where will I find him?"

"Where do you think?"

Caterina always took pleasure walking through the warren of small, interconnecting rooms, each possessing one or two overlarge windows. The maestro, she knew, preferred small rooms, believing they aroused the mind, and insisted that small windows produced too-great contrasts between light and shade, thus inhibiting good work. Like the upstairs bedroom, each chamber—one for dining, two for sitting, a music room, a library—was a feast for the senses.

Embroidered tapestries that must once have hung on royal walls now hung here. Painting and sculptures—gifts from his friends, the Florentine masters—were everywhere present, though some of the works were the maestro's own. A series of four of his sketches stretched the length of one room, all depicting a catastrophic deluge with hurricane winds and monstrous curling waves that washed away a mountaintop castle and the whole city beneath.

Underfoot, where there might have been one Turkey carpet, the maestro would have laid *three*, artfully, so that a piece of each showed through. Every possible surface was piled with treasures: an etched Venetian glass bell, a necklace of cinnabar hanging from the dismembered marble hand of a classical Greek statue. A wood carving of the goddess Isis was displayed prominently in a niche, a garland of tiny living orchids encircling her neck. And a bamboo birdcage stood in one corner, filled only with a fanciful bouquet of colorful feathers—"All," the maestro would say, "that belonged in a birdcage."

In the music room were myriad stringed instruments and horns, piles of written music and strange charts that, to an untrained eye, would make no sense. There were sketches tacked on the wall of "musical waves" traveling through the air towards a perfectly rendered human ear and the inside of the listener's head. On a chalk wall were scribbled mathematical diagrams and equations that baffled even Caterina.

She came at last to a high open archway and the one exception to the maestro's rule of small rooms. The workshop was immense, longer than it was broad, with a ceiling befitting a church. Its windows were so large, they defied imagination. But, then, thought Caterina, everything the maestro touched challenged all imagining.

She stepped into the chamber and found herself bathed in sunlight. It felt like the very cauldron of creation here. Wondrous were the sights. On a turntable was a plaster casting of a perfectly sculpted horse rearing on its hind legs. Every inch of wall was hung with sketches—of waterworks and hydraulic systems, cathedral domes, and a city designed on two levels. Drawings of a crossbow the size of a house and of a terrifying war weapon on wheels with a revolving quartet of scythes nearly covered a sketch of a fresco of the Last Supper, recently completed for the Duke of Milan.

On tables were wooden models of cranes and hoists and aqueducts. In one corner was a mysterious arrangement of eight large rectangular mirrors, all hinged together in a perfect octagon. Taking up the most space was an enormous sheet-draped device, all points and angles beneath the cover.

The maestro was nowhere to be seen.

There were numerous apprentices, though, boys from ten to eighteen working with great industry at their chores. The youngest swept the floor. Another, slightly older, stretched and nailed a canvas onto a willow panel. At a workbench two prepared an array of red glazes. The oldest, whom Caterina knew to have graduated to journeyman, was laying down the first color on a cartoon of what would later become a painting.

Her gaze lingered on one lad of fourteen, distinguished from the others as much by his demeanor as his beauty. The sulky expression he wore did nothing to dispel the perfection of his features and the extravagant headful of soft curls. He was pounding with mortar and pestle at chunks of blue stone with so much ferocity that bits of its powder flew up and sprayed his face and doublet.

Mystified by the sheeted mountain, Caterina walked toward it and behind it. There she found, staring at the wall, a tall, broad-shouldered man, his doublet deep yellow satin, his calves shapely in hose a shade lighter than above. The hair was gloriously wavy, worn loose and long. She could see that the maestro was concentrating all his attention on the wall in front of him. Here were endless obsessive sketches of bird wings, bat wings, insect wings, angel wings. Wings from every angle, paying most attention to their articulated joints. Too, there were drawings of various machines whose purpose, even to the untrained eye, were surely meant to take a man into the sky. To take a man *flying*.

"Leonardo," she said quietly.

He turned. "La Caterina." He was startled but not surprised, and clearly delighted to see her.

Indeed, the delight was shared, an emotion she felt every time she saw the man after a period of absence. Those sweet, melancholy eyes; the lush, shapely lips; the high-boned cheeks; and the nobly slender nose. Caterina always censored her urge to remonstrate with Leonardo about the full beard he insisted upon keeping. All that hair, she thought, hid the rest of his handsome face.

Still concentrating, Leonardo turned from the wall to the massive contraption, this side of which was uncovered. It was, even though she had seen the sketches, a shock to the eye. The two long bat-wings, fashioned from oiled leather and stretched over struts of pine, were clearly constructed to *move* with their mechanisms of springs, wires, and pulleys. The wings attached to something resembling a slender gondola with stirrupped pedals sticking out the bottom, and an intricate canvas harness had been designed to hold, Caterina imagined, a man inside the machine, and the wings to the man.

"I hope you do not mean to fly that thing," she said.

"Salai," said Leonardo with a wry smile, "has offered himself up for the experiment."

The sulky-faced boy looked up at the mention of his name, but the artist's stern gaze set the apprentice back to his hated task.

Caterina inhaled the pleasantly familiar smells of the artist's workshop, then released her breath in a world-weary sigh.

Leonardo's expression grew serious. "So?"

"It is done."

Their eyes met and held, tears threatening them both. Then the two embraced tenderly, Caterina's head laid against Leonardo's chest. There they stood for a time, lost in their thoughts and unmindful of the apprentices' stares.

"There are those who will call him a martyr," he murmured in her ear.

"Let them," she whispered fiercely.

Finally pushing the old woman to arm's length, he scrutinized her with a playfully exaggerated artist's eye. "So, you indulge me with a sitting today?"

"It is a day of celebration, Leonardo. Of peace. I can afford to sit quietly. I know I shall be able to breathe more easily than I have in a very long while."

"Marco, Giovanni, Alessio!" With the merest of nods, all the apprentices sprang into action. One went to the windows and with a double rope that ran, to Leonardo's exact specifications, from ceiling to floor, smoothly lowered over them a huge, folded canvas blind.

"Step away," Leonardo said, guiding Caterina back toward the workshop archway.

She saw that the other boys, having moved to four points of a square—perhaps a third of the long studio's space, closest to the windows—were working hand over hand, tugging on an intricate system of pulleys, weights, ropes, and heavy chains. Suddenly, with a loud grinding and creaking of gears, the square of wooden floor in front of Caterina and Leonardo began to rise! As it ascended on the ropes and chains, another floor was rising from the story below to take its place. Then, with the sound of heavy clanking, the new floor locked perfectly into the place of that which was now suspended high overhead. On this newly risen platform were five sheet-draped easels.

The operation complete, the apprentices returned to their various tasks, as though nothing out of the ordinary had occurred.

"Something new?" Caterina inquired of the massive contraption, with an expression of mild amusement.

"I think it should be the work, not the master, that moves up and down. Every night now I am able to put my paintings away and close them up safely."

In a sudden flurry of industry Leonardo whipped the cloth from one of the easels, then pulled a high-backed chair from beside the wall, placing it just so, in the shadows created by the now-lowered shade. He clapped his hands twice, and Marco arrived holding several down cushions that the artist instructed the boy to arrange in several configurations, none of which pleased the maestro.

Caterina had come to stand before the undraped work. It was quite small, bordered on either side by a painted pillar. The background, exceedingly dark, even foreboding, featured a winding road that led to a rocky inlet below, confined on all sides by jagged, fearsome-looking peaks and precipices. That background had always seemed a strange complement to the woman in the portrait, who sat so softly and perfectly composed in the foreground.

She was dressed in the low-bodiced olive gown that Caterina now wore, the pale green cape slung over her left shoulder. The long tawny sleeves had been pushed up her arms in many soft folds, allowing the gently crossed hands to be seen clear above the wrists. But the woman in the painting was younger than Caterina by some thirty years, and was strikingly beautiful. If there was something slightly masculine about the broadness of her face and the defiant glint in the eyes, it was balanced, if not overridden by the feminine quality of the features, and an overwhelming sense that this creature was, if not the Madonna herself, a mother who had known every pleasure and every pain of womanhood.

Leonardo's artistry had rendered more than the details of her features—the black hair parted in the center curling prettily on the softly rounded breasts, a delicate fringe of dark eyelashes, rosy pink nostrils, and pulsing blue veins in the hollow of her neck. He had imbued in the woman's smile an air of all-knowingness and deep compassion.

"Tell me honestly"—Leonardo had come to stand by Caterina's side—"did I ever look this way?" she asked.

He regarded his work for some time.

"You were far more beautiful. Your chin was more oval than square. But the eyes are yours, and the lovely high bones of your cheeks."

"Will you *ever* finish it?" she said, teasing him.

"I think it will take a lifetime to satisfy me."

He took Caterina's hand and led her to the high-backed chair, tucking the cushions into the small of her back and under her arms for comfort, arranging the center-parted hair around her shoulders and covering it with the finest black gossamer veil. He arranged her hands right over left and gently pushed the sleeves away from her wrists, into soft folds.

In the next moment Salai, all gangly legs and blue-flecked cheeks, approached the chair. "I'm going out with my friends," he announced to his master.

"You haven't finished grinding the cerulean," Leonardo said. He was met with an insolent pout.

"Alessio can do it."

Maestro and apprentice locked eyes. Salai's sparkled with mischief, past and future.

"Then you must finish when you return," Leonardo instructed, trying for sternness in his voice. But this was a clearly outrageous indulgence.

With a nod the artist gave the boy leave to withdraw. He swiveled on his heels to go.

"Salai!" Now there was steel in Leonardo's voice. He motioned toward Caterina with his eyes. The boy turned back, bent down, and deposited a perfunctory kiss on the old woman's cheek. Then, grabbing a feathered cap and tying closed the front of his doublet, he was gone.

"He's a little monster," said Leonardo, returning to stand before the painting.

"Because you allow it," Caterina said, but there was no scolding in her voice.

"Reds!" he called, and within moments Alessio had come to his side with a palette arrayed in every shade of that color.

"I so wish Lorenzo could have lived to see this day," Caterina said.

"He knew it would come," Leonardo replied, moving to one side to observe the canvas in a different light. "There was so much *il Magnifico* had already accomplished. The Academy. The library. His part in the plan." Leonardo's expression grew suddenly shy. "The two of you together . . ."

Caterina looked down at her wrinkled hands. "The Great Work."

"Have I not captured it in your portrait? All of it? The dark. The light. The female. The male. Your magic. Your memories."

Caterina sighed again. "So many memories." Her dark eyes softly tilted upward as if they were seeing it all again.

"Come, Mama," said Leonardo in the gentlest voice, "before I lose you entirely to the past . . . won't you give me a smile?"

ABOUT THE AUTHOR

Robin Maxwell lives in the high desert of California with her husband, Max, and her avian muses, Mr. Grey and Cookie.